The New Madrid Run

by

Michael Reisig

Clear Creek Press

"The kind of story where apocalyptic events occur from clear scientific logic. Where there's more at stake than just survival. Where realistic heroes turn the tide. We can't wait to make *The New Madrid Run* into a high-octane movie!"–Ronnie Clemmer, Longbow Productions, CA

WHAT IF–in just a few hours, the parameters of civilization were irrevocably shattered?

WHAT IF you survived ..?

"A roller coaster adventure ride that will have you stocking up on survival gear and buying property in the mountains!"

–The Ouachita Writers Guild

FACT: The nearly perfect alignment of the planets in our solar system, an event unrecorded for thousands of years, *will occur* in the early part of the next century.

"Reisig leads his readers into a changed world where survivors face one adventure after another and page after page, the question in the back of your mind–could this really happen?–becomes even more intense."

–Richard W. Noone,
author of *5/5/2000 Ice; The Ultimate Disaster*

FACT: Recent scientific research suggests that our planet has shifted its axis more than once in the past. Animals quick-frozen in the Siberian Tundra, and tropical forests suddenly fossilized are examples of a severe pole shift.

"Reisig has penned a page-turner that paints a graphic picture of an islander's worst nightmare–an ecological catalsym of global proportions–with a story line right on our doorstep."

–*The Key West Citizen*

FACT: Volcanic and earthquake activity is on the increase. The eruptions of Mount Saint Helen and Montserrat island, as well as the recent Los Angeles earthquakes are examples of the mounting tension of tectonic plates in the earths crust.

"Thought-provoking, frightening; the best read since Stephen King introduced the plague to modern times."

–*The Texarcana Gazette*

"An outstanding apocalyptic thriller! Reisig deftly allows his readers to sink into a fast, page-turning chain of events only he can spin. Crisp. Fresh. Fast-moving. A great new voice for the action reader."

–*The Northwest Arkansas Times*

1st Edition, July, 1998
2nd Edition–Edited and reformatted by Dorrie O'Brien, Write Way Publishing, Inc., Aurora, CO–October, 1998
Cover design by Powell Graphics

Published by Clear Creek Press and The Survival Center

Survival Center West Coast Office
P.O. Box 234 McKenna,WA 98558
1-360-458-6778

Midwest office
P.O. Box 1081 Mena, AR 71953
1-501-394-4992

ISBN: 0-9651240-1

2 3 4 5 6 7 8 9 10

Acknowledgements

A book may be penned by an individual, but ultimately, its birth on the publisher's pages is never a singular accomplishment. This novel is no exception.

There are many to whom I owe a great debt of gratitude for their support, assistance, and most of all, their belief in me.

This book is dedicated to my parents. Without their unflagging faith and countless hours of assistance, none of this would have come to pass.

Thanks to Robbie and Paula for letting me write this one on their time, and a special thanks to my buddy, Richard.

Last but not least, I offer my love and gratitude to Bonnie, who completed my editing, stoically endured the tribulations of a writer's mate and helped me keep the faith.

Thank you for believing, all of you.

"And lo, there was an earthquake: and the sun became black as sack-cloth of hair, and the moon became as blood ..."

–Revelation 6.12

FOREWORD

This planet, and ultimately its inhabitants, are moving toward the conclusion of an era, and very possibly, the end of a cycle in man's much longer history than most propose. It has happened before, it will happen again.

As with most potentially calamitous events, Mother Nature provides warnings, and explanations, if the societies affected are advanced enough to understand. It is entirely possible that civilizations before us, who experienced monumental calamity have also left us warning, if we are perceptive enough to decipher it.

This book is a work of fiction. The premise, however, and the concept that the planet earth could very possibly experience catastrophic geological and climatic changes somewhere near the end of this century, or the beginning of the next, is an extremely viable possibility.

These disastrous changes would be brought about by a unique event due to occur the early part of the twenty-first century—the nearly perfect alignment of the planets in our solar system—a phenomena that has not occurred for thousands of years.

This alignment, and the perpetually thickening ice mass of the South Pole, are part of the explanation for the approaching changes. The clearly perceptible wobble of the planet as it is affected by this gravitational pull and mass imbalance are part of the warning. The increase of volcanic and earthquake activity worldwide, the frequency and ferocity of violent meteorological storms throughout the globe, and the prediction of a devastating millennium solar storm are all admonitions by a changing planet. Yet, we can expect more ...

It is entirely possible that the coming alignment will cause sufficient gravitational pull as to change the earth's rotating axis in relation to other heavenly bodies. Due to this attraction, and the enormous weight of the accumulating ice in the South Pole, the tilt of the earth will no longer be able to overcome the centrifugal force of the spinning planet. At this point, the polar ice masses will be thrust across the earth's surface toward some point near the equator, and a shift in the planet's poles will take place.

Prior to, during, and after this shift, there will be widespread geological disturbances and climatic changes. The geodetic or tectonic plates that represent the earth's crust will, themselves, shift in numerous places–particularly in those areas of severe faults. As these large rifts expand and contract, huge sections of Terra Firma will change shape. Some of the coastlines that border major faults may virtually disappear into the sea, and new land masses will rise out of the ocean as tectonic plates are forced together and buckle upwards. Entire mountain ranges will crumple and collapse.

This massive displacement of land mass, coupled with awesome earthquakes and volcanic eruptions, will cause tidal waves of gigantic proportions, inundating coastal plains throughout the world. Areas of the globe which had previously experienced a temperate or even tropical climate may undergo rapid weather changes approaching severe northern, perhaps even arctic, conditions. Other regions, depending on location, may experience slighter climatic changes, but all of the earth will suffer alteration to some degree.

For those who survive this cataclysm, the ensuing period of recovery will be harsh indeed. In a matter of hours, the parameters of civilization, as we know them, shall have been irrevocably altered and survival may well become the law of the land. The survivors of this holocaust will face not only the dangers and challenges of a changed earth, but quite probably, the baser ambitions of their fellow man.

The possibility of a catastrophe of these proportions is not the product of the author's imagination. Rather, it is a theory already expounded upon, and becoming more readily accepted by numerous scientists, geologists, and astronomers throughout the world. Furthermore, it has become the single-most consistent prediction by those in the New Age community. From Edgar Cayce to Ruth Montgomery, the forecasts of numerous prominent psychics are patently similar.

In writing this book, I believe Michael Reisig has attempted to be as accurate as possible with the interpretive predictions of both the bona fide geological and psychic communities, using only a dab of artistic license in painting a portrait of a world gone mad. Yet, this is an adventure novel, meant to entertain. So read on and enjoy–but pay attention as you go; it could be a signpost to the future.

–Richard W. Noone

PART ONE
THE CHANGE AND THE GATHERING

"Behold, ye of little faith in God and nature. Witness the Change, bear testimony to the Cleansing.

"Save your woeful wailing, philandering Philistines, ye have squandered the gifts of God's green Earth for a pocketful of coins. Now, as sure as arrogant pride goeth before a fall, and wickedness begets calamity, it is time to pay the piper for all your dirty dancin' with Mother Nature's daughters."

—The Preacher

CHAPTER I
OF WAVES AND PLANES
South Florida, Shortly After the Turn of the Century

The sun broke clear of the moisture-filled cumulus clouds, reflected off the windshield, and warmed the cockpit of the small twin-engine Cessna as it made its approach toward the Marathon Airport in the Florida Keys.

As he prepared for landing, Travis Christian was feeling pretty damned good about life. He stretched his large frame in the seat, ran a hand through his dark, curly hair and smiled slightly to himself. This week he had celebrated his tenth year as chief pilot and owner of Islandair Charters. He was doing what he loved and getting paid for it, and that was a hard combination to beat. It had been a long and crooked path from there to here, but he had made it.

He'd been sixteen when he received his fixed-wing license. By the time he was nineteen he had been recruited by Uncle Sam and was flying helicopters in Vietnam. He was landing in places you couldn't get a Volkswagen Beetle into, then taking off with the screams of the wounded in his ears and pieces of his chopper disappearing as the enemy did their best to make his two year stay a permanent one.

After 'Nam, he finished up his commercial pilot's rating with the help of the G.I. Bill and then bummed around the States for a few years. He was licensed to fly for a living, but so were thousands of other guys who were just out of the service. Flying jobs were scarce. He traveled from California to New Mexico, across to Texas and finally down to Florida where he fell in love–not with a woman, but with a chain of islands called the Florida Keys.

The Keys: mangrove islands surrounded by gin-clear, aquamarine waters. Tall palms stretched out over small, quiet beaches. There were quaint little bars, astounding sunsets, and tourist girls from all over the world. He had found where he wanted to be; all he needed was a way to make a living. About that time he discovered his second love in life after flying: sailing.

He had been introduced to sailing by a friend who owned and chartered a sailboat out of Key West. The fellow needed a mate. His last employee, who drank even more than he did, had fallen off the dock and broke his leg. Travis needed a job, so he accepted the offer.

One bright morning, slightly hungover, Travis found himself headed toward the Tortugas on a 41 Morgan. The wind in the rigging sang to him like the Sirens to Ulysses. As he watched the sleek bow knife through the warm, clear water and tasted the salt in the air, he knew he would never be the same.

Time passed, and he learned to sail. As with any good sailor, he learned the tides, the channels, and the reefs. He also learned to pay attention to that capricious lady, Mother Nature. It wasn't long before he realized that the same ocean he found so peaceful and serene could, within a very short time, become an awesome creature, terrifying and merciless. Even so, he loved it–or perhaps, because of this, he loved it. It was the same feeling of challenge and risk that flying gave him.

He worked with his friend for about three years, sailing during the day and chasing the ladies of Key West in the evenings. Life was easy and certainly entertaining, but he still dreamt of having his own flying service. Finally he managed a part-time position with a small charter service on the island. It was also about the same time that he met a fellow pilot named Cody, and his life became ultimately more interesting.

As the runway suddenly loomed ahead, Travis got down to the business of landing his plane. Backing the throttles off, feathering the props, and dropping twenty degrees of flaps, he set up a perfect final and settled the 310 gently onto the strip. He taxied over to the ramp, killed the engines and got out. Then he helped his passengers out of the aircraft.

His clients were both engineers from Miami, working on a project in Key West. They needed two hours in Marathon to meet with an attorney. From there they were to go on to Key West, then back to Miami by the end of the day. It was a lot of bouncing around, but they were paying for it, and paying well.

Travis figured he would touch base with his secretary in the cubicle he called an office, and then have a little lunch. By that time, the engineers would be back and it would be off to Key West.

Travis was putting the chocks under the wheels of his plane when he felt a strange sense of uneasiness come over him. He stood up for a second and looked around. The feeling rushed over him like that first gust of cool air that heralds an oncoming storm. It passed, but it left something in his gut, something that said, *bad things are coming.* Most people would have shrugged it off and gone about their business, but Travis and the feeling were old friends. He didn't understand, but he knew it was the reason he was alive today. He had experienced the sensation a number of times in Vietnam. The first time he hadn't paid much attention to it, which was the day he'd gotten shot down behind enemy lines and came as close to being killed as he had during his entire tour. He learned to listen, to rely on it, and the feeling had saved his life and the lives of his crew a number of times. Now, after all this time, standing on an airstrip in an innocuous little town in the Keys, here it was again—and it was bad. He looked around again, unable to find anything out of the ordinary. Finally, with one more glance at the plane, he walked through the gate and into the building where his mini-office was.

As he entered the office, his part-time girl friend/full-time secretary looked up and smiled. "Hi, flyboy. How's it going?"

Travis attempted a smile, still occupied with his ominous vibration. "Okay. I'm okay, but it looks like it's going to be a long day. I don't expect to be back from Miami until about eight tonight."

Linda studied him for a moment—the soft lines etched into his rugged but handsome face, the touch of agitation in his bright, hazel eyes, the set of his jaw. "You all right?" she asked. "You look like you just found a finger in your jelly donut."

Travis stifled a laugh. God, she could read him well. He gave a short, uneasy sigh. "Yeah, I'm all right. Everything's fine. Anybody need flying anywhere?"

She glanced at her notes, "You've got three for Fort Lauderdale tomorrow at eight a.m., and if you're willing to hang around up there until about two, I think we're going to get another triple for Key West on the return. They're going to confirm this afternoon."

"Great. So switch on the answering machine and let's go have lunch."

"Okay," Linda replied. "I'll do a quick lunch with you, but then I've got to run over to my Mom's for half an hour. She's been really sick with the flu that's been going around and I promised I'd check in on her."

"Not a problem. Come on."

With the prospect of a good week ahead, they decided to splurge and do Mexican at the Faro Blanco. Linda had a

Margarita with lunch while Travis settled, reluctantly, for an iced tea. They had a relatively quick but enjoyable meal, discussing business and pleasure equally. Linda was always fun, and she had a good business head, which was a hard combination to find. Looking at her from across the small table he was reminded how attractive she was. Her hair was sand-colored blond, lightened by the sun and the sea, and her eyes were as soft and dark as a newborn fawn's. She had a perpetual, honey-colored Caribbean tan, and an economical little figure that reminded Travis of a college cheerleader. She was very close to what he wanted, and he cared for her a great deal, but he wasn't sure he was *in love*. She was well aware of his struggle with commitment, but she was banking on him coming around in time.

When they had finished lunch, she took her car to her Mom's and Travis drove back to the airport. He noticed, as he drove, that the nagging feeling of unease had not abated in the least. He decided that he would pay special attention to flying today. He also sensed something unusual about the air, almost as if there was an increase in the static electricity. It was difficult to describe, but he felt like the hairs on his arms were constantly prickling.

He was stopped at one of the few traffic lights in Marathon when he felt the tremor. It was distinct enough to feel while sitting in his car. Then it happened again–but stronger. He thought, *What in hell is that? An earthquake in the Florida Keys*? That was unheard of. There were no local faults. "Maybe someone's blasting a channel somewhere," he reasoned. In fact, it felt a lot like a couple of thousand-pounders the '52s used to drop in 'Nam, and it felt like they had dropped them somewhere close by.

He switched on the radio, and caught the announcer's frantic voice in mid-sentence, "... unconfirmed reports of additional major quakes in Japan and China as well as the

South Pacific. There has also been unconfirmed word of a large land mass rising out of the sea in the vicinity of Bermuda and heavy volcanic activity from the Windward Islands through Central and South America. The big news, however, is that a quake of epic proportions took place in California at approximately seven-thirty Pacific Standard Time this morning. Everything is mass confusion from Portland, Oregon, to the border of Mexico. There are no hard facts at this point, but it is believed that the majority of California, or at least, with relative certainty, the California coast, has disappeared into the sea! There are further reports of massive quakes on the eastern seaboard also, but at this time we have no idea of actual damage. The President, from Air Force One, already in the air, is calling for an emergency session of Congress to evaluate the situation here and abroad, and to determine appropriate action. We will continue to broadcast news on these and other events as we receive further information."

Travis had returned to the airport while listening to the news. He parked his car in front of the building that served as the Unicom station and the FBO offices for several flight line businesses, and got out. As he put his feet on the ground, he sensed a vibration–an almost imperceptible movement of the ground beneath his feet. Then he heard a plaintive meowing, almost a crying. At first he couldn't place the direction of the sound, but as he looked up at the roof, he saw the kitten high above him on the rain gutter. The small, orange-and-white cat was perched there looking down and complaining loudly. The kitten had been a birthday present for Linda only weeks before, to keep her company while Travis was gone on overnighters. Travis glanced over at the big poinciana tree next to the building. That was obviously the route the errant kitten had taken, but now, unable to find its way down, it was frightened and vocal.

Travis looked up again and shrugged. "What the hell, I haven't done a good deed for a while." Actually, it had been a very long while.

Travis knew where the access door to the roof was, so up the stairs he went. He found the hatch, pulled down the fold-out stairs and climbed up and out onto the roof. There, twenty feet away, still near the edge, was the kitten. He walked over slowly, speaking softly to the frightened animal. Then he stooped down and gently picked it up. As he stood and turned, he saw it.

There on the horizon, barely distinguishable at that distance, was a wall of water–a tidal wave at least a hundred feet high and running the entire length of his vision. This colossal wall containing thousands of tons of water was bearing down on the Keys with the speed and intensity of a runaway freight train. As it gathered momentum, and rose to its full height, it greedily sucked the waters out of the flats, adding to its already enormous strength. In a matter of minutes, the Keys would face not just destruction, but complete annihilation.

In a heartbeat he was bolting across the roof and through the hatch. As he raced down the stairs and out the building, the cat, frightened by the rapid movement, tore at his arm with its claws and broke loose. There was no time to worry about it. He had only seconds.

Knowing it was a futile effort, he ran to his office, slammed open the door, and yelled for Linda. She was still at her mother's, five miles away. She might as well have been in China; there was no helping her.

When Travis saw the wall of water racing toward the Keys, he knew his only chance was the plane. After checking for Linda, he raced for the aircraft, nearly knocking down the gate attendant and a couple of baggage porters in the process. There was no point in shouting warnings to anyone, and certainly no time to explain. It didn't matter. Everyone on the island was as good as dead. He knew it, and he ran.

As he reached the plane, the rumbling in the ground was much stronger. The surface of the earth was trembling, and a wind had come up out of nowhere. It was a hell of a wind, whipping at his clothes and throwing dust and dirt into the air hard enough to blind him. *Thank God this damned wind's coming down the runway,* he thought as he shielded his face and pulled the chocks away. He jumped onto the wing, ripped open the door, and threw himself into the left seat. "No pre-flight today," he whispered tensely, as he rushed through the prestart procedure. Finally he hit the starter and was rewarded as the port engine fired into life. The rumbling was growing stronger still, and everything was starting to shake. He almost screamed with relief when the starboard engine cranked over and started. He had been having trouble starting that engine lately, but thank God, not today.

There was no time to taxi down to the runway threshold. The water would be on him long before he reached it. People were shouting and screaming, running in all directions. He realized, as he frantically turned the plane's nose down the taxiway into the wind, that his chances of being alive ten minutes from now were slim.

He hammered the throttles down and gave himself ten degrees of flaps. The 310 leapt in response. As Travis concentrated on keeping her on the narrow taxiway in the gale-force winds, he glanced at the horizon for a second and gasped. The giant wall of water was aimed right at him, less than half a mile away. It was easily a hundred and twenty feet high, and as it crashed into Marathon, buildings exploded and disappeared. Instinctively he pushed the throttles tighter against the panel but there was no more power to be had, and he still needed another hundred yards to be airborne. Then he had to clear the wave.

Everything went into slow motion. He was fairly certain that he wasn't going to make it, but he wasn't frightened anymore. Life had been reduced to a contest between himself and the wave. If he won, he lived. If he lost, well, he'd damn sure go out kicking.

The plane broke free of the ground as the churning, foaming avalanche crashed across the last hundred yards to the airstrip. The Cessna was arching upward, gaining altitude despite being buffeted by fierce winds but the barrier of water loomed before him, nearly towering over the aircraft. He slammed back the yoke and threw the airplane up, almost vertically, toward the top of the wave. His first thought–natural instinct for a pilot–was, *I'm going to stall this son-of-a-bitch*. In the midst of it all he laughed fiercely to himself. If he didn't make it over the water, he was dead anyway, so what the hell.

The monstrous wave reared up and curled over him, debris from crushed houses, destroyed boats, and uprooted trees cascading down its face. Spray and foam slapped the fuselage and windshield with fat, blinding pellets.

Suddenly it was as if he was back in 'Nam, slashing through the sky and dodging tracers; the roar of fifty-calibers and the yells of soldiers numbing his senses. He felt as though he'd just mainlined a quart of adrenalin. He didn't give a goddamn anymore. The streaming, frothing fingers of the top of the wave reached out for the tiny insect that was trying to escape its grasp. The engines strained and whined as the wave struck the plane. The stall warning buzzed in his head like an angry giant insect and Travis screamed a challenge, a cry of defiance, an acceptance of whatever fate held for him.

The deafening roar of the water drowned his scream in his ears, and the sky went dark. Sheets of spray blocked the sun and the top of the wave smacked the underside of the plane like a hammer, tossing him fifty feet higher into the air. Suddenly, when Travis was certain he was dead, the aircraft broke through. He was losing what precious little altitude he had, and barely in control of the plane, but he was on the back side of the wave–and alive. There was little time, however, to take satisfaction in this tenuous piece of fortune. He had major problems with his airplane.

Besides being buffeted by winds of tropical storm strength, his starboard engine was sputtering and vibrating badly, probably from the impact of the water. He climbed, using both engines at half power. As the vibrations increased to a dangerous level, he applied opposite rudder, feathered the prop, and shut down the bad engine. The plane dropped toward the water, tossed like a leaf in a gale, as he attempted to stabilize.

Sweat poured from his face, stinging his eyes. His shirt was soaked as he struggled with the controls and fought off panic as the shuddering aircraft fell toward the sea. Finally, only fifty feet from the tumultuous surface of the water, he manhandled the 310 into straight and level flight. Slowly, inexorably, he climbed to a safe altitude of a few thousand feet. He would need the height to buy him time in a crash landing, if the other engine went. Then he glanced down at the surrounding waters–the sight took his breath away.

The Keys were gone. Below, the debris-littered water agitated like that of a washing machine. The leviathan wave had passed, followed by several slightly smaller ones. They left in their wakes complete devastation. The islands were buried by at least forty feet of water. It was as if the Florida Keys had never been.

Travis gazed down at the flotsam and jetsam that was everywhere. Anything that would float littered the surface of the sea, from palm trees and sofa cushions to huge sections of roofs. Miraculously, a few boats seemed to have survived, though most were badly damaged; a great many were capsized. He circled and watched as bits and pieces of what was left of his hometown rose and sank in the milky-green waters. There were all manner of things on the surface below, but he had yet to see a survivor. It was then that he was struck by the thought of Linda. Linda, his lover, his friend, was dead. So was every other friend he had in the Keys.

The moment of introspection was interrupted when he glanced at his fuel gauges. "Son of a bitch," he moaned to himself. "Less than a quarter-tank in each engine." He knew his chances of making Miami and the mainland on so little fuel were slim and nil. Hell, he wasn't sure there *was* a Miami anymore. It was time to make some important decisions.

While Travis was contemplating his options, which also fell into the slim and nil category, he noticed a sailboat about a quarter-mile to the west of him. His attention was piqued when he realized that it still had one of its masts and was right side up. He had to do something in the next half hour, before the engine quit and he did his flying rock act. He took another look at the sailboat in the distance and smiled grimly.

"Any port in a storm," he muttered.

Still fighting the tremendous buffeting by the wind, he dropped a wing and banked gently downward toward the boat. He made a low-level pass at about one hundred feet and got a good look at her. Then he did it again. She was beat up, there was no question about that, but she wasn't listing. Even though she'd lost a mast, the other seemed intact and appeared, miraculously, to have its sails neatly bound to the boom.

"Well, Trav, ole buddy, I think it's time to trade this girl in for a boat."

He knew that what he was about to attempt was dangerous as hell, even in the best of circumstances, but the truth was, there weren't a whole lot of choices.

He took the plane up to eight hundred feet and out a

half mile from the sailboat, then turned around and headed back toward it. Throttling back while gradually losing altitude, he aimed for a spot one hundred yards in front of, and fifty yards to the side of the craft for a point of impact. Travis unlocked his door, grabbed a life jacket from under the seat, and made sure the landing gear was up and tight. He feathered the engine and backed the power off as the aircraft glided toward the water. He was still a touch hot as the plane approached touchdown. He pulled the nose up a bit and the 310 complied by losing speed. As the last twenty feet of height evaporated and the ocean loomed up on both sides of the cockpit, he pulled back on the controls and the tail section caught the water. The jarring impact threw him forward against the controls, banging his head on the door and knocking the breath from him. The plane continued slamming and skipping across the water for a few moments, gradually losing momentum and finally lurching to a halt. Suddenly it was quiet. The only sound was the clicking of the electrical system as it shut down.

Travis, a little dazed, gasped for air as the plane settled onto the rough ocean, and instinctively shoved the door with his elbow.

The door didn't budge–that brought him around like a slap in the face.

Forgetting his sore ribs, unconcerned about the blood running down the side of his head, he swung around in the seat and hammered the door with one hand while pulling the latch with the other. Nothing. As he turned in his seat and struck the door again, he heard the sound of the water rushing into the cockpit. He looked down in terror. Seawater was bubbling into the cabin from a gash in the floor. It was already covering his ankles.

"You goddamned idiot, use the other door!"

Painfully he pulled himself across the seat to the passenger's door, knowing freedom was only seconds away. He grasped the handle and shoved. Again, nothing–it was jammed just like the other one. The water was up to his knees and the plane was starting to list, nose first, into the ocean.

Running out of time, he forced himself to look–really look–at the door before attacking it like a maniac.

He saw that the stress buckle in each door was forcing the locking mechanism against the jamb. The doors themselves weren't jammed–only the locks. Amazed at his own calmness, he suddenly knew exactly how to solve his problem: He reached into his chart compartment and pulled out a Colt .45 service model. He wasn't supposed to carry a gun while flying, but it was a throwback to another time when something like that had made him feel more secure.

The water was at his waist, and his hand was shaking noticeably as he aimed the gun at the door lock and pulled the trigger four times. The sound inside the confines of the plane was like a cannon going off, but that was the least of his concerns. Better to be deaf than drown. He brought the gun down and studied the damage that the hollow-point .45s had done. There was no longer a lock, just a six inch hole rimmed by ragged metal. He shifted his legs up on the seat and slammed his feet against the door. When it burst open, he wanted to cry out with joy.

The weight of the engines and the water in the cockpit were rapidly drawing the plane into the ocean. With only seconds left before the aircraft went down, he threw himself out the door and onto the wing where he slipped and fell into the water. Still holding onto the life jacket and the pistol, he struggled to the surface and kicked off his shoes, but lost the .45 as he attempted to don the jacket and get it buckled. He wasn't ten feet from the aircraft when, with a gurgle and a groan, it was swallowed by the sea.

CHAPTER 2
OF BOATS AND OCCUPANTS

Frantically he spun in the water, looking for the boat. The waves seemed to have no pattern; they dipped and rose and crashed into each other, throwing spray everywhere. He had only a second to look each time a swell threw him high enough to search. Then he was back in a trough, sputtering and gasping and praying he'd see the boat on the next upward swing. The bile of fear rose in his throat as he thought for the first time of what would happen if he couldn't reach the sailboat, if it drifted away, out of swimming distance.

The sea cast him up again, and this time he caught a glimpse of the mast. That was good news. The bad news was that it was a hell of a lot farther away than he had expected. Travis was a fairly good swimmer and he was wearing a life jacket. In calm water, the two-hundred yard swim would be a piece of cake. But in these seas, with the wind pushing the boat away from him, it was going to be close.

When another wave washed over him, shoving him down into the water for a second time, he came up sputtering. Each time he was atop a wave, he got his bearings, then stroked like a madman. Every few minutes he'd rest and catch his breath, allowing the jacket to support him, then off he'd go again.

After the first fifteen minutes, he could tell he was gaining, but it was tough going and he knew that this was a battle he could yet lose. If not for his excellent physical condition, he would have had little chance. He ran two miles every day and worked out in the gym two or three times a week. As he struggled through the water, he realized it was those punishing daily exercises that were making the difference.

An hour and a half later, his shoulder muscles were screaming in agony. His legs were knotting in cramps, and due to the incessant gulping of salt water, he had thrown up everything but the lining of his stomach, but the sailboat was only thirty yards away.

When Travis finally reached the hull, he realized it was trailing a stern anchor line. He grabbed the line, pulled himself hand over hand to the boat, and held on. He drifted in that position with the craft for about ten minutes–long enough to gather sufficient strength to haul himself up onto the deck and into the steering cockpit, where he collapsed.

He awoke just as the sun was beginning to set on the turbulent waters. The rise and fall of the waves cast shadows across a darkening sea. Travis rose painfully and stretched his sore muscles, holding onto the wheel in the cockpit. Up to that point, his concentration had been focused on surviving and reaching the boat. His interest now switched to just what kind of boat, and the shape it was in. There was still enough light to see below and he wanted a look inside the cabin before it was totally dark. Pulling back the hatch doors, he entered.

It was as he had expected: The place looked like a cross between a breaking-and-entering and a bomb explosion. She was an expensive boat and had been outfitted well, almost luxuriously, but damned near everything that could be broken was. Dishes, pots and pans, broken furniture, lamps and charts littered the foot-deep water on the floor. The propane stove had been torn loose from the bulkhead and lay face down in the water. Most of the electronics and navigational equipment had been ripped from their brackets.

As he walked through the debris toward the bow, Travis

thought he saw something move in the V-berth up front. "What ..." he muttered as he stopped, waiting. Again, there was a movement in the gloom. The light was fading fast but it appeared that someone, or something, was lying on what was left of the bed in the front berth. He moved forward slowly, shuffling his feet in the water to make less noise. As he reached the threshold of what was once attractive sleeping quarters, he looked in at the disarray. The dresser was shattered, drawers were broken, clothing was scattered everywhere. Expensive pictures had been ripped from the walls. The bed frame had collapsed and the mattress was askew on the floor.

But there, partly on the mattress and partly on the rug, was a dog. A huge black and brown Rottweiler the size of a leopard. Travis gasped and drew back involuntarily. He studied the creature for a moment from the doorway. There was blood in the water and on the mattress, lots of blood. As Travis inched closer he could see a raw, gaping wound on the side of the animal's head that still oozed slick and red against the black fur. The dark eyes, though dulled by pain, remained locked on the man.

The dog had apparently been thrown against something when the boat was slammed by the tsunami wave. There may have been other injuries, but God knows the one he could see was enough. Travis stood there in the fading light. The Rottwelier made a feeble effort to rise and a low growl escaped his mouth. It sounded like an attempt at a challenge, but ended in a moan.

Travis decided to take a chance. "Easy boy, easy now," he whispered as he moved forward and knelt in front of the dog.

The animal looked up at him, full of anger and pain, and bared his teeth. Another growl, deep and low, rumbled in his big chest, but this time he didn't try to rise.

Travis had seen too much devastation and death in his life, and now everyone he knew, all those he cared about, were gone. He realized suddenly he wanted to save this dog, to retrieve something from all the ruin. Travis grabbed a shirt from the water-soaked floor. "Take it easy, big guy, we're going to clean you up a bit," he said as he eased in and tentively touched the massive head. The dog watched the man's hand as Travis slowly stroked the muscled neck and spoke soothingly. Travis took the other hand and began to wipe the blood from the gash with the shirt. Again, the animal tried to raise its head only to collapse back down. Travis continued his soothing refrain as he cleaned the wound and gently inspected the animal for broken or fractured bones.

Half an hour later it was nearly dark inside the cabin. As far as he could tell, the dog had no broken bones, but was suffering from a concussion and severe loss of blood. The bleeding had been reduced, but he had nothing to close the cut with. Maybe he could find a needle and thread tomorrow, he thought. If the dog would let him, he'd stitch him up–if the dog was still alive. He stroked the dark flank once more and murmured "You hang in there, buddy. We'll see you in the morning." The animal still gazed at him, but there seemed to be less anger in those black eyes.

As he stepped back out onto the deck, gray, windswept clouds buried the last of the sunlight against the horizon, smearing reddish hues across a charcoal sky. Peering out into the darkness, Travis studied the agitated sea. You only found water movement like this in channels where the current, or fast tides, forced the water against strong winds, causing the waves to roar up and slap against each other. It was as if the whole ocean were being jostled by a giant hand. There wasn't much surface wind anymore, but high above, at three or four thousand feet, stratus clouds were racing along at almost hurricane speed. There was indeed some strange phenomena taking place.

Travis was reminded of his old friend from the Keys, William J. Cody. Cody had been a partner during a particularly exciting time in his life. He met William J. what seemed like a hundred years ago, at a bar called Sloppy Joe's in Key West. As it turned out, he, like Travis, flew for a living. The difference between the two was the cargo they carried and Cody's distinct aversion to customs clearances. Cody Joe smuggled pre-Columbian gold, emeralds and rare birds out of South and Central America, fine art of questionable ownership into Mexico and Jamaica, and money into the banks of the Cayman Islands. He had even smuggled diamonds out of Africa. The man had a reputation for being scrupulously honest in a dubious profession. He was always on time and he always delivered. He was much in demand.

The only thing Cody wouldn't smuggle was drugs of any sort. It was a hard and fast rule with him, and he never broke it, no matter how much money was offered.

As people sometimes do, regardless of occupations, the two hit it off famously, and became the best of friends, sharing a number of remarkable adventures in the process. In looks, and personality, they were much the opposites, yet they had nearly everything else in common.

Travis was tall, about six feet with dark brown, curly hair. He had bright, expressive hazel eyes that changed from shades of brown to green, depending upon his mood. His demeanor was calm and controlled. He was a large, powerful man with a deep voice that women were drawn by and men naturally paid attention to, but he seldom used his size to intimidate and rarely displayed anger. But when Travis did get riled, there was an almost tangible aura of violence about him, and one look at those fierce eyes was generally enough to quell the ambitions of the most belligerent of antagonists.

Cody was only about five foot six, with long blond hair, a droopy "Custer" mustache, and luminous blue eyes.

His personality was electric–his conversations were animated and filled with gestures, and it was rare that he wasn't the center of attention at almost any gathering. William J. was so exhilarated with life that his effervescence was contagious, but his free and easy manner concealed a sharp, pragmatic mind that planned carefully and missed little. The man was everyone's friend but nobody's fool.

Both Travis and Cody were addicted to flying, and had seen Vietnam up close and personal. They shared a passion for sailing, tequila, and blonds, and both were physical men. After many a crazy evening in those days, they had still managed to meet at the local gym the next morning to work off the alcohol.

What had jogged his memory about Cody was that his friend was always talking about a catastrophic event due to take place near the beginning of the century–something to do with the alignment of the planets in the solar system. Cody read a lot and, on that particular subject, he had studied everything that had been printed. He could quote passages from the research of professors Charles Hapgood and Albert Einstein to recent writers such as Richard W. Noone, Graham Hancock, and Professor Robert Schoch. Travis could still hear him citing names and places, weaving scientific fact and psychic predictions into the most extraordinary premise. The alignment was to create an immense gravitational pull which would cause the planet to shift on its axis, rupturing tectonic plates in the earth's crust and causing massive earthquakes, volcanic activity, and tidal waves. Land masses would rise out of the oceans, while others would be radically altered. In general, there would be major changes in the earth's surface. It was a frightening dissertation by any standard. Cody's theory, based on his aquired information, was that there were *safe* places in various parts of the U.S. and the world that would survive the majority of the geological alterations. There were also a great many areas that would just disappear. The Keys had been on the latter list.

Cody had lots of money, which was one of the benefits of late night international flying with no respect to customs. After he and Travis had become solid friends, and experienced a number of spectacular and profitable capers from the Caribbean to South America, he had talked Travis into buying property with him in the Ouachita Mountains of Arkansas. Cody had explained that Arkansas was one of those *safe* places in America.

"When the smoke from the apocalypse clears, and everyone else is trying to find their ass with both hands, I'm gonna be alive and well on my own little mountain in Arkansas."

Travis had purchased forty acres and a cabin on a quiet mountain in Polk County, about twenty miles from Arkansas's western border. He was within easy driving distance of the small town of Mena, a peaceful community of about 7,000 people nestled in a scenic valley, surrounded by the Ouachitas. He still owned the property, allowing an old man and his wife to live there as caretakers. At the time, Cody had purchased eighty-five acres and a considerably larger house about fifteen miles east of town.

It had been several years since he had seen Cody, and then only briefly. His old friend passed through the Keys every once in a while, but rumor had it that he was lying low and moving' fast–that the IRS wanted to talk to him, not to mention the FBI.

There was a side of Travis that sorely missed Cody, even as nefarious as he was. It was the handful of fairly legitimate adventures the two had shared that had provided Travis with most of his financial security. The money he'd made with Cody had bought his plane, his business and, of course, his place in Arkansas.

Looking out across the darkening water to the eerie, reddish sky, Travis muttered to himself, "So I'll be damned, the son of a gun was right."

Too tired to concern himself with food, Travis wrapped a damp blanket around himself and curled up in the cockpit. Before sleep overtook him, he thought about the dog. "Lord," he said, "I know you've already done me a couple of serious favors today, but if you could squeeze in just one more, I'd really like that dog to make it." He got up and closed the cabin hatch. "Just in case I get my wish and Buster wakes up more frisky than friendly," he said, as he curled up once more and dropped into a dreamless sleep.

The first rays of the morning sun found him shivering as he struggled awake. It was only late March and the nights were still cool. He stretched and yawned, then stood to watch a brilliant orange sun complete its rise above the horizon, changing the indigo sky to shades of pale blue and rose. After relieving himself over the side of the boat, Travis turned and looked at the hatch doors. "Time to check on Buster," he said with just a touch of apprehension. He undid the latch and pulled the doors back slowly. Nothing in the main cabin. Evidently, the animal hadn't moved during the night. Although he was a little frightened of a dog that large, he had hoped to see him standing in the cabin. There was a knot in his stomach when he thought *Maybe he isn't going to move anymore at all.*

Travis shuffled through the water-filled cabin to the forward berth. *Gonna have to get the bilge pumps working today,* he thought to himself as he sloshed along.

The dog was still where Travis had left him the night before, but he was no longer lying on his side. He had righted himself with his huge head resting on his paws, as if sleeping. As Travis came into view, the head swung up slowly as the dog bared his teeth and growled menacingly. The animal was apparently doing better, but it was also obvious that he still hardly had the strength to move. What little attempt he had made to rise had been instantly canceled.

The day before, as Travis passed through the boat, he had seen a jug of bottled water floating amid the debris. He backed away into the galley, found an unbroken bowl, and the jug. He took the lid off and tasted the contents. It was good, fresh water. He took several swallows, paused for a moment, then took a few more, luxuriating in the feeling of the cool liquid against his parched throat. Afterwards Travis filled the bowl and brought it back to the dog. Slowly, he knelt, container in his outstretched hand. Again the dog rumbled, but no fangs this time.

Travis set the water on the mattress next to the dog's head. "Here, big guy, how about something to drink? You gotta be thirsty."

The dog turned his head toward the bowl and sniffed. Travis reached out and pushed it a little closer. Slowly, but still watching Travis, the great head dipped and he lapped at the water. The Rottweiler drank all but a swallow, then pulled back and his head collapsed wearily on his front legs. Those black eyes never left the man in front of him for a second.

Travis was pleased beyond belief, but he decided not to push his luck. After a cursory look at the wound, which seemed less serious in the light of day, he backed off slowly. "I think you're gonna be okay, guy. Just hang in there and I'll see if there's anything for us to eat in here."

Again he backed out, into the main cabin, and looked around as daylight streamed through the porthole. "Lord," he muttered, "what a frigging mess." He decided to begin with the galley, knowing that food and water were first on any survival list. Surveying what was left of the pantry, most of which was on the floor, Travis discovered a fairly good stock of canned goods. The refrigerator door had stayed closed due to specially designed latches, but when he opened it up, the insides looked like a giant hand had grabbed and shaken it. Almost all the glass containers were broken, but there were a number of plastic soda bottles that had survived.

There were no fresh fruits or vegetables; the boat was not a live-aboard, but there were some good provisions otherwise. Travis found a couple of cans of corned beef–the kind with built-in openers, and a fork. He cranked the lids back, and dished them onto two serviceable plates. He wolfed his down, not realizing until then just how hungry he was.

He took the other plate to the dog. Again the animal raised his head as the man entered the cabin. "Chow time, buddy," Travis said as he slowly pushed the plate forward. Just as he did with the water, the dog sniffed the dish, then ate greedily, his eyes leaving Travis only for a second as he targeted his food.

As Travis crouched by the dog, he reached out slowly, cooing softly, and began stroking its muscled back. The dog stopped eating for a second and turned its head towards Travis's hand. Travis froze his fingers on the dog's shoulder. He could see flecks of food and saliva on the gray-and-pink maw. He could feel its breath on his outstretched arm. The mouth opened slightly, casually exposing canines curved like sabers. The creature sniffed tentatively.

Travis held his ground and whispered, "Now's a good time for us to become friends, buddy." The animal sniffed once more, then slowly turned back to the food and continued to eat. Travis exhaled and drew his arm back, infinitely pleased to have all his fingers still attached. "That's it, old boy, let's not be biting the hand that feeds you."

He spent the rest of the morning working on the batteries and electrical system. The boat had taken on quite a bit of water and needed to be pumped out before anything else could be done. Fortunately, the batteries had survived intact, but some of the wiring had been torn loose and required repair. Travis placed the batteries high and dry while he rewired the cables. When finally he hit the bilge pump switch, he was rewarded with the humming sound of the pump working. He stepped out onto the deck and double-checked to see the stream of water jetting from the hull. While the bilgewater emptied, he surveyed the boat and assessed the damage topside. She was, or had been, a beautiful craft–an Irwin 46, ketch design. Her forward mast was still intact, the other was snapped off about six feet above the deck, testimony to the battering she had received. The mainsail on the good mast was still attached to the boom. The self-furling jib had torn loose from its fittings on the deck and flapped uselessly in the light wind. The sheet lines to the good sail seemed to be in order and, with the exception of the bent and broken bow rails, she looked like she could be made seaworthy in no time.

By mid-afternoon Travis had the jib repaired and most of the water pumped out of the boat. He hoped the hull was still sound.

He found a can opener and made himself a lunch of canned peas and cold chicken soup. After lunch, he took some more water back to the dog. As he entered the cabin, the animal rose shakily to his feet. "Easy boy," Travis said gently, as he moved forward cautiously. "Just relax now, buddy. Here's some more water." The dog's lips curled slightly as the animal stared at Travis, but there was no sound from the dog's great chest, and the fire in his eyes had cooled. It was as if he understood that a pact was being made. The dog took a few tentative steps forward and drank the water, then settled down again, satisfied to rest, and heal.

Travis smiled. His new friend was going to make it.

After finding the spare anchor and securing the boat

in about thirty feet of water, he spent the next two days organizing, cleaning, and repairing it. In that time, the dog grew stronger. He limped some, favoring his back leg, and he moved slowly, but he was up and about.

From the initial truce, the man and dog were beginning to accept each other, and a bond had begun to form. Travis was able to touch the dog now without fear. In fact, *Ra,* the name Travis had decided to give him (taken from the ancient Egyptian deity, Amon Re), seemed to enjoy the affection.

Fortunately, fresh water on board ship wasn't a problem. The ship's tank seemed to be intact and almost full. In addition, whoever had owned the boat had stored three two-gallon water jugs below. Food, though, at this point, was a much more finite resource. They had sufficient supplies to carry them for a while, but Travis did not want to find himself marooned on a boat with no food and a hungry, one-hundred-and-fifty-pound Rottweiler. He could see their friendship evaporating rapidly under those circumstances.

The afternoon of the second day found Travis in the cockpit of a relatively clean and operational sailboat. Taking the winds and currents into consideration, Travis figured his position to be roughly twenty miles northwest of the Middle Keys, or the Marathon area. As sustenance had become a major issue, he'd come up with a plan. He figured the waters had receded a few more feet by now, leaving perhaps twenty-five to thirty feet of water over the Keys. It was possible some portions of the larger, stronger stores in the Keys might have survived. There had been a large shopping center in Marathon that housed the grocery and Merchandise Mart. There was diving gear on board the boat; he had discovered it while organizing. If he could find the remains of the stores, he could dive down and salvage supplies. The winds favored a cruise in that direction so, with no further delay, he upped the anchor, raised his mainsail, and set out on the first leg of his odyssey.

CHAPTER 3
THE SENSEI

The wind was crisp and the boat handled well. Running with just the mainsail, Travis was getting about five knots, and that was fast enough for a one-man crew. The day wore on and he began to observe the gruesome evidence of an inundated civilization. Flotsam and jetsam of every describable variety littered the waters: trees, roofs of houses, wrecked pleasure boats, and bodies–all the bodies ... God! It was worse than what he'd seen in 'Nam. Bloated cadavers with milky, sightless eyes, and rigid arms bobbed up and down in a grotesque collage, as if beseeching the help that never came. He continued on. There was no other choice.

As he shaded his eyes from the sun and studied the waters ahead, he saw him. Travis looked once, shook his head, then looked again. There, about 150 yards to port, was the slowly sinking wreck of what must have been quite an expensive yacht designed like an eighteenth-century Japanese sailing vessel. That, in itself, wasn't so surprising. What was remarkable however, was that on the badly listing bow, kneeling casually in *seza* position and staring right at Travis, was a Japanese man. Travis guessed him to be in his early fifties. He was dressed in traditional Old-World garb. The loose *hakama* pants and a light "Happy Coat" made him look like something out of a James Clavell novel. Travis couldn't believe it. The guy didn't wave, didn't even move. He was sitting on his sinking boat, watching Travis sail right by with no more concern on his face than if he'd been sitting on a bench feeding pigeons in Central Park. Travis could barely contain himself. There was another human being–alive.

He stood, waved his arms and yelled, "Hang on, I'll swing around and come alongside." The Japanese just looked at him and bowed slightly.

Travis came about and slid up next to the other boat. "Looks like you might be in need of some new transportation," Travis shouted amiably.

The Japanese stood and brushed down his *hakama*. "*Hei*, yes. Throw me a line," he said with a strange smile. "I have waited long enough for you." Travis reached down and threw a docking line across to the man.

"Waited long enough for me?" he muttered.

The older man turned and picked up a long, narrow bundle–something wrapped in heavy silk and tied with a silk cord. Then, with an agile leap that belied his age, he jumped the five-foot gap between the two boats, landing as nimbly as a cat on the deck in front of Travis.

The Japanese drew himself erect saying, "Higado Sensei, at your service," he said, bowing solemnly.

Travis wasn't exactly sure how to follow that act, so somewhat awkwardly, he bowed back. When he looked up, the Japanese was studying him again with that same strange half-smile.

Standing close to the man, Travis realized he could have been wrong about the fellow's age. The man had one of those inscrutable, almost ageless Oriental faces. His small, black eyes gave away nothing. He had a broad, well-shaped nose, and a narrow but friendly mouth which framed that Mona Lisa grin of his. He might have been fifty, or sixty-five; it was impossible to tell. His long, dark hair was graying, and tied into a small tail high on the back of his head, much like the Samurai warriors of the seventeenth century. He was only five feet five- or six-inches tall, but he was trim and hard-looking, and he carried a calm sense of assuredness about him as if he were a man accustomed to respect.

Suddenly Ra came bounding out of the cabin, having heard the steps on the cabin deck and the voices. Travis yelled, "Ra! Stop!" as he thought, *Jesus! He's gonna eat the guy.*

But, as the animal rounded the corner of the hatch and came at him, the man did the weirdest thing. He knelt on one knee, opened his arms to the dog, and shouted in a clear, commanding tone, "Come, Ra. Come here, now." The dog stopped dead in his tracks, suddenly uncertain. He cocked his head. The Japanese seemed to have the same confusing effect on him as he'd had on Travis. "Come, Ra," the man commanded again. The animal moved forward slowly, not sure whether to bite him or lick him. As Ra smelled his outstretched hand, the Oriental brought his other hand around in a motion that was so fast it looked like a sleight-of-hand trick, and scratched the dog behind the ears. A moment later, Ra was nuzzling him like a playful puppy.

"I'll be damned," Travis exclaimed. "Do you know this dog?"

The older man stood up. "No, but I know animals and know myself. If animal senses no fear–truly no fear, but kindred spirit–he is not so likely to do harm."

"Well, that's one of the neatest tricks I've ever seen," replied Travis. "I thought for sure he was going to eat you."

The Japanese bowed slightly, acknowledging the compliment, then looked up. "Speaking of food ..."

After they had pushed off from the other boat, they anchored up and split a couple of cans of beef stew between the three of them. Ra seemed to have accepted Higado Sensei completely, as if he had been there the whole time. Though he couldn't explain it, Travis was certain that this was an exception, not the rule, with the dog's personality.

While they ate, they talked. Through the course of the conversation, Travis came to realize that he was in rather distinguished company. Higado Sensei was the Master in one of Japan's oldest and most renowned traditional Budo retreats: a place of study for those students truly dedicated to Japanese martial arts. He taught Karate and Aikido as well as Iaido, which is the art of drawing and using the Samurai sword. The Japanese explained that his name was Higado, and that "sensei" meant instructor. He and three of his highest-ranking students had been making an historic sailing trip around the world in his specially built sailboat when disaster struck. His students had been killed when the Black Wind, as he called it, hit them. Only the sensei had survived. He had been without food or water for two days when Travis found him.

After their meager supper, they were sitting on the deck watching the sun go down when Travis turned to the man and asked, "What did you mean today when you said you had waited long enough for me? You couldn't have known I was coming."

"Oh, but I did," replied the older man. "I was in cabin of my ship when the great wave struck. Others were on deck. I was thrown against bulkhead and knocked unconscious. For a moment, my spirit passed into the void and an ancestor came to me. I was told it was not my destiny to die at sea; that there was yet a distance to travel on this path. I was told you would come and we would walk together for a while."

If someone else would have said that to Travis, he would have laughed out loud. But coming from that quiet, serenely confident man, it seemed entirely possible.

Later that night, as they prepared to retire, the sensei pulled out the silk bundle he had saved from the other ship. Travis looked over curiously as the other man laid it on the bunk and opened it carefully. Inside were two magnificent swords. One was a short sword, or *wakazashi*, the sensei explained, and the longer of the two was called a *katana*. The

Japanese reached for the long sword, and in one smooth, electric-fast motion, he had drawn the sword and laid it before him. Travis, stifling a gasp at the man's speed, thought: *This ole boy is in his fifties and he still moves faster than a cheetah on bennies. Wouldn't want to be on* his *bad side.*

Higado Sensei looked up. "I must clean my swords tonight. The salt water is not good for them." He spoke as if they were friends of his. At the time, Travis didn't realize how true that was. The sensei worked a rag across the gleaming, razor-like blade. "These have been in my family for over four hundred years, handed down from father to son for generations."

"Those little toys are quite an heirloom, Higado," Travis replied, moderately impressed.

The sensei stopped rubbing and stared at the man across from him. In an instant, his eyes had changed and Travis saw something in those bright black chips of obsidian that scared the hell out of him. "This," the sensei said, holding the point of the sword at Travis and speaking in a slow, deliberate fashion, "is neither toy nor heirloom. It is essence of what I am. This blade has drawn blood and taken lives hundreds of times. It is nexus of all that is truly Japanese. This is, as I am, Samurai."

He started to bring the blade down but suddenly stopped, still staring at Travis. "You will call me Sensei." Then, as quickly as it had come, the expression was gone and he smiled that half smile of his. "Forgive my intensity," he said as he lowered the weapon. "There is part of me that has lived so many times with the sword that it is an intrinsic part of my being. Your lack of understanding does not merit rudeness. I am sorry." He bowed slightly and then continued his cleaning ritual.

Travis exhaled. "Yeah, well, no problem. You go ahead

and clean your swords. I've had another long day. I'm going to get some sleep."

Travis went up to the forward berth and lay down. Ra followed him back and settled down in front of the door, like a fanged guardian angel.

Even with all the day's events, sleep wasn't easy in coming. When he closed his eyes, Travis could still see all the bodies in the ocean. And the discovery of the strange Japanese intrigued him. Were there other survivors? he wondered.

The challenge of survival was, in a sense, exciting, but he was plagued by uncertainty. Would he be lucky enough to find the Keys with only a compass and a guess as to his position? If he reached them, would there be anything above water to mark their position? It would be easy to sail right through a small chain of islands buried under thirty feet of water.

What if there were no Keys left to be found? What about the rest of the world? How far would he have to sail to find a safe harbor?

Travis sighed and stared at the ceiling, listening to the gentle slap of the water against the hull. He drifted from the confusing uncertainty of the future, to the past, and the paths that had taken him to this strangest of circumstance. His thoughts drifted to Linda, his girlfriend, and the times they had shared. He wondered about old friends and lovers throughout the country–who had survived and who hadn't. Travis thought about his parents.

He had experienced one of those rare relationships with both his mother and father. They had been friends as well as parents. Travis truly enjoyed their company and conversations, and they his. In all his years as a child and as an adult, he had never encountered two more loving and understanding souls, and he missed them sorely. They had passed away a year apart, only two years ago, and there were still nights when he stared at the telephone, finding it so sadly incredulous that he could no longer pick up that instrument and hear their voices.

He remembered the sprawling, ranch-style home he had grown up in, nestled in the low, green hills of Napa Valley. Travis loved those cool spring mornings when soft trellises of sunlight filtered through the windows of the big kitchen and the smells of breakfast blended with his mother's perfume as she moved about the room. It had been a wonderful home, the perfect place to grow up, but, if the radio announcer had been correct, it was all gone, entombed in the sea with the rest of California. His parents' deaths had saddened him immeasurably, but he was glad that they had been spared the terror of this calamity.

He had only himself to worry about now–himself, and his curious Japanese companion, and a dog.

CHAPTER 4
THE CUBANO AND THE BOY

Night was falling and Carlos was talking to God again. He'd been talking to God a lot during the last few days. He was speaking in English, 'cause he had used Spanish most of the time and look where he was–still floating on the rat's-ass, son-a-ma bitchin' ocean! He figured that maybe God didn't speak too good Spanish. Maybe he had a language problem, so he'd try English for a while. *Couldn't do no worse*, he thought.

Carlos was a "floater," a Cuban refugee. He was, however, one of the most unhappy floaters in the history of the Cuban exodus.

Throughout the afternoon, as he drifted under the merciless sun, he had maintained a rambling, one-sided discourse with God. He was telling God, if he had forgotten, how much trouble Carlos had gone to, only to end up like a well-done *hamburguesa*.

He was reminding God how he built a *muy bueno* raft with a wood frame from shipping crates he "borrowed" from the banana docks, and heavy-duty truck inner tubes he "borrowed" from the Departamento de Transportacion. He had stocked up on bananas, coconuts, water jugs, and some jerk pork. Finally, one night he loaded up and sneaked the raft into the water right under the noses of the Guardia Nacional. *Madre de Dios*, Carlos was scared. But he did it, and off he went, paddling to America.

As he drifted out into the gulf stream, he paused and took a last look at the moonlit silhouette of Cuba. He was not sad, he was exhilarated!

Well, the first few days were fine. The currents and the wind carried him along better than he had expected. It was just him, he had plenty of food and water. (He was not like those other *oyes*. They got to have ten people with them just to keep them company. The food and water runs out and eight of them end up feeding the sharks.)

Anyway, like he'd been telling God, everything went just like he planned it. Late morning on the fifth day he looked up after a little siesta and there was America. The Keys were no more than a mile away. He could already taste his first *hamburguesa, Madre de Dios*, he could feel that first cold American Bud-a-wiser *cervesa* sliding down his throat. He was already rehearsing his "God Bless America" act for the Coast Guard, when, out of nowhere, came this rats-ass, son-a-ma-bitchin' giant wave! Carlos looked at the wave coming at him. He crossed himself and wet his pants. He knew he was as dead as last week's chicken–all those Hail Mary's and all those candles for nothing–but even a dying man will cling to hope.

Carlos clung to the raft. He held on like a fat tick buried in the back of a skinny Cuban pig. Afterwards, the only thing he could figure was that because the raft was so light, it rode over the wave instead of being crushed by it like everything else. Carlos and the raft struck the peak of the wave and went flying over the top like a UFO. With eyes the size of manhole covers, the little Cuban screamed like a banshee and held on for dear life. When the mist had finally cleared, Carlos discovered that he had crash-landed on the back side of the wave.

The raft was broken in half. Carlos found himself clutching half the deck and one inner tube. He had a broken nose and he was sure that he'd cracked a couple of ribs, but by the most remarkable of circumstances, he was still alive.

He rested for a while, hanging on to what was left of

his raft, trying to get his nose to quit bleeding. Given the situation, most people would be thankful just to have survived. Not so with Carlos. The Keys were gone. *Cono*! One stinkin' mile to bikini contests, Bud-a-weisers and Macadonal's *hamburguesas*, and God played a stinkin' trick on Carlos. *Madre de Dios*, was God on vacation? Maybe he went to Palm Beach and forgot about Carlos?

"Hey, God, why you don't just kill me in Cuba and make it easy for both of us? I go all this way to America. *Jesus Christe* what am I supposed to do now? Just drift around and bake like a chicken in the sun? *Arroz con* Carlos, eh? Very funny joke you play!"

It had been two days since Carlos and the raft met the son-a-ma-bitchin' wave. He'd had nothing to eat or drink since then, having lost his food and water with the other half of the raft. Floating on an ink-black ocean, aware that he was becoming more than just a little delirious, he suddenly spotted something up ahead. *That sure looks like a light bobbing in the water–maybe it's the Coast Guard with a* hamburguesa. *Sí! Gracias a Dios,* it is the Coast Guard. He could even smell the fat, greasy, Macadonel's *hamburguesa.* And there was a beautiful *señorita* in a Japanese kimono gazing down at him. As he drifted toward the light, he croaked out the only words he could think of.

Travis was just about asleep when he heard the sound. At first he passed it off to a seabird, but the noise took shape as it neared the boat. *God Bless America? Somebody was out there singing "God Bless America"*! When Travis reached the deck, he saw the sensei standing by the rail, looking out at the dark waters.

"He's over there." The sensei pointed about fifty feet off the bow.

Travis peered into the night. Sure enough, there was

someone lying on the wreckage of some sort of raft. He was ranting something about no onions, ketchup *solamente*.

Carlos had not been alone in that sea of desperation. Less than a mile away, another life hung in the balance.

The boy trembled and drifted in and out of consciousness. It was dark again. He was terrified that he would drift off once more and the nightmares would return. How could it be real? Surely he was going to wake up and find himself in his warm, soft bunk on the family yacht, his father's smiling face above him saying, "Get up, sleepyhead, we're going after a sailfish today." But, the saner part of him knew that would never happen again. When he closed his eyes, he could still see the giant wave surging towards them. He could feel the shock as it slammed against the big craft. The yacht had been a fifty-two-foot Hatteras–a strong, expensive boat.

"The wealthier the man, the bigger his toys," his father used to say.

His father was rich–had been rich. (It was impossible to think in the past tense yet.) He had owned a small software company. Every summer he took a month off and the three of them, the boy and his parents, would take "The Fifty-Two," as his Dad called it, to the Caribbean.

They were loaded with provisions and headed for Eluthera Island when it happened. The boat had barely left the dock in Marathon when his father, steering from the flying bridge, saw the wave coming. The ocean was sucked out around them, leaving the craft in less than ten feet of water as the wave approached. The boy knew that his father was a brave man–a man's man, his friends called him–but when he saw the fear etched on his dad's face as he and his mother were herded below, the child sensed terror for the first time in his young life. Frantically shouting orders, his father shoved his wife and child onto the couch in the salon, dragging the mattress from the closest bedroom to throw over them. He was on his way back through the galley, to close the cabin doors, when the wave struck. It was as if a giant hand hammered the boat, shoving it downward. From behind the mattress, the boy heard the flying bridge explode into splinters and felt the craft being ground and crushed on the bottom. The room darkened as they were engulfed by the wave. The couch snapped its moorings and slid across the room as the ship cantered wildly and rolled. As he was slammed against the far wall, the lad felt a searing jolt to his shoulder. Through the kaleidoscope of terror and pain he could hear his mother screaming, but she was no longer next to him. A few moments later he heard his father's anguished cry. Finally, toward the end of the battering, the Hatteras broke free and surged to the surface like a cork.

The ship was still being tossed about, but nothing like before. He felt a hand grasp him as he struggled to his feet. It was his mother. She had a wild, frightened look in her eyes and blood streamed down the side of her face. He cried out when he saw her and she pulled him close.

"It's okay," she yelled. "Come on, we have to get out of here." He understood her panic. The boat was rapidly filling with water. They stumbled through the mangled, listing ship, wading through the rising water, grasping bulkheads for balance like drunken sailors.

They reached the galley and stopped, frozen in the knee-deep water like clay statues. There before them lay the child's father, pinned against the far wall.

The refrigerator, at some point, had broken loose from the bulkhead and come careening across the cabin. It had crashed full force against the man, crushing him to the wall. The heavy appliance lay sideways across his body; his head and shoulders above it. Blood was streaming from his mouth and nose.

"Dad! Dad!" the boy cried, breaking loose from his mother and rushing to his father's side.

The water was rising rapidly, and the ship groaned and shifted in its death throes. The refrigerator moved against the pinned man and he moaned in agony. The boy struggled to maintain his balance in the shifting hold of the ship as he struggled frantically to move the ice box, crying, begging his father to hold on. His mother, already weakened from loss of blood, did her best to help, but the heavy box wouldn't budge. The water was hip deep by then, almost to his father's chin. Blood continued to pour from the man's mouth and his eyes were beginning to glaze from shock.

The dying man turned his head toward the child, and with an effort born of desperation and love, he reached out and clasped his son's hand. "Go," he whispered. "Go now, son."

Moments later, as the waters rose over the dead eyes of his father, the boy wailed, "Noooooo! Noooooo!"

Then his mother had his arm again and he was being pulled through the cabin. With the desperate strength of maternal instinct, she dragged him through the debris-strewn water and out the hatch to the deck. By some small miracle, the Avon raft was still partially attached to the deck. Two of the four clasps that held it were gone. While the ship groaned and shuddered and began to sink, they undid the remaining clasps and freed the raft. As it slipped off the deck and into the sea, they jumped into the water next to it, and climbed in.

Gasping in fear and exertion, the two held onto the raft as the rough waters bucked and tossed them. They sat helplessly and watched as the boat that held the man they both loved, foundered and sank in a matter of seconds.

A few minutes after the boat had gone down, the boy noticed the blood in the raft. He looked over. "Mom, Mom, are you all right?" It was a stupid question, and he knew it; he just didn't know what else to say.

She lay with her head and shoulders propped against the round, inflated hull of the rubber raft. She was deathly pale. One of her hands gripped her son, the other held the boat as it rocked in the waves. The cut on her head, just above the hairline, was still bleeding, though not badly. But all the blood in the boat; where had it come from? Then, as she shifted her weight, he saw the redness spurt from the back of her leg. In the melee, something had sliced through her thigh. The wound lay jagged and open. An artery was nicked and her life's blood pumped out every time her heart beat. She had, in an incredibly heroic effort, managed to get him out of the sinking boat while bleeding to death.

He grabbed her. "Mom ... your leg!" He reached down with his small hands and tried to hold the wound closed to stop the flow. Tears ran down his face, falling into the blood-red water of the raft.

His mother had barely moved through all his efforts. Her hands had fallen to her sides and her eyes were nearly closed. As the last of her strength pulsed through his trembling hands, she mumbled, "Just gonna rest. Close my eyes for a while."

"Please, Mom, don't die," he pleaded. "Don't leave me. Please don't close your eyes." But she did anyway, and she left him.

He continued to hold her long after he knew she was gone. He held her and he cried. The pain and the grief inside him welled up like a burning, angry sun and seared his very being. He cried out in helpless rage at the night and sobbed himself breathless until, exhausted, he slept.

CHAPTER 5
ATTENTION SHOPPERS!

Emaciated, sunburned, blistered, and incoherent, Carlos lay on a bunk in the cabin of the sailboat. His small, dark frame shivered as he drifted into a restless sleep, his brown eyes fluttering open occasionally, shining with fever and delirium. Travis and the sensei had given him water and soup from one of their last cans, put salve on his worst burns, then watched him as he struggled with slumber.

Travis turned to the sensei after their ministrations. "Well, he looks a little rough, but I think he'll make it. From all the bilingual rambling about America and *hamburguesas*, he sounds like a Cuban refugee. But Cuban, American, or Afro-Hungarian, he's another mouth to feed, and with our diminishing food and water, we're going to have to get in gear tomorrow. If we don't find ourselves some signs of civilization, we're going to be up that famous foul-smelling creek without a paddle."

The sensei smiled. "Ah, the river of defecation, yes?"

Travis grinned. "Yeah, one and the same."

"We will weigh anchor and be underway at first light," said the Japanese. He motioned to the prostrate Cuban. "I will watch him tonight. You go back to sleep."

"Okay," Travis replied. "See you in the morning."

Night passed quietly. The gentle movement of the ship and the rhythmic, soft slap of the waves against the hull lulled them all to sleep.

When Travis rose in the morning, he found the sensei already on deck and together they watched as the first edges of the sun rose over the dark waters and threw tendrils of yellow and orange into the smoky-colored sky. The morning breeze skipped across the sea, rippling the waters and caressing the two men, ruffling their hair. They stood there, savoring the sweet salt air, silently acknowledging their mutual bond with the sea, when suddenly a voice croaked from behind them.

"*Donde estan*—where am I?"

Travis and the sensei turned around as one. Battered, but apparently improving, the little Cuban stood by the hatchway looking at them. Small, tight ringlets of curly black hair framed a narrow face with tired but sensitive eyes. A pencil-thin mustache dusted his upper lip. His mouth, which seemed too wide for his face, softened into an uncertain smile, conveying the image of a man accustomed to laughter. His features were drawn with fatigue but, looking at him, one expected a degree of wit, a benign roguishness.

"Who are you?" he asked.

"We're the last people left in the world," Travis replied.

Carlos gasped, "*Madre de Dios!* It is all gone?"

Travis cracked a smile. "No, it probably isn't, but as far as we know, we're all that's left around here. The name's Travis and this gentleman is Higado Sensei. I would offer you a cup of coffee, but there's no gas for the stove. Line's ruptured."

"*Mi llamo* Carlos," the Cuban replied. "Hey man, chu got any more of that soup?"

Carlos had been out when brought aboard the boat, and Ra hadn't recognized him as a threat. Carlos hadn't seen the dog at all. When Ra suddenly appeared from the far side of the cabin, cautiously padded over and rumbled threateningly, Carlos went stiff as a wooden Indian.

"*Madre de Dios*, where chu get de frigeen' dinosaur?" he mumbled tensely as the Rottweiler sniffed him.

Travis chuckled, "It's okay, Carlos. He seems to think

you're all right, but I wouldn't make too many sudden movements 'til he gets to know you a bit."

"Jesus," Carlos exclaimed, "I don' move at all if he no want me to. That son-a-ma-bitchee snap Carlos' whole leg off just for snack."

Travis laughed and called Ra over to him, allowing the newcomer to relax. "Okay, let's go get that soup you wanted," Travis said as he motioned to the hatchway.

As they shared a can of soup and a tin of cooked chicken, Carlos told them of his trip from Cuba and his meeting with the wave. Although it was basically a tragic story, Carlos's way of telling it, with his accent and his gallows humor, had Travis laughing out loud. An hour later, when the sun has risen high enough to warm the air, they were on their way. But they hadn't gone far before fate delivered them another passenger.

The night passed in dark oblivion but, when the boy woke in the morning, the crushing terror and desperation of the previous day's events wrapped around his sanity like the hands of a strangler and squeezed. His mother was gone, washed over the side by the rough seas in the night. He hated himself for the relief he felt, knowing that the terrible decision had been taken away by the sea. It all became too much for him. He slid down onto the floor of the raft, pulled himself into a fetal position, and closed his eyes. The young man stayed that way all day and into the night. He didn't really sleep. His mind, in mechanized defense, simply short-circuited and turned off.

In the early hours of the next morning, the needs of the boy's body brought him back to life. He awoke with a thirst that gave new dimension to the word water. His face and arms were badly sunburned. His skin was hot, but he found himself shivering. His mind was so numbed that he felt like a stranger in his own body. The child steeled himself to concentrate only on the present–remembrance was not allowed.

At first, even he was unaware of the deep wounds to his psyche that the trauma of the past few days had caused. It was when he saw one of his mother's sandals in the raft and attempted to cry out, that he realized he couldn't speak. Although his mouth moved to form phrases, no words issued forth. Startled, he tried to speak again and still there was no sound from his throat, no words from his lips. It wasn't like when he had laryngitis and he could just barely make the words come out. It was more like the part of him that gave him voice was gone ... just gone! Again, his mouth framed silent syllables, lost to the sound of the waves slapping against the raft and the cries of the gulls above. The boy collapsed back against the side of the hard rubber and cried–in silence.

It was thirst that brought the young castaway around once more. He lay there, cradling his swollen tongue in a dirt-dry mouth, when a thought burst into his consciousness–there was water in the raft. His father always kept a half-gallon of drinking water in a pouch in the back of the raft near the transom. In the kaleidoscopic events of the last twenty-four hours, he had forgotten all about it. The youth crawled over to the pouch and nearly ripped the zipper off getting it opened. There was not only water, but, sealed in a plastic bag were a half-dozen granola bars.

His hands shaking, he tore the cap off the water bottle and drank greedily. He paused for a moment, savoring the feeling of moisture in his parched mouth, then took another long swallow. Without missing a beat, he snapped the lid on the water and attacked the granola bars. He devoured one without even tasting it, then he slowed down and ate another, but resisted the temptation for a third. After the second granola bar, the boy had another slug of water, then reluctantly put his meager supplies away.

As the dawn gave life to the gray, cloud-filled skies, the young man tried to sleep–to escape. But when he closed his eyes, he was assailed by nightmares recounting the death of his mother and father. He sobbed in silence, his voice trapped like an insect in a mason jar, and he lay awake sweating and shaking. The sun rose and tortured him, and when it finally set, the velvet coolness of night seduced him into sleep and the nightmares came again. He awoke drenched in sweat, drank a little water and mechanically ate part of a granola bar, but he could feel the life force ebbing from him–the desire to exist, to survive, was fading. Night bled into morning again. He had long since lost track of time, and everything around him had become surreal. When he heard the voice calling, the boy thought it was his father. There was a part of him that knew it couldn't be, yet the voice persisted.

Once again it was the sensei, riding point on the bow, who spotted the raft. He pointed to the starboard as Travis changed course slightly and brought the boat abeam. There in the raft lay a boy, blond hair plastered to his head from salt spray, soft blue eyes staring up, vacant and uncomprehending, arms and face burned reddish brown. The sensei, holding a line, jumped into the raft and tied it off. He lifted the lad up to Travis on the deck. The boy didn't respond as he was picked up and handed to the man on the sailboat, but as Travis laid the child on a bunk in the cabin, the boy suddenly looked at him with frightened, pleading eyes. His mouth moved but made no sound.

"Easy son, easy," Travis whispered. "You're safe now. Just rest."

They offered him water and he drank a small swallow

but refused any food, then he curled up in a tight ball in the corner of the bed and dozed fitfully.

Travis's heart went out to the boy who, though not in bad physical shape, seemed to be suffering from shock. The lad was nearly as tall as Carlos, still lithe, but at that age where he would soon begin to fill out. The features of his face were child-soft yet, but handsome. He would grow up to be a fine-looking young man if he got the chance.

However, he was another mouth to feed, and unless Travis was successful in finding supplies, survival for the boy, and everyone else, was going to become questionable very soon, so after assigning a weak but attentive Carlos to watch over the boy, he went topside and ran out every inch of sail, his eyes constantly searching the horizon.

An hour later, almost as if he had willed it, Travis spotted the white walls of a huge, partially collapsed building protruding from the water. Dropping the jib, they sailed slowly and carefully over the area as Travis tried to verify their location. It appeared, by luck more than skill, that they were over the Publix Supermarket/K-Mart shopping center he had hoped to find.

The depth of the water was approximately thirty feet. Though the recent turbulence had clouded the sea, the water was still clear enough to discern crushed and mangled cars in the parking lot below them. Many of the vehicles had been thrown against the side of the building by the force of the wave. The walls that had received the greatest impact of the wave had been completely destroyed; part of the back wall had held, but the roof was gone, carried away or broken into pieces and mingled in the carnage. The contents of the building were scattered over a couple of blocks. Travis tried to keep himself from wondering how many hundreds of people had died screaming in the wreckage below.

There were two sets of snorkeling equipment with masks,

fins, and snorkels stored in the forward compartments of the boat. Accompanying them was a single dive tank and regulator, miraculously undamaged, and registering twenty-two-hundred PSI. At a depth of thirty feet, an experienced diver like Travis could squeeze out about an hour and a half of bottom time–if he took it slow and easy. He decided to tackle the grocery store first. Afterwards, if he still had air, he'd try the K-Mart for whatever hardware and supplies he could find there.

Travis checked the boy before preparing to dive. The child still slept, but occasionally he would thrash back and forth silently. Looking down at him, Travis knew that the kid had been through a rough time, but at the moment, there was nothing more he could do for him.

They anchored the sailboat over what used to be the center of the Publix store. A cold northern wind whipped at Travis as he stripped to his T-shirt and underwear, and it occurred to him that the weather had suddenly become unseasonably cold for this time of the year. He wondered if the damages the earth had received could have already begun to affect climatic conditions. If he could find supplies they needed, he was for heading north. If there actually had been some sort of polar shift like Cody used to talk about, and the weather was getting colder in the tropics, it made sense that it might well be warmer farther north.

He donned his gear and consulted with the sensei about the dive. The plan was for Travis to take a quick exploratory look to determine what, if anything, was below. If the initial dive showed promise, Travis would go back down with the two nylon catch bags they had found with the snorkeling gear, and fill them with goods. He would then tie the catch bags to a line from the boat and the sensei would pull them up.

Just before he dropped into the water he told the sensei,

"Watch for my bubbles on the surface. It will give you an idea where I am—not that you'll be able to do much about it if anything goes wrong, but it'll make me feel a little better knowing you're paying attention to me."

The sensei nodded. "I will watch for you, Travis-san."

When Travis hit the water, he noticed that it too was reacting to the cooler weather, and had a bite that was well beyond cool and refreshing. He paused for a second, floating on the surface, and let his body adjust to the temperature while studying the bottom. Drifting directly above the store, he could see the bent and broken remains of the aisle shelves that had displayed food. The people and the goods in the store had been blown away with the ferocity of a high-pressure hose on an ant colony. Nevertheless, he could see canned goods scattered across the floor, their round bottoms looking like giant pieces-of-eight from a recently gutted Spanish galleon.

Travis treaded water and yelled to the sensei, "Throw me the rope. I'm going down here. Looks like shelved goods below us."

Grabbing the rope as it was tossed to him, he tied the end to the catch bags, and dove for the bottom. He drifted silently downward, his eyes scanning the scattered ruins of what was, until recently, his world. He swam past an overturned car and observed a grisly reminder of the killer wave—an arm extended out of the passenger window, moving stiffly up and down in the current, almost as if beckoning him. Travis shivered and swam on until he came to a large overturned display rack. On either side were hundreds of cans. He settled onto the bottom and began sorting, then loaded his bags. When the two bags were stuffed with corned beef, tuna fish, baked beans, etc., he hauled them closer to the boat and tugged on the rope. Up they went, as the sensei pulled from above. Two minutes later, the bags were back, and he began to fill them again.

That went on for the better part of an hour. In the process, they accumulated everything from fruit juices, canned fruit and jars of almonds, to peanut butter, canned peas, corn, and dog food. They had recovered sufficient supplies to last them at least a month. Travis surfaced with the last load and checked his pressure gauge. He still had eight hundred pounds left–enough time for a short dive on the other store. Handing his tank to the sensei, Travis pulled himself up over the stern. He put on some warm clothes they had found in one of the dressers on board, then they upped anchor and repositioned the boat about two hundred yards back, over the K-Mart. Travis, deciding to go below and warm up for half an hour, was greeted by an exuberant Carlos. The diminutive Cuban, an open can of beans in one hand and a jar of peanut butter in the other, praised Travis as he entered the cabin.

"Hey man, chu a pretty amazin' son-a-ma-bitchee. Most *hombres*, they go in the ocean, they catch a *pescado*, maybe a lobster. But chu man, chu catch peanut butter!"

The boy was awake, huddled in the corner of his bunk, his legs drawn up to his chest as he watched Travis and Carlos, but said nothing. Beside him sat an empty can of beans, a sign of a returning appetite, anyway.

Travis reached down and picked up a can of peaches from the pile of canned goods on the floor. He popped the pull-top, walked over to the boy, and knelt in front of him. "Hi, little buddy, how ya doin'?" he asked, extending the can of peaches. "How about splitting these with me?" The lad looked up at Travis for a few seconds, then nodded his head. Travis pulled a slice out for himself, then handed the can to the boy, who slowly reached out and took it. "You eat the rest," Travis said.

Travis got up and sat on the bunk next to the youngster, and a moment later Ra came over to him and nuzzled his hand affectionately. The lad watched with a mixture of curiosity and concern. Ra, who seemed to understand intrinsically that the rules had changed regarding his protection of the boat, raised his head and sniffed the newcomer.

Travis stroked the dog and said, "His name's Ra. He won't hurt you; he's just big, not mean."

The boy nodded solemnly, holding his can of peaches with both hands.

"What's your name, son?" Travis asked. The child paused for a moment, then his mouth moved to form words but there was no sound. Obviously struggling with himself, he tried again, still without success. Suddenly his face became a mixture of pain and frustration, and tears ran from the corners of his eyes. Travis realized then that the boy couldn't speak. He felt angry with himself, and embarrassed for the pain he had just caused the child.

Doing his best to mollify the situation, he said, "Hey, it's okay. You just hang out, relax and catch up on a few meals. We'll take it slow and let everybody get to know one another in their own time, all right?" He stood up. "I'm Travis. This is Carlos, and I guess you can call the Japanese guy on deck, Sensei. I've got to get back topside and do a little diving, but Carlos, here, will watch out for you. If you need anything, let him know."

As Travis moved up the stairs to the deck, Carlos called after him, "Hey Travees, chu see any Bud-a-wiser on the bottom of that ocean with de peanut butter?"

Ten minutes later Travis was back in the water. It was late afternoon but daylight wasn't a factor as he had only about half an hour of air left. Even so, the next round of underwater shopping was extremely important. There were a number of things they needed to enhance their chances of survival. Among those items were fishing gear, propane gas or a grill for cooking, foul weather gear, and a hundred other things, not the least of which were weapons.

Cody's words of long ago echoed in Travis' ears: "When the shift comes and the damage is done, there won't be any law for quite a while in the majority of this country. It's gonna be every man for himself and I guaran-friggin'-tee you, it's gonna get sticky. When the people left alive in the cities have eaten everything but the cardboard advertisements in all the grocery stores, there's gonna be a mass exodus toward the rural areas. Trust me, when they arrive, they'll kill you for a candy bar if you can't protect yourself. By the end of the first winter after the shift, better than half of the original survivors will be dead from disease, starvation, exposure to the elements, and exposure to their fellow man. The only way to survive will be to have a place far enough from the cities and difficult enough to get to, that you filter out the majority of the predators. You arm yourself like Patton and treat aggression like Attila the Hun. A few heads placed on stakes, marking the boundaries of your property, is a relatively effective deterrent to unwanted guests."

Travis had to smile when he thought of Cody. What a character. But damn if he wasn't right so far.

He glided toward the bottom in the cold water and studied the area for the items they needed. There was no determining departments in the store anymore. Everything was scrambled and strewn everywhere. He'd just have to work fast and cover as much ground as possible. After five minutes of precious time, he had worked his way back to the partially existing wall when he began to recognize sports equipment. Soon he had found two good fishing rods and reels, a couple of raincoats, a hunting knife and, under an overturned display rack, packages of hooks, sinkers, and lures. Travis dragged the load back and tied it to the rope which the sensei promptly pulled up, then he was off again.

It appeared that the sporting goods department must have been near the surviving wall, as much of it was piled against that crumbling barricade. He rummaged through the debris, eventually coming to a smashed and broken display case. Remembering that weapons at K-Mart were kept in such cases, he began to dig around and, sure enough, there before him in the wreckage lay a Smith and Wesson nine-millimeter pistol. Moments later, a few feet away, he found a .38 revolver with a four-inch barrel. Travis stowed the guns in his bag, then swam over to the remains of the display case. The glass was scattered all about, but the solid lower compartment was still intact. He pried open the sliding door, and was rewarded with the sight of ammunition cartons. *Thank God for sealed boxes.* He found six boxes for each weapon, which he added to the catch bag, then continued on.

Making his way back to the boat, he picked up a spear gun and some lubricating oil. He also found a small gas-operated Hibachi, but no propane gas. When that load had been transferred to the boat, Travis checked his pressure gauge. The remaining two hundred and fifty pounds was enough for one more run. He worked quickly now, gathering such miscellaneous items as fishing line, suntan lotion, oil for lanterns, etc. He was about one hundred feet from the boat when he saw the barrel of a rifle protruding from beneath a huge display rack. The metal rack lay tilted on its side, supported by surrounding debris, creating a cave-like effect. The gun lay in the back, wedged beneath the base. Travis, excited by the prospect of having a more powerful weapon to add to his arsenal, quickly swam under the metal shelving, grabbed the barrel and pulled. The rifle broke free with a lurch, but in doing so disturbed the delicate balance of the structure above him.

There was a grating sound and a shift in the rack as the surrounding supports gave way and it fell. Travis had just enough time to turn around and begin to move out, head first, when the entire unit came crashing down on his waist and legs, pinning him painfully to the bottom.

For a moment he was stunned, but as the realization of his predicament set in, the pain in his legs was far out-shadowed by the cold, knife-like fear gripping him. He struggled maniacally to free himself. Most of the weight was centered on the back of his legs. There was no way he could reach around, or gain any leverage to lift it off. He was trapped. He looked at his pressure gauge–fifty pounds left, and fading fast. He struggled again, so violently that he could feel the flesh of his ankles tearing against the metal. Fear and the exertion were rapidly depleting the last of his air. The tank was already becoming harder to draw on. He shifted again and frantically glanced at a gauge that no longer offered any hope. He had only moments left.

The air faded as he struggled madly, his tortured lungs screaming for oxygen. Then, inhale as he might, there was nothing more coming through the regulator. Terror gradually faded to surrender, then acceptance, and his struggles were reduced to feeble, helpless movements. He was dying. As everything dimmed to shades of gray and black, he thought he saw a large shadow pass above him. His last cognizant thought was: *Probably a shark–not bad enough I have to die like this, I have to get eaten as well.*

Then suddenly, as the darkness began to overtake him, he felt something grab him and roughly drag him out from under the heavy metal frame. He was beyond caring. The next thing he remembered was being pulled across the surface of the water, throwing up saltwater and trying desperately to inhale the sweet, life-giving air into his lungs.

As the sensei pushed him up to the boat, Carlos dragged

him on board and unceremoniously dumped him on the deck. "Hey, Travees, Travees. Chu okay, man? Chu don't look so *buenos*, man."

Travis couldn't move. He lay on the deck gasping, incredibly thankful just to be alive. Across from him, the sensei slipped up and over the rail of the boat in nothing but his birthday suit. He knelt next to Travis and quickly examined him, nodded an approval, then went to get his clothes.

Ten minutes later they were all gathered in the cabin. Travis had recovered sufficiently to speak again, and the color of his skin was no longer gray and mottled.

He turned to the sensei. "How'd you know? How'd you find me?"

The Japanese looked at him, "You say to watch bubbles. When there was no more, and you had not surfaced, I swam over to last bubbles and dove down."

Travis shook his head in grudging admiration. "Not a bad free dive, considering you had to deal with lifting that rack off me and getting me to the surface."

"Japan is surrounded by water," said the sensei. "Part of training at Dojo is daily two-mile ocean swim."

With new respect in his eyes, Travis stared at the Oriental. "Well, Higado Sensei, the first port we reach, I owe you the best bottle of saki in town. I'm in your debt and I won't forget." He stood and bowed slightly to the sensei.

The Japanese smiled, and returned the bow. "The debt is already paid. You forget that it was you who rescued me from my sinking ship."

"Then we'll just split that bottle of Saki when we find it," Travis replied.

Carlos, who was sitting next to Travis, shook his head sadly. "All this talk of liquor and not one stinkin' Bud-a-wiser for Carlos."

Everyone laughed–except the boy.

CHAPTER 6
COUNTRY CLUBS AND SINKING SHIPS

The sun descended slowly into the sea, piercing the evening sky with fiery daggers, surrounding the gray storm clouds on the horizon with a crimson luminescence.

They all sat together on the deck, watching nature's light show, each lost in his own thoughts for the moment. Memories of other times, friends and lovers, other places, flashed through their minds in pinwheel fashion. Their lives had been changed forever. There was no going back. The past no longer existed, and the future–who knew what that held. They were embarking on a journey into the new world, as if they were ancient mariners, setting out in search of new lands.

Aside from the tragedy that had brought him to that point in time, Travis couldn't help but once again find himself excited, intrigued by the possibilities and uncertainty of the trek ahead. *Born once more to adventure on the sea*, he thought to himself as he watched the last rays of the sun burnish the darkening waters. He smiled, remembering adventures he and Cody had shared on the ocean.

The first waft of the cool night breeze brought him from his reverie and he shivered.

"It getting *muy frio*," Carlos muttered next to him as he stood, his arms wrapped around his skinny frame.

"Yeah," replied Travis. "I think its time to head below deck." As the others stood, Ra, who had been lying next to them, rose and led the way to the warmth of the cabin.

Carlos had stored all the goods they had found. He had also cleaned everything from the walls to the floor and laid out a cold dinner of beef, carrots, potatoes, and chocolate pudding for dessert. Ra devoured the couple of cans of dog food prepared for him, then lay contented by the cabin door–the ever faithful guardian.

During supper, they learned a little more about one another. Carlos began by telling them of his life in Cuba. The small, animated man with dark, curly hair and an easy smile recounted working for the Cuban equivalent of the U.S. Department of Transportation. He had repaired their trucks, from engines to two-way radios. To hear him tell it, he was nearly a genius–forced to repair antiquated equipment with inadequate tools and very few spare parts. Nonetheless, Carlos convinced them that with talent and tenacity, he had kept nearly the entire Cuban government running. There was some confusion, however, over the disappearance of several radios in the trucks he had repaired. It had prompted an investigation, but he left before any conclusions could be drawn. He was innocent of course, but in Cuba one was guilty until proven guilty, so he decided not to wait around for the verdict.

Travis told them of his flight service and how he had survived the wave. The sensei listened quietly and interjected a question or a statement here and there. The boy seemed to be gradually shaking off his lethargy, but there was a heavy aura of sadness around him that was almost tangible. He did, however, begin to show interest in the conversation, and when dinner was over, he lay down beside Ra on the floor. His tentative strokes to the animal's flanks were answered by a huge sticky tongue licking his fingers. It seemed that both the boy and Ra were pleased with the exchange.

The sensei retrieved his swords from behind his bunk and performed his ritual cleaning. He brought the cloth back and forth across each blade and spoke, for the first time, of his personal life in Japan. The boy and Carlos, fascinated by the swords, listened intently as the modern-day Samurai told of his school, his home, and, with a touch of sadness, his family. He had left a wife, two sons, and three grandchildren in Japan, hoping to return to them by late summer.

"Now," he said, as he paused and his gaze fell away, "I must learn patience and practice faith while I await the judgement of powers greater than my own."

An hour later, they extinguished the two oil lanterns and everyone retired to their berths.

Ten miles to the north, two people fought a desperate, losing battle with rising water in a badly damaged 32-foot Chris Craft. The overworked, hand-operated bilge pump was failing and, with it, their chances of survival. They were bruised and bloodied and weary to the point of collapse. Still, they refused to give up.

If not for the cuts and the oily grime, one would have said that they were a handsome couple. Both of them were tall; he was six feet, and she, about five-ten. He was slim, with the well-defined muscles of a runner, or a raquetball player. He wore his styled blond hair straight back. His aquiline nose and intense blue eyes gave him the look of a seductive predator: handsome, sophisticated, perhaps a little dangerous. He was college-educated and street-wise; congenial when he needed to be, formidable when it was necessary. The man was a remarkable communicator, a salesman extraordinaire. He called himself an investment broker, and it was true that he had made considerable amounts of money for some people, but regardless of the situation, he rarely failed to profit himself. Many of the peripherally legal "special opportunities" he so generously offered his clients never materialized, disappearing like the investor's money. There were times when it really wasn't his fault, but generally, it still presented a problem. If his welcome began to wear thin in one place, he simply moved on. There were lots of country clubs packed with people who had more dollars than sense.

She was the epitome of the stunning blond; her hair was a tawny, strawberry color, thick and long, cascading down her shapely shoulders. Her bright green eyes and perfect skin were complimented by a figure that left gawkers walking into walls wherever she went. She was a flawless combination of breeding, sensuality, and intellect. Her father had been a consul for the State Department. She had attended secondary school in Europe, and spoke fluent French and Spanish, as well as English. Her mother's family had been American ranchers in Mexico, where they raised cattle and horses. The summers spent with her grandparents on the ranch had given her an earthiness, a love of the land that complimented perfectly her more sophisticated qualities.

She had graduated college, spent three years with the Peace Corps in Central America, then returned to school. While in her second year of graduate studies for a law degree, her parents had been killed in an airplane crash, leaving behind a sizable estate. The tragedy, and the ensuing wealth, did not alter her ambitions, and she had continued her education. She met Jan at a party in Fort Lauderdale while in her last year of studies. He had attempted to impress her with position, resources, and significant acquaintances. She decided early on in the evening that his looks were definitely his best asset.

They were well-tanned, well-endowed and well-connected–yacht club material–equally at home at a cocktail party or on the tennis court, but as they struggled grimly in the water-filled cabin of a foundering boat, that life was a million miles behind them.

The engine was ruined, the electrical system down, radios broken. Their food and water were running low; the life raft was untied and ready.

He levered like a machine on the manual bilge pump. She bailed with a bucket, filling it from the cabin, taking it up to the deck and dumping it overboard. They both knew the water was still rising, regardless of their efforts, but neither would be the first to admit defeat. That was the way they were with each other. It epitomized the time they had spent together for the past few months. They shared their lives in cohabitational competition: neither showing weakness to the other. It wasn't that they didn't care for one another–they did. In fact, the challenge that each represented made the relationship all the more interesting. They had begun to date casually at first, becoming more serious when they discovered how much they enjoyed each other's company. The relationship had evolved from *the possible big one* to a pleasant contest of wills, generously seasoned with great sex. They both recognized that they made an attractive couple, and in the world of business lunches and country clubs, looking the part had its advantages. But at that moment, the only advantage they had was that they were still alive, and that was waning.

A few hours later, near early morning, Jan had just begun to work the bilge pump again after a few minutes rest when, with a sickening wrench, the valve in the pump gave out. The handle slid effortlessly up and down the pipe, and the stream of water ceased. He looked up at her.

"Well, Christina, the party on this yacht's over. Time to move on to a less mechanized, more rubberized form of transportation."

She gave him a somber smile. "You always did have a way with words."

"I make my living with words, dear," he replied. "Put the correct syllables in the proper sequence. Combine that with timing, which is the essence, from commando raids to orgasms, and you can elicit practically anything from anyone."

"Everyone has a weakness and everyone a price, eh, Jan?"

It was curious, she thought. They stood there bantering back and forth as if they were at the club when, in reality, their boat was sinking in the dead of night, they were nearly out of food and water, and the only thing they had left that floated was a pathetic little rubber raft that looked like it came from some second-hand concession on Miami Beach. To top it off, they were in the middle of the ocean, God knows how far from civilization–if there still was a civilization. For all their spit and polish, she thought, they were tough.

They had been diving off Alligator Reef, just east of Marathon, the day the wave struck. They were preparing to pull the anchor, to move farther down the reef, when Jan saw the thin line forming on the horizon. He had witnessed a small tsunami once before, in the Phillippines. He knew immediately what it was. He also recognized that the size and speed of this one dwarfed anything in history. There was no running from it, no getting around it. He glanced back at the slender string of islands to the stern, then forward to the approaching leviathan. He decided to head straight for it at full power. It was a desperate gamble, perhaps suicidal, but the alternatives weren't any more promising. There was a small chance they might force their way through, or over it–a small chance. He quickly explained the situation to Christina, wondering how she would react to the prospect of imminent disaster.

She moved quickly to the bow rail and gazed out across the sun-sparkled sea, staring at the oncoming apocalypse, then turned to Jan. "I'll get the anchor," she said. "You get the engines going."

Strapped to captain's chairs inside the reinforced bridge, they drove their fragile craft into the heart of the wave. Still, there was really no reason why they should have survived.

Neither of them remembered much after striking the wave. When the pummeling finally subsided and they came to, the Keys were gone, and Jan's beautiful boat was a floating wreck that was taking on water at an alarming rate.

Both had been cut and bruised badly but neither had received any debilitating injuries. The last three days had been a dazed nightmare of painful, perpetual motion. It hurt just to move, but they had to to keep their boat from sinking. They had slept little, eaten scarcely enough food to sustain them, and had suffered the fear of the choices that were left to them. With the breaking of the bilge pump, those choices had become even more limited.

Exhausted, they sat on the deck, hand in hand, their backs against the cabin, and watched the waning of the full moon–its brightness illuminating the phosphorescent tips of the waves around them. It was a good two hours to sunrise. The boat would last until then. With the sunlight, they would load the raft with the few provisions left and cast themselves adrift.

The moonlight on the water was mesmerizing, and weariness overtook them. They huddled against each other seeking comfort and warmth, and fell asleep.

As the sun rose, its warmth roused them. Jan woke with a start as a wave gently crested the gunnel of the boat and caressed his feet. "Jesus Christ! Wake up, Christina. The goddamned boat's sinking!" he croaked as he shook her and rose painfully to his feet.

"Get the raft untied!" he yelled as he stumbled toward the hatch. "The water's nearly filled the cabin. I'm going in for the supplies, then we've got to get off. She's going down!"

He struggled through the chest-deep water, took a quick breath and submerged himself, grabbing the packages of goods they had prepared. She untied the raft and stood by, frightened but ready. He came out of the cabin with two bundles as the boat made a distinct canter toward the ocean floor. "Push the raft over the side!" he yelled. "No time for more." Slipping the raft into the water, she tied the slipknot they had practiced onto the rail, jumped in, and took the bundles from Jan. He leaped into the dinghy behind her and pulled the knot loose as the yacht's bow entered the water.

They quickly pushed away and watched the death throes and the gurgling, bubbling disappearance of *The Caribbean Joy*, their last refuge in a ravaged world. They sat for a moment in post-adrenal silence, then Jan took a cigarette from the waterproof case in his shirt pocket and lit it.

He leaned back against the rubber rail and exhaled, squinting at the rising sun. "Nice day for a tan," he said. "Did you bring the oil?"

Morning broke, and the sun turned the slate-gray waters back to blue with its usual sleight-of-hand. Once everyone was up, Travis called a meeting before breakfast, which was being prepared by Carlos, the self-appointed resident chef. To hear Carlos tell it, he was once the head chef at one of Cuba's major hotels, where people came from everywhere to eat his "*Pollo* Fidel" and his "Veal Picasso." But there'd been a little problem–something to do with the disappearance of several forty-pound rounds of beef that were later discovered at a roadside restaurant that was owned by Carlos's brother-in-law.

Gathered around the table in the cabin, Travis explained to the small group the necessity for conservation of food and water, and the need to assign responsibilities to each person, from maintenance of the ship to fishing for dinner. They had been thrown together by fate, but they were a team now, and they had to work together to survive. It was agreed that Travis and the sensei would handle the sailing and navigation of the vessel–something Carlos, to the surprise of everyone, said he knew nothing about. Navigation was limited to the compass and the stars as all the direction-finding equipment had been destroyed by the wave. The sensei, however, felt he could keep them headed toward the mainland without much difficulty. Carlos agreed to handle the meals, using the hibachi and driftwood for fuel. He also agreed to handle the maintenance of the cabin. The boy, who was gradually shaking his catatonia, was assigned the task of fishing when at anchor and trailing a feathered jig when they were sailing. Fish would become an important supplement to their diet of canned goods. Water, at that point, was generously rationed at a glass with each meal and an occasional sip during the day as needed. With the ship's water tanks almost full and the extra gallons stored onboard, it was not yet a problem. Travis explained a plan he'd thought of to reach the mainland and determine the status of the rest of the world. It was agreed upon unanimously.

With the meeting completed, Carlos served a breakfast of canned pears and peaches with a scoop of peanut butter and a glass of warm Pepsi from the defunct refrigerator.

The sensei and Travis had estimated their position the night before, so they upped anchor and sailed for the mainland.

The boy proved to be an adept fisherman and in no time had a feathered lure skipping the surface behind the boat. It was he who sighted the boat in the three o'clock position off their bow. Remembering that they had agreed to check any floating objects for survivors and supplies, the boy ran nimbly along the deck, back to the steering cockpit where Travis was, and pointed urgently. Travis gazed out across the water and squinted.

"Something out there, huh? Yeah, sure enough, looks like a sinking boat." A moment later he added, "With a couple of people on board. I'd say we arrived just in time, from the looks of things."

They moved closer and watched the figures scramble off the craft moments before it submerged. They could see them in the life raft with their backs to the sailboat. As they moved within hailing distance, the sensei took the wheel and Travis moved forward to the bow. The dinghy was no more than fifty yards away when Travis hailed them.

"Hello there! Need a lift?"

The figures in the raft snapped around as one, relief and joy on their faces. The big man in the raft yelled back, "Hell yes. We don't even care where you're going!"

Carlos and the sensei dropped the sails as they slid up to the raft. Travis caught the bowline tossed by Jan and tied it off. As the boats came together, Jan rose and held the rail of the sailboat while he helped Christina up to Travis and into the boat.

As the woman stood, Travis got his first good look at her. Even with the bruises and the cuts, and no make-up, she was easily one of the most attractive woman he had seen in years. Moreover, it seemed as if he already knew her, or had known her from somewhere, or some time. Only once before in his life had he experienced such a profound feeling of *déjà vu*, and that had been with his wife, Michelle, many years ago, on the island of Haiti. Her death, several years later, had left a void in his life no one had ever filled.

His feelings must have shown on his face because, as she reached for his hand, she gave him a quizzical smile and asked, "Are you all right?"

Quickly regaining his composure he replied, "Gee, I would have figured I was supposed to be asking you that question."

She gave a throaty little chuckle. "It was just that you looked ... Oh well, never mind."

Travis helped her over the rail and onto the deck. Christina moved out of the way, and Jan climbed aboard behind her.

"Gentlemen," he said, "I can't tell you how glad we are to see you. That's just about the most remarkable timing that I've ever seen."

Introductions were made all around and the couple were taken below. There, Carlos insisted on treating their cuts and abrasions, explaining that he once studied to be an assistant doctor–whatever that was–at one of Cuba's finest medical facilities. He would probably have been a physician's assistant by now, but there had been a problem with missing medical supplies that turned up on the black market in Havana. Naturally, Carlos had nothing to do with it, and fortunately, they couldn't prove he had. But it tainted his medical career, nonetheless. So, as the might-have-been Doctor Carlos treated the couple, they told a story of what was to be a simple ten-day cruise to the Keys, and the chaotic struggle to survive on a wrecked boat with a breached hull.

As Jan and Christina related their experience, Travis studied the couple. That is to say, he mostly watched Christina–the thick, honey-red hair and sensuous mouth, the high cheekbones and almond-shaped, emerald-green eyes. Perfectly shaped breasts strained at the soft cotton shift she wore, and her tanned legs were so long they seemed to go on forever. *She was the kind of girl who could bring out the best and the worst in a man,* he thought. Glancing over at her partner, he had to admit, begrudgingly, that the man had probably never suffered with too much rejection from the ladies–*tennis pro type, never too far from a slim waist and a tall drink.*

He was dragged from his reverie by a question from Christina. "Tell us, Travis, what are your plans? Where are you all going?"

Caught by surprise, Travis stumbled for a moment, then

caught his verbal balance. "Well, ah well, we've decided to shoot for the mainland and find out what's happened to the rest of the world."

"Good plan," Jan interjected. "Just what I'd do. By the way, Travis, seeing as we'll be traveling with you for a while, if you need any help sailing this baby, I'm your man. I've put in my fair share of time behind the tiller."

Travis thanked him for the offer, saying that it was quite possible but, for the first day, they were to just relax and catch up on some badly needed sleep.

After making the couple comfortable below, the others excused themselves, Travis saying, "We've got to get underway again. Get some sleep and we'll talk tonight at supper." As Travis left the cabin, he stole one more glance at Christina. He was pleasantly surprised to find her studying him with a bemused little smile.

Ra, who had remained aloof, followed the group out to the cockpit and lay by Travis's feet. The man scratched him on his head. "What's up, Ra? Getting too crowded down there for you?"

After raising the sails and setting course again, the sensei came and sat down across from Travis. "Well, my friend, we are gathering quite a cross section of the world, eh?"

"That we are, Sensei. That we are. I wonder how many more survivors we've got out there."

"Not many more," said the sensei, his tone somber. "There were probably very few, if any, survivors on the islands themselves. Even if they survived the battering of the wave, which I believe is next to impossible, after four days in cold water with no food, they would have died of exposure. I think the only people who survived were on large boats in open water. There is, of course, the exception of Carlos, who was on a vessel so light that it rode over the wave rather than being crushed by it."

"Well, we'll keep our eyes open," Travis said, "just in case."

But they saw no more survivors that day.

That afternoon, while under sail, the boy hooked a fat, ten-pound grouper, enticed by the feathered jig. He fought it silently, refusing help, as everyone cheered him on. Jan and Christina, refreshed by a few hours sleep, came up on deck to see what the excitement was about. Travis watched as Christina clapped excitedly and encouraged the lad. Seeing her refreshed and animated, he was once again taken by how attractive she was. He mentally shook himself, with a quick reminder that this was another man's woman he was gaping at. The boy wore the fish out and brought it alongside. Carlos, lying stomach down, reached over the side and grabbed it by its gaping mouth. He pulled the grouper up and over the deck while everyone cheered again. Then, for the first time since coming aboard, the youngster smiled.

Carlos removed the lure from the fish's mouth. Holding it aloft, he congratulated the boy. "A hot-damned *bueno pescado, muchacho*! Tonight I make my famous *Pescado Cubano*. Once I even make *Pescado Cubano* for that pig, Fidel, himself, when he come to the hotel *restaurante*, but before I serve it to him, I spit on it." Carlos laughed. "He come to me afterwards and say, 'Carlos,'–he call me Carlos–he say, 'I never have pescado that good in my life.' I tell him I put some special seasoning on it, just for him only." Carlos was still laughing at his own joke as he took the fish forward to clean it.

Travis raised the sail again, having dropped it while the boy fought the fish. A brisk wind filled the canvas, and the ship knifed through the water as they sped northward. The sensei moved to the bow, and Jan and Christina settled into the cockpit with Travis. Jan's eyes scrutinized the sails, looking for any luff. Travis took satisfaction in knowing there was none. The boat was trimmed as well as she could be.

Jan looked at Travis. "Tell me, what's the story with the navigational equipment and the radios below. Anything working?"

Travis shook his head. "The ship took quite a beating, and with the exception of the VHF, most of the equipment was literally torn from the brackets. The VHF radio is still in place, but there's nothing but static on it. Carlos says if it can be made to work, he'll fix it. Unfortunately, we only have part of an antenna left topside, but he said he may be able to rig that, too. He's going to look at it tonight."

"Excellent," said Jan. "That is good news. I'd love to know what the hell's going on out there."

"That makes two of us," Travis agreed.

Christina sat back, her head against the rail, her arms up resting on the sides of the cockpit. "God," she breathed, "it feels good just to be safe."

"It does, indeed," echoed Jan, "considering our predicament only hours ago. If we haven't mentioned it before, Travis, thanks."

"No problem. Glad to have you aboard."

The day wore on as the three of them talked. Travis told them a little about his charter service, and Jan gave a peripheral explanation of his investment business. Christina related a short account of her travels, and her studies toward a law degree.

When the day ended, and the sun fizzled into the dark-green ocean, they anchored and Carlos served dinner. He had grilled great slabs of fish, added several cans of black beans with spices he had discovered on board, then baked the whole thing on the hibachi. It was one of the first hot meals any of them had eaten in days and it was wonderful. The little Cuban fairly glowed while basking in the praise.

While Carlos and the boy drew saltwater for cleaning the dishes, the others sat in the cockpit, under the yellow glow of an oil lamp, and talked of the past and the future. The concept of the world having shifted on its axis was discussed at length. The general consensus was that it seemed a distinct possibility, though Jan had more reservations about that theory than anyone else.

Travis told them of Cody's theories concerning the damages the Americas would, or could possibly, sustain; the loss of the east and west coasts due to the faults and, most dramatically, the creation of an enormous inland waterway from the Great Lakes through the Mississippi Valley and out into the Gulf of Mexico. As Cody told it, the shifting of the poles would cause a dramatic expansion of a major fault, the New Madrid Fault, in the central United States. A combination of these two devastating occurrences would cause the waters of Lake Michigan to be thrown violently northward. When the merger of gravity and topography stopped the monumental flow, it would turn southward in one gigantic wall of water that would plunge through, and gouge out the Mississippi Valley, expelling itself into the Gulf of Mexico, creating a new inland sea.

When Travis had finished, Jan said, "Sounds all too incredulous to me, like the end-of-the-world doom-criers carrying their signs. My bet is, there may have been a good-sized meteor strike somewhere, and if there's even been a shift of the earth, the damage has been minimal in the States. Maybe coastlines and such."

Travis gazed out at the stars. They looked like pinholes in a black blanket being held against a brilliant light, and the constellations seemed out of place. "I hope you're right, Jan, but my gut tells me that something powerful, something tumultuous, has taken place, and I won't rest easy until I know for sure."

Moments later, the unusually cold night air drove them into the cabin where sleeping arrangements were decided. The ship had more than ample bunks for everyone. Jan and Christina took the forward berth. Travis and the sensei took berths near the stern to facilitate the operation of the boat. The youngster was still suffering from terrible nightmares, thrashing and moaning at night, so Travis placed the lad between his bunk and Carlos's, allowing one or the other to watch over him.

The boy seemed taken with Christina, and through a series of questions answered by a shaking or nodding of the head, she discovered that his name was Todd. When she inquired about his family, it was obvious that what had happened to him was too traumatic for him to handle, so she stopped her questions and Todd withdrew into himself once again.

During the evening, Carlos had taken apart the VHF radio and, having found a couple of loose connections, repaired them. When it was reassembled, the radio no longer produced the continuous static it had before, but without an antenna, they still received nothing in the way of broadcasts. Carlos said he would attempt to rig one the next day.

Everyone prepared to retire. Travis went topside to check the ship once more before turning in. The dark waters rhythmically slapped the side of the hull and the wind gently rattled the rigging as he stood on deck gazing at the pale moon. If he was correct in his calculations, they should reach the mainland by tomorrow evening or the following morning–if, of course, the mainland was still there.

He was dealing with something else, as well–something he hadn't yet mentioned to anyone else, not even the sensei. He was beginning to get that old gut-level premonition of danger again. It wasn't all-consuming, as before, but he was starting to feel it just the same.

"Is something bothering you, Travis?" asked a voice from the shadows next to him. Travis started as the sensei appeared. "Forgive me if I startled you."

"Jesus Christ," Travis exclaimed. "Don't you ever make any noise when you move? I'm gonna have to tie bells on your ankles just so you don't scare the hell out of me every time you show up when I think I'm alone."

The sensei chuckled. "You must learn to hear with more than your ears."

"Forgive me for being so western, Sensei, but I've been using my ears to hear with all my life. As far as I know, they're the best I've got for that."

"They are good, yes," replied the sensei, "but they are not all you have, Travis-san. You can learn to identify by vibration, exercise sense of smell and, most of all, learn to feel the presence of others. It can be done with patience and practice. They can become valuable assets in times like these." The corners of his mouth turned in a small distant smile as he gazed out over the water. "I tell my students, he who sweats much in practice will bleed less in war."

"An old Japanese saying?"

"No," replied the sensei, "from coach of Dallas Cowboys. Now tell me, what were you thinking about when I shattered your concentration?"

Travis grinned, beginning to recognize an adroit sense of humor in his stoic companion. "Well, Sensei, this may sound strange, but I sometimes get these premonitions of danger, and I'm starting to get one again. I think we need to pay close attention to what we do for the next few days; we might be in for some trouble."

"It is wise to listen to the voices of your ancestors," the sensei acknowledged. "If it is as you expect, and civilization has changed, the times may lend themselves to those who have no conscience about taking what they want from others. Let us prepare, and proceed cautiously. It is better to have the arrow notched and not need it, than to find you are too late to the quiver."

Travis just looked at him. "I'm not even going to ask." A moment later Travis yawned. "Well, I feel better having told you. I'm going to hit the sack. We've got another long day tomorrow."

An hour after daybreak the next morning, they were once again underway. The rising sun had yet to drive the cold from the air and Travis, at the helm, was thankful for the sweater he had found among the clothes in the forward cabin. There was a light, quartering tail wind and the seas were relatively calm. *Nice day for a sail on a normal day*, Travis thought. *Only this isn't just a sail, and nothing is normal anymore.* That disquieting feeling was still dancing around on the periphery of his consciousness, as unsettling as an anonymous, threatening letter.

Christina came up from below, bringing a couple of cups of instant coffee, one of his most valuable acquisitions from the dive a few days before. "Just a wee bit chilly today, huh?"she said as she passed him a mug and sat next to him.

"Yeah, it is, but it'll warm up as soon as the sun gets a little higher. Still, it's nowhere near as warm as it should be for early April."

"Could be just a cold winter."

"Yeah, I suppose," Travis said as he tightened the lines on the main. "But the air feels different. There's less humidity than there should be. It's like sailing on the Great Lakes in late spring."

"Do you think we'll reach the mainland today?" she asked.

"I think we'll reach where the mainland used to be, but it stands to reason that if the Keys are thirty feet under the ocean, the better part of South Florida is going to be treading water."

She threw her head back, the wind rippling her hair like water, and chuckled. "Fort Lauderdale under water," she said quietly. "The inundated offices of Gridder, Shyborg, and Ripstein, what was to become home to this new attorney. I can hear old man Gridder now, screaming at God as the wave carried him away. 'You can't do this! I've got connections! I'll sue, I'll sue!'" She laughed a soft, infectious laugh that caught Travis and he joined in. Then, more seriously, she said, "Money was their only source of pleasure and power, their only real God. To whom do they pray now?"

"Yet you wanted to be one of them?"

She turned to him. "For some reason, it was the crowd I ended up in. Who, when running with the wolves, would want to be a sheep?"

He laughed at the appropriateness. "Yeah, I suppose you're right," he said, looking at her. For a moment their eyes locked, and in that split second, like the instantaneous green flash that is sometimes seen with the setting of the sun over water, something passed between them. Christina broke the gaze as she turned to watch the gulls darting downward at a school of baitfish off the bow. "It's so peaceful and pretty today," she said. "Sitting here, it doesn't seem possible that the world ... has changed."

"The thought pleases me no more than it does you," said Travis. "But I'll bet you dollars to donuts that it has."

Moments later, Jan came through the hatch. "Sensei wants to see you down below. Something about our course. I'll take the wheel for a while. I promise not to get too far off."

Travis found the sensei at the chart table. As he approached, the Japanese turned and bowed ever so slightly. The American returned the bow. It was a courtesy to the man, he told himself. But quite frankly, it just seemed like the right thing to do around him.

The sensei grinned with that half smile of his. "If I had time, I could make you a good Japanese," he said.

"I'm barely managing to be a good American. Don't confuse me," said Travis.

The sensei gestured to the chart. "Come, let me show you where I believe we are. I estimate us to be here, forty miles south-southwest of Miami."

"Okay," Travis said. "I think you're right about that. Now what do we do? With the water depth we're anticipating, we could practically sail into downtown Miami."

The older man frowned and started to speak. Travis raised his hand and stopped him. "I'm only kidding. That would be like trying to sail the Bahamas without charts. We'd lose the bottom of our boat on the roof of somebody's house."

The sensei nodded. "There are a number of things to be considered–" Shouts from the deck interrupted him.

As Travis reached the deck, he saw the focus of the commotion. A sailboat floated perhaps a quarter of a mile away. Jan set a course for it while Travis prepared to board. As they neared the boat, they could see it was sinking, but not from damage by nature–along the water line were two neat rows of holes. Travis had seen that kind of damage many times in Vietnam–automatic rifle fire. The breaches in the hull and the shattered port holes indicated some sort of fire fight. *Who*, thought Travis, as they slid up beside the craft, *and why?*

Before boarding the other boat, Travis went back down to his cabin and pulled out the nine-millimeter pistol from under his mattress. He checked the clip, shoved it back in with a satisfying snap, put the gun in his belt at the small of his back, and went topside.

"Everybody hold tight," he said to the excited group as

he came out. "I'm going over and check it out. Everyone else stays right here." Before anyone could argue, he moved to the rail and jumped across to the other boat. His sense of self-preservation was jammed into high gear when he got to the cockpit and saw all the blood: The Fiberglass siding was splashed dark red; there was a quarter-inch of dried black blood on the floor.

He pulled the gun from his back and chambered a shell, with a "watch your ass" feeling crawling all over his spine like sugar ants on an Eskimo Pie. The semi-dried blood squished and stuck to his shoes as he moved across the cockpit to the hatch doors. He kept his attention on the cabin and did his best to keep his breakfast where it belonged.

The first thing he saw when he opened the hatch was the woman. Her head was leaning back against the stairs that led down to the interior of the cabin. She'd been tied spread-eagle on the floor of the cabin. Whoever killed her had used her first, and they had taken their time on both counts. Travis stepped over the woman, into the dim room. It appeared that the boat had been badly buffeted by the wave, but it had also been thoroughly ransacked, and gutted of anything valuable. He moved slowly, cautiously, working his way forward. In the front berth, he found a man lying on a blood-covered bed, his hands tied behind his back. He had been shot several times in the head, leaving him largely unrecognizable. Travis stared, awestruck, at this brutal carnage. An anxious hail from above brought him around, and he quickly worked his way out of the ship. He found himself gulping drafts of fresh air as he reached the deck and the sun.

"What's happened? What's going on?" shouted Jan.

Travis glanced over at the sensei. The look on Travis's face was enough. The Japanese turned to the rest of them, his voice no longer soft now, but commanding, like someone who is accustomed to demanding and receiving attention.

"You will all stay here, no noise. Wait!" Without another word, he turned and leaped over to the other boat. There was something so absolute about him that everybody did exactly as he said–even Jan.

Travis showed his companion the grisly discovery. When they got back up on deck, the sensei turned to Travis. "Your feelings were well founded. These people survived the natural disaster only to be murdered by their fellow man. Violence like this smacks of no concern for authority, or no concern with retaliation by authority. It indicates that damage to this region may be as bad as you suggested, leaving breakdown of civil law enforcement."

"Yeah," said Travis. "It all adds up to 'watch your ass' from now on. Let's get back to the boat. There's nothing we can do here."

As he turned toward the rail, he noticed that the VHF antenna on the sinking boat was still intact and bolted to the deck. "Carlos," he shouted, "get over here with a wrench and get this antenna."

"Aye, aye *Jefe*," Carlos called as he went below for his toolbox. In minutes, he had the antenna and cable off and reattached to the fittings on their boat. Carlos's work on the other craft had been expedited by the sight of all the blood in the cockpit. He said nothing, but his hands were still shaking when he finished.

CHAPTER 7
THE PREACHER

As soon as the installation of the new antenna was completed, they were underway again. While they sailed, Carlos repaired the wiring to the VHF radio, then called them all below. Everyone gathered around as Travis turned the radio on and ran through the channels one by one. It appeared to be functioning okay; there would be silence on some channels and static on others, but as they came to the end of the channel cycle, there was still no voice from the outside world. He ran through the cycle again, broadcasting himself periodically, with no better luck than the first time.

"Well, we may have to get closer to the mainland. This radio has line-of-sight limitations and is only good up to about fifty miles," Travis said as he ran the dial one last time. He was about to give up when, faintly in the background, behind the static, he heard a voice.

"Hey! Wait!" urged Christina as she heard it, too. "There's someone out there, someone talking!"

Travis adjusted the squelch, tuned in the channel as best he could, and turned up the volume. Behind the light static a man was speaking in a sonorous, rolling, southern baritone attributed to Bible-belt preachers. They listened for a few moments and realized that, sure enough, that's exactly what he appeared to be. There was, however some "local color" to the sermon.

"This here's the Reverend Jimmy Johnson, bringing ya regional news, spiritual reflection, and ecological insight. I'm a broadcastin' from the shrimp boat *Jesus's Love*, settin' here in the waters over not-so-beautiful downtown Miami, and a-lookin' at the crapped-out skyscraper skeletons all around me. Jesus is comin', you miserable sinners, and He's pissed. The sins of the fathers shall be visited on the children. Ain't it the truth! Oil spills, ozone holes, and acid rains didn't even slow ya down in your mad, mindless rush into the technicolored dawn of the new age, did it? Well, how do you like it now, you fluoro-carbon flaunting assholes? Where are your petrol-guzzling, gas-belchin' dinosaurs of transportation now? At the bottom of the friggin' ocean, that's where! How do you like them malathion-treated apples, you tight-tied, tight-assed, money grubbin' sons of bitches? Huh? Huh?

"I been a-shrimpin' from Florida to Louisiana and a-preachin' everywhere I went. I been yellin' at you the whole time. Didn't I tell you that you was cuttin' down trees faster than anyone coulda possibly growed 'em? Didn't I tell you that you was a-poisonin' the rivers and pollutin' the seas? Jesus! You was makin' handbags and hats out of God's most glorious creatures, or worse, killin' them for fun. Rhino's and gorillas slaughtered and ground up to make powder for your peckers. God! Of all the stupid shit I've ever heard! Listen to me, you myopic, self-serving bastards. You was livin' in cities where they had to have daily air reports–daily air reports!–to tell you whether it was okay to go outside your houses and breathe the gal-derned air! In Japan they was a-sellin' oxygen on the street like they was vendin' hot dogs! I told you what was gonna happen, but did you listen? Noooo, you didn't listen. Noooo, nobody listened to ole Reverend Jimmy. They said he's just a doomsday crazy. Well, what do you think now, you baby-boomed IBMers? Pretty friggin' tough treadin' water with your computer, huh? Huh? Well, it's intermission time. I gotta take a leak–drain the ole dragon. This commercial break is being brought to you by my dear friend Jack Daniels and his fine sippin' whiskey."

Throughout the environmental evangelist's tirade, Travis

and the group stood in tongue-fettered silence. The effect of the one-sided conversation was rather like somebody telling you a funny joke while poleaxing you. Travis thought to himself, *this guy is three sheets to the wind, and funny as hell, but if he has his facts right, the local world is flat-assed screwed.*

The radio squelched and there was a loud burp over the air. "Well, I'm back. And now, for those within the sound of my voice, it's time for a status report on the country ... I call it the NBC report–notable bullshit and commentary. Anyway, I've been gettin' messages from people up and down the New Coast, as we're callin' it. They've been receivin' and relayin' information darn near across what's left of the U. S. of A. It ain't a pretty picture, but I'm a-gonna tell you about it anyway. One, because I always wanted to be a newscaster, and two, because I just luuuuv being right!

"First off, it appears it weren't no meteorite that caused this mess. That is to say, nobody's reportin' any major holes anywhere. It looks more like some massive shifting of the earth's surface in places. Some areas seem to be in terrible shape or just plain gone, others fared a little better. No one got away without payin' the piper. There ain't no more Florida, except for a piece of high ground near the panhandle. Did I hear ya gasp? Well, that's about as good as it gets.

"California's damned near disappeared–lock, stock, and tomahawk. There was a country song about waterfront property in Arizona a few years back. I think it's available now! How about a little good news-bad news? The good news is that there won't be any more cost-of-living riots in New York. The bad news–and I don't know if it's all that bad–is that there ain't no more New York. There ain't much of an Eastern Seaboard left, for that matter. From what they're a-tellin' me, it made a big, crumbling sound and dropped off into the ocean.

"Now here's a little info that I'm not too happy about–

there don't seem to be much of a Louisiana anymore. Looks like the Mississippi Valley filled with water from somewhere and rushed through New Orleans like a case of clap through a whorehouse! I reckon with the way things look, I could putter this here little shrimper right up to the Great Lakes. 'Scuse me just a second folks, got to pour a little more refreshment. Ah, Dr. Jack. Good for all that ails ya; soothes the nerves, numbs the past, brightens the present, but unfortunately, don't do squat for the future."

The group listened in shocked silence to the world report given by the drunken shrimper/preacher.

"He can't be right," Jan whispered, a stricken look on his face. Christina, obviously shaken as well, reached over and put her hand on his shoulder, almost as if to console them both.

Travis looked across at the sensei, who maintained his impenetrable expression throughout. *He could be listening to the sports scores for all it shows,* thought Travis. *Never play poker with that son-of-a-gun.*

Carlos and Todd stood to the side. Carlos's expression was one of a fatal acceptance tempered with an I'm-still-alive optimism. The boy, who had been through so much already, accepted the news with a subdued indifference.

Carlos shook his head. "*Jesus Christe,* now I never get a *hamburguesa.*"

The others smiled. "You hang in there, Carlos," said Travis. "I'll find you a *hamburguesa* yet."

"I heard it, but I still can't believe it," muttered Jan.

"By God, my buddy Cody was right on the money," said Travis. "I mean, *right on.* If I ever see him again, I owe him a bottle of Jose Quervo. That was the bet." Then, with a sad shake of his head, he said, "But, I don't suppose there's much chance of him collecting on it."

Snapping out of his melancholy, Travis reached for the

radio. "I want to try to get this guy on the horn here, see if there's any more he can tell us." In moments, Travis located the preacher's frequency and was broadcasting to him.

"Preacher, Preacher, this is *The Odyssey*"–it just happened to be the name of the boat; it hadn't seemed important up to this point, but when he used the name for the first time, he considered the significance–"This is *The Odyssey* calling the Preacher. Come back, Preacher, come back."

A few moments later, the preacher's slurred voice boomed through the speakers. "Well howdy, you God-forsaken, useless sinner. What can I do for you? Are you a-lookin' for the way to Heaven or do you just need another can of aerosol hair spray–or could you be callin' for our leather-bound, gold-embossed first edition of *The Animals That Used To Be*, the thrilling story of a boy and his bird, 'cept the bird is extinct, along with about a hundred other species you managed to extinctatize in less than a century. Yeah, I said extinctatize. May not be a word, but I like it, and I'm damned near writin' the rules now. So what's it gonna be, Sinner? God's a-waitin' and so am I."

Travis decided to fight humor with humor. "I'll take three cans of hair spray and a copy of the book. I'm sure it's gonna be a best seller. I'll bet your publisher's swamped, so to speak."

The preacher's belly laugh echoed across the radio. "Well said, Sinner, well said! God likes a man with humor." The preacher paused while he took a noisy sip of whisky, then continued, "Tell me, Sinner, have you been saved?"

"Have I been saved?" Travis said to himself as much as anyone. "In the last week I've been saved from an airplane crash, I've been saved from drowning, and I've been saved from starving. I'd say, offhand, that I've been saved about as much as anyone I know."

"No, no, no, Sinner. I mean, have you been saved by Jesus?" the preacher responded loftily.

"Well, I'll tell you, Preacher, if it ain't Jesus who's been saving me, then the devil's working overtime."

"He's doin' that for sure, Sinner," the preacher bellowed. "He's doin' that for sure."

In a more serious voice, Travis spoke again. "Preacher, we heard your report. Can you give us any further details? Clarify the situation somewhat?"

"How clear do you want it, Sinner? The world's gone to hell in a bread basket."

"Yeah, I know," said Travis, "but have you heard anything that relates to the authorities? The government? If we've lost the coastlines, what's the condition of the central U.S. and the rest of the world?"

"Well, I'll tell you what I'm hearin'. It ain't much, but I believe it's solid. I got a Ham and a sideband radio on this ole tub, so I figure, for information, that puts me on par with CNN–if there is a CNN anymore.

"The government, huh? Well, from what I'm a pickin' up, there ain't much cohesive government left in the U.S. of A. right now. Oh, there's a few military bases that didn't get hit too bad, from Langley in Virginia to Fort Benton in Montana. These folks seem to still be functioning but they've all got their share of problems, and martial law has been declared. The story is, about half the armed forces just up and left, trying to get to wherever they're from to help save their own.

"Nobody seems to know if we have a federal government at all. Communications are down everywhere, so no one's got the foggiest what anybody else is doin', but then that's just about par for the government anyway. The federal and the civil authorities are in a state of collapse. The civilian population is on its own. My guess is it's gonna be years before we see any real semblance of order."

"To top it off, it looks like we've had a couple of major nuclear accidents where earthquakes upset reactors. Meltdowns have occurred where California and upstate New York used to be. Most of the coast of Texas is gone, too, and they're reporting a nuke melt outside Dallas.

"As for the central U.S., it seems to have survived the best. Oklahoma, Arkansas, Kansas, up Montana and Colorado way—those areas did a lot of shakin', rattlin' and rollin', but they're still intact. Big news is that inland sea in the center of the country now. And there's a report that Oregon broke off from the coast and is now an island, but that's third- and fourth-hand news at this point, so I don't know for sure.

"The armchair estimators out there figure that somewhere near a hundred million people are dead and gone. Lots more are gonna die from radiation, starvation, and each other. As far as what's happened to the rest of the world, who knows?" The preacher paused for a moment and took a noisy swallow of whisky, then continued. "I'll tell ya, Sinner, I don't think we're gonna be givin' a tinker's damn about other countries for quite a piece to come. We're gonna be pretty gal-derned busy shuckin' our own peas for a while, let alone anyone else's."

"What about the Turkey Point nuclear reactor in South Miami?" Travis asked.

"If that had been a problem, son, we wouldn't be talking now, we'd be a-sizzlin' like a couple strips of bacon in a frying pan. Evidently they got it shut down ahead of time, or maybe the reactors were down for repairs. Who knows? There weren't no earthquakes here, just a little shaking and lots of water. All I know for sure is that it didn't blow up or melt down, or whatever they do."

Travis stared at the radio, thinking, as the preacher talked. After a few moments he said, "Listen, Preacher, I figure we're about twenty to thirty miles southwest of your position. I'd like to talk with you some more before we make any major decisions. If we can find you, how about if we tie up sometime tomorrow morning and let us treat you to breakfast? You pick the restaurant."

The preacher laughed again. "Sounds good to me, son. I could use the company. If you're pretty sure about that southwest position, just set a forty-five degree course and look for what's left of the big buildings off South Miami Beach. Stay east of them, in deep water, and come in from that direction. Look for the tallest building. I'm anchored just east of it. I'll give you a holler on the horn tomorrow morning, just to make sure you're on target."

Travis replaced the microphone and turned to his companions. "This is the way I figure it: The guy may be a little bourboned-out, but he's got access to incredibly valuable information which can help us make intelligent decisions for any course of action we take. This isn't a dictatorship. I want your input. But for my money, I'd like to sit down with this fellow for a day or so and learn as much as I can before continuing on."

Everyone agreed with Travis's plan.

"All right, that's that," Travis declared. "Let's set course and get underway. We still have three hours of daylight left."

They sailed without incident for the rest of the day, a light sea and favorable winds giving them a chance to relax.

Young Todd caught two nice mackerel during the afternoon and Carlos treated them to another delicious dinner. Spirits were, for the first time, almost optimistic. The worst was over. Civilization was still out there and they were going to find it. Travis had listened carefully to what the preacher said about the inland waterway and the central U.S. being intact. He was beginning to formulate a plan, but he needed more information before he spoke with the others.

When supper was finished and the dishes done, Carlos brought out a slightly water-warped deck of cards he'd found on board and the group played poker for about an hour. The sensei sat off to the side and cleaned his swords. As the game began to break up, Travis went topside to check everything before bed, as was becoming his routine. He sat for a moment on the cabin roof, watching the dark waves crest and fall, when he heard footsteps behind him. He turned, surprised, to find Todd standing a few feet from him. The boy looked at Travis, uncertain, then stared past him at the cold, moonlit water. Travis studied the child for a few seconds, then, in one of those rare moments of mutual understanding, raised his arm and beckoned the young lad to him. The relief of being understood flooded across the boy's face as he came forward. Travis put his arm around him and held him. No words were spoken–none were needed–as the pair sat and watched the reflection of the yellow moon dance on the blue-black water.

CHAPTER 8
THE QUICK AND THE DEAD

The following morning Travis was awakened by the sunlight as it streamed through the porthole and flooded his bunk. He opened his eyes and he realized that something else had roused him–voices. Cuban voices, not Carlos's, were coming from topside. As he quickly pulled on his shirt, that familiar feeling crept over him, and something deep inside shouted a warning. He grabbed the nine-millimeter from the drawer next to the bunk and shoved it into his belt at the small of his back as Jan showed up.

"There's somebody up top in another boat. Cubans, I think." He was attempting to be casual but his eyes betrayed him.

Travis looked at the other gun in the drawer, then on impulse took it out. "Can you use one of these?" he asked.

"Yeah, no problem," Jan answered confidently.

Travis handed him the weapon. "Keep it tucked in your back, out of sight." Jan nodded.

The others were awake and standing by the stairs to the hatch as the two men reached them. "Jan and I are going out. You folks can't do any good up there and I don't want them knowing how many of us there are. We'll talk to them, see what they want." The others nodded tensely. Travis could tell that the sensei was not happy with the arrangement, but saw the wisdom of it.

The pair moved up the hatchway and out onto the deck. There, anchored about twenty yards from them, was a fifty-foot Cuban fishing boat. Beside the forecastle of the trawler stood two men. One was of medium build; jet-black hair greased back against his skull, his dark eyes quick and nervous. The other was a large mulatto. The wide, African features of his face were framed by ringlets of long, wet hair. His dirty T-shirt was strained to capacity by heavy shoulders and a bulbous belly. Most ominous of all, however, were the M16 rifles they held casually at their sides.

Travis and Jan halted in front of the cabin, and the big one spoke: "*Buenos dias, amigos. Habla Espanol?*"

"No, we don't speak Spanish," Travis answered, even though he did speak some.

The mulatto grunted disdainfully, as if the reply had been a rebuke. Then in broken English he asked. "How many people you have with you, *amigo*?"

Travis recalled the bullet-riddled boat they had seen the day before, and red warning flags danced across his mind like a fourth of July parade. "Just a couple. How about you?"

"Jus' me and my *amigo* here, tha's all, man." Travis was positive he had heard at least three voices–maybe four–before he went topside. Every instinct in his body told him it was all about to hit the fan. The big Cuban smiled, exposing a mouthful of crooked, yellow teeth, like discolored tombstones at the mouth of a cave. "Tha's a very nice boat you have, *amigo*. How come you have such a nice boat like that?"

"I won it in a raffle last week."

The smile drained from the Cuban's face. "You know, *amigo*, we need some food. Maybe you have some you could give us, huh? Maybe if you don' have too much food, maybe you have some valuables you could give us so we could buy some food somewhere, huh, *amigo*?"

"Listen, buddy," replied Travis, "my partner and I are nearly out of food and water and about the most valuable thing I've got is the shirt on my back. How about if we just up anchor and we'll go our way, you go yours."

The mulatto turned and casually spit over the gunnel,

then brought his attention back to Travis. "Maybe we do that man, maybe we do that." Then in a staccato burst of Spanish, he spoke to his friend, who moved over about ten paces.

Carlos's voice came urgently from the hatchway. "He just tell his *compadre* to move down so to get you in a crossfire, *Jefe.*"

Jesus Christ, Travis thought, *after all we've been through, now we have to get caught in an ocean version of the O.K. Corral.* "Slide over some, Jan," he whispered. "When they start to raise their guns, you shoot the one on the left. I'll take the big guy with the Colgate smile." Jan nodded and moved down slowly, obviously frightened, but maintaining.

The one thing nobody knew, least of all the Cubans on the other boat, was that Travis was an expert with a handgun–a natural, they called him. He had carried a service issue .45 in Vietnam for two years, and after the service had still practiced consistantly.

Suddenly, without warning, the big Cuban shouted and started to raise his rifle. Travis had been standing with his hands on his hips to give him quick access to his gun. When the other man made his move, Travis dropped to one knee, drew his pistol and clipped off three rounds. Instantly, a trio of messy red dots appeared in the mulatto's chest, throwing him back against the forecastle of his boat, arms flailing. A split second later, automatic rifle fire sprayed the top of the cabin next to Travis, missing him by inches as he dove to the deck. The other man was still standing, about to fire again, when Travis got off three quick shots in his direction. Unfortunately, the rolling of the boat threw the rounds off slightly, splintering the wood next to the Cuban's head and sending him flying for the cover of his gunnel. Travis found himself lying wide open in the middle of the deck, and in a hell of a quandary. If he got up and ran for the safety of the steering cockpit, the Cuban could pop up and kill him easily with that automatic rifle. But if he stayed where he was and waited for the fellow to come up from behind the gunnel, he had to get him right away, or he was dead for sure. *Six of one ...* he thought to himself. Just then, the Cuban stood up as though he was John Wayne in *Rio Bravo*, and started to fire. Travis aimed quickly and touched off four more rounds. The smaller man did an imitation of his friend as a red line stretched up from his stomach to his throat.

"*Adios*, you son of a bitch," Travis muttered grimly as he watched the man slide down the blood-splattered wall of the cabin.

As he stood, Travis realized he hadn't heard any fire from Jan. He looked over his shoulder to find his compatriot sprawled out across the top of the cabin. Jan's chest and back had been laid open by the murderous 5.56 rounds that had sprayed the boat; his sightless eyes stared vacantly at the sky. Quickly, Travis moved over to him, knowing already that it was too late. He was kneeling by the dead man when a movement on the bow caught his attention. He looked up to see another Cuban pulling himself up over the bow with a rope attached to a gaff hook. The man had swum across and hooked the gaff to the bow rail while the fire fight was going on. As the Latino stood up, Travis raised his pistol and pulled the trigger, but instead of the deafening report he'd expected, there was an impotent click as the hammer fell on an empty chamber. He immediately pulled the trigger again. Another click.

Realizing the situation, the Cuban smiled and reached down to pull a pistol from his belt. Travis braced himself for a rush at the man, knowing it was suicide, when suddenly from around the other side of the cabin came a hundred and fifty pounds of snarling muscle and teeth. Flying low, Ra struck the Cuban in mid-air as he straddled the bow rail. The dog hit the startled man with such force that he flew backward a good six feet before he even started to fall, Ra's fangs buried in his throat. The bandit didn't have a chance. He was dead before he hit the water, but Ra refused to release him until he began to sink. Only then did the animal break away and begin swimming toward the stern of the boat.

Travis exhaled the breath he'd thought to be his last, stood up, and turned toward the rear hatch.

There, standing on the stern, dripping wet, gun in hand, was yet another Cuban. That one, having crawled over the back of the boat, had obviously witnessed the last exchange. He wasn't frightened and he wasn't in a hurry. He had things in control and he knew it. The bandit motioned with his gun to the others in the hatchway.

"Up, up, all of you. *Andele*! Quickly!"

Carlos and Christina moved up and out first, then Todd. The sensei came last. As the Japanese cleared the cockpit, Travis noticed that he was wearing his sword.

The Cuban saw it as well. "Take knife off, now!"

The sensei was a good five feet from him when he started to comply, but as he reached across to undo the belt, his hand brushed the hilt of his sword. In a millisecond, so fast that the blink of an eye would have missed it, there was a blurring arc of steel. The Latino's gun, and the hand that held it, suddenly leaped from his wrist. The astonished bandit had only enough time to look down at his wrist, mouth gaping in surprise, when another arc took his head cleanly from his shoulders. Before the body could even recognize it was dead, the sensei spun and side-kicked it over the rail. Then he turned, flicked the blood from his sword, and sheathed it. His expression never changed.

The entire transaction took less than two seconds. The Oriental looked over at the other boat and the two dead men, then swung around to Travis. As their eyes met, there was new respect from both: credibility which can only be earned by absolute deadly experience.

The moment was shattered by a scream as Christina discovered Jan lying across the top of the cabin. She ran over and knelt beside him. The girl reached out to him, but stopped and drew her hands back to her mouth, a look of horror and revulsion on her face. "Jan. Oh Jan. God no. No," she moaned, swaying slightly as she stared at the torn and bloodied body. Travis moved quickly to the girl's side, lifting her up by the shoulders, and holding her.

"I'm sorry, Chris," he whispered. "There's nothing we can do. He's gone." As she sobbed, he pulled her away from the body and took her below.

He helped Christina onto the bunk, then sat down beside her. As she cried quietly, Travis was, for the first time, aware of her vulnerability. He realized then that beneath the practiced exterior of confidence and independence was an innocence–not virginal, but child-like–and he wanted more than anything to take the girl in his arms and tell her that he would see her through this sadness and protect her and ... but he didn't. He brushed the hair from her face and eyes and gazed down at her. God, even then, in all her sadness, she was so incredibly beautiful! His hand lingered on the side of her face and she reached up and took it, holding it tight with both hands against her cheek. They stayed like that until her sobs quieted and her breathing relaxed, and she slept.

Travis left her sleeping and went up on deck. He noticed immediately that Jan's body was gone, and turned to Carlos as he cleaned the blood off the deck. "What happened to Jan?"

Carlos pointed to the sensei. "He tell me 'throw him overboard,' so I did. I no gonna argue with that hombre."

The sensei had pulled Ra aboard, and was up front

inspecting the damage done by the gunfire. Travis walked over, his sense of propriety disturbed by the inadvertent throwing of Jan's body into the water. "What's with tossing Jan into the sea? No funeral, no words, no nothing?"

The sensei looked up from his inspection of the bullet holes, and paused. His cold eyes almost made Travis flinch. "What would you have us put him in? We have no sheets, extra canvas, or blankets to spare. Would you like her"—he said, motioning below—"to have another look at his butchered body, just for old time's sake? We are in daily life-and-death situation. If we are to survive, we must think like survivors. Let us concentrate on the living so that we might have less dead to contend with. The dead can take care of themselves."

The sensei stood up, his voice softer. "Travis-san, these people respect you and look to you for guidance. You must begin to think differently now. You can no longer think simply in terms of yourself, nor can you practice judgement with antiquated ethics. Lives have been put into your hands, and their survival is dependent on you. I will help when I can, but these are your people; they will not follow me. You are their leader. Think like one; become one."

Travis looked out over the waters and thought about what had just been said, then turned to the Japanese. "I haven't had to worry about anyone but myself for a long time, Sensei. I'm going need some practice at being a leader again. Stay close. If I get out of line, slap me on the back of the head."

"It will be my pleasure, Captain," said the sensei as he smiled and bowed to Travis, who, having become comfortable with the custom, returned the bow, and the smile.

CHAPTER 9
RECOVERY AND DIRECTION

When the sailboat had been cleaned up and the cabin top patched with a can of Fiberglass putty from the hold, they decided to have a look at the Cuban's boat. They upped anchor, sailed over to the other craft, and tied up. Travis reloaded his pistol, then he and the sensei boarded the vessel. Once on the deck, they took the M16s from the dead men before going below.

The hold was a disaster. Empty beer cans and tequila bottles littered the floor, along with half-eaten cans of food, dirty dishes, and *Penthouse* magazines. Pictures of nude women in various, provocative positions were nailed all over the walls. The only thing that seemed to have any semblance of order was a row of boxes that were stacked against the rear bulkhead. Stenciled boldly on each box, in military script, was **PROPERTY OF NATIONAL GUARD**.

Travis looked at the sensei, then back to the boxes. "Looks like someone hit a National Guard Armory and maybe an ammo storage facility." They went over and pulled a case down. The lid was loose, and lifted off easily. Inside, cleaned and greased, lay ten M16s; two had already been removed from the original dozen. With a screwdriver Travis found nearby, they pried the lid off another slightly longer box. Inside were six brand new, ready-to-use Squad Automatic Weapons–SAWs–devastating belt- or magazine-fed machine guns that used the same 5.56 cartridge as the M16. Opening the third case, even the sensei's usually inscrutable face changed slightly. There, packaged in neat rows, were four dozen fragmentation grenades. The *pièce de resistance*, however, came when they removed the boxes of ammunition from atop a large, flat case and opened it. Inside were four M-72 Light Anti-Tank Weapons System–LAWS–a one-round disposable device that had replaced the Army's bazooka.

Someone certainly knew what they were shopping for, thought Travis as he studied the deadly arsenal around him. "Looks like someone was planning to start a war," he muttered.

"Or, at very least, seeking to discourage opposition to their plans," said the sensei. "When negotiation fails, a sharp sword is your best persuasion."

"Ah, another Japanese saying," said Travis.

"General George Armstrong Custer," replied the Oriental with his half smile.

An hour later they had transferred their new-found armory to the sailboat. They had also discovered several heavy-duty flashlights and a case of Budweiser beer. Carlos was estatic! The most important acquisition, though, aside from the weapons, was an operable Global Positioning System–GPS–a navigational device that determines a position by satellite and can computer-plot courses. Carlos installed the new GPS into the brackets that had accommodated the previously damaged model, and as the dark screen lit up, the little Cuban smiled. Travis stepped over, and in moments was able to determine their exact position.

They finished storing the last of the goods as the VHF radio crackled to life. The preacher's voice boomed across the speaker. "Good mornin', sinners and sinnerettes. Have you fallen on your bony knees and thanked the Lord for your useless lives today? Well, what ya waitin' for? By the way, where's that fella who promised me breakfast? It's damned near halfway through the mornin' and I'm hungry enough to eat my boots."

Travis picked up the microphone. "Preacher, this is the breakfast boy. Unfortunately, we had a problem this morning with some people who'd decided they would look better in our boat than we would. We got into a firefight and lost one of our men." Travis paused for a moment, then continued. "Listen, Preacher. We just got our GPS working again. If you'll give us your exact position, we can probably reach you inside a couple of hours."

"Right, son." The preacher gave his position: 25 degrees, 47 minutes, 30 seconds north; 80 degrees, 11 minutes, 10 seconds west. "Sorry about your loss, son. May his soul rest in peace."

"Thanks," replied Travis gratefully. "We'll see you soon."

After one more look through the other boat, they upped anchor and departed. They left the Cuban vessel where it was; the craft was of no use to them.

As she lay on her bunk below, Christina felt the boat heel and move off. She was awake and the tears were gone, but the pain and the horror still gripped her. It clawed at her insides like a writhing, living thing, unable to be contained. Her mind kept flashing back to Jan, sprawled out on the cabin. The girl tried to stop it, but the scene played over and over again. Though she had not truly been in love, she had cared deeply for him. They had shared their hopes and dreams for tomorrow; but for Jan, there would be no more tomorrows.

Christina lay there staring at the ceiling, small tears returning to the corners of her eyes, when she saw a movement at the door. Todd was standing in the passageway, a cup of coffee in his hand. He hesitated for a moment, until he was sure she saw him, then slowly walked into the berth. He went over to the side of the bed as she sat up, drying her eyes with the back of her hands. The youngster stopped by her side and offered her the coffee. She gratefully took the warm cup and did her best to smile. Christina took a couple of sips, then set the cup on the nightstand by the bed.

"Thank you, Todd," she said, turning toward him. Slowly, haltingly, he took her hand in both of his and held it, his eyes saying all the things his lips could not. There were tears in both their eyes. Instinctively, she understood that they were sharing the tragedy of their losses, and painful as it was, they no longer had to face it alone. They would help each other, and from that moment on, they would both become stronger. She drew him to her, and willingly he came into her arms, clutching her with silent, grateful need.

Half an hour later, just after they spotted the landmarks mentioned by the preacher, Christina came up from the cabin. Her eyes were still red from crying, but her hair was combed and her walk was straight and controlled. She paused, one hand on the rigging, and looked out at the sea, letting the cool salt air wash over her. The sun broke clear of the clouds and she welcomed its warmth on her face and arms. As she stood there, eyes closed, face lifted to the brightness, she heard Travis's voice next to her.

"How ya doing, Chris?" he asked.

"I'll be all right, I guess." She involuntarily looked over to the cabin top where Jan's body had been, then glanced at Travis. The question remained unasked, but it was there all the same.

"I'm sorry about Jan," Travis said. "He was a good man, and he was there when the chips were down. You can't ask for more than that. We buried him at sea while you slept." She nodded, staring intently at the water, small tears running down each cheek.

Travis put his arm around her shoulder. "I know that the pain you feel now has to pass in its own time, but I think you need to ask yourself what Jan would have wanted of you. He was a man who loved living. He loved you. Jan wouldn't want you broken and sad, he'd want you to hold your head up and go on."

"I know you're right," she said, "but the pain's just too new, and it's hard ..."

"It'll get easier. You have to take it one day at a time."

They stood there in silence, watching the morning sun glisten off the rolling waves until the sensei called out, "Eleven o'clock off bow, one mile out–the preacher's boat."

Travis peered across the sea in that direction. There, bobbing gently over the waves in the distance, was the forecastle of a shrimper. He gave Christina's shoulder a squeeze and said, "I'm gonna go below and get the preacher on the horn–make sure that's our target."

She nodded, and as he turned to go she called after him. "Travis."

He turned. "Yeah?"

"Thanks," she said with a weak smile.

Travis paused, staring at her. "No problem, Chris. Anytime."

Travis contacted the preacher, confirmed that it was him they saw, then asked Carlos to whip up a special breakfast.

Fifteen minutes later they were abeam the shrimper. As they slid up to the larger boat, the door on the forecastle opened and the preacher emerged. He was a large man, probably six-one, with a barrel chest, longish graying hair, and a three- or four-day salt-and-pepper stubble of a beard. He had piercing gray-blue eyes the color of Bahama waters on a cloudy day–eyes that looked 30 years younger than the craggy, sun-bronzed face they were set in. There was an distinct and immediate robustness about the man, a straitforwardness that matched his radio personality, and the sense of humor that showed in the laugh lines of his face complimented his more obvious qualities. Travis liked him immediately, guessing his age to be a very healthy fifty-five to sixty.

"Welcome, Sinners!" he yelled as they tied off. When they finally faced each other for the first time, the preacher shouted, "Where's that breakfast you promised me? I've reached a critical victual situation on this ole tub." He held up a near-empty bottle of Jack Daniels. "I been on a liquid diet for the past day-and-a-half and I'm a-running out of liquid!"

Travis laughed. "Come aboard, Preacher. Breakfast is just about ready."

They all settled into the galley while Carlos served a breakfast of cold fish, mixed vegetables, canned peaches, and coffee. After introductions, the preacher ate heartily, and in the process, told his story.

He had been outside Everglades City when the wave hit. He had just finished installing a new diesel engine in his boat and had taken it out for a test ride. Having cleared the harbor, the preacher looked back to see the wall of water rushing over the land toward him. He immediately turned the craft into the wave and, after some "serious rockin' and rollin'," found himself and his boat banged up but serviceable–which was more than he could say for Everglades City. He took his deliverance as a sign of God's reward for his faithful preaching. Further evidence of God's favor came later, when he found a case of Jack Daniels sippin' whisky floating amid the debris–lost, he was sure, from one of the many bars in Everglades City. Sign from God or not, it had really brightened his week.

Travis, in turn, related his tale, including how he had met the others and of the recent firefight with the Cubans.

"Sounds like a Louis L'Amour novel," declared the preacher. "You get through this, son, you ought to write a book. That's providing there's a publishing house left to publish it, or someone out there who cares about reading a book, and who ain't too busy just tryin' to survive."

Travis laughed. "I suppose you're right, Preacher, but the books that will be in demand now are going to be the 'how to' books: *How to Grow Vegetables, How to Build a House, How To Dress a Deer and Cure Meat–"*

"Or *How To Keep Your Neighbor From Shootin' You For What You Made With Your 'How To' Books,'"* the preacher interrupted with a laugh.

"You sound like an old friend of mine," Travis said, thinking of Cody.

The sensei, who had been listening quietly, interjected, "Have you heard anything new from rest of the country? Or beyond?"

"Well, I tell ya," the preacher began, "things seem to be a tad worse than I thought. Seems like after the initial shock passed, people sorta woke up, shook themselves, and began a wholesale panic that has swept the entire country. Even places that weren't hit real bad have experienced at least some breakdown of law and order. From what I'm a-hearin', looting is widespread throughout the nation. The police and the Guard tried to stop it at first. Finally a lot of them just gave up and went home, or joined the looters. You only hold out against the Indians if you know the cavalry's a-comin'. In this case there ain't no more cavalry and there ain't no percentage in dying for a lost cause.

"The nation, geographically, is shot to hell. The north-east coast is definitely gone–clear down to somewhere near Virginia, and inland up to a couple hundred miles. The west coast, from what I hear, is still havin' major quakes and is still losin' ground to the sea as far inland as the Rocky Mountains. The continent is about split in two by the new waterway where the Mississippi Valley used to be. They're havin' storms like this country has never seen up north and on the coasts. Torrential rains and flash flooding in the midwest have killed thousands who thought they'd survived the worst. It ain't good news, and the way I figure it, there's worse coming. If you're alive today, what do you eat? Where do you live? How do you live–especially when winter hits? My guess is that by the end of this winter, we'll have lost two hundred million people, which makes this little event just about the greatest catastrophe in the recent recorded history of man. Right up there with Noah and the great flood.

"Been a-gettin' some feedback on the rest of the world, too. Some pretty solid info seems to be coming out of Langley Air Force Base via satellite. It ain't pleasant. The Hawaiian Islands are gone. So is Japan, Hong Kong, and a good portion of China. Central America's been banged up pretty bad too, lots of volcanic activity. And most of the Bahamas are under water."

At the mention of Japan, the sensei's normally tranquil face tensed for a moment and a small sigh escaped him.

Travis turned and placed his hand on the man's shoulder. "I'm sorry, Sensei," he said, not knowing what else to say that would ease his companion's loss.

The Japanese took a deep breath and brought his head up, his features once again as proud and inscrutable as if chiseled from stone. "Thank you, Travis-san," he said in a quiet voice that all but betrayed his appearance.

The preacher continued. "Europe's had some major changes too, from what they say. England, Scotland, and most of the coast of France–gone. This is all second-hand, but it looks like there was some sort of partial shift in the planet's poles. Huge, previously populated areas of the earth are now covered with ice, just as if they were never there."

Travis decided to ask the question that was the basis of the plan he had been forming. "What have you heard specifically about the Arkansas area?"

"Well, son, I had a chat with a fella up in those parts a couple of days ago. Seems they got shook up pretty damned hard–somethin' to do with a large fault called the New Madrid. Somewhere near St. Louis, I think. Looks like there's a lot of waterfront property in Eastern Arkansas, now that it borders that new inland sea. Mostly, they've survived okay in west and northern Arkansas, but they're havin' to pick up a lot of the pieces." The preacher paused for a moment, took a sip of coffee, then continued. "My best advice for anyone still alive is to head for the hills, literally. Find someplace away from the cities. Cities are gonna be death to anyone in and around them. Get up in the mountains somewhere. Get a garden started. Shoot some game and dry the meat, like Travis said. Then beg, borrow, or steal every piece of solar or turbine energy-makin' equipment you can find. Arm yourself and wait this whole thing out."

"God, if you don't sound like my buddy, Cody," Travis remarked, amazed at the similarity in their thinking, and pleased that the preacher's thoughts coincided with his own plans. "What are you going to do, Preacher? What are your plans?" he asked.

"Well, son, I don't rightly know, to tell ya the truth. I didn't have much family left to speak of before the big change. Wife's gone; left me for a gal-derned piana player ten years ago. She was a might younger and I guess she needed more than me and Everglades City could show her. No kids, only a couple a cousins and a sister I ain't seen in a coon's age. I reckon now I ain't got no one at all. There's nothing left of my home, or Florida for that matter. Guess I'll head north and see how far I get before the ol' girl runs out of fuel. Got almost full tanks, so that's gonna last a while."

Listening to the preacher talk, Travis decided this was as good a time as any to present his plan to the group. When the preacher finished, he stood up.

"Listen, everybody. Having heard what the preacher has said about the condition of the country, I've decided what I'd like to do–what I think would give us the best chance for survival. But I'd like your vote of approval, so let me tell you what I have in mind." Looking over at the preacher, Travis said, "You're welcome to come in with us on this, too. In fact, I'd like to have you."

"Thanks, son. Let's hear what you have to say."

Travis looked around at the group once more, then continued. "I own forty acres of beautiful, fertile land in the Ouachita Mountains of Arkansas. When I bought it, there were deer and wild turkey everywhere, not to mention a creek that runs through the property that's chock full of bass and perch. There is, or at least there was, a nice house on the property, plus a guest trailer. If I can make it to Arkansas–if *we* can make it to Arkansas–by way of this new waterway, we can walk to my property from where we leave the boats. I can't think of a better place to regroup and sit out the changes this world is in the process of making. I won't tell you the trip will be a piece of cake. I don't even know for sure we can negotiate a sailboat all that way; but I do know, gut level, that if we can make it there, we can survive. For those of you whom this plan doesn't suit, I'm sure we'll make a number of landfalls and anyone is free to leave anytime they find a better situation for themselves."

After Travis made his speech, he prepared himself for the arguments he felt would come. Instead, he was surprised to the core when Christina spoke up without the least bit of hesitation. "Travis," she said, "I think if anybody can do it, you can. I'm in."

The preacher stood up and lumbered over to Travis, his arm extended. He mauled Travis's hand with his huge paw and bellowed, "I'm in, too, son. Anywhere you can get the keel of that sailboat, I can follow with *Jesus's Love.* Hot damn, I'll be the first shrimper in Arkansas!"

Next the sensei stood and bowed slightly. "When do we leave, Captain?"

Travis grinned at the sensei, and returned his bow respectfully, then walked over to Todd, and put his hand on the boy's shoulder. "Okay with you, Todd?" he asked. The lad looked up at Travis, put his arm around the man's waist, and nodded solemnly.

Suddenly Carlos piped up, echoing the preacher's expression with his Cuban accent, "Hot damn, *Jefe*. Time for *cervesas* for everyone!"

And so, with Budweisers in hand, the group celebrated their survival, toasted their captain, and planned the next leg of their odyssey into the new world, until the beer ran out, the sun set, and the cold, moonless night wrapped its dark arms around the little flotilla.

The next morning, which was Sunday, the preacher insisted upon a short service before the company departed. Standing on the forecastle of his boat, he gazed down at his small congregation, and cleared his throat. He extended his arms, Bible in hand like a prophet out of the Old Testament, lifted his eyes to the heavens and began. "Lord!" he cried, "Great Shepherd! Gathered before you today are the remainder of your flock in these 'ere parts. We ask Thee—nay, we beseech Thee—watch over, guide, and protect the last of your lambs. With your sword of righteousness you have struck down the sodomiting, insectaciding Philistines, the Sodom and Gomorrahs of the east and west coasts, pregnant with pollution from noxious emissions and toxic wastes. Your lightning and your sword have taken those who would ravage nature, who defile and destroy without conscience, the creatures of your making. The sinners of the earth have forfeited their miserable lives for pleasures of the flesh: fox furs, elephant tusks, and alligator shoes.

"Guide us now, Lord. Deliver us to the New Eden. Let our flesh be the flesh of the New World!

"These things we ask in the name of the Father, the Son, and the Holiest of Ghosts. Amen."

"Amen," repeated everyone aboard the sailboat, relieved at the brevity of the sermon and anxious to be under way.

Travis had gone over charts and courses with the preacher and the sensei the night before. They planned to stay with the "BC" coastlines–before the change–an expression the preacher had coined. That way they were fairly safe from underwater obstacles. As they neared northern Florida and southern Georgia, they would look for coastlines where they could make landfall for information and supplies. The Global Positioning System would allow them to pinpoint their exact location.

The boats were to be kept in sight of each other at all times, and would anchor close together in the evening for mutual protection. The adults would take shifts standing guard at night. Carlos agreed to travel with the preacher and Christina took over Carlos's duty in the galley of the sailboat.

All things in order, they upped anchors and set their course and their hopes for the north.

PART TWO
HOMEWARD

"To the hills, those of you destined for the New Eden, to the hills.

"Far from the hungry cry of doomed and ruined cities.

"Journey forth, and witness the birth of a New Age. Take your place in the history of the world.

"But keep your eyes peeled and your powder dry, for there are still those who would steal your dreams."

—The Preacher

CHAPTER 10
DELTA CAMP, NORTHWEST ARKANSAS

Colonel "Dutch" Rockford stood on the deck of his Quonset hut and surveyed the camp below: Delta Camp, base of operations for the Arkansas Militia, military branch of "The New Provincial Government of Arkansas." Colonel Rockford, the conceptual architect of the Provincial Government and Commander in Chief of the Arkansas Militia, was witnessing the fulfillment of a life-long dream.

It probably wouldn't have come to pass in such timely fashion without the recent catastrophe, but then he had allowed for that. No, actually he had planned on it. From the reports coming into his communications center, the rest of the nation was in a shambles. The Federal Government had collapsed, and most local authorities had all but given up. That too, fit nicely into his plans.

Arkansas had been shaken badly, as close to the New Madrid Fault as it was. Most of the eastern delta was under water, and possibly a third of the dwellings in the state had been badly damaged or destroyed. Casualties were in the tens of thousands. But the backbone of the state, the Ozark and Ouachita Mountain ranges, had absorbed the shockwaves and buffered much of the populace. The nuclear plants outside Russellville had survived intact, which was perhaps the greatest saving grace. If it had been any other way, there would have been nothing left for him to salvage.

Rockford gazed out over the activity below: supplies being unloaded and stored, troops drilling, newcomers being oriented. He smiled, savoring the taste and smell of rising power. *The New Provincial Government of Arkansas.*

As a young man fresh out of high school, Rockford had joined the Army. A few years later, when the struggle in Vietnam became an unofficial war, he found himself in the Mekong Delta fighting a brutal, elusive enemy who tried his patience and his courage. Fortunately for him, he managed to display these selfsame qualities and earned a field commission. He survived his first tour, then did a second. His latter tour, however, was cut short by a board of inquiry, and accusations regarding his treatment of VietCong prisoners. There were rumors, very strong rumors, that Captain Rockford was far too enthusiastic in the interrogation of prisoners. It was also said that his participation was close-up and personal, with his own favorite knife on several occasions, to the point of the unfortunate demise of the suspected VC.

When all the legal smoke cleared, the bottom line on the inquiry was that there were no witnesses who would come forth and testify to the allegations. Actually, there had been one–a Lieutenant Billingsly–who filed a statement, but he was killed on night patrol only a few days before his testimony was due. The official report read that he had been shot in the back by friendly fire when he accidentally extended his position too far forward.

The captain had proven himself to be an exemplary soldier otherwise, so it was decided by the Board that he would be sent stateside, to a training facility near his home town of Fort Smith, Arkansas. In a twist of fate, the slightly psychopathic Captain Rockford, who, at the very least, should have been courts-martialed, returned home a hero.

In the ensuing fifteen or sixteen years, the captain became a colonel and eventually retired from the U.S. Armed Forces. He did, however, during that time, lay the groundwork for a long-term goal he intended to realize upon leaving the service: The formation of a paramilitary organization that would serve as a protective agency for the civilian populace of the State of Arkansas, superseding federal and state authorities at such time when those authorities could no longer ensure the safety, defense, and welfare of the population.

Colonel Rockford was a bit of a visionary; a less than perfectly balanced one, but a visionary nonetheless. He foresaw, at some point in time, the collapse of the central government, and that it would be brought about by one of three things: a mass uprising of the impoverished minorities in the cities, spreading outward across the country and developing into full-scale civil war; or a limited nuclear war, leaving the country devastated and crippled, but functioning in some "clean areas" less affected by the bombs and fallout; or a natural disaster of catastrophic proportions such as what had actually taken place.

The majority of the colonel's career having been spent in Arkansas, he had managed to establish a number of powerful connections in the socio-political framework of the state. After retirement, he began to work in earnest on the founding of his Arkansas Militia. Rockford purchased a large, remote tract of land just south of Fort Smith in the foothills of the Ouachita Mountains, and began developing the property. He gathered a core of followers, many of whom had served under him in the Army, and they began to spread his doctrine. The colonel financed and supported the group with his own considerable wealth, and discreet contributions from people who could not afford to be overtly connected to him, but who sympathized with his concepts. In the end, what he achieved was the establishment of an organization that attracted a primarily white, Aryan survivalist mentality, but fostered loftier ideals such as patriotism, defense of hearth and home, and loyality to the militiamen and the State of Arkansas.

In true Machiavellian style, the charter of the New Provincial Government sanctioned the confiscation by eminent domain any property that was necessary for the establishment of militia training areas, military bases of operation, buffer zones, and communications or headquarters facilities.

In essence, should a national disaster actually occur, Colonel Rockford and those few power brokers who had supported him would find themselves with an unparalleled opportunity to gain control over as much choice Arkansas property as their greed would allow. With the demise of central government, that control might easily extend throughout the entire state, or even farther.

In the few years since its inception, the organization had prospered. Active membership, those who participated in maneuvers and held other jobs, and those who were full-time soldiers and staff, was approximately four thousand before the change. A week after the disaster had struck, the troops who hadn't deserted to safeguard home and family numbered about a thousand.

It wasn't long, however, before the organization began to gain new momentum, as those who had lost everything, and those who had nothing to lose, began gravitating toward the promises of food, shelter, and "the new beginning" being offered by Rockford and his cronies.

Before the change, the militia represented little more than an opportunity for groups of pro-survivalists to gather together on weekends, play soldier, and reinforce each other's slightly biased philosophies. When the devastation that Colonel Rockford had been predicting actually occurred, his credentials were considerably enhanced. Being an opportunist at heart, he had immediately taken advantage of the situation by securing control in his area with the militiamen and declaring himself leader of the new, independent State of Arkansas. The governor had been killed when a part of the capitol building collapsed during the initial earthquakes; consequently, there was virtually no organized government at a state or federal level to monitor, oppose, or resist him. It wasn't as if the state had accepted him *ad hoc* as the new leader. On the contrary, with poor to non-existent communications, half of the state didn't know he was alive and the other half didn't care. But that didn't matter to Colonel Dutch Rockford. Opportunities like this did not come along often and he was not going to let this one pass him by.

He held no illusions about his new government. As he put it, "democracy no longer fit the times." It was to be a benign dictatorship–that is, for those who agreed with him. Those who disagreed would find him less than benign.

He had devised a simple solution to the acquisition of land via eminent domain. Shortly after the initial disaster, while confusion was still at its peak, he sent teams out to rob banks in the small towns around the countryside. Any resistance was answered with the throaty roar of an M16. Inside of a week he had stockpiled over three million dollars, earmarked for the purchase of property. There was, of course, the small problem of owners not wanting to sell, which was solved by offering options to the occupants of the properties. Option number one: accept the money, take all their possessions, and leave quietly. Option number two: be buried on their property. Nearly all the people they dealt with chose the former.

Delta Camp had existed prior to the cataclysm. Alpha Camp, about twenty-five miles northwest of the town of Mena, was in the process of being established on some of their newly-aquired land. The colonel had chosen well on his second camp. Five separate purchases had provided him with over one hundred acres of prime land, three large country homes for an additional headquarters and officer billeting, ample outbuildings for storage of supplies and equipment, and sufficient area for personnel compounds. The location was ideal, as it was only a fifteen miles from the small municipal airport of Waldron, which would become his first air base. He was considering the purchase of one more piece of property, which would give them an overview of the valley and serve as an observation post. With that acquisition, the new base would be complete.

As the colonel watched the movement of men and vehicles, he was joined by one of his captains. "Sir!" the captain barked as he snapped to attention and saluted. "We're prepared for your inspection of the armory." They had been able to salvage some valuable equipment from the National Guard Armory in Fort Smith: two armored personnel carriers with .60 caliber machine guns, three transport trucks, and several cases of M16s. But a rival survivalist group and a street gang had chosen the same night to pillage the depot, and a firefight ensued. Rockford's troops suffered a number of casulties as they were forced from the compound in retreat. The loss of men hadn't bothered the colonel, but he was livid at being beaten back by the rival groups. He shot two of his own soldiers that night for failing to hold their position under fire.

Prior to the firefight, they were also able to procure various other complements to their existing equipment, from mess kits and tents to field radios, so it had been a profitable evening regardless. There was no ammunition available at the armory, but that wasn't a problem. With some inside help, they had already raided an ammo storage facility: Several dozen cases of ammunition were stored in Delta Camp's munitions bunker. In the colonel's eyes, the loss of a few men was insignificant compared to what they had gained materially. The men could be replaced; there were other warm bodies. Trucks, armored cars, and machine guns gave him leverage–powerful leverage.

Colonel Rockford and the captain walked through the bustling compound to Delta Camp armory–a large, recently erected metal shed. The trucks and armored personnel carriers, which were parked in a neat row in front of the building, gave the colonel a new sense of pride and purpose as he strode past them. With dedicated men and equipment like this, in a few short months he would eliminate all opposition to his new government. He didn't give a damn about the rest of the country. Let it wallow in indecision. Let it remain in collapse for all he cared. He and his new Provincial Government were going to lead Arkansas into a new era. Arkansas would become the shining star of America, and he would be its undisputed leader!

Capitalism, communism, democracy–those were expressions of the past. He thought of himself more as a warlord, using power, cunning, and ruthlessness to consolidate and maintain his government. The old world had held room for bleeding-heart liberals, charity balls for starving Africans, and hospitals crammed to capacity, preserving the deformed, the diseased, and the mentally useless. The new world would be closer to nature's way. The strong would survive; the weak would succumb, and the world would be a better place for it. There would be few, if any, prisons packed to capacity with pampered prisoners enjoying fancy food and color-TVs. If you committed a crime, you'd pay. There would be no such thing as a stay of execution. Justice would be swift and sure: There were lots of trees and plenty of rope.

As the colonel walked through the doors, the "army" smell assailed his nostrils, and it pleased him. The armory not only held their present acquisitions, but also the equipment they had been amassing for years. Racks of weapons lined the walls; cases of supporting materials were stacked nearby. Two field pieces, 105s, stood at ease in the back. He smiled to himself in pride and anticipation of events to come.

He strolled through the building checking weapons, trying bolts, examining various pieces of equipment while the captain, like a faithful dog, followed behind, hoping for a word of praise.

"Well, all seems to be in order," the colonel finally said, straightening up and rubbing the palms of his hands together slowly. "Let's have a look at the ammunitions depot."

The ammo bunker was a hundred yards away, on the other side of the compound. Another metal shed covered a concrete block cellar, where virtually all the munitions for the camp, from 105s to M16 rounds, were stored. Rockford walked through the rows of boxes, checking the integrity of cases and looking for moisture or mildew. When he was finally satisfied, he dismissed the captain and walked back to the cabin that served as his headquarters.

Rockford hung his hat on the peg inside the door and surveyed the interior of the cabin. It was furnished in what he referred to as "Spartan elegance." It was uncluttered, containing only the basic necessities in furniture, but each piece was of unquestionable quality. From the antique cherrywood secretary and desk to the huge, four-poster, mahogany canopy bed, every piece had been selected with care.

As he moved past the full-length mirror in the hallway, he paused and studied himself for a moment, smoothing down the front of his uniform. The pale blue eyes that stared back at him still harbored fierce passion, yet they carried the cool detachment of a predator. His dark hair, close-cropped military style, was only beginning to gray at the temples. For a man who had just turned fifty, he was still tall, trim, and capable-looking, but the lines on his face told a tale of the triumphs and the tradgedies of a soldier's life.

He had been married twice; both had failed. The truth was, like so many men, he was married to what he did, and pleased with who he was. Unfortunately, it left little time for any other conjugation.

Rockford moved on to the desk and sat down, lit a Havana cigar from the teak humidor, then pushed the seat back and put his hands behind his head. He exhaled a small blue cloud toward the ceiling, and for a few moments, mentally reviewed the next stages of his strategy.

First, he had begun a political campaign, not to solicit votes, but to inform the citizenry of his intentions in a fashion that would be acceptable to them. His men had commandeered several radio stations and were broadcasting hourly messages detailing the catastrophic conditions of the Americas, emphasing the collapse of federal and state governments. The last half of the broadcast was a taped message from Rockford extolling his virtues as a leader and explaining the necessity of the new government. The colonel also had teams delivering flyers with the same message across the countryside.

Secondly, he intended to form a group. That is to say, his Captain Reynolds, an unsavory but useful man, would form a group for him. The colonel would not–could not afford to be–directly affiliated with them. The band, under Reynold's leadership, would terrorize the remaining enclaves of civilization in Arkansas. Although the state had suffered severely from the disaster, there were still a number of areas where damage had been minimal. There was a "wait and see" attitude from the people in those locations. They felt the Federal Government might still come to the rescue, and had resisted Rockford's overtures. They, and some of the bureaucracy clinging tenuously to their positions in various parts of the state, were going to need some prompting. And prompt them he would. When Reynolds and his bandits were finished, the citizens of Arkansas would be clamoring for some form of law and order. At that point, when most of the state was begging for deliverance, he and his troops would crush the offenders. There would be no more dispute as to who was in control.

As an incentive for his band of thugs, he would, for the time being, allow them whatever they wanted in their pillaging. He would have Reynolds assure the leaders that when the time came he would stage a mock raid on their camp. The encampment would be destroyed, and the outlaws would disperse with their newly acquired wealth.

Truth was, when the time came, Reynolds would assist the colonel in destroying the bandits to a man. There would be no witnesses to his collusion. Even Reynolds was in for a surprise.

CHAPTER 11
DANGEROUS SEAS

After departing the sunken remains of Miami, the first two days of sailing were relatively uneventful. Todd hit several schools of mackerel while trolling lures, so fresh fish, for the time being, was no longer an issue. Carlos experimented with smoking the fillets, storing them in the cool of the hold in plastic bags that he'd found aboard the preacher's boat. The fish, supplemented by canned goods, formed the basis of their diet. It was healthy, albeit a bit monotonous.

They saw an occasional boat on the horizon, but no one approached them. They posted a guard at night and took turns with the duty, breaking it into shifts. Christina was recovering from the trauma of losing Jan. It was obvious to everyone that she was suffering, but it was equally evident that she possessed an inner resilience that would not permit useless emotion such as self-pity or unfounded guilt. She was going on with her life. The girl was a survivor.

Travis and the others talked for hours as they sailed, and Ra stretched out on the deck like a big black cat, enjoying the sun. Todd never spoke, but he was out-distancing his emotional fugue, and it was very apparent that he had taken to Travis. They spent hours together fishing, or sitting on the bow watching for turtles and dolphins, and Travis was teaching him to sail.

One evening, after an early supper, Travis and the preacher discussed weapons. The preacher had served in the Army in his early days. When Travis showed him the LAWS anti-tank weapons they had taken from the Cubans, he nearly flipped.

"Call it what you want, son, that's a bazooka to me. Hot damn! God have mercy on the next unlucky sinner bent on doing damage to this flock."

They all decided, for the safety of the group, that they would keep one of these devilishly powerful devices on the shrimper, and the rest on the sailboat. The following day, everyone practiced preparing, aiming, and dry-firing one, which turned out to be simple. As the preacher had said, the LAWS was a smaller, more manageable model of the bazooka. It was nothing more than a tube with an enclosed round. The operator simply popped off the front and rear covers, extended the weapon to firing position, shouldered the device and centered the target in the pop-up V-sights. Nonetheless, it was formidable. It had an accurate range of at least 400-hundred meters and the explosive delivery equivalent to a full stick of dynamite. Each of them also took an M16, along with six clips of ammo. Travis spent half an hour with Christina, teaching her how to use the rifle. She proved to be a quick study, having hunted grouse and quail on her grandparents' ranch in Mexico. They also broke into the box of grenades and stored half a dozen within easy reach on both the sailboat and the shrimper. They were not going to be caught flat-footed again.

It was late that afternoon, when all the weapons had been put away, the boats anchored, and supper was being served on the big boat, that they noticed the weather change. There had been a fair southeasterly breeze for the past two days, with light rolling seas. Suddenly, within a matter of minutes, it was as if Mother Nature had taken a deep breath and held it, sucking up all the breeze and calming the seas flat as ice. Christina was the first to see the blackness creeping up on the edges of the horizon.

The preacher gazed out at the ominously darkening sky and frowned. "I been a-hearin' about these storms the rest of the country's having and I been a-wonderin' why we ain't seen one. I think we're about to."

Travis got up from the table. "All right, everybody, let's get back to the sailboat. We've got to batten down everything that moves. Preacher, I don't have to tell you the drill. You've been there before." Looking at the blackening sky, Travis spoke again. "We'll probably get separated if this is as bad as it looks, so the best we can do is ride it out and stay in contact by radio. We'll find each other after the storm blows itself out."

"Right you are," bellowed the preacher. "The Lord will protect. Believe ye of little faith, witness Him work His mighty wonders. Now get the hell out of here, and prepare yourselves for a little of God's non-aerosol cleansing." He lumbered off to secure his boat, Carlos trailing behind.

The storm rolled in like an ebony chariot, a nightmare of unearthly speed and power. Horrendous clouds billowed and mushroomed across the sky, turning the day into night in minutes, and from the dark center came a howling wind, shrieking and screaming at them like a chorus of demons. Lightening erupted across the sky; daggers of fire split the heavens, striking and illuminating the sea with incandescent flames.

Travis reefed the sails, battened the hatches, and tied down everything that jiggled. The two boats separated, to give each other the safety of distance while fighting the storm, then aimed their bows into the approaching onslaught and prayed as they faced a sailor's greatest fear. After firing up the diesel engine to help maintain direction and inertia, the sensei and Travis tied themselves into the safety harnesses in the cockpit and Travis took the wheel. The others remained strapped in below.

The rigging rattled and shook as the relentless wind tore at it, and the boat slammed into ever larger and more frightening waves. A solid wall of cold rain struck them hard enough to make Travis wince. The rain continued to sting and blind the two men while the vicious waves battered the boat and attempted to wrest control from them.

In their struggle against the gale, time became an indiscernible factor. When Travis's cramped and numbed arms could no longer hold the wheel against the seas, he gratefully turned it over to the sensei, who took over with equal tenacity and skill. For hours, while the tempest raged around them, they switched control: when one of them could physically go no further, the other sensed it and took the helm. As the storm peaked and finally waned, a friendship emerged from the relationship that already existed. They had sailed through hell together and looked the devil in the eye ... and the devil turned away.

Although they had been tossed about like a matchstick in a white-water river, damage to the craft seemed to be minimal. The good mast had held. The sails were still reefed and nothing topside was broken. The Avon raft, tied behind the boat, was the one major loss they sustained. In the worst of the storm, while changing places, they had nearly lost control of the boat as it was broached by a huge wave. The line to the raft slackened, then sprang tight, snapping with the sound of a rifle shot.

As the winds and seas subsided, the sensei took the wheel and Travis went below to check on the others. Thanks to advance preparation, the inside of the cabin was still intact. Christina and Todd had strapped themselves to their bunks and, other than a little seasickness and a bruise or two, had come through it well. Ra had allowed himself to be bound to a mattress in the forward berth, and had survived the storm without injury. They had been lucky. Unfortunately, there had been less luck aboard the preacher's boat.

***

The preacher held the wheel as he faced the onslaught in grim silence. The little Cuban, white with fear, stood beside him, witnessing the monstrous storm rushing toward them.

The winds hit them like God's own hammer and the waves tossed the fifty-foot shrimper from crest to crest like a toy. The tempest was just reaching it's full fury when the preacher realized he had left his VHF antenna in the Up position. There was no question that they would lose it if it remained that way. The preacher was torn between leaving the wheel to an inexperienced seaman like Carlos while he went out, or sending Carlos out to face the dangers of a slippery deck and enormous waves. He yelled his dilemma over the clamor of the storm, and the Cuban instantly volunteered to lower the antenna. There was no time for discussion; the preacher nodded, and Carlos left.

Carlos was hammered against the cabin by gale-force winds and sheets of blinding rain. He grasped the cabin door handle, orienting himself and attempting to get his racing heart under control. It was no use–he felt the same mind-numbing, incapacitating fright he had experienced as a child when his father, drunk and angry, would smash his way into their one-room shack, seeking to vent the frustrations of poverty and position on his woman and the scrawny child she had borne him. Seared into his memory was the sight of his father, the screaming, angry giant looming over him, deriding him for his weakness, his frailty, and his size. Overwhelmed by the same helplessness and terror, he stood rigid as death, welded to the wheelhouse door with both hands.

At that moment, a large swell broke over the bow and washed across the forecastle. The cold water drenched him, cutting into his senses like the blade of a knife. The wave had been the "slap in the face" Carlos needed. He shook his head like a dog, rising out of the miasma of fear and uncertainty. He was no longer a frightened child. He was Carlos

Venarega, a man, and he would do what was needed of him, or die trying!

He swallowed his panic–he physically pushed it down inside him and buried it under a layer of determination. He moved away from the door, struggling to remain upright on the bucking boat while keeping his balance against the slippery deck and the crushing waves. Finally, after a few terribly long minutes, he made it to the rear of the wheelhouse where the antenna was. Holding an empty equipment rack with one hand, he loosened the adjustment lever on the Fiberglass antenna, pulled the rod to a horizontal position, and tightened the adjustment again to keep it safely in place. Pleased with his success, he turned to begin his trek back to the wheelhouse door when the boat, struck sideways by a wave, lurched crazily to starboard. Carlos was in the process of switching grips when the boat tipped hard to the right and ran a rail into the water. Losing his balance, he was thrown backward, and found himself sliding toward the buried rail and the ocean. With a shriek, Carlos made a desperate grab for safety, missing by inches. The back of his thighs hit the rail and he was tossed head over heels into the angry sea. Death opened its arms and waited to embrace the small, brave man.

Patches of stars in the coal-colored sky began to break through the thinning cloud cover. The seas were still jumbled but far less dangerous and beginning to calm. Travis thought to himself that, once again, Mother Nature had thrown her best at him and he had survived. Having made sure that Christina and Todd were all right, Travis went to the radio and tried to raise the preacher.

On the third try, the older man's tired, gravelly voice came over the air. "I read you, Travis. I'm here. The boat's a little banged up but she made it." There was something in the preacher's voice that Travis didn't like, it sounded as flat as day-old beer.

"Preacher, you all right? You don't sound good."

"I'm okay, but I lost Carlos–"

Travis, shocked and instantly frightened for the little man, keyed in, "How? When? What happened?"

The preacher spoke again, regret etching every syllable. "My antenna was up–he went out in the storm to put it down. We got hit sideways by a wave about that time. I heard him scream, then he was gone, washed over the side. God rest his soul."

"Oh no," Travis moaned. *Lord,* he thought, *just when things were looking so positive–when we were all feeling so confident–to lose Carlos!*

They had been together only a short while, but had suffered so much collectively that losing one of the group was like losing a family member. Moreover, it made death and destruction tangible again. Just when there seemed to be a small light at the end of the tunnel, when it seemed they might all survive, the storm from hell had rolled through and snatched someone, just to remind them all.

Travis paused for a moment, then keyed the mike again. "It wasn't your fault. You didn't have anything to do with it. You go on from here, you hear me."

"I know, I know," replied the preacher wearily. "It's just that, damn it, man, if I hadn't forgotten to put the antenna down–God! I sent him out into that."

Travis broke in immediately. "If I know Carlos, he volunteered to go. He made the choice, Preacher, not you."

"I guess it don't much matter now," sighed the older man. "He's gone and I can't bring him back, though I'd take his place if I could."

Travis decided to change the subject. "Your GPS still working? If so, give me your co-ordinates so we can tie up."

"Yeah, it's workin'." The preacher gave his coordinates: 25 degrees, 39 minutes, 20 seconds north; 81 degrees, 24 minutes, 5 seconds west.

"Okay, gotcha," said Travis. "Stay there. We're gonna get some sleep and start out at first light tomorrow. We're only about three hours from you, so hang on. We'll see you in the morning." Travis hung up the mike and turned to see the tears in Christina's eyes.

"Oh God, Travis. He made it so far, he fought so hard, and now ..."

He took her in his arms and held her as she cried, tears of frustration and pain filling his own eyes.

Carlos's first sensation was that of being immersed in cold silence as he plunged below the surface and a following wave churned over him. He fought his way to the surface, gasping and choking, but before he could fully catch his breath, he was lifted by another wave, slapped to the bottom of the trough, and buried again by a ton of water. Once more, he struggled to the top, his lungs crying for oxygen, his movements already slowing and confused. He tread water as best he could, continuously fighting the mountainous waves, sucking in air when he was able, but the cold water was burning down the adrenalin in his system and he was tiring. He knew it was only a matter of time.

Ever the faithful Catholic, as he neared the end, Carlos prayed. He didn't pray to be saved from the situation. He figured that God was probably a little short on miracles for useless, inattentive *Cubanos*. Rather he prayed for his soul, which he was certain would be in the hands of the Lord in minutes. Another wave caught him and drove him down, tumbling him over and over under the sea. With his lungs nearly bursting, Carlos knew, almost peacefully, that was the last time he would make the surface. The Lord had chosen to take him, and he was ready.

But, at the last minute, as his head and shoulders broke clear of the water, Carlos felt something hard and rubbery hit him in the back of his head. Exhausted but startled, he turned to find the Avon raft nudging him in a freak moment of calm between waves.

"*Madre de Dios*!" he croaked, as he grabbed the side and clawed his way into the raft. He lay flat on his back in the dinghy, alternately gasping and vomiting while watching the swirling clouds above.

Carlos remained like that as the raft was tossed by the colossal waves and slid down troughs that would have been the envy of any Wiameia Bay surfer. The waves crashed over him, leaving him choking and gasping. The raft filled with water dozens of times, only to be emptied on the next jarring toss. Carlos kept his death-grip on the ropes of the dinghy and begged for deliverance. Lord, the deals he made: no more drinking, no more "borrowing" things. He swore he would never miss Mass again–if he could find a Mass again! For what seemed like hours, he was pitched and pummeled, intermittently praying and puking. But eventually the storm abated, and, as the waters settled, Carlos relaxed, then slept.

He awoke to someone shouting at him. His battered and fatigued body barely responded as he roused himself and looked over the rim of the raft.

In front of him were, not one, but three boats! The largest was a fifty-five foot Coast Guard cutter. The other two were fairly expensive sport-fishing types, about forty feet each.

Carlos's first impulse was joy: The Coast Guard had found him. There was still an America. The man on the cutter shouted at him again and he looked up at the crew. They were not Coast Guard servicemen; their hair was shaggy and long and they were dressed in jeans and sweatshirts. There was nothing military about them. *Don' matter*, Carlos thought, *Attila the Hun would be a welcome sight, long as he was in a dry boat.*

"Toss him a rope," the big man on the deck ordered. Within moments, a rope hit him across the face and chest. He grabbed it and they pulled the dinghy to the side of the larger vessel. Carlos struggled up the rope ladder, was pulled aboard and unceremoniously dumped on the deck.

"Looks like we got ourselves a *Cubano* here."

One of the others sneered, "Yeah, I think you're right."

The fellow who appeared to be in charge stood over Carlos. "Hey you," he said, kicking the prostrate Cuban in the leg. "Speakee English?"

Carlos looked up at him. "*Sí*, I speak English."

"Well, that's just great," replied the man, "cause I need a cook and a cleaner on this tub and you just got elected! Keep quiet, do what you're told, and you'll get to enjoy adventure on the high seas. Screw up, and the best you can hope for is to be back in that raft. *Comprende, amigo*?"

"Yeah," replied Carlos wearily, "I *comprende*."

CHAPTER 12
CONFRONTATION AND RESURRECTION

Travis lay on his bunk, staring at the ceiling. For all that he'd been through, and as tired as he was, sleep just wouldn't come. He kept thinking about losing Carlos, and what a psychological blow it had been to the group. Moreover, for the first time in quite a while he found himself apprehensive about the future.

The responsibility for the lives he directed lay heavily on him. He closed his eyes. "Lord," he said. "I know it seems the only time I talk with You anymore, is when I need something, and I guess this is no exception, but I've got some people here relying on me and I need a little guidance. Just help me make the right decisions to get us through this, please. And Lord, take good care of my little buddy, Carlos. He did his best while he was here."

The sensei woke him just after sunrise. Christina, Todd, and the two men had a quick, cold breakfast, then upped anchor and headed for the preacher. There was little conversation. The loss of Carlos had stolen the triumph in their survival of the storm.

The weather had cleared but there was still a stiff wind and a rolling sea. They'd been sailing for about two hours; the sensei had the wheel when Travis decided to go below and touch base with the preacher. He was in the midst of a brief conversation with the shrimper when the sensei appeared at the stairs of the cabin. Something in the old warrior's eyes brought Travis immediately to attention.

"We have company on the horizon–three boats and they're headed this way."

Travis got up, that watch-your-ass feeling crawling all over him. "I don't want company. Let's run from them, see if we can make the preacher." He brought the mike up again. "Preacher, we're about five or six miles west-southwest of you and we've got company I don't feel good about. Put it in gear and get over to us as quickly as possible. And break out your bazooka."

They put out every inch of sail she had and the boat moved out swiftly, but she was no match for the powerboats behind them. In less than twenty minutes, two of the craft had circled them in a pincer movement, positioning themselves directly in their path. The other boat, the bigger of the three, stayed behind them and moved up slowly. Travis dropped the sails; they weren't going anywhere.

The ship in the rear was a small Coast Guard cutter. Normally that would have offered them some security, but as the boat neared they could see that something was amiss. It hadn't been maintained like a government craft. The men on board didn't look like any military crew they'd ever seen, and there were marks along the cabin that looked distinctly like bullet holes. Travis and the sensei glanced at each other, and without another word, headed for the cabin and the guns. Just as the three vessels lined up in front of the sailboat, the preacher called.

The sensei and Travis were loading their M16s when the preacher's gruff voice rolled over the radio.

"*Odyessy*, this is the preacher. I can see you and the boys. I'm about a mile away and coming up from behind them. I don't think they've spotted me yet."

Travis grabbed the mike, a plan forming. "Listen, Preacher, get in range with that anti-tank gun and kill your engines. Christina's gonna be on the radio. If she says, 'do it,' take one of them out. You got it?"

"Yeah, I got it, son."

Travis turned to Christina. "Listen carefully, Chris: Watch from the rear hatch with the mike in your hand. If I raise my right arm, or they start shooting, you tell the preacher to let 'em have it. Understand?"

"Count on it."

The sensei and Travis stood on the bow with their weapons and faced the three boats. A tall, heavyset man with dirty blond hair tied in a ponytail moved to the bow of the cutter and looked down at Travis. The man smiled but it was more the smile of a cat that has just cornered a mouse and knows he can take his time.

"Why, Captain, you seemed so unfriendly, trying to run away from us like that." His two crew members chuckled, guns resting casually in the crooks of their arms.

"Sorry if we offended you," replied Travis. "Just didn't feel like company, it being such a nice day for a sail and all."

"Yes, it is," the man said. "Tell me, Captain, where'd you get those weapons you have there?" pointing to the M16s with his own gun.

"Well, I'll tell you," answered Travis, "we met some guys a while back who sort of inadvertently gave them to us. Guess you could say they didn't need them anymore."

"Yes, we've met a few people like that ourselves," said the fellow, with a sinister smile. His companions snickered again.

"Listen, we'd love to stay and chat," said Travis, "but you're holding up lunch, so I guess we'll just be on our way. We'll wish you boys luck at whatever it is you do."

As Travis started to back off slowly, the man spoke again. "Not so fast, Captain. We thought you might invite us to have lunch with you, give us a chance to get aquainted."

"Sorry," said Travis. "A tin of spam only splits comfortably four ways. Maybe next time."

The man's smile hadn't strayed, but his eyes went hard as he spoke again. "Well then, perhaps you'd like to give us those weapons you have, as sort of a parting gift." Then, looking past Travis to Christina, whose head and shoulders were sticking out of the hatch, he continued. "And maybe we might like to borrow your friend there, too. We promise to return her."

That tore it for Travis, but he kept his composure. Looking at the man across from him he spoke slowly, menacingly. "Tell you what, *Captain*"–he spat the word back–"there are a number of possibilities here: One is that I might give you the girl and the guns, but there are probably a couple of other possibilities that are more likely, and a smart man like yourself should weigh all the odds before taking action, don't you think?"

The big man looked down at Travis and nodded, curious.

"One of the distinct possibilities is that we could have a little shoot-out here, and seeing as how I know my chances of surviving are slim, I'm gonna do one thing for certain. I'm gonna make sure I cut you right in half with this M16 before anything else happens."

The man started slightly but held his position, saving face.

"There is one other important possibility that you should consider before you decide on anything," Travis continued, "and that is, the boat you see about four hundred yards to your rear has a Light Anti-Tank Weapons System–a bazooka for you laymen–aimed at you boys."

The crewmembers of the three ships jerked their heads around as one, eyes coming to rest on the shrimp boat in the distance.

"And if I raise my right arm," Travis continued, "he's gonna vaporize one of you."

The leader's head swung back to Travis. Unfortunately, he was still smiling. "That's a nice bluff, Captain, but I'm not buying it."

"That's what I thought you'd say," replied Travis as he

raised his right arm. There was a moment of tension on the other vessels, but when nothing happened, the crews began to laugh. Travis had just begun to feel stupid when there was a whooshing sound and the boat on the far side of the cutter disintegrated into a fireball, hurling pieces of the craft for a hundred yards in all directions.

Everyone was thrown to the decks of their respective boats, but Travis seized the moment by rising quickly and raising his rifle to the place where his antagonist had been standing.

"Get ready," he shouted to the sensei. Travis waited until the big man stood up, then gave him a burst from his stomach up to his head, pretty much keeping his promise to the man.

The sensei, with his rifle on full automatic, cut down the two lieutenants by the wheelhouse before they could recover.

Travis fired a burst over the heads of the terrified men in the other boat. "Drop your guns, all of you. Fire one shot at us, and we'll blow you out of the water." Guns clattered to the deck.

Just then Travis heard a voice he thought he recognized, screaming, "*Jefe*! *Jefe*!" No, it couldn't be ... but out of the cabin door of the cutter burst Carlos yelling, "Don't shoot, *Jefe*! Don't shoot! It's me, Carlos!" Travis simply gaped in disbelief as the diminutive Cuban raced across the deck and shouted, lapsing into Spanish, "*Madre de Dios me Jefe, esta Carlos, me Jefe*!" Carlos paused only long enough to spit on the prostrate form of the man on the bow. "You stinkin' son-a-ma-bitchee," he barked.

Recovering, Travis shouted to Carlos, "Glad to have you back. Now grab one of those guns and keep the guys in the other boat covered."

The Cuban did as he was ordered, enjoying the role as

he yelled at the terrified men. "Make one move and Carlos shoot you like the stinkin' pigs you are, you bastard son-a-ma-bitchees!"

Travis could barely repress a smile; they had done it. They'd taken the pirates, and to top it off, Carlos was back. He turned to the sensei, whose normally inscrutable face was broken by a wide grin. As their eyes met, the Japanese bowed slightly. Travis smiled and returned the bow.

After collecting the weapons from the outlaws on the other craft, they tied them up and stripped the two boats of anything valuable, from food and radio equipment to basic supplies. The preacher was given the option of taking one of the boats as his own, but he declined, saying he couldn't leave *Jesus's Love* just a-driftin' at sea. She was a little beat up, but she was his. They filled their fuel and water tanks from the cutter and set it adrift, then gave the three men just enough food and water to make land and let them go in the sport-fishing boat. With no weapons, little food, and a pretty boat, they were likely to become victims of their own kind.

That evening, when they anchored for the night, the reunited crew discussed their position and future plans. The sensei had plotted them to be a couple of miles from the area that used to be Tampa Bay, and, as if to confirm that, the setting sun glinted off the bent and jagged remains of the Sunshine Skyway Bridge rising out of the water.

"From the looks of that, they must have received some pretty serious earth tremors around here," Travis remarked, staring at the twisted metal in the distance.

The sensei also studied the bridge. "I suspect the farther north we go, the more damage we will see from earthquakes."

There was still no land to be seen, and they all looked forward to dispelling that empty, disconnected feeling with the sight of some solid ground.

Dinner was served on the shrimper by the resurrected Carlos. He had to tell his story several times before everyone was satisfied hearing it—he had been so incredibly lucky. But then, they all had. They survived an encounter that, by all rights, should have been disastrous.

"Not without," the preacher reminded them, "the will of the Almighty and the Lightning of His right hand!" Which was the preacher's new name for the LAWS. With eyes as bright as Christmas tree lights and his face aglow, the ecological evangelist described how he, the right hand of God, reached out and smote the fornicating Philistines with the rod of the Lord, wreaking righteous vengeance on those unholy aberrations.

Ah, thought Travis, *there's nothing like a man who enjoys his work.*

Carlos had his own name for their new secret weapon, which was probably more appropriate. He simply called it, "*El Grande* Boom Boom!"

Travis and his crew returned to the sailboat via the *Amazing Avon*, as they'd taken to calling the raft. Carlos and the preacher bedded down in the shrimp boat.

When everyone was safely aboard the *Odyssey* and settled into the cabin, Travis headed topside to stand the first watch. As he reached the stairs, he heard Christina call from behind him, "Mind if I join you?"

"Not at all, come on up." He held out his hand, and she took it. They sat together in the cockpit, looking out at the ever-constant movement of the gentle sea, illuminated only by the diamond-bright stars. Travis turned slightly, putting his arm on the rail behind Christina, looking into those incredible green eyes. "Are you doing okay?" He hesitated, not wanting to remind but to assure. "I mean with all that's happened, today, and ..."

She smiled slightly, with just a touch of melancholy.

"Yeah, I'm okay, I'll be fine. How about you, Captain?" she asked. "You're the one who's having to deal with all the excitement we keep running into."

He smiled. "I'm fine, no problems."

Sitting there in the starlight, she studied him for a moment; the confidence about him, the rugged, attractive features of his face, yet the gentleness in his eyes. *A rare combination in a man,* she thought to herself. "Tell me, Travis Christian," she said in that frank fashion of hers, "was there no one in your life before all this– this– this catastrophe?"

His eyes showed a small flash of recollection. "I had a friend," he replied. "I don't think I was in love, if that's what you mean."

She nodded solemnly, carrying it no further. It was quiet for a few moments, then she looked at him again. "Were you ever married?"

This time his face softened at the memory, though sadly. "I was married once, a long time ago. She was a French girl from Haiti. Her father owned a sugar plantation there. I met her while on an adventure with my old friend, Cody."

"What happened?" she asked.

His face went sad and hard at the same time, and Christina knew she shouldn't have asked. "I'm sorry. It's none of my business," she said quickly.

"It's all right," he replied. "Like I said, it was a long time ago. She was killed in an attempted robbery while Christmas shopping with a friend in Miami."

Christina touched his arm. "Please forgive me for bringing it up. I didn't mean ..."

But Travis went on, staring hard at the dark waters, as if he hadn't heard her. "She was Cody's friend, too. The police in Miami came up empty-handed as to who did it. Hell, half of them couldn't find their ass with both hands, let alone solve a crime. It was just another shooting to them, something that happens five or six times a day." He sighed angrily. "I guess, in all fairness, the cops are outnumbered and overworked most of the time. They just do what they can, and the rest just falls through the cracks. Anyway, when the police couldn't find the killer, Cody and I went to work on it. I hired the best detective agency I could find, and Cody put the word out to all his connections in the area. It took us six months–six months of beating the bushes, but we found them. Two guys, brothers, crack addicts, looking for a quick fix to their financial problems. Yeah, we found them."

The savage look on Travis's face made asking the obvious question unnecessary. Christina didn't want to know.

He looked back to her again, and his face softened. "I apologize," he said. "You didn't need to hear that."

"It's okay," she replied. "Maybe you needed to say it."

As they sat there looking at each other, the cool wind rippled the water and she shivered slightly. Instinctively Travis put his arm around her and she, in turn, with a sense of comfort and ease she had not felt in a long time, moved toward him. Travis thought how natural and relaxed the moment was, without the tenseness and indecision usually found in new relationships, if indeed, this, in any sense, could be considered a new relationship. Intuitively, he knew he must keep his emotions in check. For her, it could very well be no more than one person comforting another after a rough day.

He gazed out at the water and spoke: "You're one hell of a woman, Christina. You didn't even flinch through that whole experience today. You were really brave."

She pulled away and looked up at him incredulously. "Me, brave? Good Lord, you're the brave one. You looked like something out of a Harold Robbins novel, telling that guy and his little army they had to leave now because he was interrupting your lunch."

It was so amusing, the way she said it, that Travis had

to laugh. "Well, it was either that or give him you and the guns, and I really hated the idea of losing those guns."

She pulled away and slugged him in the chest, laughing. "Thanks a lot, you crud. Shows me where I rate."

In an attempt to stop her from hitting him again, he instinctively pulled her to him, and suddenly their eyes locked. Like the flow of the tides or the movement of the moon, they both knew that there was nothing that could stop the slow, inexorable path their parted lips took as they came together. There was an electric moment of mutual need as they embraced. Then suddenly, Christina pulled away, breaking the spell.

"Travis, I'm sorry. I can't–it's too soon. I need time."

He reached out and held her gently, looking into her eyes, which reflected green fire like emeralds. "Take all the time you need, Christina. I'm not going anywhere."

She held his eyes with hers. "I still have a lot of emotional baggage to shed with Jan's passing. I think you know we weren't 'in love', but we shared a lot. We were close. I can't just put him behind me that easily–especially after the way he ..."

She broke his gaze, and he replied softly, "It's all right, Christina. Like I told you, I'm not going anywhere. But if and when you're ready, I'm here."

They continued to hold each other, watching the dark waters in silence. The wind whispered soft promises to the rigging, the stars bathed them in cold brightness, and both suddenly found themselves more content than they could remember.

CHAPTER 13
EMINENT DOMAIN

Colonel Rockford sat at his desk, going over the paperwork that assembling an army required. There were requisitions, supplies, personnel rosters, and a hundred other things that had to be compiled during the day-to-day operations as he and his aides tried to turn civilians and weekend warriors into real soldiers. Yet that was but a small part of the gargantuan task of creating an infrastructure for a new, independent government.

Of primary importance was the reduction, then the elimination, of opposition. He was actively working on the problem.

The lieutenant-governor, who survived the initial disaster and had attempted to take the reins of leadership, had been shot to death while leaving his residence a week ago. The colonel had attended the funeral and consoled the widow.

Several of the leading senators who opposed Rockford's rise to power had mysteriously disappeared. Dissension in the ranks of the remaining jumble of influence peddlers and lawmakers had diminished greatly since then. His campaign to promote himself to the people of Arkansas was moving along well. He had plans for a state-wide tour, and was beginning to schedule speeches in various locations. Rockford had, through Captain Reynolds, activated his campaign of terror in those enclaves still resistant to his concepts, loyal to whatever form of state and federal government they hoped might exist. He had no time to waste coddling those people. A slap in the face was always more effective than "excuse me" for getting someone's attention, and slap them he would! His army of bandits would shock those pockets of resistance into submission. Then he would rescue them all by eliminating the marauders, demonstrating his leadership in ultimate fashion.

There was a knock on the outer doors, and one of his aides ushered Reynolds into the room. The doors closed and the captain sauntered over to the colonel's desk.

Rockford looked up from his paperwork, "You salute a senior officer, Reynolds, especially your Commanding Officer."

"Begging your pardon, Sir," responded Reynolds with a touch of sarcasm as he executed a sloppy salute.

You're just like a bad dog, the colonel thought, looking at him. *I'll keep you on a short leash, aimed at the enemy, and I'll keep a close eye out, because you could turn at any moment.* Reynolds served a purpose for the time being, though, and when he was no longer needed, like any animal that had gone bad, Rockford would have him put down.

"Tell me, Captain, how are you progressing in your program to convince the people of Arkansas of their need for our new government?"

Reynolds smiled and relaxed. "Well, Colonel, me and the boys have been fairly successful in puttin' the fear of God, and anything else that goes bump in the night, into the local citizenry. We raided Russellville two nights ago. Judge Hawkins was at home when we arrived; he won't be giving you any more trouble. He's survived by his wife and daughter who'll probably be needin' to rest for a couple of days, after entertainin' the troops. The boys got a little carried away and burned down some of the town, but all in all, you could say folks got the message. We been conductin' weekly raids into the well-to-do areas of Ft. Smith, Hot Springs, and Little Rock. They've been very profitable. We've got them people so goddamned scared, they'd elect the devil himself governor, if he promised to stop us."

The colonel smiled. "Good, Reynolds, good. I want you to concentrate on the smaller communities in the Ozarks and the Ouachitas for the next few weeks, those who don't already support us. We have to convince the independent-thinking people of those areas that it's in their best interests to cooperate with us. Prove to them that they need us, but keep your dogs in check, Reynolds. I don't want everyone killed. I just want them scared."

"Right, Sir," Reynolds replied. "Oh, by the way, Colonel, there's a little matter of the bonus you promised me. I think the number was twenty thousand ... in gold ..?"

"I haven't forgotten," Rockford snapped. "You take care of your end and I'll take care of mine. When the job's done and we've disposed of your crew, you'll get your money."

Reynolds smiled. "No problem here, Colonel. Just making sure we're still on the same page."

Rockford stood up. "All right, that's all. Report to me again this time next week. Dismissed."

Reynolds saluted with that same sarcastic grin on his face, and sauntered out of the room.

"I can't wait to pay you off," muttered the colonel under his breath as the doors closed.

The phone rang. It was Richards in armaments. "Sir, I've got some great news. We've found a jet pilot. He's one of our new recruits. Seems he recently gave up service life—lost his family in some local violence and decided to join up with us. Says he worked out of Little Rock Air Force Base, and if we can put him inside the airfield, he can get one of those F-Sixteens out of there. We'll have to get arms and fuel, but I can pull it off if you give me enough men. I don't think they've got much of a force guarding the base anymore; the soldiers still there are just hanging on halfheartedly, hoping for some sort of federal miracle. The pilot knows where they keep the armaments, and a fuel truck's a piece of cake to steal."

"Splendid," declared Rockford, "let me know what you need; I'll supply it. I want that plane, Richards. Once it's in the air, have the pilot fly it to Waldron Field. The airport has a good four thousand feet of runway and there's a large hanger at the end of the field. Put the jet in there and leave a dozen men on guard twenty-four hours a day. I repeat, I want that plane! Pull this off, Richards, and I'll remember."

Two days later a force of one hundred men, the colonel's best, hit the base. A little C-4 explosive and a small fuel depot at the end of the field created a nice diversion. The guards at the main gates were quickly neutralized. With inside help, well paid for assistance and information, they accessed the ammo for the cannon of the aircraft and grabbed a handful of heat-seeking sidewinder missiles. The snatching of the plane went like clockwork and resistance was light; no one wanted to die for a cause they weren't sure existed anymore. In minutes, the pilot was in the air and headed for the colonel's airfield. Richards himself drove a truck full of fuel through the open gates and into the night.

Rockford was ecstatic. He had the beginnings of a real air force. He already owned a number of small twin-engine aircraft and one DC-3 for troop transport. Pilots for those were no problem. Now he had a fighter jet and a pilot to fly it. Finally, his air force had teeth. If all went well, and the facilities of the military became his by bona fide acquisition as the leader of the new government, fine! If not, and he had to fight for it, then fight he would–with everything he had in his arsenal.

The parcel of land Travis had purchased years ago sat on the side of a gently sloping mountain, offering a magnificent view of the surrounding countryside. Probably the only piece of property that offered a better viewpiont was the land just east of him, owned by the Jacobs. Edith and Jeb Jacobs had lived on that forty acres for most of their adult lives–since 1954.

Jeb was twenty years old when he and his new bride bought the land with money borrowed from his dad, and built themselves a home. They raised three children in the interim, all of whom had grown up, married, and moved away. Jeb had finally retired from the local saw mill, and he and Edith were enjoying the autumn years of their lives.

From the large porch of their lovely old farmhouse, they could watch the whole valley as it glistened with morning dew, then turned golden as the sun crept over the hills and light splashed across the trees, rivers, and roads. They had often remarked that, with this view, there wasn't much going on in the valley that they didn't know about. Recently the Jacobs had noticed an increase in military vehicles going in and out of the properties that had been confiscated by the so-called "New Provincial Government." From where they sat, they could see the camp and the roads leading to it quite clearly; they had an excellent vantage point.

Willy Snead and his wife, Sara, had taken care of Travis's property for the past seven years. About six months ago, Willy's wife of forty-five years had died after contracting a virulent strain of flu that developed into pneumonia. The old man was alone, and the loneliness ate at him, so he spent much of his time visiting his friends, the Jacobs, to keep his sanity in check, and to kill time until he could be with his Sara again. He often took a stroll through the woods to have a cup of coffee with his neighbors. They would sit on the big porch, take in the view, and talk of old times. He was on his way to the Jacobs's one morning, an hour or so after sunrise, walking the well-worn path between the two homes, when he heard shouting.

Quietly, cautiously, Willy moved forward on the trail. He was no longer a young man and a good portion of his courage had escaped with his youth. Easing into the bushes as he reached the clearing where the Jacobs's house sat, he saw several men in fatigues holding guns and standing by two military vehicles.

He watched as his friends were dragged from their home by four soldiers. They were forced to stand there while a document was read to them by a man who had stepped forward from the parked vehicles. Willy's old ears weren't as good as they used to be but he caught enough of the conversation to realize that the Jacobs were in the process of having their property confiscated by eminent domain. Something about a necessary vantage point, an out-post for the security of the new base.

Jeb Jacobs wasn't buying it. He was shouting at the man, telling him where he could put his paper and his new government. The man with the paper just smiled coldly and told him he could take his offer, or he would make him another one he wouldn't be able to refuse. The men around him chambered shells for emphasis. Jeb seemed to calm down then. He asked permission to go back into the house to take one of his heart pills before signing the document, and the men released him. The old man had only been in the house for a moment when he burst out of the front door with a shotgun. The first blast of the twelve gauge blew the guy with the paper right off his feet, sending him flying backwards as if someone had tied his collar to a passing bus. The second round took out the two men who had dragged him from his house. He was chambering a third shell in the old Remington pump when the soldiers who held his wife pushed her aside and cut loose with their

M16s. They caught him low in the legs and the old man screamed as the bullets tore away chunks of bone and flesh. He fell, but he wasn't finished. As he hit the porch, he pumped out two more blasts of buckshot, taking a good portion of the head and shoulders from both his assailants. The men near the trucks opened up with a fusillade of bullets that literally ripped the front porch apart. Jeb was bounced back against the wall and torn to shreds.

Watching in horror, his wife screamed, struggled to her feet, and ran toward her husband. She hadn't gone ten feet when, by accident or design, the fury of the weapons cut her down. The bullets jolted her as she spun, eyes wide in shock; then, like a discarded doll, she crumpled into a heap at the foot of the porch steps.

Willy's breath was coming in ragged gasps, and his hands were shaking so badly that he had to clasp them together to keep them from jumping off his wrists. He crouched lower in the bushes, like an animal that has sighted a predator.

The remaining men moved out from behind the vehicles, their weapons pointed at the house, but the Jacobs were past being a threat to anyone. It had been a costly morning for the militiamen, and someone would have some serious explaining to do. Five of their men had been killed, and in the process they had shot up the house they wanted. It would require major repairs before it would be habitable again.

Willy figured he'd seen all that his nerves and heart could stand; so, quietly and slowly, he backed out of the bushes and onto the trail that would take him home. Once safely on the path, he shuffled along as fast as his aging legs would carry him, back to the safety of his house and his bedroom where he hid until late that night.

CHAPTER 14
MA AND THE BOYS

Cries of seabirds pierced the stillness of the gray dawn as Travis shook the dew from the sails and tightened riggings, while the sensei upped anchor. The preacher waved from his boat as he hit the starter, and the rumble of the big diesel was followed by a belch of exhaust from the stern.

They headed out of the Tampa Bay area and sailed north for three more uneventful days. The morning of the fourth day brought the long awaited words that have excited mariners throughout the ages: Land ho! There, rising out of the early morning mists, was the dark and distant shape of terra firma. The GPS put them somewhere near the Georgia border south of the Florida panhandle, but the entire coastline had changed. Bays and inlets ran for miles over and through areas where, before, there had been solid ground.

As the boats moved closer, the crews could see the tops of large pines emerging from the water. Here and there, a church spire broke the surface, marking a lost community. They were careful not to get so close as to endanger the keels of the boats, but they were near enough to be awed by the topographical changes.

Sailing around a bend in the new coastline, they passed a sleepy-looking little country town, perched on a high knoll about a quarter of a mile from the shoreline. Smoke rose lazily from several of the chimneys and a few folks could be seen moving about, but as the two vessels came into sight, the bell in the church steeple rang out urgently.

They motored in close enough to see a line of grim-faced men and women assemble at the front of the town, weapons in hand. There were no waves of greeting, no smiles, just a hard look of determination on the faces of the gaunt and hollow-eyed people as they watched the boats pass by.

"Well, I think we can scratch that off our list of places we want to visit this vacation," Travis said.

Christina shook her head. "God! It seems like in such a short time the whole world has become angry, suspicious, and dangerous."

"That's the way it's going to be for a while," he replied. "There's going to be a transitional period where mankind plays a giant game of musical chairs. A lot of folks are just going to end up without a chair, and out of luck. Interaction between people will begin to take place again, as order and security are re-established. Maybe, from all this devastation, a new society will emerge–one that remembers the mistakes and the shortcomings of the old, and refuses to live like that again. The decision belongs to us."

Travis felt a hand on his shoulder. It was the sensei. "You are beginning to sound like a leader, Travis. It could be that you are becoming a good American after all."

"I figure it's now or never," replied Travis.

They turned west at the panhandle of Florida and stayed with the new coast. The days passed, and the travelers on the two boats drew closer. Ra and Todd were becoming inseparable; the preacher and Carlos had become the best of friends. Carlos was spending so much time around his companion he was beginning to develop a Southern Baptist/ Cuban vernacular–"Pass dem 'taters, *por favor, amigo.*"

Christina and Travis were becoming closer every day, and both looked forward to their nightly ritual of watching the stars before bedtime.

The sensei and Travis had long since established one of those friendships that a man finds only a couple of times in his lifetime.

Nobody in the group could say what the future held, but the present, tenuous as it was, felt good.

The only problem they had, as they sailed toward the new inland waterway, was lack of fresh meat. Todd still caught a few fish, but they had eaten all the canned chicken and beef. They would exhaust their other supplies too quickly trying to substitute them for meat, so something had to be done.

Travis and the preacher, both having done a considerable amount of small game hunting, came up with the idea of a hunting trip into the interior. The little flotilla was near the Mississippi-Alabama border, and Travis figured there would be deer, wild turkey, and probably boar in the surrounding woodlands. The group decided to anchor their boats in a bay near the shore, while the two men took the *Amazing Avon* in and looked for game. Travis and the preacher would leave at sunrise the next day and be back by sunset, with or without success.

The cold dawn crept over the misted trees and fog-shrouded water of the small bay. The hunters were ready; Christina had packed them a tote-bag with a couple of cans of fruit and vegetables, as well as a half-gallon of water. Both of the men carried an M16, and Travis had his nine-millimeter pistol, stuck in his belt under his sweater.

After a goodbye that included a less-than-hasty kiss from Christina, Travis stepped down into the raft with his companion, and they paddled to the shore. There, they tied up the boat and headed inland.

The first hour was spent crisscrossing through the brush trying to find a game trail. The preacher finally located one with fresh spore–deer for sure. They followed the trail for about an hour, the old shrimper periodically doing an excellent turkey call just in case there might be a bird in the area.

It was midmorning when the path finally broke into a

clearing. There in the center of a small meadow stood a six-point buck. They quietly knelt out of sight and, without taking his eyes from the deer, Travis said, "Go ahead, take him."

The preacher raised his gun and fired. The deer's head snapped back as if it had been slugged, its legs buckled and it dropped to the ground. When they reached the animal, Travis realized his friend had gone for a head shot, a credit to his confidence with a rifle.

The preacher saw him examining the deer. "A heart shot with this kind of bullet would have torn up too much meat."

"Nice shooting for a shrimper," remarked Travis.

The preacher laughed, "Son, give me a good gun and I can neuter a bullfrog at a hundred yards. Now let's get his fella hung and dressed."

While they were dressing the deer they heard the turkey. "An ole gobbler for sure," said the preacher with a smile. "He ain't far from here, let me go take a look; maybe I can add a bird to the larder."

Travis agreed and continued to dress the deer, quartering it and storing the meat in canvas gear bags from the sailboat.

For the first fifteen minutes he could hear his friend calling and the turkey responding. Eventually, both became fainter until finally, there were no more sounds from either one. He wasn't concerned for the first half hour as he was kept busy getting the deer packed; but, as a half hour moved into an hour and there was still no word from the shrimper, Travis started to worry. It was afternoon now; they had their meat and he wanted to get back before dark. He walked to the edge of the clearing and called. No answer. He went back, picked up his rifle, and began to follow the trail the preacher had taken.

Travis called a couple of times as he walked, but the farther he got into the bush, the less he felt comfortable about yelling and giving away his position. *Giving away my position to whom*? he thought, the back of his neck prickling ever so slightly.

He'd been following what he thought to be the preacher's trail for about twenty minutes when he heard a sound up ahead. Cautiously, his gun ready, he rounded the bend in the path. There, in a small clearing, lay the inert body of his companion. Travis looked around quickly and, seeing no one, ran forward and knelt beside the older man. There was still a pulse, but he'd been badly beaten. There didn't appear to be any major wounds, just a number of cuts and bruises. Travis was bringing the preacher around when he felt the cold muzzle of a rifle pressed against the back of his neck.

"Well, well, here's the boy we been waitin' for. This other fella just weren't the talkative type, didn't wanna tell us nothin', but he made good bait. Now you drop that fancy gun, mister, and turn around real slow."

Standing in front of Travis were two characters right out of the *Beverly Hillbillies*, before they moved to town: patched and ragged pants, only one of them with shoes, crumpled hats, dirty shirts, and unkempt beards. They would have appeared humorous were it not for the malevolent eyes in their dull faces.

Suddenly, the one in the rear started shuffling back and forth nervously, and in a moronic southern drawl, began to whine, "Can I shoot 'em, Billy? Can I shoot 'em? Come on, Billy, you always get to shoot 'em. Let me shoot these ones!"

As the dimwitted little brother danced over to Travis and started to raise his gun, the older one knocked it aside and pushed him to the ground.

"How many times I gotta tell you, you don't do nothin' 'less I tell you to. We ain't gonna shoot 'em here. We gonna take 'em back to Ma. Maybe they belong to them boats in the bay. Ma wants to know."

"It ain't no fair, Billy, it ain't no fair. I never get to shoot nobody," the little one moaned, getting to his feet. "You know what's gonna happen if we take 'em home to Ma. She gonna have all the fun, and all we get to do is bury 'em! Come on, Billy, 'least let me shoot the beat-up one. He called me names. He deserves to be shot. He called me a inbred bastard, called me a devil's spume, and I wanna shoot him. Come on, Billy," he whined, "just let me shoot him a little bit."

The older one swung around and raised his hand as if to strike his demented younger brother, who yelped and danced back. "I'm only gonna tell you once more," he growled. "We ain't gonna shoot 'em here. Now get your rope out and tie their hands."

The preacher was roused with a kick to his ribs, then he and Travis were forced to kneel with their hands behind their backs. While they were being tied, the smaller brother maintained a steady stream of one-sided conversation.

"Billy, what about them shiny guns? Can I have one of them, Billy, can I have one?"

Billy had set down his older model shotgun and was attempting to figure out the action on the M16.

Travis looked up at him. "If you'll untie me, I'll show you how that works."

Billy looked at him disdainfully and pointed at his brother. "He's the idiot, mister, not me. I'll figure it out. Until then, you just shut up and do what you're told, or I just might let Walt have you."

Seconds later they were dragged to their feet and pushed along the trail by Billy and his brother, who reminded Travis of a sadistic Howdy Doody. As they walked, the preacher related what had happened.

"The sons of bitches caught me by surprise. One steps

out onto the trail and says, 'Howdy, stranger,' just as polite and friendly as can be. The other one sneaks up on me, quiet as a cat, and clubs me with the butt of his gun. When I came to, they wanted to know who I was, how I got there, whether or not I'm with the boats in the bay, and the moron keeps wantin' to know what kind of goodies I have for him–whatever *that* means. When they didn't get the answers they wanted, the pair decided to bounce me around a bit, to see if they could tenderize me. Somewhere along the line, they hit me too hard. Thereabouts, I guess, you came into the picture." The preacher paused to catch his breath. "Travis, I think I got a handle on these boys. Wasn't long ago a buddy of mine was telling me about some of the backwoods families in the wilderness area along this here southern Mississippi-Alabama border. There's a handful of people who live back in the swamps and lowlands that ain't never had much truck with the outside world. Some of them have been known to be less than hospitable to strangers; that is to say, people sometimes disappear in this area–hapless travelers who get a little off the beaten path, hunters who just never come home–situations like that. Even the law don't get back here much. First off, these people, with the exception of our little buddy here, ain't that stupid. They ain't gonna leave anything for the police to find. Secondly, sometimes even the police disappear. I hate to say it, son, but I'll bet you fifty bucks to a hatful of shrimp that's exactly what we've stumbled into here."

"You don't paint a real encouraging picture," Travis said. "Reminds me of a movie I once saw. I can almost hear the banjo music in the background."

The preacher smiled. "Yeah, I remember. But this ain't Hollywood, son, and if we don't pay attention, these sons of bitches are gonna kill us. Let's just keep our wits about us; maybe we can catch them with their guard down."

"I hope they untie our hands first," replied Travis dryly.

They walked for about an hour on a rough and winding path. The land became higher and drier with more pine trees. Finally the path opened into a hummock of oak and pines. On the far side of the hummock sat a small wooden house, smoke curling out of the chimney. There was a well-maintained chicken coop, a handful of pigs in a small pen, and a narrow barn-like structure in the back of the compound. In the center of the clearing, a little way from the house, sat the stump of an old oak about two feet high and two feet across. From a distance it looked like someone had coated the top and most of the sides with a reddish-black paint. Buried in the center of the stump was a short-handled axe.

They were being forced across the clearing toward the barn, when a woman emerged from the house. She could have been any country boy's mother. Her graying hair was pulled back in a bun. She had a cherubic face flushed from working near the stove, and a chubby but solid body with strong-looking shoulders and arms. The only things out of place in that picture were the two wolf-like dogs that came out of the house behind the woman and moved up, one on each side of her.

Dressed in a gingham dress with a cooking apron, she smiled when she saw her boys, and waddled over. "Well, well. Looks like we have guests," she said amiably as she studied Travis and the preacher. "You boys wouldn't be from those boats over yonder in the bay, would you?" Neither the preacher nor Travis said anything. "My, looks like the cat's got you fellas' tongues, huh?" she added, still grinning as if she was at a church social.

She turned quickly to Billy, who flinched involuntarily as she swung her heavy body towards him. "Take 'em to the shed and wait for me. I gotta get a pie out of the oven."

"Yes, Ma," Billy said dutifully. Little Walt hung in the

background and said nothing, following Billy as he walked to the shed with the prisoners.

The barn—or shed, as they called it—had a large open area at the entrance, and a couple of stalls for domestic animals, though Travis could see no cows or horses. Various types of farm equipment lay stored against or hung on the surrounding walls.

Once inside the building, Travis and the preacher were pushed to the ground. While Travis sat there on the hay-covered floor, he observed something unique about the two brothers—both were missing fingers. Billy was missing an index finger, and little Walt was lacking an index on one hand and a little finger on the other. Travis wondered what they did that was so hazardous to the hands.

Walt seemed to be more animated, now that Ma wasn't around. He slid up to Travis with that goofy, malicious smile of his and put the barrel of his shotgun in front of Travis's face. "Open your mouth, Mister. I wanna see if my gun fits in it!" When Travis didn't respond quickly enough, he pushed the barrel against his face hard enough to split his lip. "I said get it open or I'll shove this gun into your mouth and out the back of your head!"

Billy stood to one side, smiling, a sadistic glint in his eyes.

Travis looked up at the little moronic monster. Blood was running down his chin from the badly lacerated lip. "First chance I get, I'm gonna kill you, you retarded little prick."

Walt's eyes grew wide at the insult, then narrowed to brutal slits as he drew back his gun, preparing to thrust it at Travis. Just then there was a hoarse shout from the door. "Walter!"

Little Walt wilted like a daisy in a microwave as his mother stood silhouetted in the doorway. "I wasn't doin' nothin', Ma. I just ... he called me—"

"I don't care what he called you," she spat at him, the "sweet old lady" façade melting off her features, leaving a cold, rock-hard face that would make a steelworker flinch. "I told you to put them in the shed. I didn't tell you to touch them, did I?"

"No, Ma–Ma'am," Walt stuttered. "It's just–"

"Shut up," she growled. "You have offended me, Walt. Don't offend me again today. You know the law." The implied threat was ugly, sinister, and Walt wilted even more, his head down, eyes cast to the floor.

The heavy woman was no longer concerned with her image. She lumbered over to Travis like a refrigerator with legs, her cobalt eyes as hard and merciless as a cobra's. Looking down at him, she pointed to the preacher. "Who's your friend here?"

"Don't know," Travis replied, looking her in the eye. "Never saw him before."

The preacher was sitting on the floor beside the woman, totally unprepared for what happened next. She turned casually, reached into her apron, and pulled out an extremely sharp-looking pruning knife. Before anyone realized what was happening, she grabbed the preacher by the hair and said, "Then you won't mind if I cut him some, will you?" Drawing the knife from the temple, next to the preacher's right eye, she ran it down his cheek, laying it open. The older man cried out and pulled away, sprawling onto the floor, blood pouring across his face.

As she reached for the preacher again, Travis yelled, "Okay, okay, don't hurt him anymore. I know him. I know him!"

She turned back to Travis with a mirthless smile. "That's better. Now, I'm going to ask you some questions and, as long as you're answering, I won't have to cut him again. Tell me, are those your boats out there in the bay?"

Travis hesitated just slightly, and once again, she reached for the preacher.

"All right, all right. They're our boats."

"How many people are with you on the boats?"

"Four more, that's all."

"I hope you're telling me the truth," she said, riveting Travis's eyes with hers. "You offend me with your lies and there will be hell to pay. Do your friends have any more guns on them boats?"

"A few," replied Travis truthfully.

"I'm thinkin' I might like to make a trade with your friends on them boats–you and this here fella for whatever they have that I want. I think that's a real good deal, don't you, Mister? You two think on it. The boys here will snug you up while I finish my work in the kitchen. We'll check in on you a little later."

Travis and the preacher were bound hand and foot, then dragged over and tied against the wood slats that framed the stalls.

The brothers left, and as soon as the doors closed, Travis turned to the preacher. "Listen, I've still got my pistol tucked into my belt under my sweater. Those idiots didn't even search me. If one of us can get untied, we've still got a chance."

For the next twenty minutes, they struggled with their bonds.

The preacher finally collapsed, exhausted and exasperated. "It ain't no use. I'm trussed up tighter than a Sunday goose."

Travis, pouring with sweat, spoke through clenched teeth, "I'm beating it, Preacher. My wrist ropes are giving just enough." Then, with a short lurch of his shoulders, a hand broke free. "Got it," he whispered as he pulled his other hand loose and struggled to his feet. Seconds later he was standing, free of the ropes. "Now you," he said, but as he bent to the preacher they heard footsteps outside. With no time to plan, Travis pulled his gun and scrambled over against the wall next to the doors.

A moment later the brothers sauntered through the door, expecting to see their trussed turkeys. Just inside the room, they stopped dead when they saw only the preacher sitting there against the stall. Travis moved in behind them, kicking the younger brother in the base of his back and sending him sprawling across the floor. At the same time he put his gun to the temple of the older brother. "If you want to keep what little brains you have inside your head, you'll drop that gun, now!" As little brother scrambled up, grabbing his gun, Travis stepped behind Billy, his gun still at the man's temple. "Drop it, Walt, or I'll blow your brother's brains out."

Walt looked like he was just about to co-operate when Travis saw him smile. Travis realized why a fraction of a second too late. He was just starting to turn when something hard and heavy smashed against the base of his skull, delivering an explosion of pain, then darkness.

The sun was just beginning to set as Travis awoke. His first sensation, past the blinding pain in his skull, was the constriction of his right arm. When his head cleared and his eyes focused, he found himself in front of the house, tied to the ominous tree stump he had noticed earlier. His left arm was secured tightly to his side, and his legs were tied together. His right arm, however, had been laced to the top of the stump, held by cords that were fastened to spikes nailed into the side of the old tree. It was bound so tightly that he couldn't move his wrist a quarter-inch in any direction, and the pressure from the ropes was numbing. Most ominous of all, though, was the axe blade buried in the wood only inches away. He looked closely at the red-black matter that covered the old oak and his stomach convulsed: The entire stump was covered with dried blood. He suddenly knew, with terrifying certainty, that it wasn't just from unlucky chickens.

The reality of the situation zapped him into alertness like a bucket of cold water. He strained at his bonds and was attempting to survey the area when he heard footsteps behind him. A moment later he saw Ma waddle into sight, flanked by her pair of wolf-dogs, whose cold eyes scrutinized Travis with the deadly intention of hungry sharks. Behind her came the two brothers, pushing a trussed-up preacher ahead of them.

"I see you're awake," she purred. "That's good. I want you awake for this."

Travis's insides did a backflip at those words. "Listen, wait a second–" he croaked, trying to keep his wits about him.

"No, you listen," she snapped, her face contorted in anger as she leaned down next to him. Her breath washed over him, hard and foul. "You have offended me. Your right hand held a gun to my boy's head, and the Lord says 'smite the hand that offends.'"

Oh my God, thought Travis. *This can't really be happening.* "Listen," Travis started again. "I don't know exactly what you want, but I'm sure we can work this out. This ... this just isn't necessary. You can't–"

"Oh, but I can," she said, snatching the axe from the stump, a maniacal gleam in her eyes. "Now you will learn to obey," she hissed as she raised the axe.

"For God's sake, no!" Travis cried, and as the axe fell he screamed again. He shut his eyes at the last moment, as the blade sliced through his flesh and thunked into the wood.

When he opened his eyes again, Travis was immediately assailed by two emotions: The first was major relief, as he discovered his hand was still attached to his arm. The second was a combination of pain and nausea when he realized that the axe had cut into and through almost a half-inch of the meaty part of his forearm before burying itself in the stump. He was bleeding considerably from the wound, but it was small change compared to losing a hand. Looking up, he could see the boys behind Ma, giggling like demented elves, and the ugly smile was still fixed on the old woman's face.

The preacher stood by with a look of stricken relief.

"Now that I have your attention," she whispered coldly, "this is what I want from you, and it better happen just as I say, or that axe will fall again. And the next time, I promise you, I won't settle for a piece of your arm."

"You," she said as she stabbed a finger at the preacher, "are going to go back to your boats with my boys. Walt's gonna wait on the shore while you and Billy go pick up the rest of your friends and bring them back to the bank. If anything happens to Billy, Walt's gonna fire his gun. In fact, if I even hear a gun go off, I'm gonna come over to this stump, cut this man's arm off and let him watch himself bleed to death. You understand? Billy's gonna have a look at your stuff and when we've taken what we want from your boats, then you'll be free to go."

Right, thought Travis, realizing what was going to happen. *You'll let us go when pigs learn to fly.*

"Do you understand?" she said, staring at the preacher.

He sighed and looked at Travis, "Yeah, I understand. I understand completely."

The woman swung around to her sons and pointed at the shrimper. "You boys take him back to the shed, then get some sleep. I want you out of here before dawn." She glared at the preacher once more. "Remember my words, old man. I hear a shot, and your friend here dies."

As they started to drag the preacher off, he hesitated, and turned to the woman. "Can I say goodbye to my friend?"

She paused, then shrugged, "Sure, why not."

He was released, and walked over to Travis. The old shrimper, his hands tied behind him, knelt beside Travis. His eyes were tired and worried and dried blood was caked down his cheek and neck. "I'll do everything I can, son, to get you out of this."

Travis did his best to smile and failed miserably. "I know you will." Then, in a last effort toward salvation he told the preacher, "Tell the sensei, 'remember *katana*.'" The preacher looked puzzled, but repeated the phrase dutifully. "Just tell him that," Travis emphasized.

His friend rose reluctantly. "God bless you, son," he said, in a tone that sounded far too much like a eulogy to please Travis.

It was a long night. The preacher, contemplating the possibilities of a no-win situation, didn't sleep much. Travis, tied up like Houdini at show time with an axe buried in the meat of his arm, hardly shut his eyes.

Just before dawn, Travis heard them pass behind him. Moments later he could just make out their shadows as they reached the trail in front of the clearing. "Good luck, Preacher," he whispered.

The boys knew the trail well, so they tied a rope to the preacher's hands and pulled him along. They moved fast and failed to sympathize with the man's inability to see in the dark. When he stumbled and fell, they dragged him until he managed to get to his feet again. He learned quickly to pay attention. An hour after dawn, they arrived at the shoreline and the preacher showed them where the *Avon* was.

Billy turned to his brother. "You remember what Ma said, Walt. Now I'm gonna go on out and look around on them boats." He turned to a big tree on his left, about fifty yards away. "If I'm not back by the time the sun reaches the top of that tree, you high-tail it back to Ma and finish off that fella, you hear?"

"Yeah. Yeah, Billy, I hear," answered Walt nervously. "I'll wait, but you're comin' right back, ain't you, Billy?"

"Yeah, I'll be right back. This should only take a few minutes." Billy looked at the preacher. "All right, mister, let's go meet your friends."

When they reached the sailboat, the preacher yelled out and the sensei came on deck, along with Ra. The Japanese's face was a mask, but his eyes riveted on the man with the gun. Billy instantly stiffened at the sight of Ra, who growled menacingly. "Have 'em tie that thing up now, before I come on board."

The preacher called to the sensei, "There's been some problems. We're coming aboard to explain. Tie Ra up."

As the sensei complied, they pulled the raft alongside and secured it. The rest of the crew was on deck by then, anxious to know what was going on.

Pointing the gun, Billy yelled, "Everyone back away, I'm coming up."

The preacher's voice boomed out behind him, "Let him come, don't do anything!"

Billy reached the deck, keeping his gun leveled on the confused group. The preacher climbed aboard behind him and put his hands out, palms up. "Whoa, listen everybody."

"Yeah, you tell 'em, mister," Billy interrupted, obviously nervous, still waving the gun.

The preacher continued. "This man and his ..." he paused for the right word, "his family, have taken Travis prisoner. They want to trade Travis for whatever goods they need that we have on our boats. We're supposed to go ashore now so they can check over the boats. If we do anything wrong–if there's a gunshot–the one on shore will signal them to kill Travis."

There was an audible gasp from Christina, and Carlos muttered under his breath, "*Madre de Dios.*" The sensei remained stoic.

Looking at the Japanese, the preacher remembered Travis's last words. "Sensei, Travis said to tell you, 'remember *katana*.'"

There was no change in the sensei's face, but his eyes came alive. "Yes," was all he said.

"Everybody inside," Billy yelled. "I want to see what kind of goodies you got in here."

Billy kept everyone in front of his gun as he examined the gear, the food, and the equipment he planned to steal. When they reached the forward cabin where the National Guard guns were stored, he demanded, "What's in those boxes?"

"Nothing much," replied the sensei, "old clothes, extra sails, that sort of thing. If you promise to let my friends go, I have something very special I will give you."

"Oh yeah, what?" said Billy, turning away from the army cases.

"I have a sword given to me by my grandfather. It is four hundred years old and the hilt is made of gold and silver."

Billy's eyes lit up at this. "Yeah? Show it to me, mister."

Everyone, sensing what was about to happen, slowly moved back. Billy just thought they were frightened, and paid little attention. The sensei turned to his bunk. "It is here," he said as he reached under the mattress.

Billy backed up, leveling the gun on the Japanese. "Slowly, mister, slowly. One wrong move and I'll blow you in half."

"Do not worry," said the sensei in his softest voice. "I just want to give it to you so you won't hurt my companions."

As the sensei turned to present the sword, he subtly

clicked the scabbard release. When he reached out to hand it over, he tilted the weapon just slightly. The sheath immediately slipped from the blade and fell to the floor.

Billy tensed, as did everyone else in the room. "Oh, so sorry, so sorry," said the sensei as he went into his best Japanese act and bent over to pick up the scabbard. The barrel of Billy's gun was just in front of and above the sensei's head. The unsheathed sword was in his right hand. The sensei reached for the scabbard with his left hand, when suddenly, in one lightning-quick motion, he swept the barrel of the gun aside and struck. It was an instant replay of the last time he had drawn his sword. There was a whir, then a snap as the blade sliced through the man's wrist as if cutting butter, and cleaved into the butt of the shotgun. The hand and the gun dropped to the floor.

"Jesus! You cut my hand off!" Billy cried incredulously as he stared at the bloody stump. Without a moment's hesitation or a whisper of pity, the sensei turned and drove his sword–his *katana*–up under the base of the man's chin and into his brain. Billy's eyes opened wide in shock, his body shivered in a death tremble, and he fell, the sensei withdrawing the blade as he collapsed.

The preacher broke the tomb-like silence as he whispered in awe, "They told me about you, but I couldn't believe it ... I never seen anyone *move* like that."

If it was a compliment, the sensei didn't acknowledge it. He simply turned to them and said, "There is another on shore. We must take him before he suspects anything and sounds alarm."

"You're right," agreed the preacher, "but we're gonna need some sort of plan. Let me tell you the situation quickly."

As they talked, they moved away from the body and the preacher looked down. "You know, I got an idea already. Sensei, you're just about the same size as this guy. If you put on his clothes, and sat in the bow of the boat on the way to shore with that hat pulled down and your back to his brother, we might be able to get him close enough to take him. The other one's a bit retarded, but he's as brutal as Stalin on a bad day, so don't take any chances. Just get him. Remember: he can't fire that gun or Travis is dead."

The sensei studied the man on the floor and thought for a moment. There wasn't much blood on the jacket or the pants. It just might work. "Very well," he said. "Help me with his clothes."

Once the sensei was dressed, he took the tattered hat, pulled it on so it covered his head down to his neck and turned to the rest of the group. "I will sit in the bow and keep the shotgun leveled on you people. My sword will be hidden next to me. If necessary, I want you, Preacher, to create a distraction, to draw him closer to the boat." He didn't need to say anything else; everyone knew what would happen then.

They all climbed into the *Amazing Avon* and headed back to shore. The sensei sat in the front, the preacher rowed, and the others huddled in back. As they neared the shore, they could see Walt standing in plain sight about thirty feet from the water line.

When the boat finally touched land, Walt hollered, "You got''em all, Billy, huh? You got 'em?" He moved closer to the dinghy, but unfortunately, instead of walking right up to the boat, he stopped about ten feet away, his instincts picking up something unnatural about the way his brother sat. "Billy, Billy, let's get 'em out of the boat. Come on, Billy, you know you promised me ..." Then, more cautiously, talking to the sensei's back, "Billy, how come you ain't gettin' outta that boat?"

Suddenly, the preacher cried out, "Don't shoot us, Billy,

please don't shoot us," as he fell to his knees in front of the sensei. "You can have everything, just don't shoot us, Billy!"

The outburst pulled Walt a couple of feet closer, but his guard was up. "What's goin' on, Billy? How come you ain't talkin'?"

The preacher paused and looked up. The tension was so thick it was nearly tangible. Suddenly, the sensei sighed with resignation, and slipped his sword free from the scabbard as he turned. Walt was a good eight feet away and the sensei was still in the boat as he swung around.

"You ain't Billy!" Walt exclaimed as he started to bring his gun up. The sensei held his sword by the very back of the hilt, his arm straight down at his side and slightly back, with the point of the blade aimed at Walt. With almost superhuman speed, he threw the sword underhand, blade first, like a softball pitcher, at the man in front of him. Before Walt could bring his gun to bear, the blade pierced his chest, the inertia driving the bloodied point out his back. The man's legs buckled and he collapsed to his knees, frozen in that position for a moment as he examined the hilt of the weapon protruding from his breastbone with a surprised expression.

Slowly he raised his head to the others, who stood there, stock still, willing him to die. "Ma's gonna be very mad at you," he whispered. Blood trickled from the side of his mouth and dripped onto the weapon in his lap. Walt looked down at his gun. As if seeing it for the first time, the corners of his mouth turned upward in a small, sick smile, and the fingers of his right hand crept toward the trigger.

"For God's sake, die you son of a bitch!" hissed the preacher. The sensei braced himself for a desperate leap at the man, when suddenly Walt's eyes went wide, and he gasped. He exhaled softly, the smile fading with the life in his eyes, and he tumbled face forward onto the soft earth.

The shotgun slid from his fingers and thumped to the ground. There was a simultaneous sigh of relief from the others in the *Avon* when they realized that the sensei had pulled off the impossible.

"*Gracias a Dios*!" whispered Carlos as he crossed himself.

The preacher shook his head as if to clear it, and quietly said, "Years from now, when I'm drunk in some bar and tellin' this story, nobody's ever gonna believe me."

The sensei turned back to the rest of the crew. "He was the only one on shore, yes?"

"Yeah, he's the only one," answered the preacher. "But we've still got to deal with the old lady and her dogs. Don't sell her short; she's as mean as God makes human beings and her two dogs would have you for lunch and still want dessert."

The sensei nodded. "Very well, everyone back to the boat. You and I, Preacher, are going after Travis. Carlos will stay with Christina and Todd."

Half an hour later, the two men stood on the shore with rifles in hand. "All right, sensei, follow me," the preacher said. "Let's go get my boy."

Driven by anxiety, the preacher kept a hard pace. Two hours later, they approached the clearing where the house stood. Ma was feeding the chickens, not more than forty feet from where Travis lay tied to the stump. The ever-present wolf dogs stood by her side, eyeing the chickens with poorly suppressed malice.

The two men were a good fifty yards from the woman and fairly well hidden, but they failed to take into account the dog's keen sense of smell. The wind at their backs blew their scent across the compound, and as it reached the dogs, they bristled and turned as one. Ma jerked to attention, followed the dogs point with her own eyes, and caught a glimpse of the preacher's red flannel shirt.

In a second she realized what had happened. She dropped the sack of grain she held, stabbed a finger at the men, and screamed to her dogs, "Go! Go!" They didn't need a second invitation. The animals were off like two gray blurs.

The woman paused long enough to look across at the preacher. Her cold, venomous smile promised retribution. In the next second she was running, surprisingly fast for a woman of her size, toward Travis–and the axe.

The preacher stood up. "You take the dogs, Sensei, I'll take the woman. Now!"

The pair raised their rifles together, with the dogs less than fifteen yards away.

Grimly intent on reaching Travis, the old woman had covered better than half the distance already. As they fired, one of the dogs slammed into the earth, its front legs collapsing as the bullet smashed into its chest. The preacher's bullet caught the woman high in the shoulder, spinning her slightly as her huge body absorbed the impact of the round. She stumbled and fell no more than ten feet behind Travis.

The sensei pulled the trigger to take out the second dog, but nothing happened. The first shell had not ejected cleanly and had jammed the mechanism. He threw the gun aside and swiftly drew his long sword, facing the charging animal with his blade high.

The preacher had no time to help; he had his own problems. Blood-splattered but coldly resolute, Ma had struggled to her knees and was crawling toward Travis, who was trapped between them, inadvertently shielding her from the preacher's gun. Try as he might, the shrimper couldn't get a clear shot at her as she crawled closer and closer to the axe.

The sensei stood his ground, awaiting the onrushing dog. When the distance closed to six feet, the dog leaped, fangs bared. Flexing his knees, the sensei drew the sword back, and thrust it into the animal's chest as the dog flew into him. The Japanese was bowled over as man and dog careened backwards. When they finally stopped rolling, the sensei found himself staring at the creature's jaws, only inches from his throat. The angry, glaring eyes of the dog were just beginning to glaze in death. The sword had entered his chest and the impact had forced the razor sharp blade through his heart and into the vitals of the body cavity.

Ma, using Travis as protection, had nearly reached the stump. The preacher, beside himself with frustration, still didn't have a clear shot and he knew he would get only one chance.

Travis watched helplessly as the maniacal creature with death in her eyes clawed her way toward him. Spittle and blood flew from her lips with every ragged breath she expelled.

Die! his mind screamed at her. *Please God, make her die! Don't let her reach that axe!* But on she came, slowly, inexorably, with hatred emanating from her like heat from a steel mill furnace. She was five feet away–then two–then her hands were on the stump.

"Now," she wheezed through clenched, blood-covered teeth, "now you pay! The law! My law!" She ripped the axe free, drew herself up onto her knees, and raised it over her head.

It was *déjà vu* terror for Travis as, once again, the woman held an axe above him and began the downward swing. As the blade descended, he wrenched desperately at the ropes that held him, shrieking incoherently.

The axe was only inches from Travis's arm when he heard the ear-piercing sound of metal striking metal, followed by a ricochet. The weapon went flying from his assailant's hand, bouncing to the ground several feet away. For a moment, both of them were stunned–too surprised to act. Then, in frustration and rage, the woman screamed, swung her huge body around and scrambled for the axe. In a supreme effort, she grabbed the handle and rose haltingly to her feet. With her blood-red, bulging eyes centered on Travis's head, she raised the blade one more time and charged the remaining few feet with the single-mindedness of a wounded rhino.

Travis was straining like a madman at his bonds when he heard the slapping impact of bullets into flesh, and two bloody holes appeared in the breast of the woman standing over him. She stopped dead in her tracks and wavered like a tree sensing the breeze, shock and confusion suddenly tempering the bitterness in her eyes. The axe was slowly slipping from her fingers when a third shot punched a hole in her throat, snapping her head back and toppling her to the ground.

Wearily, Travis let his head fall on his arm and sighed the mother of all sighs. Seconds later, the sensei and the preacher came into sight, as they walked across the clearing. The sensei had blood all over the front of him and was limping a bit. The preacher wore an ear-to-ear grin as he reached Travis.

"How'd you like to get away from that stump, son? That's providing you haven't got to likin' it so much you want to take it with you."

Travis looked up at his friend with a tired smile. "Untie me, just untie me."

As the preacher worked the ropes, Travis remarked, "That was the most amazing shot I've ever seen, hitting that axe blade in mid-air."

"Nope, it wasn't," the old shrimper said noncommittally.

"What do you mean, 'nope.' At that distance, with the blade moving that fast—"

"Wasn't aimin' for the axe. Was aimin' at her head."

Travis looked at the preacher incredulously. "You mean

to tell me you missed her head by a foot and hit the blade by mistake?"

"Yep, guess I did."

"What was all that about you neutering frogs at one hundred yards then, huh?"

"That was if them frogs was sittin' real still on a lily pad with their asses up in the air a bit. None of them frogs was chasin' anyone with an axe or a-tryin' to cut off a friend of mine's arm."

"I see," said Travis.

A moment later, Travis was freed from the stump, and as he flexed his arm to circulate the blood, he looked over at the sensei. "What happened to you?" he asked, pointing at the blood on the man's coat.

"I had a disagreement with a wolf," he said with a grin.

"Very funny," said Travis. "You know, I think with a little more time, I could make you into a pretty good American."

"Never mind," said the sensei. "I am having trouble enough maintaining any sort of Oriental austerity as it is."

"Touché," Travis chuckled, as he pointed at his friend with an arm miraculously still attached to his body.

Before leaving the compound which had been home to Ma and her sadistic offspring, they raided the pantry and the smoke house, stocking up on vegetables, hams, sausages and venison. They also took time to turn out the chickens and other stock so they could roam freely.

Two and a half hours later, they were back at the shore, looking across the bay to where their boats rocked gently at anchor. A jubilant Carlos, Christina, and Todd waved from the deck of the sailboat. Travis returned the wave, thanking God in a silent prayer that he was still able to do so.

"Let's get out of this place," he said. "I'm going to have

nightmares about fat women and axes for a month of Sundays."

The sensei smiled. "It is better to return home bearing terror of the battle, than to have not returned at all. Lunacy can be treated, death is incurable."

"Ah, Oriental wisdom."

"Winston Churchill."

CHAPTER 15
MONROE, LOUISIANA

After storing their newly acquired supplies, they upped anchors and were off again. With his "trip to hillbilly hell" behind him, Travis opted to rest for an hour or so. The preacher, equally worn out, followed suit. The sensei took the wheel of *The Odyssey* and Carlos kept the shrimper on course.

The winds kept the sailboat heeled and headed in the right direction, and the weather seemed to be warming slightly as they sailed northwest, making the trip even more pleasant. Travis slept for three hours, then went topside with Todd, who had stayed below with him while he slept. The boy appeared to be afraid to let Travis out of his sight.

As they sailed into the golden-red sunset, Travis recounted his harrowing adventure with Ma and the boys.

At the end of the story, Christina shook her head, "Travis, I don't think I've ever met anyone with such a propensity for attracting trouble as you. On the other hand, you seem to be blessed with just enough luck to stay one step ahead of it."

"If that was a compliment, I thank you," he replied.

"I'm not sure it was," said Christina as she smiled from across the cockpit, "but you're welcome, anyway." She paused for a moment, looking at him. "I'm glad you're safe, Travis."

Later that night, after supper had been dispensed with and everyone prepared for bed, Travis and Christina slipped away to the cockpit. They sat, holding each other while watching the soft reflection of the stars on the water.

"Travis? When we get to Arkansas, will we be safe? Will

you stop trying to get yourself killed then? Couldn't we just raise some chickens, have a garden and wait out all this madness?"

"To answer your questions in order, yes, we're going to be safe in Arkansas. We're going to hide like two little fleas on a shaggy dog. As for me trying to get myself killed, I'm real tired of that sport. Dangerous living isn't all it's cracked up to be. Gives me acid indigestion. I'd love to raise some chickens, bag a deer or a turkey every once in a while, do some trout fishing, and cultivate a garden full of Miracle Grow vegetables." He turned to her. "What about you? A few weeks ago you were worth a fortune, a prominent member of the South Florida social register. Will you, the aspiring attorney, the Miami jet setter, be content with life in the country, farm animals, first-hand fertilizer for your garden, a pot-bellied stove and a fireplace for heat when winter rolls in?"

She smiled at him. "You have no idea how a part of me has always longed for a life like that. Past the dance lessons, debutante balls, and all the glittering gifts of my childhood, I remember more than anything else, the summers I spent on my grandparents' ranch in Mexico. The feel of a horse beneath me, the musky-sweet warmth of a hay barn in summer, new calves calling to their mothers at the end of the day." She looked up. "Don't worry about me. You get us there and I'll be just fine. Would you kiss me?"

"Yes, I would like to kiss you." Then he did. And then he did again.

For the next few days the sailboat and shrimper traveled the new coastline of Mississippi. They passed the inundated remains of Gulfport without bothering to stop. Their goal was still the mouth of the new inland waterway–the body of water they hoped would take them all the way to Arkansas. They were beginning to see a number of other boats; probably survivors from the Gulfport area. All seemed to be wary and stayed a good distance away, although now and then, a few of the occupants waved.

Late one morning, after a group breakfast on the shrimp boat, the preacher took a reading with the GPS, went topside, and looked at the coastline and the sun, then came down and checked the GPS and the charts again, a puzzled look on his face. Travis had been watching him. "What's up? You look confused."

"That's as good a word as any," the older man muttered. "I've checked our position twice now, to be sure; then I checked the sun just to be double sure. What's up is, we're running out of coast or, that is to say, the coast is receding radically northward along the east side of the Mississippi Valley. We're in the area of Biloxi, right now, but there don't appear to be much Mississippi left to speak of. I think, gentlemen and lady, we are entering the inland sea of North America. If my fathometer is right, and I think it is, there must have been one hell of a wall of water come through here diggin' a giant trench, or one monster fault ripped itself open here, 'cause we're anchored over what was dry land before–and now we're in seventy feet of water." The preacher paused and looked around at everyone, "Lord have mercy on the souls of new adventurers."

Before getting underway, the preacher, the sensei, and Travis did a little guesstimating on the width and depth of the inland waterway, trying to determine what course to plot. The consensus was to head west-northwest, into and across the sea, keeping them in what should be fairly deep water as they aimed diagonally for the coast on the other side.

The decision made, anchors were pulled and off they went. The wind was still crisp and favorable; the day was clear and the waves light. All the omens seemed good, so, like true adventurers, they faced the unknown with excitement rather than trepidation, and sailed undaunted into the morning mists of a new sea.

They journeyed for four days, seeing fewer and fewer boats as they entered the interior of the waterway. According to the GPS readings, they traveled through Mississippi, into Louisiana, and continued on a northwest course across that state. On the fifth day of their sail, they began to observe more traffic again. Trawlers and smaller fishing boats dotted the horizon periodically, as well as a couple of freighters. There appeared to be less tension in the air when the other craft passed, and it was apparent that commerce had begun again to some degree.

During that afternoon, they saw a fishing boat off the starboard beam about a quarter-mile out. A small man wearing a yellow slicker and a weathered ball cap waved frantically at them from the deck.

Travis radioed the preacher. "You see him out there?"

"Yeah, I see him, son. Whatcha think?"

"Looks like he has a problem. Let's go over and check it out. But we go with weapons ready and you flank him in the shrimper. I'll do the talking; you keep him covered."

"Got it," said the preacher. "Let's go."

Alvin Plummer was having a bad day. He'd gone out to try to catch a few fish in a body of water that hadn't decided if it wanted to be fresh or saltwater, and it was throwing the fish off their feed. He had less than a hundred gallons of gas left in the boat. When that was gone, he'd have to barter part of his catch for incredibly expensive fuel. To top it off, fifteen miles from shore his fuel line ruptured and he had nothing with which to repair it.

When he saw two boats headed his way, he was both hopeful and apprehensive. He figured either they were coming to help him, which would be great, or they were pirates, in which case a ruptured fuel line would no longer be one of his major concerns.

Since the big shake there wasn't any Coast Guard, and people in his position just had to rely on help from somebody else, but nearly everyone else was busy helping themselves. Somehow or another, he had to get back to Monroe. He had a wife and kids to feed.

It's funny, he thought, *how quickly we get over being thankful that we survived yesterday, when we have to worry about surviving tomorrow.* If they could get all the dead buried and keep disease under control, a good portion of the remaining residents of Monroe might make it.

After the collapse, what with the looting and all, people were killing each other like flies, and a good portion of the people just upped and left. Somewhere along the line, between the fighting and the talking, there began to emerge a glimmer of organization. Those strong enough to fight for what they had, sometimes got to keep it–if they won the fight. Those folks ended up as the new commodity brokers; maybe they owned a gas station or a vegetable farm, a grain mill or a liquor store, something to barter with. There was no longer much stock put in paper money. It had worked at first, in a largely inflated sense. People paid hundreds of dollars for a few canned goods or a little gas. Then everyone wised up to the fact that the money wasn't much good if there wasn't any federal government to back it. Finally people began trading in gold and silver, jewelry, and services, as they had a couple hundred years ago.

As far as crimes and violence, there was still a lot of that going on, but it wasn't as mindless and uncontrolled as it had been at first. In the beginning, justice was a rope or a bullet. But there were a few people picking up where the authorities had left off, and order was slowly but surely coming around. The whole thing reminded Alvin of the old west he used to read about as a kid.

A good portion of the towns and cities that ran their electric plants on natural gas or nuclear energy were still getting power—provided the local generating station hadn't been damaged, the gas lines ruptured, or the transfer lines knocked down. Others, where the quakes had been the worst, or the storms had hit, might be years getting back on line. Everything was still hit or miss, but it was a hell of a lot better than it had been in the terrifying, uncertain beginning.

The unique thing about the town of Monroe, located until recently in the center of Louisiana, was that it had become a seaport. The earth had trembled and shook. There had been a thundering sound like that of a million horses in stampede, and the survivors of the initial onslaught staggered to their feet to witness the changing of the earth's surface as a wall of water, a hundred miles wide, roared through the Mississippi Valley. It ripped apart cities and towns in a single breath, and gouged out thousands of square miles of forests, rivers and hills.

When it was all over, and the waters had stopped rising, a third of Monroe lay underwater, making it the newest city on the inland sea. Because its new topography gave Monroe a fairly deep harbor, it became a natural port. In the weeks that followed, people with boats from Louisiana to Eastern Texas began to congregate there. In less than two months, a small fishing industry had begun to form, which was what had attracted Alvin in the first place. The other, probably more important factor that had helped establish Monroe as a seaport, was the enterprises of three ruthless brothers named Lafont.

The brothers, Louisiana Cajuns, had owned part of a timber business at the time of the destruction. When everything stopped moving and the water quit rising, they saw the potential in the construction of docks that a seaport would need. They had been minor partners in their lumber business, but the scuttlebutt was that they felt it was just too good an opportunity to share. It seemed their partner, Jack Thompson, a well-respected citizen of Monroe, met with a hunting accident shortly after signing an agreement that deeded the business to the surviving partners should something happen to him. Everyone figured that they knew what happened, but no one was going to call the Lafonts on it, especially when there were people still shooting each other for a gallon of gasoline or a can of beans.

The Lafonts trucked in hundreds of sixty-foot logs. Cut in twenty-foot lengths, they spiked and chained them together to make two docks, or walkways, and floated them out into the water about a hundred yards apart. At twenty-foot intervals, they interspersed sixty-foot logs on each of the walkways, to create forty-foot berths on the inside of the catwalk. The two catwalks were about two hundred yards long, running parallel to each other, creating a channel in the middle with berths along both sides. The whole affair was anchored by heavy chains to the bottom, fifty feet below. It was crude and temporary, but ingenious, and it worked to accommodate trawlers, salvers, and fishing boats. There were even a few small freighters and tankers anchored outside the marina, close enough to run a skiff to the docks and shore. The boats inside were protected from pirates at night by two large trawlers that were pulled across the entrance, bow to bow, blocking it off. Some people said it also kept the boats inside from leaving in the night without paying the exorbitant docking fees that the Lafont's charged. But no one said it too loud.

It was obvious to all that the Lafonts had become the "teamsters" of Monroe, and they didn't mind conducting business with a gun or a baseball bat. In fact, that approach seemed to suit them well. Their new acquisitions in the town extended well past docking fees and marine supplies.

Alvin stood and watched the sailboat and the shrimper move in on him. When he saw the automatic weapons, a shiver ran down his back.

Travis stayed twenty yards off and yelled to him, "What's the problem?"

"My fuel line's gone and I've got no replacement."

Travis looked across to Carlos and the preacher. "No *problemo*," Carlos yelled, "we got plenty extra. I can fix plenty quick."

"All right, Mister," said Travis, "we can straighten that out for you, it seems. Stand by and we'll tie off."

Moments later they were alongside. Alvin introduced himself, and while Carlos repaired the fuel line, the others pumped the fisherman for information, which he gladly gave, which was how they learned of Monroe, its occupants, the docks, and the Lafonts.

In no time at all, the fuel line was fixed and Alvin was so grateful he was beside himself. Travis and Carlos virtually had to pull themselves away lest the little fellow pump their hands off shaking goodbye.

Intrigued by the thought of solid ground, they decided to pay a visit to the city of Monroe. After wishing Alvin luck, they took the bearings he gave them and set off. Two hours later, the western coast of America's inland waterway came into view.

The new seaport looked like a scene that might have been painted by an angry Dali: The town ran right into the water, or vice versa, giving it an amphibious feeling. Of the section that was above water, part had been collapsed by quakes and part had been consumed by fire–the place looked like Savannah after the siege.

Fortunately, repairs and recovery had begun in earnest for those who had decided to stay. In the salvageable sections of town, some electricity was being restored, the natural gas lines to the city electric plant having been temporarily repaired. Badly damaged buildings were being torn down and their lumber used to restore more viable structures. People scurried everywhere, working, hustling, trying to find something valuable, then trying to sell or barter it for something they needed. The one notable difference between the people there, and those before the shake up, was that almost everyone carried a gun.

Of course, the newest and most outstanding addition to the town was the dock system at the eastern end, near the new bay. It extended into the water like parallel log runways. There were perhaps twenty boats tied to their individual berths inside the docks. The two large trawlers Alvin had mentioned sat at the mouth of the docks, prepared to close it off. Armed guards strolled the catwalks, looking bored but dangerous as they made their rounds. Three small freighters and a salvage boat lay at anchor just outside the marina.

Travis and the sensei dropped the sails and motored in, the shrimper following. At the land's end of the docks, there was a small, newly constructed building above which hung a sign that said simply: **LAFONT BROS. DOCKAGE, REPAIRS, SUPPLIES**

Underneath the sign stood a dark-haired man of medium height with a strong, stocky body and muscled arms. He waved them into two adjacent slips. As they were berthing, the fellow strode toward them with an obvious air of authority. While still a distance away, with a broad, wide-toothed smile, he hollered, "Howdy, sailors, welcome to Monroe!"

Travis leaped off the bow onto the walkway, tying off the boat. The sensei helped Christina and Todd down, then followed. The preacher had backed his boat in and he and

Carlos climbed off the stern onto the dock. As the fellow moved toward the group, another man, slightly taller but equally capable-looking, came out of the building and joined him. The newcomer appeared better dressed and a touch more sophisticated than his associate. He was a handsome man with long, dark hair and good features, but there was a cruel set to his eyes.

That's a man who appreciates pain, Travis thought.

The shorter of the two men extended his hand to Travis: "Henry Lafont's the name. This is my brother, Peter," he said, nodding to the man next to him as he shook Travis's hand with the grip of a Sumo wrestler.

Introductions were completed, and Travis couldn't help but notice Peter Lafont's eyes as they rolled over Christina. He didn't even try to be subtle. She, too, was aware of it and flushed.

After a pause, Henry Lafont continued, "How long will you folks be staying with us, and are you going to need any repairs or supplies?"

"No repairs," Travis replied, "Maybe some supplies. We'll probably be here a day or two."

"Good, no problem. Where are you coming in from?"

"The Florida Keys, or where they used to be."

"Gone, huh?" asked Lafont.

"Gone as can be."

"Well, I guess a few years from now, we'll truck in a couple of loads of sand and become the new Miami Beach," laughed Henry. As he talked, he appeared to be a congenial enough fellow, but there was something about him that said that as soon as you didn't please him, you'd see a different attitude. His brother was less subtle. There was a look of dangerous arrogance about him–a man used to getting his way.

As Travis studied the Lafonts, Peter spoke for the first

time. "Tell me, how will you be paying for your dockage here?"

"Well, that depends," said Travis. "Why don't you tell us what the rules are and we'll tell you if we can play by them."

"Well put," said Peter, his eyes sharpening. "As you may or may not know, with the federal government pretty well shot, paper money isn't worth much, so perhaps you have something of value that we'd be able to barter for your stay here?"

"Sounds possible," said Travis. "Let's say we're here for two days, what would be a reasonable payment for that length of time?"

Peter looked at him. "What a reasonable payment might be no longer applies in these times. We're not just supplying dockage, we're offering protection as well. We'll barter food, fuel, engine parts, guns, ammunition, and radio equipment."

Travis thought for a moment. They had taken the radios from the cutter and the sports fisherman a while back. They could spare one of those. "Okay, how about a like-new VHF radio and antenna for our stay?"

Peter paused for a moment and looked out across the dock. "That and twenty gallons of fuel."

"Good Lord, man!" Travis exclaimed. "I don't want to buy the berths. I just want to use them for two days!"

"You want the berths, that's the price," Peter said, a slight smile turning up the corners of his mouth as he did his best to stare Travis down. Travis knew he'd been had; they needed the security of the docks. Anchored off shore they wouldn't last ten minutes before somebody shot Ra and broke into them.

"Well, I guess we have no choice but to accept your gracious hospitality," Travis answered with just a touch of sarcasm.

"Intelligent decision," said Peter. "But to make you feel

better about the deal, I invite you to one of the few operating saloons in Monroe for drinks, on me."

"I suppose you own the saloon, too," said Travis.

"As a matter of fact, I do. Why don't you stop by around seven and we'll get to know each other?" Peter asked as he flashed a look at Christina. "Well, I've got things to do. Henry will arrange for the radio and fuel, and give you directions. See you about seven." He started to leave but turned back around for a moment. "It'll be dark then, so dress appropriately. That means carry a gun that's not real obvious."

After securing the boats and settling up with Henry, who, in an unusual gesture of magnanimity, threw in some sugar and a box of powdered milk, they prepared to see the town.

Earlier in the trip Christina had discovered a few pieces of jewelry in one of the drawers in the forward bedroom—a gold bracelet, a necklace, and some earrings. They took these to barter with, should they need anything in town. Ra was taken for a half-hour walk, then left to guard the sailboat, as always.

They were directed to the section of town that had survived most, or perhaps had been destroyed the least. It was still a mess, but commerce was taking place amid the rebuilding.

Noticing that people looked at them warily and few spoke, it was the preacher who offered an explanation: "Take a good look at us, son. We may have been tourists at the start of this little vacation, but we look more like mercenaries now. From the M-Sixteens to the Samurai swords, we look like we work for Genghis Khan." It was true—even Christina carried the nine-millimeter, and Todd carried one of the hunting knives tucked into his belt, its scabbard and blade up, imitating the sensei.

They found a place that served food—not really a restaurant, more like an open-pit BBQ selling grilled chicken and baked potatoes. Christina bargained a few links of the gold bracelet in exchange for everyone's dinner. The sun began to set as they sat at the candlelit tables, ate half-cooked chicken, drank warm beer, and thought they'd died and gone to heaven. Afterward, spurred by the prospect of a free drink or two, the preacher and Carlos urged the rest of the group to search out Peter's "Sea Dog Saloon."

Night was falling, and after a short walk through nearly deserted streets, they found the tavern. It had once been Maryann's Bar and Grill, but Maryann had been made an offer that she couldn't refuse and a new sign was nailed over the old one–an increasingly common business practice of the Lafonts. The bar was small but, considering the times, well stocked. Fortunately, the supply room had just been stocked when the catastrophe struck. She and the Lafonts were peripheral friends, and they had sent over a few men to help her keep the looters at bay. When things quieted down, the Lafonts, in much the same manner as Colonel Rockford, gave her a couple of options.

A dozen or so stools lined the bar and about the same number of tables were scattered around the dimly-lit saloon. A sign above the bar read: ALL GUNFIGHTS TO BE TAKEN OUTSIDE, OR WE SHOOT THE WINNER–THE MANAGEMENT. Four men sat at the bar, and another eight or ten sat at the tables. A well-armed bouncer leaned casually against the end of the bar.

In the back, seated at a table against the wall, was Peter Lafont and another man, whom Travis immediately identified as the third brother. He had the same dark hair and swarthy complexion. He was as tall as Peter, but not as heavy. Where Peter appeared arrogant and dangerous, the other was just plain cold to the bone. He had a large, hooked nose and a thin, white scar that ran from his cheekbone to the edge of his jaw, adding considerably to his sinister appearance. Every shift of his empty, black eyes said he could kill you at lunch and not miss a spoonful of dessert at the memory.

Peter saw the troupe as they walked in and waved them over while making some comment to his brother. As the group moved toward the table, the two men, who had been playing cards, put the deck aside and stood.

Peter flashed a big smile. "Welcome! I'm glad you accepted my offer. This is my brother, Chad." After introductions, everyone was seated around two tables that had been pushed together. Peter called the bartender over and drinks were ordered. For the next hour conversation ranged from the Lafonts' success, and how fortunate they had been "to be in the right place at the right time," to the history of the newcomers, and their adventures. Peter carried most of the dialogue while imbuing it with a number of sexual innuendoes directed at Christina.

The older brother questioned Travis about the changes they'd seen in their travels. His eyes occasionally darted to Christina but, by and large, he kept himself within the bounds of good manners.

Unfortunately, that was more than could be said of Peter, whose rudeness and arrogance began to increase with each drink, and he was drinking steadily. The rest of the group had two–maybe three drinks–including Chad; Peter was on his sixth whisky and water, and the last two were very short on water. The more he drank, the less he hid his desire for Christina. She was an incredibly beautiful woman and it wasn't the first time that a man had been "taken" with her, but Peter was used to taking what he wanted.

While Travis and the preacher talked travel with Chad, Peter decided to become more earnest in his affections and moved his chair around by Christina's right side, ostensibly so they could chat more easily. Travis sat on Christina's left, facing Chad, which left him turned partially away from Christina. Todd and Carlos sat back from the table, watching. The sensei had gone to the restroom. From a portable disc player on the bar, a slow country song whined of lonely rooms and unrequited love. Peter, by then loaded to the gills, decided he wanted to dance–Christina decided she didn't. It got worse from there. His entreaties went from a moderately forceful requests to demands, and suddenly, before anyone could stop him, he was dragging her from her chair, pulling her to him in a sloppy excuse for a slow dance.

Travis had been attempting to keep his cool for the sake of his people. When he turned around and saw what was happening, he swung his head back to Chad, looking for assistance. Chad just sat there smugly, with a whisper of a smile, staring at him.

All right, thought Travis, *if that's how you want it.*

In a split second he was up. He grabbed Peter's left hand, which was holding Christina's shoulder, and pulled it down and back, twisting the wrist as he moved. Peter yelled in pain and released Christina as he was forced away from her. "That's enough," said Travis. "Leave her alone."

"You're right. I'm gonna leave her alone for now," Peter grimaced through clenched teeth. "I'm gonna fix you first, then I'm gonna have her!" He turned and swung at his opponent's head with his right hand. The blow glanced off Travis without really hurting him, but it forced him to break his grip. The Cajun turned with a fierce gleam in his eyes and the smile of a man who'd been in his share of fights and had grown to like it.

Travis glanced quickly at the others. Christina was rubbing her wrists, a frightened look on her face. Todd and Carlos were back against the wall, Carlos protecting the boy. The preacher was calm but ready for a signal. Chad just sat there, unconcerned, amused, certain of his brother's abilities.

Travis decided to make it short. A long fight with a guy

like that meant a chance of losing. Before Peter could move, Travis stepped forward and gave him a crude but effective side kick to the inside of the knee. The joint snapped like dry timber as Peter screamed and collapsed. Travis took another step forward and front-kicked him in the face, nearly lifting him off the ground and slamming him against the back wall—a technique Travis had learned from a good friend who had been a drill sergeant at Fort Benning. He had seen his friend use the same method time and again when outmatched or outnumbered, always with the same brutal success.

Peter, with his nose smashed flat, front teeth powdered and his leg broken, was out for the count. Travis turned just in time to see Chad rising out of his chair, his hands clenched, an entirely different look on his face. He was a man bent on revenge. But he was barely erect and reaching for the gun in his belt when he felt the barrel of a rifle under his chin.

The preacher rose slowly beside him, keeping his gun tight against the man's neck, and said, "Now he won that fight fair and square, boy. He don't have to do it again." Then, as he took the Cajun's gun, he said, "If you move a muscle, the only thing you'll be fightin' for will be air through the hole in your neck. You got it?"

Chad looked at him, murder in his eyes.

"I said, you got it?" the preacher emphasized with a push from the barrel of his weapon that lifted Chad to his toes. Chad nodded.

During this performance the bouncer had slowly made his way across the bar and was raising his gun at the preacher's back when someone tapped him on the shoulder. Surprised, he turned his head. He shouldn't have. The sensei, having returned from the restroom, watched it all happen and stood quietly in reserve. He was ready when the guard made his move. The sensei tapped the man on his left shoulder while standing to his right; the guard turned his head and looked the opposite way from the Japanese, who reached in, lifted up the gun, exposing the man's side, and delivered a punch that broke three ribs and ruptured a kidney. The guard was no longer an issue.

Travis looked at Chad, then to the rest of his crew. "Well, I think we've worn out our welcome. Time to go. Sensei, take the point. Preacher, bring your friend along just for safety's sake. We'll let him go when we're clear. Christina, Todd, Carlos, stay in the middle as we go out. I'll take the rear. Let's move!"

Just as they started out, another guard appeared in the doorway and leveled his rifle at the group. The sensei had just turned back to check on the group when the man came through the entrance and caught him unawares. As the guard aimed his gun at the sensei's back, Christina, without the slightest hesitation, shot the intruder three times with her nine millimeter pistol. The man bounced out the door and hit the ground, the soles of his feet sticking up, holding the door open. The sensei, swinging around at the sound of the shots, quickly realized what had happened. He looked at the man's feet, then at Christina, and smiled that half smile of his, bowing ever so slightly. Travis just shook his head in amazement.

"All right, let's go!" yelled the preacher, snapping them back to attention. Guns ready, they moved out into the night, leaving the handful of shocked, gaping patrons at the bar.

As the doors closed, the bartender, who had no particular love for the Lafonts, turned to the man seated next to him. "I'll bet there'll be blood on the moon before this night's done."

He wasn't far wrong.

They moved quickly through the dark streets as they

headed back to the docks. As the preacher put it: It was time to get the hell outta Dodge.

Chad Lafont made his move when they were a couple of blocks from the docks. He had begun to lag, and he and the preacher had fallen behind. Suddenly, Lafont faked a twisted ankle and fell. When the preacher bent to pick him up, he sprang forward, knocking the man's gun aside and hammering the old shrimper in the jaw with a quick right. The preacher staggered to his knees, dazed, and Lafont was up and gone down a dark side street. Travis raised his gun, but Chad was out of sight before he could shoot.

"That rips it," muttered Travis. "Ten minutes from now we'll have every thug Lafont ever knew after us." He went back to the preacher and helped him up. "You all right?"

"Yeah, son, I'm okay. He just tricked me, then sucker-punched me."

"Okay, let's get going. We've got to get to the docks and get out of here."

As Travis and his crew ran toward the marina there was, unbeknown to them, another important scenario playing itself out in the evening fog offshore, about two hundred yards northwest of the docks.

Jefferson Davis was in the process of negotiating his eighty-foot freighter into Monroe Bay, hoping to purchase lumber which he intended to sell when he returned to Texas. He was having a couple problems, though. First was the fog that had settled in early that night; second, Jefferson, named after that famous Southern president, was damned near blind drunk. It had been a long trip. The friggin' lazy crew did only about half of what he told them, and the weather out of Texas had been a bitch, so he decided to celebrate making port just a little early. Half a bottle of scotch later, he was squinting drunkenly over the wheel into layers of fog and running his ship at a speed no sober man would have ever considered. He had no idea that a hundred and fifty yards ahead sat *The Yellow Peril*, an aging, hundred-foot salvage boat painted a garish yellow. Even the hull's bright color wouldn't save it from the course that fate had plotted for it that night.

The captain of *The Peril*, Ted Nickels, had survived the catastrophe in Mobile, Alabama, and had headed up the coast of Louisiana, looking for ships and equipment to salvage. In his hold was a large tank that held twenty-five hundred gallons of gasoline to run the onboard pumps and motors. In the last month, he'd been miserly in its use, fuel having become so valuable, so almost two thousand gallons remained. *The Yellow Peril* was anchored less than two hundred yards from the Lafont's docks.

Far too late for his liquor-laden mind to react, Jeff Davis saw the huge yellow ship looming ahead in the fog. He threw the wheel hard to port, and, with a jarring, grinding crash, the bow of the freighter plowed into the starboard side of the other ship, just below and to the right of the large gasoline tank, gouging a six-foot hole in the outer hull and a two-foot gash in the tank itself.

Even as Travis and his people reached the dock, gas was pouring out of the hole in the salvor and the wind and tides were blowing it quickly over the surface of the water toward the docks.

The group made it to their boats just as Lafont returned to the bar and radioed his brother, Henry. His orders were emphatic, simple. "Stop them! Kill them if you have to, but stop them." He would be there himself in minutes with more men.

The two trawlers that blocked passage out of the marina were anchored nose to nose, with their bows chained together. When they had reached the docks, and Travis had taken a discouraged look at the blocked waterway, the preacher yelled, "Don't worry, son, me and *Jesus's Love* can knock those boys apart."

Travis looked over at him. "You're crazy! You'll lose your boat! You'll crush your bow getting through that!"

"Son, it's either that or we stay here and fight it out. You know we can't win here, so get in your boat and let's get the hell out of here. Just stay tight behind me."

Travis and his compatriots were untying and shoving off as Henry came running out of his office, gun in hand, hollering to the guards.

The first thing the preacher did after they were untied and Carlos started the engines was to grab one of the SAWs he had stored on his boat. Smashing open a box of ammo for the devastating weapon, he threw a couple of belts over his shoulder and headed for the forecastle.

Reaching the wheelhouse, the preacher turned to Carlos, who was watching the RPMs on the engines. "Get out of here, Carlos. Go get on board with Travis; this ain't gonna be no ride at the county fair."

Carlos looked at his friend. "Preacher, I can no leave you. You need help. Carlos stay!"

"Sorry, Carlos, no time to argue," said the big man as he bodily picked up the Cuban, carried him to the starboard rail, and threw him into the water by the stern of the sailboat. Then he ran back to the wheelhouse, revved her up, and shot out of the slip.

By the time Carlos was pulled aboard the sailboat, the shooting had begun. They started up the small diesel engine and pushed out quickly. The sensei took the wheel while Travis, Carlos, and Christina opened fire with their rifles. In moments they had managed to take out three of the guards on the walkway, but Henry Lafont and his hoodlums were gradually moving in, continually returning the fire. As the craft moved forward in the channel, they had to deal with the gunman on the trawlers at the mouth of the marina as well.

Everyone on both sides was so preoccupied that no one noticed the pervading smell of gasoline as sheets of the flammable liquid blanketed the water surrounding the north side of the docks, while the wind and the waves worked it into the berths and the inside of the channel.

The spark that gave the inert gasoline terrible new dimension came from a ricocheting bullet. In seconds the whole place was a scene from hell; the entire northern catwalk lit up in a flaming barrier as the fuel ignited. With an enormous whooshing sound oxygen was sucked from the air, and a wall of fire swept across the fuel-slicked water. In moments, boats and catwalks were ablaze and being consumed. Huge patches of the flammable liquid were swept into the channel and exploded around the boats, including the shrimper and the sailboat. Seared by the heat, and illuminated by the flames, they suddenly became even better targets, and were beginning to take serious fire from the shore and the trawlers.

The preacher, realizing that his friends were unprotected in the sailboat and couldn't possibly survive the withering gunfire from the trawlers, decided to even it up a bit. Locking the wheel of the shrimper in place, headed straight for the bows of the two ships, he grabbed the SAW with several belts of ammo and climbed up on the forecastle.

As they sailed through the blaze of the manmade inferno, Travis heard the Squad Automatic Weapon open up. When he peered ahead, through the smoke and flames, he couldn't believe his eyes. There stood the preacher on the top of his boat, legs straddled for balance, ammo belts flung over his shoulder like some hero in an old war movie, the gun cradled in his arms, chattering away. Flames licked up around the *Jesus's Love* and part of its deck was already burning, but he was pouring such ravaging gunfire into the trawlers that the effort directed at Travis and his crew had all but ceased, fire from the trawlers having been redirected at the preacher. Travis watched as the shrimper surged toward the bows of the two ships. Bullets ripped up the planking around the man, but he just stood there like a statue, illuminated by the fire that had begun to consume his boat and the flames in the water surrounding him.

Suddenly, a round hit him in the thigh and he was thrown to the deck by the impact. A shrapnel of splinters tore into his hands and legs as more bullets hammered into the wood around him. He grunted in pain as he rose to his feet again, and once more the chatter of his weapon cut the night. But a moment later, he was struck in the shoulder. The shot spun him and knocked him to the roof of the wheelhouse one final time, only seconds before the boat hit the trawlers. The preacher, on his hands and knees, blinded by the smoke, his blood-soaked clothes smearing the wood beneath him, slowly crawled for his gun when a final bullet found him. He shuddered, then collapsed as his pride and joy, the *Jesus's Love*, smashed into the bows of the barricade.

Travis watched the impact and saw the preacher thrown from the top of the wheelhouse into the water as the boat crashed through the two trawlers, thrusting them apart, and crushing the port side of the shrimper's bow. He could see the old man struggling feebly in the fiery water as the preacher's boat passed through the opening and veered off to the left, leaving the passageway clear.

They were drawing out of range of the men on the catwalk, and the impact had slowed the return fire from the decks of the two ships for a moment, but it was picking up again. Just then, Carlos yelled and stumbled against the cabin, a crimson patch spreading across the upper arm of his shirt. He staggered to his feet, grabbed his gun with the other hand and continued firing as blood ran down his arm and dripped onto the white deck. They had to get past the opening in the trawlers quickly or they would be shot to pieces at such close range.

"Take us through!" Travis yelled to the sensei, who pushed the throttle full forward and centered the craft on the breach.

Thick billows of oily smoke swirled in, choking and blinding them, while the flames surrounding *The Odyssey* bubbled the paint on the Fiberglass hull. Bullets smacked into the cabin and deck all around the crew, shattering portholes and ricocheting off the metal rails, but they held their ground and returned the fire, as the boat raced toward the gap.

Through the nightmare of smoke, fog and flames, Travis glanced over for a moment and watched Christina slap another clip in her rifle, raise the weapon to her shoulder and drop two men from the bow of the closest trawler. Carlos knelt on the deck, balancing his gun on the cabin, firing one-handed, his bloodied arm dangling at his side. The sensei stood rock solid at the wheel, eyes centered on the break in the two boats ahead. Bullets slashed and hammered the Fiberglass cockpit around him; he never even blinked. Todd, who had been told to stay below, was dodging rounds and running clips of ammo to the crew.

The boat finally surged past the breach. They were still surrounded by flames, and taking heavy fire, but before them lay open water. As they cleared the opening, Travis once again caught sight of the preacher, about twenty yards forward of the bow and perhaps ten yards to the starboard side.

Travis yelled to the sensei over the gunfire, "I'm going for him!" as he dropped his gun and kicked off his shoes.

The Japanese grabbed his arm. "You cannot save him! Let him go. You can't help these people by dying as well!"

Travis swung around fiercely, an angry determination in his eyes. "I don't give a damn what you say: He's still alive and I'm *not* gonna leave him. Slow down a little and throw out the stern line. I'm gonna get him and swim over to the line as you drag it by. If I miss, you just keep going. It's your show then."

He ran to the bow and jumped into the flaming water.

Travis swam below the surface as far as his breath would allow. Fortunately, the water outside the mouth of the passageway was not totally covered with gas and fire, and he managed to come up in an area free of flames, get his bearings, and take a breath. The preacher was only a few yards from him, struggling desperately to stay afloat. There was fear in the old shrimper's eyes. Travis battled straight through the last of the flaming water so as not to lose sight of his friend. The patches of fire seared his skin, and singed his hair and eyebrows.

Despite his efforts, he was still ten feet away when the last of the preacher's strength failed and with a final look at his friend, the old man disappeared into the water. Travis watched helplessly as his companion's wide-open eyes, filled with terror and resignation, sank beneath the surface. A single hand reached up out of the depths, grasping desperately for the salvation that wasn't there. Then it too was gone.

Travis screamed and thrashed his way the final distance. He spun around, treading water, desperately looking for any sign of the man. He took a deep breath and dove. Struggling in the depths of the inky-black water he flailed about, grasping nothing but cold emptiness until he thought his lungs would explode. He rushed to the surface and gasped in life-giving air. There was a part of him that already knew he was wasting his time, but Travis gathered another breath and dove again. Once more he thrashed about in the dark water, reaching out desperately, begging for the touch of something solid; and once more he ran out of oxygen. But this time, as he turned to surface, his foot kicked something firm. Instantly he jackknifed and reached down below him. Travis knew he only had one shot, his lungs were on fire, he was only a moment away from passing out himself. His hand touched the water-soaked flannel of the preacher's shirt. He grabbed a handful and frantically kicked upward, feeling the weight of his friend beneath him. When they burst to the surface, Travis drew a few badly needed breaths then grabbed the preacher and swung him around into a cross-chest carry, reminiscent of his lifeguard days. The old man, his burned face streaked with oil and etched with pain, coughed up several mouthfuls of water, looked at Travis and whispered hoarsely, "Leave me, son. Get outta here, save yourself."

Travis grasped him tighter and lashed back, "You ain't getting out of this life that easily, Preacher. You hang tight and keep breathing. We're gonna make it."

Ignoring the gunfire from the ships, the sensei slowed the boat to buy more time for Travis. The stern line was out and trailing. It all came down to timing, and luck.

Travis started back with the preacher as the stern of the sailboat was passing them about twenty feet away; but there was only a hundred feet of stern line. He kicked and swam like a madman, pulling the dead weight of the preacher with him. He could no longer see the line, it had sunk below the surface. In a frenzy of determination, he swam on. When he reached the wake of the sailboat there was still nothing and his mind screamed, *"God, no! I've missed it!"* He could see the anxiety-ridden faces of the sensei and Christina looking back at him from the stern of the boat. On he swam, toward the center of the wake, hoping against hope he would find the line.

At the last moment, when Travis was certain his cause was lost, he felt the rasping of the rope against his waist as it played past him. In a panic, he grabbed for it with his free hand, almost losing the preacher in the process. Before he could exert enough pressure to stop it, the first six feet ran through his hand, taking the skin from his palm. He clenched his jaw against the pain and bore down. They were being towed, but the water was rushing up and over his face and head, nearly drowning him. He turned his head from the flow, gasped for air, and held on.

Bullets slapped into the surface of the water around him with smacking sounds. Another two feet of rope slipped through his palm, and his torn and bloodied hand throbbed in agony. The water continued to inundate him, depleting his oxygen and sapping his strength. The strain of holding onto the preacher while being towed was all but wrenching his arm out of the socket. The pain and the lack of oxygen were beginning to overwhelm him. It would be so easy, just to let go of the rope ...

There comes a time in the life of many a man who lives occasionally on the edge, when he faces a choice between life and death–to survive or to succumb. At that crossroads, there is oftentimes a point when giving up is easier than going on. It is there that his desire, his determination to survive, is tested. Some reach that point and succumb; they accept and endure the pleasure of darkness over the suffering of survival. There are, however, those people whose spirits cannot abide a defeat by death, whose minds simply cannot entertain surrender to that ultimate adversary, and they force themselves beyond the wall of human endurance–past ordinary physical capabilities and continue to grasp at that which appears unattainable. Not always, but sometimes, at that point they are rewarded by retaining what they have fought so hard for–life.

Travis had reached that crossroad and the gauntlet of choice lay in his hands.

He felt the line slip again and another two feet ran through his mangled hand before he could gather the strength to stop it. In minutes they would be out of range and safe, but minutes had become terrible eternities of misery and faltering will. He began to contemplate the pleasures of release when, once again, the rope ripped through his hand, and this time he felt the end of it slip past his waist. He cried out with the realization that unless he stopped it there and then, he was lost.

At that moment his decision to survive was made. All thought of giving up dissipated, dissolved like snow under the sun. Galvanized by the fear of losing the rope, he bore down on his grip to stop it. He was not going to die there, and he was not going to let his friend go. As the last few inches of the line neared, Travis felt a large knot the sensei had tied at the end. He grasped it with a single-minded tenacity found only at the gates of death, and held on. Moments later he felt his forward motion slow, then stop, as the sensei cut the engine. He was being pulled gently forward. In seconds there were hands on him, dragging him and the preacher aboard.

While Travis was slumped on deck, gasping, the sensei and Christina carried the preacher below. Suddenly Carlos rushed over to Travis, who was propped up against the cabin. "*Jefe*! *Jefe*! They come!" he said as he pointed with his gun toward the mouth of the harbor.

There, through the flames, came a big sports-fishing boat. Travis could just make out Chad Lafont with half a dozen men on the bow. He was sure that Henry was in the wheelhouse. Shaking his head to clear his fatigued brain, he stood up, took one more look at the oncoming boat, then turned to the Cuban.

"Get me one of those anti-tank guns, Carlos. We don't have to worry about blocking the channel now." In a minute Carlos was back with the weapon. Kneeling on the deck, they armed it, and as the boat behind them closed the gap to seventy-five yards, Travis lifted it onto his shoulder and aimed.

"Goodbye, Mister Lafont," he whispered as he pulled the trigger.

The explosion lit the night as the craft disappeared in a fiery mass of flying debris. Huge pieces of the ship's flaming hull soared though the night like comets, striking the water all around them and sizzling into silence. Travis watched for a moment, then exhausted, dropped the weapon, fell into the seat of the cockpit and closed his eyes. The sensei took the wheel and piloted them into the still, fog-shrouded night while behind them, the docks of Monroe burned to the waterline.

CHAPTER 16
HEALIN', WHEELIN' AND DEALIN'

After an almost sleepless night, the first rays of a cold, red sun crept across the misty waters and touched the ragged, battle-scarred sailboat. The sensei and Travis had spent the night in the cockpit, to watch for further pursuit. The skin on Travis's face and arms was oil-smeared and burned, his hair was singed and his muscles ached. He stood up slowly and stretched. The sensei followed suit. Travis looked over at him. "The preacher?"

"He was alive last time I checked," answered the sensei, his eyes offering little promise. Travis reached for the hatch door and they both went down into the cabin.

Christina, kneeling by the preacher's bunk, looked up. Her face was tired and drawn, her eyes worried. Todd stood next to her, as he had most of the night. Ra, who had been locked in the front cabin during the firefight, lay at his feet. Carlos had a fresh bandage on his arm, and was slumped against the far bunk, hollow-eyed and pale from loss of blood.

As Travis came down the stairs Christina turned her attention back to the old shrimper. She wiped his ashen, feverish face with a damp cloth. "We've cleaned and bandaged the wounds as best we can. He was hit in the shoulder, the leg, and the left side. Carlos says he has a chance, since none of the bullets struck anything vital. The side is more of a flesh wound, and all the bullets passed through. The problem is loss of blood and shock. From here on it's up to the Lord that he prays to so much."

The preacher, in the midst of delirium, raised his head,

his unfocused eyes staring upward. "I'm a-comin', Lord!" he cried. "Open the gates wide, I'm a big man!"

Travis quickly eased him down. "Take it easy, friend. Take it easy. I don't think heaven is ready for you yet, and I'm sure hell's afraid you'll take over, so you may have to stay awhile."

For a moment, the preacher's eyes focused as he looked up at Travis. "Travis, son! Did we make it out?"

"We made it. Everybody's fine. You just relax."

"Yeah, tired," mumbled the preacher wearily, "real tired." And he closed his eyes.

Travis turned to Christina. "You've been here all night, haven't you?"

She stood up, stifling a yawn. "Yes, I couldn't leave him. I was afraid–"

"Yeah, I know," said Travis. "You and Todd go get some sleep. We'll watch over him and keep things on course."

She nodded, grateful to be relieved.

"And how are you, *amigo*?" Travis asked Carlos.

The Cuban offered a tired smile. "I be okay, *Jefe*. I hurt, but I be okay."

"Good man, Carlos. *Fuiste un hombre bueno anoche*. I was proud of you."

Carlos perked up noticeably at the compliment from his *Jefe* in his own language. "*Gracias, Jefe*," he replied, head up, proud.

The sensei and Carlos went topside to assess damages and Todd slipped away to his bunk after a quick hug from Travis.

Christina turned to do the same but Travis reached out for her and turned her towards him. "Christina, you're the bravest, most beautiful woman I have ever known."

"And you," she said, "look like a cross between a chimney sweep and an out-patient from Hiroshima, but I think I love you anyway."

Travis's eyes widened with surprise. He pulled her close and they kissed with the passion of a first-love romance. Todd, who had peeked around the bulkhead of his bunk, smiled, very satisfied, then pulled the covers up around him and went to sleep.

After a few hours of motoring, they anchored in a small cove about fifty yards from shore, somewhere near the Louisiana-Arkansas border. There they made breakfast, then cleaned and patched the bullet-ridden hull and sails as best they could.

Travis continually monitored the preacher, wiping his forehead and face with a cool cloth and checking his bandages. There was no change in the man's condition; he held on, barely.

If the coastline continued its northward recession, the sailing part of their journey would end in a few days. They had ample food and water so they decided to hole up and rest for a while. Hopefully, to give the preacher a chance to recover.

They spent the next three days in the cove. By the second day the preacher's fever had subsided and, though in considerable pain, he was beginning to sleep normally. He was going to make it.

That afternoon, Travis and Christina took Todd and Ra ashore in the *Amazing Avon*, which once again, had miraculously survived. There they spread a blanket and picnicked in the woods. Ra, who thought he was in seventh heaven, chased squirrels and frolicked with Todd like a puppy.

Gazing across the blanket at Christina, Travis suddenly realized that although he'd just been through one of the most traumatic periods of his life, he couldn't remember being happier. He felt as if every inch of his being was alive, and Christina brought out feelings in him that he thought had died and been buried forever.

The afternoon wore on and Todd took Ra back to the boat, promising to return for them later, and displaying more intuition than was common for a twelve-year-old. Christina smiled at Travis as Todd paddled away. "I feel like we're being 'handled' a little bit by him, don't you?"

"Yes, I do. I think he likes this situation between you and me, but then, that's okay, because so do I."

Christina chuckled and caressed him with her eyes. "Me, too." For a moment they both watched Todd paddling in the distance, then, almost as one, they turned and their eyes locked again. Without a word, Christina moved across the blanket and into his arms.

The fire and the need between them had been driven to blast-furnace intensity by sweet anticipation and self-imposed restraint dictated by the close quarters of the sailboat. When their bodies touched and they were finally loosed to their own desires, the white-hot emotions of love and lust drowned their senses in a sea of uncontrollable passion. Clothes instantly became inhibitors to be torn off with trembling hands, so that flesh could join flesh. And in the final moment of union, so intense that its pleasure bordered on pain, their cries startled the creatures of the cove.

By the fourth day, the preacher was able to sit up and was sounding like his old self. He leaned back in his bunk and took a glass of water from Christina. "Got so many galderned holes in me you could stick a hose in my ass, set me on the lawn, and use me for a sprinkler."

Travis descended the cabin steps and looked over at the two of them. "Amazing what a pretty nurse will do for a man." He walked over, put his arm around Christina's waist and looked down at the preacher. "Well, buddy, looks to me like hell got all panicky for nothing. The nurse here tells me you're going to live."

"And it's a damned good thing, son, 'cause somebody's got to keep you out of trouble." The preacher paused for a moment, as if searching for words, which was rare for him. He looked up at Travis, his face serious. "Son, I want to thank you for what you did back there–comin' after me like that."

"Forget it, you'd have done the same for me."

"Maybe I would've–maybe I wouldn't. You never know for sure 'til the chips are down, and there ain't no more cards to turn. All I know for certain is that I'm here now because of you. When it comes to things like this, thanks ain't much of a word, but you got my thanks and my friendship for as long as you want it."

Travis reached out and touched the older man's good shoulder. "That's payment enough for me, Preacher. Now I'm going topside and get this ole girl moving, so we can get to Arkansas and I can start my vegetable garden." He winked at Christina as he turned to leave.

The winds had calmed, so they motored along the new coast of Arkansas for the next three days. The evening of the third day found them in a little bay about seventy-five miles northeast of Little Rock. By GPS reading and the new coastline, that seemed the best place to strike out across land for the Ouachita Mountains and their new home, so there they anchored *The Odyssey* for the last time. The matter of new transportation became an issue.

They would no longer need the sailboat, so the plan was to find someone with a land vehicle who would perhaps trade with them. The following morning, Travis and the sensei decided they would hike into the nearest town and find someone who would like to make a deal. The rest of the Armageddon Gang, as they had taken to calling themselves, stayed in the boat.

After going ashore in the *Avon,* Travis and the sensei took a road that virtually ran into the water near the sailboat, and headed inland. They had been walking for almost two hours when they saw several spirals of chimney smoke curling up in the distance. Fifteen minutes later they found themselves on the outskirts of Newport; population 8,565, read the sign, but there appeared to be considerably fewer occupants. Like most of the towns near the New Madrid fault, it had sustained significant damage. Those who had stayed were in the midst of re-organization and re-construction and, just like a hundred and fifty years ago, they carried guns and were wary.

The two men had barely made their way into town when a group of armed citizens in a couple of pickup trucks appeared. A small, wiry man, carrying a shotgun, got out of one of the cabs and approached them. He wasn't smiling but he didn't appear ready to shoot, either. "What can we do for you, gentlemen?" he asked. It was posed as a polite question, but it really meant: What the hell do you want here?

Travis looked at the men in the trucks, then back to the fellow in front of him. "We need some transportation. A van, or a pickup truck–something like that."

"And what exactly do you plan on paying for it with, mister?" the man asked skeptically.

"Well, strange as it may sound, we just sailed up from Florida in a dandy little forty-six-foot sailboat. It's anchored about ten miles east of here, and we'd like to trade it for something with wheels."

One of the men in the other truck had been listening intently to the conversation. He got out and walked over, a look of interest blending with disbelief on his face. "You sailed up here all the way from Florida, huh? That musta been quite an adventure."

"You have no idea," replied Travis.

"What kind of sailboat?" the man asked.

"An Irwin forty-six."

"Whew. That's a nice boat, man! I used to be a pretty fair sailor when I was younger. I wouldn't mind sailing again–just never figured I'd get the chance here. You're tellin' me you want to trade that boat for a truck?"

"Well, yeah," said Travis, "a nice truck, or a van would be even better."

"Listen, mister," the man continued, "I just happen to own what's left of a used car lot. If what you're telling me is the truth, I'll make you a deal on a real nice 'ninety-six Ford van that made it through the quakes without much damage."

Travis turned to the other men. "We're not looking to make any trouble. We just want some transportation, and we'll be gone." Then he turned back to the man interested in the boat. "Why don't we have a look at your van? If it's what we're after, we can drive it down to the sailboat and close the deal there. If it'll make you feel more comfortable, bring a few of your friends."

"Oh, I will," said the man with a wary smile, "I will. Now let's go get my van. I want to see this boat of yours."

Eric Dever, the sailing enthusiast, got in the cab of his pickup with Travis and the sensei; three of his buddies jumped in the back. They drove to his house on the outskirts of town, a rambling, ranch-style home, part of which had rambled down the hillside during the recent earthquakes. Off to the side of the house was a row of vehicles, the salvaged remains of Eric's used car business.

The van was roomy and clean. It had a heavy-duty transmission, four-wheel-drive, and two gas tanks. Travis thought it was perfect for their purpose. They all piled in–Travis and the sensei up front, Eric and two of his armed buddies in the back, while the other one followed in the pickup. The drive back was quiet and quick. In no time at all, the bay and the sailboat came into sight. Living in a time when no one took any unnecessary risks, Eric and Travis rode the *Avon* out to the boat while the sensei remained on shore in the company of Eric's friends.

As they pulled up in the dinghy, Eric took a look at the missing mast and the bullet holes. "She's a bit rough. Looks like you did have some exciting times getting here."

"Let me put it this way: You aren't the first person to want this sailboat; you're just the first person willing to pay us for it."

Eric laughed. "It's like living in the wild, wild West."

Travis looked over and smiled. "Yeah, I've made that comparison more than once myself."

They were helped aboard by Christina, and Eric spent the next hour trading stories and looking over the craft. When the hour was done, so was the deal. Eric knew he was getting a bargain, even with the bullet holes. The agreement was that Travis and his crew would get the van plus two extra five-gallon containers of gas. Eric would have himself a slightly used, but serviceable sailboat–one of the very few in Arkansas.

For the next two hours, Travis and the gang unloaded their gear from *The Odyssey* and packed it into the van. More than a few eyebrows were raised when the National Guard guns and ammo were brought out.

"How'd you come by that, if you don't mind me askin'?" queried Eric.

"Parting gifts from some of those people who wanted our sailboat."

"I see," said Eric.

When everything was loaded, and most everyone was

onshore, Travis and the sensei went back for the preacher, helped him into the *Avon*, and paddled it back to the bank. The three men stood for a moment at the edge of the water, one on either side of the old shrimper, supporting him as they looked back at *The Odyssey*.

"Sorta reminds me of my first car," Travis remarked wistfully. "She was a beater, but I had some incredible times in that car and hated to let her go—even though I was trading it for a newer model."

"Yeah, I sure understand that," said the preacher. "Felt the same way about the *Jesus's Love*."

The sensei looked at both of them. "Come, my friends. Save your regrets. I have a feeling that all the incredible times are not yet over."

They said their goodbyes to Eric and his friends, piled into the van, and rode off toward the setting sun.

PART III
EDEN

"Welcome traveler, to the new Eden.

"Look around you; tribulation borne of woeful judgements in the past.

"The land has changed. Have you?

"Draw wisdom from these old hills, and seek your new destiny carefully.

"For there are still as many snakes out there as apples."

–The Preacher

CHAPTER 17
HOME

Travis drove, equipped with his memory of the area and a road map of Arkansas. The sensei rode shotgun. The preacher was made comfortable in a make-shift bed in the back, and the others sat in the middle seat. Ra wedged himself in at Todd's feet.

An hour later, when night began to fall, they pulled off onto a side road by a small stream and set up camp. Carlos built a fire and warmed a meal while the others laid out the sleeping gear taken from the boat. After supper, they sat around the campfire and talked of the future, and what they hoped it would hold. The sensei, as always, cleaned his swords.

When the flames had burned to embers and the excitement of the day caught up with them, everyone retired to their individual bedrolls. Travis, whose blankets were next to Christina's, leaned over and kissed her goodnight, whispering, "I can't wait 'til we have the privacy of our own room."

"Mmmmm," she murmured sensually as she kissed him once more.

The misty morning air chilled them as they awoke to a cool, gray dawn. Carlos and Christina built a breakfast fire while Travis and the sensei packed the sleeping gear. The preacher was doing remarkably well; his wounds were healing and he was able to stand for small periods of time, but he tired quickly. After breakfast, everyone gathered around the road map and Travis showed them where they were headed. From what they had seen, the roads in Central Arkansas had suffered a fair amount of damage due to the quakes and tremors, but with a little luck and the van's four-wheel-drive, they would make it.

Shortly after sunrise the group was once again packed into the huge van and underway. Even with the bad roads and delays, Travis figured it was no more than a day and a half to his mountain homestead. He was trying to keep himself in check, but he was becoming excited. They had survived the worst. In one more day they would reach the safety of home.

The travelers avoided the larger cities and kept to secondary roads as much as possible. They encountered a number of people in the small towns they passed through that morning. Some waved and some didn't. Everyone seemed intent on whatever they were doing; no one chit-chatted like in the old days. It was amazing to Travis that, in a matter of a few weeks, life on the planet earth had been so completely altered–not simply in terms of how people went about their daily lives, but how they thought, and how they interacted with their fellow man.

Catastrophe brings out the worst and the best in people, thought Travis.

They passed through places where it was evident that the citizens had banded together and struggled for the return of harmony–not just in the physical sense, but in a spiritual sense as well, discovering the pleasures of giving and helping. But, there were other areas where it was obvious that the contest of good against evil had been lost, and the baser side of man's nature prevailed; hollow-eyed, frightened people moved quickly and silently into the shadows of broken, deserted buildings, appearing to have abandoned hope. The Apocalypse had come, and it had stolen their faith, leaving suspicion, deception, and envy as its legacy.

The countryside itself had changed as well, nearly as much as the people who populated it. There were great fissures, gaping wounds in the flesh of the earth that ran for hundreds of yards. Landslides still buried portions of the roads and forced four-wheel detours. Here and there a stream or a river had been re-directed. The weather was noticeably warmer also; daytime temperatures were reaching the mid-eighties, and for spring in Arkansas, that was unusual.

The day wore on and they stopped for lunch by a broad, tranquil river, finishing off some of the last canned goods. Ra splashed in the icy water, chasing fish, while he and Todd explored up and down the bank.

Sitting there on the grass by the water, Travis watched the boy and the dog playing, then turned to his friends. "Lord, I can't wait to drive that van through the gates of the old homestead. I'm just praying it's still there."

The preacher was lying on his back, a blade of grass in his mouth. "It's gonna be there, son. It's gonna be there, and you and I are gonna get to do some turkey huntin' and maybe a little bass fishin'."

"And I get my vegetable garden," Christina chimed in.

Travis smiled over at her. "Yes, you get your vegetable garden." Then he looked over at the sensei. "And what can we do for you, my friend, to make you more comfortable in our little mountain home?"

The elder man looked at Travis with his familiar smile. "In an attempt to resist the process of Americanization," he said, "I would like a cherry tree, so that this time of year, its fragrance and its blossoms will remind me of who I am and where I come from. That token of my heritage may help quell the desire to scratch my genitals in public while addressing my peers as 'yo, buddy!'—and perhaps suppress my urge to consume greasy hamburgers and guzzle beverages of fermented wheat while watching giant men in helmets knock each other senseless in their pursuit of an oblong pigskin."

The preacher laughed so hard he swallowed the blade

of grass he was chewing and nearly choked. Travis, still chuckling, said, "Sensei, I will personally find you a cherry tree, if I have to rummage every remaining nursery in Arkansas." Then, more seriously, "By this time next year, my friend, you will have your cherry blossoms and their fragrance." And once again, as their eyes met, he bowed slightly to the Japanese, who returned the bow, never breaking eye contact.

When lunch was completed and the cooking equipment was cleaned and stored, they filed back into the van, anxious to be underway. The excitement was building. Travis was sure now that by the following morning they would reach home.

It was late afternoon; the group had been on the road for about four hours when they found themselves traveling through an area of well-to-do farms and ranches. Each was at least forty acres or so, and the houses that could be seen from the road were large and expensive. Suddenly, as they reached a rise in the road, they heard shots–short staccato bursts indicative of a firefight.

Travis slowed the van and listened. "That's not a trigger-happy deer hunter. That's somebody in trouble–I'd bet on it." He turned back to the others as he stopped the van. "Whatever's happening is taking place on the backside of that hill."

"I can see your sense of American justice and fair play has been triggered," said the sensei with a sigh. "Let us have a look."

Travis told Christina and Carlos to keep their guns ready and their eyes open, then he and the sensei took their M16s and headed for the top of the ridge. Rapid bursts of automatic weapons shattered the still afternoon, and as they neared their vantage point, they could hear men shouting to each other.

They reached the crest, and cautiously peered down through the sparse woods at the confrontation. Below them was a large ranch house and a barn, enclosed by an attractive four-foot rock wall, accessed by a pair of large gates in the front. It was a lovely home by any standard, but the house and its occupants were under siege. One group of attackers was moving in from the front while another group worked their way around back. They were using the wall for protection while they poured round after round into the building. There were signs that the defending forces were suffering. Several of the windows in the home were shattered and there was a body on the corner of the porch, apparently one of the defenders who hadn't made cover in time.

Suddenly a child, perhaps four or five, burst from the door of a small guest house about a hundred feet from the main structure. She was quickly followed by a lass in her late teens; they were running for the larger house. The two must have been trapped in the smaller building when the shooting began and they were trying to reach the safety of their home and family. The older girl snatched up the little one and continued running. Suddenly, a door was thrown open in the main house and a large man came flying out, his head down, his eyes ahead like a fullback going for the winning point. The men behind the rock fence saw them and began firing. Rounds kicked up the dirt around the man's feet but he just kept going. Even the girls started picking up fire as bullets zinged and hammered the ground around them. They were only about fifteen feet apart when the man was hit in the thigh; it spun him and he fell, but he was back on his feet again in a second, lumbering toward the girls, oblivious to the blood streaming down his leg.

Travis didn't need to say a thing: He and the sensei raised their guns at the same time and opened up on the men behind the wall, who were in plain sight to them. In seconds, four of the ten men below were dead and the rest were scrambling for protection, having given up on both the girls and the man. The fellow grabbed the two girls and raced back to the house, pausing only for a split second to look up at Travis.

Travis shouted to the sensei as he fired, "Go back and get Chris and Carlos. Bring a handful of grenades and more ammo. I'll hold them 'till you get back."

Without a word, the sensei was gone, silent as a falling leaf. Travis continued peppering the attackers with short bursts to conserve ammunition until the sensei returned. He fired and moved continuously, to give the impression that there was more than one assailant, and to keep them from nailing him down with return fire.

It seemed only a minute or two and the sensei was back with Christina and Carlos at his side. "Okay, this is the situation," Travis said as he grabbed a clip and reloaded. "We've got four men behind that brush pile down there and two or three in that stand of trees at the corner of the wall. There's another group of maybe six or eight working their way around back–that's who you hear firing now. Sensei, take Carlos and work your way around high on this hill, without making contact until you're above those guys in the rear of the house. Don't let them see you, and don't open up until you're in position if you can help it. No need to get into a firefight; take two or three grenades and lob them. If there's anything left, clean it up with your rifles. Chris and I will take the ones in front the same way. Okay, move!"

Travis continued to fire, keeping the men below pinned down while Carlos and the sensei moved around the hillside to their position above the other assailants. The house was still receiving gunfire from the men in the back, who were bunched up in two groups behind the wall. They were confident, certain they were safe and secure, unaware of

Carlos and the sensei creeping through the woods a hundred feet above them.

Travis waited for five minutes, then took a deep breath and turned to Christina. "Okay, let's get 'em." He took a couple of the grenades Christina held. "I'm going to put one in those trees and one in that brush pile. Anything that comes out of the trees, you shoot. I'll take the brush pile."

She threw the bolt on the M16 expertly and tossed her hair back, the way she did when the chips were down. "Let's do it," was all she said.

Travis still had a little of his sandlot quarterback arm. That and a little luck put the grenades right on top of his targets. The deafening explosions were followed by screams; two men came out of the woods, firing as they ran. Christina got one of them. A couple more scrambled from the wood pile–one already limping. They hadn't gone thirty feet when Travis took them both. Just then there were twin explosions from the back of the house near the wall.

Carlos and the sensei sat on the hill above the men by the rock wall and waited for Travis's signal. When the grenades went off out front, they each took one and tossed it down the hill. The angle of the incline caused the grenades to roll down to the wall and stop right next to the men.

Carlos threw his grenade at the group on the left and watched it roll down, hit one of them in the leg, bounce against the wall and settle. The man looked at it in disbelief, then up at Carlos, who smiled and whispered, "Have a nice day, *amigo*." Realization dawned on the fellow about the same time the grenade went off. A second later it was followed by the explosion of the sensei's grenade. There were no survivors.

The one man who had eluded Christina's gun paused on the ridge above the house long enough to take a good look at who he was certain must be hired mercenaries. As

Travis moved out into the open and shouted down at the house, the hair on the back of his neck prickled. His eyes were drawn to a man standing alone on the ridge above him, about a hundred and fifty yards away–a big red-headed man, staring hard at Travis and Christina.

Reynolds took one more look at the people below, then turned and headed for the jeep he had hidden in the woods. The colonel would want to know about this development.

After getting an all clear from the sensei, Travis yelled again, "Hello! You, down there in the house, we're friends. Hold your fire!"

The front door opened slowly, and the man who Travis had protected earlier emerged, gun in hand, his leg bandaged. "Get your people in the open," he shouted back, "hands on the butts of your guns–no sudden moves!"

Travis called to the sensei, and after a quick perimeter check for any enemy survivors, the four of them joined up at the front of the open gates. The man, who had watched from the house, waved Travis and his people in.

When they reached the porch, he said, "I don't know who you are, mister, but I think I'll just call you the Lone Ranger. I'm in your debt–my family is in your debt." The man limped forward and extended his hand. "I'm Ben Harcourt, Circuit Judge for Montgomery County–or at least I was–until about seven or eight weeks ago. This is my house and my family you just saved."

Travis introduced himself and his companions and they were ushered into the living room by the judge. There they met his wife, their two daughters, and an assortment of help from cooks to groundskeepers; the people who comprised Harcourt's sparse defenses. If Travis hadn't stumbled onto them, they wouldn't have had a chance.

Judge Harcourt insisted that they have supper and spend the night at his home. After some refusing and more insisting, the group finally accepted the offer. Travis and the sensei went back for the van, accompanied by one of the gardeners who was to show the way into the property.

When they reached the van, Todd ran silently to Travis and wrapped his arms around him in a bear hug. "Hey, little buddy, I'm okay," Travis said as he held the boy. "Everybody's okay."

The preacher looked out at his friend from his seat in the van. "Hot damn, son, I been as nervous as a housefly at a lizard convention. What the hell happened? Where is everybody?"

"Everybody's just fine," Travis repeated. "We ran into some bad guys; they lost, we won–another page out of the Old West." Travis smiled and turned to the sensei. "Let's go, Tonto."

"Tonto? Who is this Tonto?" asked the Japanese.

"Never mind, just a joke," Travis said, chuckling to himself as he got into the van.

Once they were all in, Chester, the gardener, showed them the road which led to the house. An hour later, everyone was sitting in the large living room, drinks in hand. The preacher was propped up on the sofa with pillows all around him and a whiskey and water in his big paw. The judge and his wife sat across from Travis, Christina, and the sensei. Carlos and Todd shared a divan on the far side of the room, while Ra was afforded the luxury of the cool, hardwood floor next to them. Judge Harcourt had begun to explain the unique political circumstances existing in Arkansas. Harcourt, no particular friend of Colonel Rockford, was detailing the colonel's political aspirations and his own theories on the reign of terror that the survivors in Arkansas were experiencing:

"The man isn't interested in the due process of a democratic political system. He doesn't want to run Arkansas–he wants to own it. This country was established, and has survived for over three hundred years, on the concept of certain basic, intrinsic, freedoms. We've survived depression, civil wars, and inept leadership because the principals of the country are strong, as are the innate values of the system.

"Rockford wants to throw all that away. He wants to be a new-world Ghengis Khan, and he wants to make Arkansas his own version of Little Mongolia. Sure we had a shake up. Things are a mess. There is little or no federal government and I know we'll be on our own for a while, but that's no reason to depart from our basic ideals. He's using this catastrophe as an excuse to usurp a state from the United States of America, and if he's successful here, there's no stopping him from moving into Oklahoma, Missouri, or Tennessee. His capricious applications of eminent domain, which is, in essence, stealing property from people for his new government, has got a lot of people frightened and angry."

The judge paused. "I'll admit that I sympathize with some of Rockford's philosophies. He's right that the liberals of this country had taken us to the brink of economic and socio-political collapse prior to this disaster. They tried to accommodate the masses with failing welfare systems that taught the people it was easier to take than produce. They constantly treated the symptoms and never really treated the disease. Our borders bulged with people who couldn't make it somewhere else, then found that they couldn't make it here, either, because America wasn't a panacea for poverty and ignorance. It was just another country that, at first, had done better than most.

"I agree with Rockford that criminals in the old system got away with murder–literally. Justice was never sure and very rarely swift, and culminated only after every conceivable loopholed appeal had been exhausted. We need to alter that. We have to change some things to fit the times in which we now live. Laws for these times need to be simple, exact, and clear; justice swift and sure, but only after due process has been served by a court of law—not a group of vigilantes with a rope and a tree. The new laws have to work for the honest, law-abiding citizen, not the attorneys, and not the criminals.

"Like I said, I'm not at odds with all Rockford's ideas. It's his methods I don't agree with."

Harcourt took a sip of his drink, then continued. "As for what happened today, I have my own theory with which a number of my constituents agree. The majority of Rockford's opponents seem to have health problems, mostly trouble with foreign objects in their systems—like shrapnel, or bullets. Or, they leave a note about how they can't go on, then shoot themselves several times after cutting their own throats; or, they just disappear. A lot of us who don't think Rockford and his new government are the answer, have begun to suffer with bandit raids, home invasions, and all the above maladies.

"Rockford claims it's gangs of minority riff-raff from the cities, and the homeless have-nothings looking for somebody else's something who're causing the trouble. He claims they've joined together in some sort of bandit army that raids the surviving well-to-do areas of the state. He's made a lot of noise about his militia crushing these bandits once and for all, but, as of yet, it hasn't happened.

"My guess is that Rockford himself is behind the attacks, but many of the people here are frightened enough to settle for anyone who can stop the raiding and the killing. If Rockford can pull that off, it won't hurt his credibility. He knows he'll never be 'elected' into power. If he has to wrest control away from someone, he will; but even a bullheaded egomaniac like our Colonel knows he'd be better off with some type of a general mandate from the people. It would buy him time to consolidate control over everyone before they realize what they've bought with their consent. It also affords him the perfect opportunity to kill off a lot of the dissention before coming to the rescue."

"Wonderful," said Travis sarcastically. "We've battled bad weather, bad guys, and bad luck for fifteen hundred miles, thinking we'd be safe and secure here, and now you tell us we've got to deal with the man who would be king, huh?"

"That's about the size of it," Harcourt agreed.

Travis paused for a moment. "Tell me, is anyone making a concerted effort to stop this psychopath?"

"He has only one serious rival; a congressman named Turner who's doing his best to form a democratic caucus. Turner's a smart cookie, and so far, he's managed to stay alive–which is more than can be said for most of the competition. He has the support of the majority of the legitimate government–the ones the colonel hasn't paid off–but like I said, most of those people are running scared because of Rockford's methods of reducing political dissent. There're a handful of us who refuse to be intimidated, and have openly supported Turner. I truly believe most of the populace is on our side, but you got a taste today of what we've been dealing with. Like it or not, this is a political fight to the death. It's a battle for democracy in America. What happens here could very well decide the political direction and the governmental policy of this country for the next few hundred years. I, and others like me, have sworn not to allow our freedom to be taken until we're lying stiff and cold and we don't need it anymore.

"Travis, I know you've been through a lot already," Harcourt continued, " and I'm not asking you to make any decisions right away, but we need men like you. Arkansas needs men and women like you folks now, more than ever. We are going to have to fight fire with fire, and from what

I saw today, you're pretty good at that. None of this will go away; if we don't do something, it'll just get worse.

"If you can live with a government that can take anything from anybody at any time with complete impunity—fine. If you can accept a governing body that controls through fear rather than democratic process, then again, you'll do just fine, and you don't need me. But I'll bet last year's salary that none of what's going on now will set well with you. Go home, and get settled. You know where to find me. I have a feeling our paths will cross again."

Travis took a slow, thoughtful sip of his drink. "Well, Judge, first off, I've got to get to our little neck of the woods, make sure the quakes didn't get it, and that it isn't owned by some new government. Providing none of the above is the case, we need time to settle in and get ourselves organized. I can't promise you anything at this point. I need to see the picture for myself, and it's not my decision alone to make. We're a team, a family, and we decide together."

It was the first time Travis had used the term "family." He suddenly realized how appropriate it sounded.

The cook announced supper and they gathered around a large table in the dining room. The preacher said grace and they sat down to their first home-cooked meal in almost two months. After dinner, there were more drinks and conversation until finally, the guests were shown to their sleeping quarters and the luxury of large mattresses, goose down pillows, and rooms that didn't sway to the rhythm of the sea.

The following morning, the travelers said their farewells to the judge and his family, Travis promising to call on Harcourt in a week or so. Then they headed for Polk County, and home.

They drove for three hours, the detours from damage becoming fewer as they reached the insulation of the mountains. At last, Travis took a deep breath, exhaled, and pointed at a narrow dirt road. "There's our turnoff. The house is about a quarter-mile down that road." The gravel path was still as bumpy as ever, but in a sense, that continuity pleased Travis, instilling confidence that the old place might also be the same. They rounded the final bend, and there before them stood the farmhouse, the guest house, and the barn—still in place, everything intact.

Travis breathed a sigh of relief. He had been terrified that he might have taken his friends all that way, through so much, only to find their final sanctuary destroyed or usurped.

With his fears assuaged and his prayers answered, Travis smiled and turned to the others, his arm extended toward the property. "Gentlemen and lady, we're home!"

As they pulled up in the driveway, the screen door opened and the barrel of a shotgun poked out. "Don't got nothin' you want here. Now get, afore I shoot!"

Travis opened the door of the van and got out. "Hey, Will, you old codger, it's me, Travis. I've come home to roost."

Will Snead peeked around the door, sticking his scrawny neck out like a curious tortoise. His watery blue eyes suddenly brightened as he recognized his friend. "Well, I'll be derned. Travis! It is you!"

"Well, you gonna invite us in, or shoot us?" Travis yelled.

Will stepped out and brought the gun down, brushing back the last wisps of hair on his balding head when he saw Christina and the others. "Come on in, come on in."

Half an hour later, they were sitting around the big kitchen table drinking some of Will's precious coffee. The triumphant homecoming had been dampened somewhat by the old man's account of the slaughter of his neighbors and the acquisition of their property. The group sipped their coffee in silence as Will continued his story.

"They drug them from their home and told them they

had to leave, just like that, with a handful of belongings and a fistful of useless paper money. I'm not surprised ole Jeb did what he did.

"I went back the next day. They'd buried Jeb and his wife in a common grave by the shed and looted the house of anything valuable. A few days later, a team of carpenters showed up to fix the place. Now there's a crew over there twenty-four hours a day. They're a mean, rowdy bunch; been over here a couple of times, just to check me out and let me know how important they are. Since they took up residence, I've lost a sheep and one of my dogs. I know they killed 'em, but I can't prove it and, even if I could, what difference would it make? Like the Chinese say, 'To whom do you complain, when the Emperor steals your wife?'"

Travis sat looking out the kitchen window at the valley below as Will spoke. *The Emperor*, he thought to himself; it seemed a damned appropriate term from what he'd been hearing. Well, he would just have to let the future bring what it would. They all needed to rest, relax, and recover–and that was about all he planned to do in the immediate future.

Christina made the preacher comfortable on the couch in the living room, and changed his bandages after re-dressing Carlos's arm. They were both healing nicely.

While she worked, the others unloaded the van and stored the equipment.

Pretense dispensed with, Travis and Christina moved into one bedroom, while Carlos and Todd bunked with Will in the other. The preacher and the sensei chose the small guest house. Ra thought he was in heaven, with so much land to roam and Will's female Labrador to play with. By the end of the day, when Will served a supper of fried chicken and fresh mashed potatoes, life was beginning to feel pretty good.

As he sat at the table, looking at Christina and his

close friends, Travis was just about as content as he could remember feeling. "A toast," he offered with a glass of Will's homemade mulberry wine, "We made it, my friends. We made it."

"Praise the Lord," echoed the preacher as he threw down his wine in one gulp, using his good arm. "Not bad, Will," he said, smacking his lips, "not bad at all. You got any more of this?"

After dinner, and two more bottles of wine, Travis and Christina went for a walk. They reached the yard as the huge yellow moon rose above the distant trees. Hand in hand, they strolled the perimeter of the pasture bordered by pines and oaks in front of the main house. Christina paused to gaze up at the moon. "Oh Travis, I can't believe we're finally here. It's even lovelier than I hoped. I keep thinking I should pinch myself just to make sure I'm not going to wake up on my bunk in a lurching, rolling sailboat again."

"We're here, sweetheart, and we're here to stay," Travis said emphatically.

Christina, catching his tone, stopped and took his hands, looking into his eyes. "Travis, do we have to become embroiled in this political war? Couldn't we just sit back quietly and wait for the federal government to re-organize and take care of guys like this Rockford?"

Travis looked away. "We might be able to. I'm going to give the situation the benefit of the doubt for the time being. Maybe it's not as bad a picture as the judge painted it." He turned back to Christina. "I'll try not to get in anybody's way and I'm not going to make trouble, but I'll be damned if I'll let anyone take my land. I don't care what their reasons are." Then, suddenly recognizing his intensity, he calmed and his face softened. "It's okay, Chris, we'll be all right. I'll be a good boy; I'll go fishing with the preacher, raise my chickens and my vegetables, and enjoy every minute of it as long as I have you with me."

The old homestead had fallen into some disrepair, with only Will living there, so the next few days were spent in a leisurely effort of restoration. Fences were mended, the barn was cleaned and organized, the chicken house was redone, and Will and Christina went to work clearing and planting the garden. Toward the end of the week, Travis and Todd cleaned the fishing gear in the shed, then took off for the Ouachita River. That afternoon they returned, sunburned and hungry, with enough smallmouth bass for supper. Todd was ecstatic, and beamed with pride when he displayed the fish and Travis recounted their adventures.

Life seemed to be settling down by the end of the first week. They'd had no contact with the outside world and that suited them fine, especially Christina. She and Travis had what she deemed the perfect romance, and Todd, as he had intended, was becoming their adopted son.

The sensei practiced with his swords in the early morning and had begun to teach Travis and Todd the art of Iaido. The preacher was up and moving about with the aid of a crutch that Carlos had carved for him.

Everything seemed too good to be true–and often times, when a situation seems too good to be true, it is.

CHAPTER 18
OLD FRIENDS

With all the new occupants at the homestead, it wasn't long before they needed supplies. The group decided on a trip into Mena, which was the closest town of any size. It would also afford them an opportunity to pick up on any news, local or otherwise.

Everybody wanted to go except Will, who made it quite clear that he didn't care if he ever left the property again. Early the next morning, everyone loaded into the van, and half an hour later they were at the outskirts of the small community. Diesel fuel for the generator, seeds for Christina's garden, a handful of tools, shotgun shells for bird hunting, and some kitchen supplies were the main items on their shopping list. Travis figured they would start at a local hardware store, if one was still in business. That and the barber shop, were certainly the best places for information in any town.

Most of Mena had survived the cataclysm. Repairs were being made on the few buildings that had suffered minor damage, and people moved about freely, talking and bartering goods. There were far fewer weapons on prominent display than many of the places they had been through, but an air of caution and a watchfulness still prevailed.

On their way into town, Travis had noticed a large number of military-type vehicles on the road. When they reached the hardware store, there was a Jeep and a small canvas-covered transport truck parked out front. A group of men in camouflage uniforms was gathered around the entrance.

Directly across the street was an open-air market, selling fruits, vegetables, homemade jams, poultry, etc. As they parked the van, Christina leaned forward and told Travis that she and Todd would try the market for some fresh vegetables, and the seeds she needed, while he and the others took care of their business.

In an attempt to appear civilized, they opted to leave their weapons in the van. With Ra inside, no one with any use for their extremities would try to steal anything.

As Christina stepped from the vehicle, the soldiers, almost as one, turned their heads. There was a low whistle from the center of the group. She smiled, then continued across the street with Todd. A sharp command from the platoon leader brought the men back around, and he dispersed the majority of them while Travis and his people exited the van and headed for the hardware store. Travis walked into the store followed by a limping preacher with his crutch, but as the sensei started into the building with Carlos behind him, the officer and his remaining soldiers stepped in front of the entrance, blocking the door. "No chinks allowed in here," he said.

The sensei stopped, his eyes hooded and went cold, but he kept his composure. "I am not Chinese. I am Japanese," he said evenly.

"Don't make no never mind to me what kind of slant-eye you are. You ain't buying nothin' in this store. You ain't even goin' in."

The man's three companions closed in around him to emphasize his words, their guns in hand. The fellow looked over the sensei's shoulder at Carlos. "No spics, either. This place is for Americans. In fact, this state is strictly for Americans now, so why don't you get your asses out of here before I lose my patience and my temper."

The sensei paused, studying the men, when the one in

the center raised his rifle in a menacing fashion and growled, "Did you hear me, you slant-eyed son of a bitch?"

Not wanting a confrontation, the Japanese turned to go back to the van. But as he did so, the man behind him raised the butt of his gun, intent on bashing him in the back. The weapon had just begun its forward motion when the sensei spun, hammering the stock with such a powerful forearm block that it slammed into the face of the soldier to the right, smashing his nose and knocking him out. The sensei immediately sidestepped and, with the blade of his hand, chopped the man still holding the rifle on the side of the neck. The movement was so smooth and quick that the fellow actually looked puzzled as he collapsed to the pavement. In the next moment, the Oriental performed a violent ballet: While the soldiers on either side of him reacted by moving away from the door and raising their weapons, he grabbed the barrels of both the guns and held them away and up. In almost the same motion, he roundhouse kicked the soldier on his right squarely in the head. Before the sensei's right foot had even touched the ground, his left foot was in the air, delivering a vicious sidekick to the chest of the other soldier. In no more than six or seven seconds, the four khaki-clad figures lay inert on the ground around him.

Inside the store, another ballet of sorts was unfolding. There were two soldiers in the back, purchasing supplies when the ruckus started. Dropping their goods, they charged down the main isle, rushing the sensei, who was framed in the doorway. But as they ran by the preacher, paying no attention to the injured, older man, he swung the heavy, solid oak crutch in a swift, horizontal arch, catching both of them solidly in the forehead. Their feet went out from under them as if they'd run full bolt into a low-hanging tree limb–which, in essence, they had.

The preacher looked down at the cold-cocked men on

the floor, then admiringly at his crutch. "Damn, that's some fine wood, that oak!"

The owner of the establishment walked over to Travis and the preacher, shaking his head and grinning. "I don't know what you boys need, but if it ain't too expensive, it's on me. I ain't seen nothing that entertaining since lightning struck ol' JJ's chicken farm exhibit at the county fair. Don't care much for these fellas and their attitudes, anyway, and they take too much and always pay late, if they pay at all."

Travis took out his list. "If we could get these few items we'd really appreciate it, and I suppose we should be as quick as possible. I'd like to be gone before these guys come around."

The man took the list and looked it over. "No problem. I'll have it for you in two minutes."

As the shop owner was finishing with their order, Todd came dashing across the street and stumbled through the doorway, out of breath. One look at the lad's expression was enough to tell Travis that something was seriously wrong. "What is it Todd? Is it Christina?"

The boy nodded vigorously and pointed to the other side of the street. "Show me," Travis said. "Preacher, you get the goods loaded, and be ready to get out of here. Sensei, Carlos, let's go."

Todd led them to the far side of the open-air market where there were some old storage buildings. Behind them was a large, dilapidated barn. When they neared the barn, they heard Christina cry out. They rounded the corner of the entrance to see her being dragged into the back of the old structure by two of the soldiers who had broken away from their comrades earlier.

The two, with their backs to the barn door, were so intent on Christina that they failed to notice Travis and the sensei charging them until it was too late. The Japanese took the one on the left, Travis the one on the right. Carlos stood by the door. The sensei spun his man, kicked him twice in the ribs before the fellow could blink, then struck him hard under the chin with the palm of his hand. The man's head snapped back violently and he crumpled like a rag doll. The other soldier saw the sensei grab his friend and turned to face Travis. He was smaller than Travis, but there was no fear in his eyes. He was trapped, but he wasn't going down easy.

The guy took his best shot and Travis blocked it without missing a step. The big man closed his hands around the soldiers's throat, lifting him completely off the ground, then carried the fellow choking and squirming to a roof post of the barn, where he slammed him repeatedly until the old wood gave and the six-inch post collapsed. When the red cleared from Travis's eyes, his antagonist lay sprawled in the dirt.

Travis was headed for Christina when a hard, gravelly voice from the barn doors yelled, "Nobody move!" In the opening stood four more Arkansas militiamen with their guns leveled at Travis and his companions. One carried a rope. The officer in the middle, with the harsh voice, looked at the two men on the ground, then at Travis and his friends. "I don't know who you boys are, but you've gone and caused your last bit of trouble." Behind them appeared their battered companions, the ones the sensei had dealt with earlier, pushing the preacher along. They shoved the old shrimper into the center of the barn, and he moaned with pain as he struck the ground.

The others moved into a semi-circle around Travis and his group while one of them threw the rope over a beam. The leader stepped forward. "You boys are about to get a taste of Provincial Government justice. In your case it'll be your first and last. As for the girl, we'll save her for a while–"

Travis charged forward only to be stopped by a rifle butt to the side of the head, felling him.

The man looked down. "Don't be in such a hurry to die, mister. Hell ain't goin' nowhere."

They dragged Travis to his feet and slipped the noose over his head. One of them pulled an old milking stool from a nearby stall and forced Travis to balance on it while the rope was drawn tight, making him stand on his toes. Then they tied it off on a post.

The leader walked over to Travis and stared up at him, smiling. "Say hello to the devil for me," he said, and kicked the stool away. Just as the weight of Travis's body tightened the noose, the deafening thunder of a Thompson machine gun shattered the silence in the old barn. The rope, as well as the beam that held it, splintered and split, dropping him to the floor. As the startled soldiers spun around, a line of automatic weapon fire stitched the ground up to and between the feet of the officer, who instinctively released his gun and put his hands up. Another burst of a Thompson echoed out, and the dirt in front of the other militiamen shuddered from the impact of heavy .45 caliber slugs. The soldiers immediately threw down their weapons and raised their hands.

In the doorway, flanked by two huge, almost identical-looking men cradling machine guns, stood a short, stocky man with long blonde hair, bright, iridescent blue eyes, and a droopy "Custer" mustache–William J. Cody! Travis, working the rope off his neck, couldn't believe his eyes.

Cody quickly surveyed the scene, his eyes widening as they stopped on Travis. "Well, I'll be damned! Travis Christian! You been hanging around here long? Bad joke–sorry. You okay, ol' buddy?"

"I am now," replied Travis as he jerked the noose over his head and threw it down.

Cody noticed the blood on the side of Travis's face,

and his eyes flashed back to the soldiers. There was an angry glint in those iridescent orbs. "Which one of you hit that man?" he demanded. For a moment no one spoke, but a burst from the Thompson at their feet brought fingers pointing to the leader. "Cover them," Cody Joe said casually to his friends as he walked over to the man. Stopping in front of the fellow, he smiled disarmingly; then, without a word, slammed the butt of his gun between the man's legs with enough force to lift him off the ground. The soldiers's eyes went wide with pain and surprise as a guttural scream escaped his mouth. He hit the floor and doubled up in a fetal position, moaning, not moving.

Cody turned to Travis. "You feel better now? I do."

Travis chuckled. "Yeah, I feel much better."

"Okay, Travis," Cody said, "have your people get their weapons." Then he turned to the soldiers. "Now listen, boys, I want you to take your clothes off–every goddamned piece. You've got thirty seconds. Anybody with a stitch of clothing on after that, I shoot."

There was a moment's hesitation from the soldiers. "Twenty-nine, twenty-eight, twenty-seven," yelled Cody as he raised his gun, and the men began tearing at their clothing. Cody looked at the officer on the floor, then at Travis. "I'm not worried about that one. He'll be lucky if he's walking in a week and he'll never sing bass again."

Travis laughed. "God, Cody, I've missed you."

"Missed you too, buddy."

Travis grabbed the rope that would have hanged him, and he and Carlos tied the naked soldiers to one of the beam posts.

When that was done, Travis turned to his old friend. "Well, I guess we better get the hell out of here just as quickly and quietly as we can."

"We've got some catching up to do, Travis. Your place or mine?"

"Come on out to my place, and I'll treat you to a bottle of ol' Will's mulberry wine."

"Done," replied Cody. "Let's go. We'll save the introductions 'til we're clear, okay?" he said as he looked at Christina and the others and winked.

They grabbed their supplies from the hardware store, thanking the owner once again, jumped into the van, and headed out of town with Cody Joe and his boys following in their Jeep.

By mid-day the gang was back at the ranch. Introductions dispensed with, and refreshments in hand, they sat on the porch while Cody entertained them with stories of earlier adventures. Cody's large companions, who were identical twins who resembled lumberjacks on steroids, guarded the drive and the front of the house.

"Security," Cody said with a grin. "A habit of mine which has preserved my health and lifestyle."

They reminisced for a while, then the conversation turned to politics. Travis looked at Cody, who was slouched in an old rocker in the corner of the porch. The smaller man's long hair was pulled back in his usual ponytail. There were a few more lines around his eyes than the last time Travis had seen him, but those incredible eyes of his still glowed with mischievous exuberance; he still had that aura of barely contained energy about him. *Same old Cody,* thought Travis warmly, incredibly pleased to see his friend again.

"What do you know about this Rockford guy and his New Provincial Government?" he asked. "From all that I've seen and heard, I've got a problem with him. The whole thing smacks of Hitler's Germany–like Adolf gone Country."

"Well, up until today, my people and I have done our best to avoid the thugs he calls soldiers," said Cody. "We haven't made any political waves, and he's known we're a pretty tough bunch, so there's been no percentage in hassling us. But now, the complexion of this whole thing will probably change.

"Rockford's boys aren't used to being manhandled. They're the only organized force in the area, and they've taken advantage of that. In fact, they've enjoyed it. We'd both better pay attention for a while in case they decide to retaliate.

"As for Rockford himself, I think your Hitler analogy is pretty close. I don't believe for a moment that most of the people are on his side, but he's the one making the most noise, and his opposition keeps having accidents. He does have a core group of followers who stand to benefit from his rise to power; they range from a handful of crooked politicians and power brokers to the conglomeration of have-nots that he calls an army. They all want what he's promising–a chicken in every pot, the minorities in their place, and prosperity from a new world order."

They talked through the afternoon and polished off a couple more bottles of Will's dwindling supply of wine. Cody brought Travis up to date. Cody had never really given up "the business," as he called it; he'd just slowed down and chosen his times and places more carefully. The FBI however, had been breathing down his neck for the past year, so the big shake was just about the best thing that could have happened for him. The down side was, with the present condition of the world, there was little demand left for the finer things in life, and virtually no restriction on imports or exports, which all but put Cody Joe out of work.

Cody was an unusual fellow: an outlaw with a conscience. There was no doubt that he could have made a fortune smuggling cocaine or heroin–several times more money than he made on the gems or paintings he dealt in–

but he didn't care much for drugs. He'd seen what they did to people, close friends, and he didn't like it. He enjoyed the game of smuggling: the excitement of challenging his intellect and his talent, with freedom as the wager. And he liked the money. But what he brought in didn't hurt anyone. Cody always said he wouldn't be responsible for importing someone else's misery, and he lived by it.

He invested his money wisely in "things," as he put it, having anticipated the natural disaster all along. He owned several airplanes, a handful of vehicles from four-wheel-drive trucks to Corvettes, and, until the islands disappeared, a number of very expensive boats. His home in Arkansas was state of the art–alternative energy, powered exclusively from solar and turbine sources. He had a two-thousand-gallon natural gas tank and a two-thousand-gallon fuel tank buried on his property. He owned real estate all over the west and paid a loyal crew of men exorbitant salaries to pay attention to his business and his back. Even with the change, or perhaps because of it, he was about as well set as a man could be.

But with the day's events ... The conversation came back to the problem with Rockford. Travis stood and paced the length of the porch once, then turned to his old friend. "I don't see any way around this but to fight this guy. What it really boils down to is, do we take him out now, or later? I say let's get him while he's still organizing. A year from now, if he does end up in control, we'll have a harder time dealing with him. His system might be so entrenched that his followers could simply pick up where he left off. Once a form of government is established, it's harder to shake. I don't want to give him that time to settle in.

"Now, I'm not saying that you and I should take him on single-handedly. What I am saying is this: There's some solid, but poorly organized opposition to Rockford out there. It revolves around a congressman named Turner."

"Yeah," Cody interjected, "I've heard about that guy. Sounds like a pretty good man."

"From what I hear, he is. I met one of his supporters the other day; I'd like you to meet him, too. His name is Judge Harcourt."

"Heard of him, also," Cody said. "He's been getting in Rockford's way, politically. I'm surprised he's still around."

"He wouldn't be if we hadn't come along when we did. It was sort of a fortunate meeting on both our parts. Anyway, he wants to go after Rockford and his army–he's just not sure how. The guy's got good connections and I think he's a man of his word. I'd like to take you to meet him tomorrow. We can sit down and talk, and perhaps we can find the colonel's Achille's heel. What do you say?"

"Well, I guess you're right. We fight him now or we fight him later."

About six that evening, after dinner and one more bottle of Will's wine, Cody and his men headed back to their ranch, which was less than an hour from Travis. He had agreed to return the following morning so he and Travis could meet with the judge, and figure out "how to kick Rockford's ass," as Cody put it.

After Cody Joe had gone and everyone was settling in for the evening, Travis and Christina sat on the front porch and watched the yellow Arkansas moon crest the pines and bathe the valley in soft luminescence.

Travis put his arm around her as they looked out over the pasture. "Well, what do you think of Cody?"

"You talked about him so much on the trip, I felt like I already knew him. But to meet him is something else. He's like a small ball of perpetual energy."

Travis smiled. "He's always been that way. That's Cody. But don't be fooled by that 'let it all hang out' attitude.

He's one sharp cookie; he plans things out, and he doesn't make many mistakes."

"I hope not, because you two are about to play hero again and, Travis, I don't want to lose you."

He pulled her to him, their faces only inches apart. "Honey, I'm sorry about this. I know I promised you we'd be safe here. I just didn't know–how could anyone have known?–that we'd have to deal with some maniac who wants to be king."

CHAPTER 19
CHERRY TREES AND PLANS OF WAR

Cody showed up early the next day, and after a quick breakfast, he and Travis were off. They took Cody's Jeep, leaving the van for the others should they need it. As they drove, the two reminisced over Key West summer nights and the Caribbean capers they had shared. Cody was in the midst of telling a story about a smuggler he knew who used to fly so low coming into the Keys, that he always had pieces of flying fish stuck to his windshield, when Travis looked up and saw a sign that read CHERRIES FOR SALE.

"Cody wait! Take this road coming up!"

"Travis, cherries are out of season. There won't be any for another couple of months."

"I know, I know. I want a tree, not the cherries. I promised the sensei a cherry tree to remind him of his home."

They pulled into a drive next to the faded sign and drove up to a quaint little farmhouse nestled in an orchard of blooming cherry trees. Travis looked out at the blossoms and smelled the fragrance. "God, the sensei would love this. I'll have to bring him here sometime soon." Then, turning to Cody he said, "I owe that man more than I can ever repay him. I wouldn't be here if it weren't for him–not once, but several times. He wants a cherry tree and, by God, if I have to dig it up and carry it back myself, he'll have one."

"Okay, okay, so we get the guy a cherry tree," Cody laughed, a touch more impressed with the quiet Japanese.

Travis honked the horn and a fellow emerged from the house, shotgun in hand. They got out of the Jeep slowly and Travis called out, "Good morning. We're in need of a cherry tree, and this seemed a likely place to start looking."

Still cautious but warming, the man at the door smiled a little. "Well, I can see you're a man of vast deductive powers. Now, the question is, if I had a tree, what would you give me for it?"

Travis, having nothing with him of value to trade, was stumped. Cody reached into his pocket and pulled out a coin, then tossed it to the man who deftly caught it. "How about that?" Cody asked.

The man's eyes lit up when he saw the solid gold Krugerrand in his hand. "Follow me, gentlemen. I've got half a dozen nice little trees in bushel baskets, ready to be planted. He glanced at the gold coin again. "You boys can have your choice."

Travis looked over at his friend. "What did you give him?"

"A Krugerrand."

"God, Cody, that makes for a pretty damned expensive tree."

"It's okay. Through the years I converted most of my money over to gold, silver, Krugerrands, etcetera. Trust me, it's not the only one I have."

"Yeah, I'm sure of that, but thanks, man. Thanks a lot."

They picked out a perfect six-foot tree. The fellow wrapped the branches in burlap, so it wouldn't become wind-burned on the trip home, and laid it in the back of the Jeep. As they turned to leave, the man called out, "You boys need any more trees, you be sure and come back, you hear?"

About an hour later, Travis and Cody pulled up at the gates in front of the judge's homestead and sounded the horn. The gardener let them in as Judge Harcourt waved from the porch.

The judge, still limping a little, greeted Travis with a

smothering bear hug. "Good to see you, Travis, good to see you. I thought perhaps you'd decided to play ostrich."

"No, I didn't even get a chance. Before I decided if I wanted to see the mountain, Mohammed and his provincial government brought the mountain to me."

The judge stepped back, surprised. "You're telling me you already had a run-in with Rockford's boys?"

"Yeah, sure did."

"Well, tell me about it, but introduce me to your friend here first."

"Sorry, judge, my manners seem to be slipping a bit. This is my good friend, William J. Cody, named after Buffalo Bill Cody, the famous Indian fighter, to whom he is distantly related. You can call him Cody. Everyone else does."

The judge's eyes narrowed slightly at the mention of Cody's name. "Yes, it seems I've heard that name before–mostly in law enforcement circles, if I remember correctly. But, Mr. Cody, if you're a friend of this man, you're a friend of mine. Right now we need all the help we can get and if my memory serves me well, it seems to me you were spoken of with grudging respect for your ability to fly an airplane. Who knows, we might have need of your talents."

Cody smiled. "Actually Judge, I'd like to talk to you and Travis about a plan I've been forming that applies exactly that element."

"All right, gentlemen," the judge said as he motioned them through the door. "Come in, come in. Your timing is excellent–uncanny, actually–because in less than an hour Congressman Turner will be here with a handful of Rockford's most powerful rivals. We've decided we're no longer political foes. We are Rockford's enemies, and a number of us want to do something about it."

After they had settled on the big couch in the living room, Travis told them about the militiamen in town.

Harcourt listened, then added somberly, "Baptism by fire. Now you're one of us whether you like it or not." The judge turned to Travis's friend. "All right, Mr. Cody–"

"Cody, or Cody Joe, please. That 'mister' stuff makes me feel too much like an adult."

"Okay, Cody, tell us about this plan of yours."

"Well, first off, I have one of my men in Rockford's Delta Camp; he joined the New Provincial Government last night. He's a quick study with lots of military experience. He'll ask the right questions and we'll have some idea of what the good colonel's up to from now on." The judge nodded as Cody continued. "As for my plan, I figure there's no more mister nice guys now. We need to take Rockford out, along with as much of his organization as possible. We have to shock his weekend warriors enough to where, if they do survive, they won't want to play anymore. I have an airplane in the hanger next to the strip on my property. It's a P51 Mustang, which was probably the best ground support fighter in World War Two, if not the finest fighter, period. The unique thing about my plane is that it's armed. The fifty-caliber machine guns are still in it and operable–and I have lots of ammunition." The judge's eyebrows rose perceptibly.

Undaunted, Cody continued. "I also have a set of jetisonable wing tanks. This is what I propose: We take the wing tanks and fill them with a mixture of castile soap and gasoline, which makes a hell of a poor man's napalm. It works damn near as well as the stuff we spread all over 'Nam. The plane's altered to seat two people, with dual controls. Travis and I will take her up tomorrow and hit Rockford's Delta Camp a little after dawn. I already know that the major ammunition dump for Rockford's army is in that camp; by tomorrow morning I'll know exactly where. If we can hit that dump with a handful of rounds from the fifties on the plane, or one of those homemade napalm bombs, we can most likely take out the colonel and a good portion of his army. At the very least, after we've attacked that base it'll never be the same, and a lot of his so-called soldiers will be considering alternative life styles."

Travis looked over at Cody. "How in hell did you get live ammo and machine guns for a Fifty-One?"

Cody smiled. "Hey, all it takes is money, and that's never been one of my problems."

The judge turned to Travis. "Well, what do you think? This is your forte, not mine."

"To tell you the truth, I think it's a hell of an idea. A Fifty-One, armed, like the one Cody's talking about, will make a mess of that camp."

"Right you are," agreed Cody. "They'll think the devil himself grew wings and came for them."

Harcourt pushed himself back in his chair, and clasped his hands together under his chin. "Well, I'd like to run this by Turner and his people, but my guess is that he's going to buy it. Turner's preparing a grass-roots campaign to bring himself to the attention of the people of Arkansas. He's having a hard time now because of Rockford's violent methods of dealing with competition. With the colonel out of the way, getting Turner elected as the new governor of Arkansas would be a piece of cake. The people know him; he's got solid credentials and a good track record. He probably would have been the next governor anyway, if not for the disaster."

At that moment, the housekeeper announced that Congressman Turner had arrived with his constituents.

Turner was a slender man of about forty five, with slightly receding, gray hair and intense, dark eyes. He radiated a straight-forwardness and honesty that seemed remarkably non-political. His handshake was firm, and when he talked, he looked you in the eye. Travis liked him immediately. He was accompanied by three other men, two of them were congressmen, the third, another judge. Since the arrival of Travis and Cody, the focus of the meeting had shifted from aggressive defense to outright confrontation and, when Cody's plan was revealed, it was agreed upon unanimously.

While they talked, another conversation was being conducted miles away in the officers' quarters of Delta Camp.

Reynolds nodded as he listened to the men who were reporting the incident of the day before. The description of the big man with dark hair and the woman coincided with his memory of the people at the judge's place. Not only had they again gotten the best of his men, but it appeared that they had joined forces with the guy who owned the fortress-like property on the western edge of town. Reynolds was unaccustomed to being "had" by anyone once, let alone twice. He wanted those people. He wanted to settle the score personally. Jotting down the descriptions of the people and the vehicle, he dismissed his men, then called Communications.

"Dickens, this is Reynolds. I want an all-points bulletin put out on a vehicle–a late model, blue Ford van with Arkansas plates. I want everybody we've got to know about this. You're looking for two big guys; one in his late forties, the other maybe fifty-five or so. There's a good-looking woman with them. She's got reddish-blonde hair and a body that'd stop a clock. There's a Jap and a Latin guy with them, too. Find 'em for me, Dickens. Find 'em–you understand?"

"Yes, sir."

"Good, now get on it," he said, and hung up. Reynolds sat back and thought about the situation for a moment, then decided to go over to the colonel's office and fill him in. These were some pretty tough characters he was dealing with. If something went wrong, he didn't want to be the only one around to take the blame. He had seen how Rockford dealt with that kind of incompetence.

Rockford was not happy to hear that the opposition was fighting back with hired mercenaries. He was livid when he heard that his men had been made fools of in town.

"Reynolds, I want to know the minute you find these people. I'll be in on this when we go for them. When we're done, no one will try this again."

An hour after his conversation with Reynolds, Dickens, the Communications Officer, was on the radio to the outpost adjacent to Travis's property–the house that had belonged to Jeb and his wife. Newton, the officer in charge there, took the message, then walked into the living room where the others were lounging around. "Got some hot info here, boys. We're to watch for a blue late-model Ford van and a handful of people Reynolds and the Colonel want found: two big guys, a good lookin' woman, a Jap and a Mexican. We're to pay attention to the local roads in the valley. Sounds like they want this bunch real bad, so keep your eyes peeled."

"I've seen that van," a voice said. Newton looked at the man in the back of the room, who was cleaning his pistol on the kitchen table. The soldier paused, putting the gun down. "I saw that van turn into the property next to us a couple of days ago."

"You sure?"

"Well, I'm sure it was a blue Ford van. I ain't sure it's the one you're wanting."

"Okay," Newton said. "Take Carlin and Blair and go over there. Borrow a cup of sugar or something and check the place out."

"All right, soon as I finish cleaning my gun."

Newton went around quickly to the front of the table. "Hey, mister, I said now! Not tomorrow! This comes straight from Reynolds and has top priority, understand? That means if you don't do what you're told, when you're told, you could end up feeding the Colonel's dogs–and I don't mean handing them the food."

"Okay, okay, I'm going," the soldier said reluctantly. "Blair, Carlin, let's go!"

Christina and Carlos were in the garden with Will, trying to get some tomato plants started, when she saw the three men come off the path and into the clearing. It was obvious that they were NPG military. They strolled over with the cocksure attitude of soldiers who know that their actions, however inappropriate, are afforded complete impunity. *The Gestapo Syndrome*, she thought to herself.

As the soldiers approached, Christina rose and brushed down her skirt. Carlos and Will stood on either side of her. Ra, who had been playing with Todd, lay in the tall grass about twenty feet away, watching–not moving.

Corporal Eastern, the soldier who had been ordered to the house, was not in a terrific mood. He was a man with a quick temper and he was already on edge. He stopped in front of the woman and her friends. "You folks own that van over there?"

Christina paused for a moment, wishing Travis was there. "Yes, it's ours."

"I'm looking for a big guy, dark hair. Is he here?"

Christina tossed her hair back with a shake of her head. "That's a pretty broad description. It probably fits fifty percent of the men in Arkansas. If you can give me a little more information, then maybe I can tell you I haven't seen him."

The corporal stepped forward menacingly. "You'd be wise not to give me any trouble, lady. Now just answer my question and don't jerk me around."

"Or what? You going to put me against a wall and shoot me?" The man's eyes narrowed, but before he could do anything, Will stepped in front of Christina. "I think you fellas ought to leave now. Far as I know, working in the garden ain't illegal yet, even by your standards. So, unless there's something else we can do for you, it's time for you to go."

The corporal's short temper was ignited when Will stood up to him, and he lost what little control he had. "Yeah, there's something else you can do, old man. You can get the hell out of my way." He grabbed Will and threw him to the ground, then reached for Christina.

Ra covered the distance between himself and the men in three bounds, like a wounded lion coming out of the tall grass on the Serengetti. The corporal had just enough time to turn pale before Ra hit him in the chest in typical Rottweiler fashion, using his body weight to knock his opponent down. Few people do well with a snarling one-hundred-fifty-pound dog on their chest, and the corporal was no exception. He lay there in an excellent imitation of a frozen fish filet, not moving a muscle, as Ra stood on him, a slow, throaty growl issuing from his bared teeth.

As the other two started to raise their guns, bringing them around toward Ra, Christina pulled her hand out of her apron and, aiming her trusty nine millimeter, fired a shot into the dirt between them to get their attention. "I wouldn't even consider shooting that dog, gentlemen. Try it, and I'll bet you funeral costs that it's the last thing you ever do. If you're not convinced that I can take you, look over at the house." The sensei was at the front door with an M16 and the preacher was at the window, rifle in hand. Christina stared at the soldiers. "It's your call, boys." The two men looked at each other, then down at the corporal, and slowly lowered their guns.

Christina smiled. "Prudent, gentlemen, prudent. Now drop your magazines and empty your guns." They did as she requested. She looked at the soldier on the ground, "Okay, Ra, let him up. Back, boy." Reluctantly, Ra moved off the corporal, who exhaled shakily and slowly rose to his feet.

"This was a mistake, lady, a big mistake on your part."

Christina glared at him. "Personally, I think the mistake was not letting him rip your throat out, but I could fix that with a simple command. Ra!"

The growl from the huge dog was enough to put the three men in full retreat.

"Okay, okay, we're going," said the corporal as he moved backward, "but we'll be back."

Christina, looking braver than she felt, stared him down. "We'll be here."

By late afternoon, Turner and his group had mapped out a political battle plan to start after Rockford and Delta Camp were eliminated. They knew that the new Alpha Camp would also have to be dealt with, but it was staffed by fewer personnel, and they figured, with the head of the snake gone, dealing with the tail would be easy. They all agreed that there was no point in delay. Cody would prepare and arm his aircraft that night. The following morning, he and Travis would attack Rockford. They worked out most of the details and the meeting broke up.

Cody dropped off Travis and his cherry tree and they agreed to meet at Cody's just before dawn. As Cody Joe drove away, Christina came out of the house and, although she gave him a big hug, the look on her face told Travis something was wrong.

After a brief embrace, he held her at arm's length. "What is it?"

"Come on in Travis, supper's almost ready. I'll fix you a whiskey and tell you about our little brush with the Colonel's boys today."

"The Colonel's boys?"

Christina sat him down in the living room and told

him about the incident with the soldiers, Carlos and Will adding to the story. When they were done, the preacher limped over and sat down noisily. "Way I figure, it's a damned good thing we're goin' after them, 'cause it's a sure bet they'd be comin' for us real soon."

Travis nodded. "Yeah, you're probably right. But with any luck at all, by day's end tomorrow, Rockford and his camp will be history."

"Amen," said the preacher. "May the Lord guide and protect you as you serve as His scythe of retribution on the wheat of the damned."

Travis smiled. "Amen."

CHAPTER 20
FLYING AND DYING

Rockford paced across the room, then turned sharply to Reynolds and his two Lieutenants. "So you've found them, eh? Good. I want this bunch."

"No more'n I want 'em," Reynolds replied, lounging in the big high-backed chair by the colonel's desk. The other men sat stiffly on a nearby leather couch.

The colonel looked out over the encampment from the picture window, dismissing Reynold's statement. "We've encountered resistance before, but these people smack of professionalism. Three times you've had contact with them and three times they've made your men look like fools. This is it, Reynolds. This is where it ends."

"You're right there, Colonel. "They're as good as dead."

"No, I want them alive–or most of them alive, if at all possible. I need examples. There'll be a public hanging in the center of Fort Smith. The folks around here are going to see first-hand what this kind of opposition buys. Now tell me, what intelligence information do we have on these people?"

"Well, after my men located them and reported to me, I put two sentries in the woods watching the property. They're all there now–the big guy showed up with that Cody fellow about four that afternoon. Cody left the rest of them there and headed back to his place about half an hour later. We can deal with him and his boys after we finish with this bunch. I've got my best men standing by. I figure to hit 'em first thing tomorrow morning–surround the house and burn 'em out."

"Right, Reynolds, but we take them alive if we can, you understand? Alive! I'm going to direct this personally. I want you and your soldiers assembled and ready at oh-six-hundred hours. All right, captain, you're dismissed."

Reynolds got up and executed a shoddy salute. "Roger, Colonel. We'll be ready." His lieutenants stood up, snapped salutes, and followed the captain out.

Rockford clasped his hands behind his back, and stared out the window at the compound below. He suspected these people were tied to Congressman Turner somehow. They had to be if they were protecting Judge Harcourt. All along, Turner had represented the greatest threat to his control over Arkansas. The man was smart, Rockford had to give him that. He had managed to consolidate strong support among the surviving politicians, while avoiding the hit squads the colonel had sent for him.

Rockford smiled grimly. "That's okay, Turner," he muttered. "First I'll get your dogs, then I'll take you."

When Cody got back to his place, he called together the people who worked on his planes with him and told them what he intended to do. He assigned part of his crew to fueling the aircraft, arming and testing the .50-caliber machine guns, and checking the plane mechanically. He and the lumberjack twins took two fifty-five gallon drums of fuel and mixed several gallons of liquid soap into each one, creating a highly effective ersatz napalm. After achieving the right jelly-like consistency, they transferred the solution to the large wing tanks of the P51. When the wing tanks were full, they sealed them and carefully epoxied dynamite blasting caps on the nose and sides of the fuel cylinders. The impact on the caps would provide sufficient detonation to set off the napalm. After sealing the tanks, they attached the deadly cylinders to the quick releases under the wings of the plane.

When they were finished, Cody stepped back, looked

at the P51, and grinned. "The colonel's gonna get a wake-up call from hell tomorrow."

While Cody Joe worked on his plane, Travis and his people reviewed their plans for the following day. The sensei and the preacher would take Travis to Cody's in the morning. On their way back, they would stop in town and pick up diesel fuel for the generator at the house. Carlos would stay by the CB radio at home, waiting for word from Travis. Everyone would remain armed throughout the day.

When Travis and Christina went to their bedroom, Chris closed the door and pressed her back against it, looking at Travis, who stood by the bed. Her green eyes danced with the fire and the urgency of need, compounded by a clear and poignant desperation–a fear of the impending dawn and what it held for the man she loved.

"God, I love you," she finally said, summing up the turmoil in her heart.

Travis moved to her and took her in his arms. "You talk too much," he said softly as he picked her up and carried her to the bed.

Dawn came sooner than Travis wanted. The new sun crested the surrounding mountains, promising a clear and cloudless late spring morning. In the chill of the early hours, they all drank a cup of coffee. There was no breakfast–no one was hungry.

The preacher and the sensei climbed into the van as Travis gave Todd a hug and ruffled his hair affectionately. "I'll see you soon, son," he said, for the first time using that term of endearment with the boy. "Next week we'll go catch some more of those smallmouth." The young man smiled bravely and hugged Travis again.

Travis gave Ra an affectionate pat on the head, then turned to Will and Carlos, "Hold the fort down, you two, and keep a sharp eye out."

"*Sí, mi Jefe,*" Carlos said.

Travis took Christina's hands, pulled her close, and she clung to him. Then she pulled away and shook her hair back in that typical fashion of hers. "I love you, Travis Christian. Now get this done and come back to me."

"I will, Chris, I will. And I love you, too."

He got into the van and they were off. Travis looked back as they pulled out of the driveway. Christina and Todd stood holding hands, watching, with Will and Carlos next to them. For a second, as he looked at them, he was hit with a wave of discomfort, like someone had splashed a few drops of cold water down his back. Travis returned to his driving and the feeling passed, but left him slightly unsettled.

"Are you all right?" the sensei asked from the seat next to him.

"Yeah. Yeah, I guess. Listen, I want you two to get back to the farm as quickly as you can. Drop me off, get that gas, and get back there, okay?"

The sensei nodded. "*Hei*, Travis-san. Yes, we will."

When they reached Cody's place, he and the plane were ready and waiting on the strip. Cody Joe, ever the showman, had on his worn flight jacket and a leather aviator's cap, complete with goggles. With his long hair protruding from the bottom of the cap and falling across his shoulders, he looked like a cross between a small Viking and a World War II flying ace. His bright eyes danced with anticipation.

"Glad you could make it," shouted Cody, motioning Travis with a sweep of the arm toward the foot-up on the wing. "Let's go kick some NPG butt."

Travis laughed, waved goodbye to the sensei and the preacher, then hopped onto the wing and into the specially designed rear seat of the cockpit. Cody climbed into the cockpit in front of him, handing him a set of headphones.

"Put these on so we can communicate while this whole thing is happening."

In seconds, Cody had the big engine fired up. The twins removed the chocks from the wheels and a moment later the plane was rolling down the strip, the engine roaring in their ears and the tail of the aircraft coming up off the ground, enhancing the increasing speed.

Cody applied a little more right rudder, offsetting the asymmetrical thrust of the propeller and keeping them centered on the strip, while applying more back pressure to the controls as they reached optimum take-off speed.

"Hang on, buddy, here we go!" he shouted as he drew the controls back and the plane leapt from the ground and streaked toward the sky. Cody took it up to three thousand feet, did a wing-over, then rolled it upright again to check the controls. He fired a quick burst from the machine guns to double-check their operation. "We're good-to-go. Everything's doing just what it should. Now let's go find Rockford."

In a plane that cruises at close to four-hundred MPH, it doesn't take long to travel seventy miles. When they were about twenty miles from the camp they saw a small convoy of two trucks and a Jeep headed away from the compound. They debated hitting them, but it seemed too small a force to bother with. Besides, it might spoil the surprise attack on the main camp, so they flew on.

Rockford looked up as he heard the roar of the '51, three thousand feet above him and about half a mile to the west. "Where in hell did that come from?"

"Don't know, Colonel," Reynolds replied. "Seems to me I heard someone in the valley owned one. I just don't know who."

"Find out!" Rockford snapped. "Now how much longer?"

"Maybe an hour. No more."

***

Christina made herself busy around the house for the first hour after the men had left. Carlos and Will were outside working on the new smokehouse, something the family would need. She was doing her best to appear calm and organized for the others, especially Todd, but she was so worried she could barely concentrate. Taking a World War II fighter plane out with homemade bombs–no parachutes, no way to communicate with her if something went wrong–to attack a camp bristling with men and automatic weapons. It was idiocy! God save her from boys who never grow up and their heroic aspirations. But what was a woman to do, really, when she loved the boy?

It had been a little over two hours since the men had left. Christina was in the living room, trying to concentrate on a book. Todd and Ra lay in front of her on the floor. The dog and the boy were almost inseparable these days, but it was obvious that Todd was also fidgety, and worried. He carried the added burden of not being able to voice his concerns and exorcize his fears. He kept it all inside of him, but his eyes showed his anxiety. She looked down at him.

"They'll be all right, Todd. He'll be back soon." Todd looked up at her, his soft blue eyes pleading with her to be right. Just then she heard shouting outside. And rifle fire.

Travis's mountain could be approached only from the roadway side. The back side of the property dropped off sharply in a ninety degree incline of jagged granite outcroppings surrounded by the loose soil of the mountainside. It afforded a spectacular view of the valley, but access was difficult. The woods around the front of the house had been cleared, leaving a field with a driveway to the main road in the center. The cleared area was just over a hundred yards square. Forest wrapped the edges of the field, the densest part facing the house where the driveway ran through and out to the road.

Reynolds' men had reconnoitered the property and recognized their limitations. A frontal assault was their only option. It offered easy access and cover up to the field in front of the house. The convoy stopped on the main road and Reynolds sent in a squad to determine the immediate situation at the homestead. Rockford was furious when they returned with the report that the van was gone and the only ones who appeared to be there were the old man and the Latin, who were working on something in the yard, and the woman and a boy, seen through the windows of the house.

The colonel snapped around. "What the hell is this, Reynolds? Where are your goddamned Intelligence people?"

Reynolds shrugged his shoulders. "All I know, Colonel, is that at five a.m. this morning, they were all still there, sleeping. That was the last report I got."

"Well, the ones we wanted are gone," the colonel shouted, then paused for composure. "Okay, all right. We'll just make the best of the situation. Actually, this may work out better. This bunch will be easy to deal with. We'll take 'em, then come back for the others. Split up the men. Send in two squads, one on each side of the road in the forested area. Once everyone is hidden in the woods as close to the house as they can get, rush the compound. From the corners of the field, where the forest ends, to the house is only seventy-five meters or so. You should be able to cover that distance before the two outside know what's going on. The woman and the boy in the house shouldn't be any trouble. Remember, Reynolds, take them alive if you can."

Carlos and Will were in the process of building a new smokehouse, between the barn and the main house, when Carlos went to the barn for another hammer. Just as the little Cuban entered the barn, Will looked up and saw the line of soldiers charging across the clearing. He grabbed his gun and headed for the house, shouting for Christina. Because of the location of the smokehouse, Will had to run diagonally toward the line of advancing men to get to the front door. The old man was twenty yards from the porch when Corporal Eastern, the soldier with the bad temper and a score to settle, raised his gun and fired. Eastern smiled as Will tumbled to the ground.

The shot drew Carlos from the barn. When he saw the line of men approaching and Will on the ground, he knew he couldn't make it to the house from that direction, so he sped out the back, and along the precipice near the rear of the homestead, trying to gain entrance to the back porch.

Corporal Eastern saw the little Cuban dash around the barn and head for the house. He could hear Reynolds shouting at him as he raised his gun again, and pulled the trigger. The shot rang out, Carlos threw his hands into the air and fell off the cliff, down the hillside. Eastern turned just as Reynolds came running up to him. "Got him, sir!" he yelled.

"No, got you!" Reynolds shouted as he shot the corporal between the eyes with his pistol. Reynolds swung around screaming, "The next man who even fires his gun gets the same thing. I want the woman and the boy alive! Now take them!"

When she heard the shots, Christina raced to the window just in time to see the soldiers moving in on the house. Quickly, she ran to Todd, grabbed him, and headed for the cellar trap door in the floor of the kitchen. She threw back the rug that covered it, grasped the ring, and opened the hatch. She thrust the silently protesting boy into the opening and, for protection, also ordered Ra down into the dark stairway. "Don't make a sound," she shouted, "and stay in there until I tell you to come out!" Christina slammed the door shut and threw the rug over it again as a third shot rang out, followed by more shouting. Taking her nine-millimeter pistol from the counter in the kitchen, she walked to the center of the living room, calmed herself, and waited for them.

The first four soldiers that burst through the living room door never lived to see the sun set. Two others were wounded. There would have been more, but she ran out of bullets.

They grabbed Christina and threw her hard to the floor, tying her hands and feet as she struggled, then they ransacked the house looking for the boy. It wasn't long before the men found the trap door. An over-anxious soldier lived just long enough to regret his haste when he opened the hatch and a hundred and fifty pound version of hell with teeth hit him in the chest. The dog seized the man's throat, his front paws practically draping over the shoulders of the militiaman, his back feet still on the stairs of the cellar. As the man gurgled in a macabre dance with the dog, the soldier next to him, unable to shoot for fear of hitting his companion, reversed the gun and swung it like a club, hammering the butt of the gun against the big dog's head. The impact was so great that the stock snapped off the weapon and the animal tumbled down the stairs into the dark cellar. No one was overly anxious to go down the dimly lit stairs, so they shouted to the boy from the door above: "Come out! Get out of there now or we'll shoot you and your goddamned dog!"

Alone in the darkness, Todd realized that Ra had been hurt, and not wanting anything further to happen to the dog, he acquiesced. The men moved back from the door as they heard movement on the stairs. Seconds later, when the boy's head and shoulders appeared through the opening, they grabbed him and dragged him out, quickly slamming the trap door.

A few minutes after Cody and Travis passed the small

column of vehicles, Delta Camp came into view. Cody Joe checked the instruments one more time and took a deep breath. "It's show time, Travis. Hold on tight, here we go." He rolled the wing over and dropped down on Delta Camp like an avenging metal angel. As he descended almost vertically, Cody yelled, "I'm going to chew them up with the fifties on the first pass; that'll get them all outside, like stirring up an ant hill. On the second pass, we'll go for the ammo dump and use the napalm."

Cody leveled out with the terrain about a quarter mile from the camp and throttled back in order to get as many rounds into the compound as possible. He knew there would be little or no return fire on the first pass, so he came streaking in one hundred feet off the ground, clobbering the headquarters, the newly built officer's barracks, and the rows of tents for the enlisted men. The big .50 caliber rounds carved twin rows of mayhem as they ripped through buildings like a shredding machine. Tents and huts collapsed, men screamed, and complete panic ensued in a matter of seconds.

Cody ran the plane out past the camp and stomped on the left rudder while pulling the controls back hard and to the left. The responsive aircraft jackknifed up and over as he applied a little more stick and rudder to bring it smoothly around for another pass. Travis's stomach was thrown up and down so fast, he felt like a blind man strapped to a Brahma bull.

Cody missed the communications post on the first pass. The radioman, who was taking a break on the front porch when the plane attacked, saw it all. In a flash, he was at the radio. "Colonel Rockford! Colonel Rockford! This is Sergeant Dickens at Delta Camp. Come in, come in!"

Rockford, in his Jeep, heard the urgent broadcast. "Right, Dickens, this is Colonel Rockford. What is it, man?"

"Colonel, we're being strafed by a World War II fighter. The guy's stomping the hell out of the camp!"

"What the– All right, sergeant, this is what you do. Get on the horn to our air base and get that F16 up and over there double time. You hear me, Dickens? Do it now!"

"Right, Colonel."

Fredrick Marshall, the F16 Falcon fighter pilot, was playing cards with the maintenance people when the call came through. That was about all he did anymore: play cards, eat and sleep, then play some more cards. When he heard about this development, he was ecstatic. Not only would he have a chance to fly again, he was going to get some target practice at an aging WWII aircraft.

Cody's plane was anything but aging. In fact, Cody's plane was better, faster, and more dangerous than most of the P51 Mustangs that saw combat in the war. His magnificent engine had been beefed up to provide maximum horsepower and performance. Furthermore, he had an engine booster system installed wherein a water/alcohol mix injected into the cylinders delivered instant cooling, giving an extreme burst of power for short durations, greatly increasing the already remarkable speed of the '51. The original P51 Mustangs were equipped with .30- and .50-caliber machine guns in the wings. Cody had installed all .50-caliber guns, eliminating the need for two kinds of ammunition and providing the airplane with greater devastation at a longer range.

Still, with all the innovations on Cody's aircraft, it was nowhere near a fair match-up. The F16 had a 20-millimeter Gatling gun pod mounted on its underside that fired up to seven thousand rounds per minute and was armed with two heat-seeking sidewinder missiles. It wasn't going to be a fair fight, but then, Captain Marshall didn't really want a fair fight, he wanted a little excitement. He was going to get to do a little fancy flying, knock the hell out of some joker pretending to be a WWII ace, and be back in time for supper. Yeah, it was going to be fun!

Minutes after the call, Marshall was taxiing his plane onto the threshold of the strip, nervous excitement cranking up his pulse and slicking his palms. With a final check of the instruments, he moved the throttle forward and the magnificent metal beast all but leapt into the air, climbing away from the earth. *Let the games begin*, he thought to himself with a smile as he knifed through the sky towards the P51 and its unsuspecting pilots.

Cody stood on the rudder and cranked the plane around for another pass. He had picked out the ammo dump on his first time through. It was right where his man had said it would be. He came in hot and low, reducing the margin for error as much as possible, and offering only a brief target to the men below. The camp loomed up in front of him again and he could see the soldiers spilling out of the buildings and tents, many with guns in their hands, firing up at the plane. "Now it's really gonna get interesting," he muttered under his breath as he opened up with the .50s once more. After a solid burst of three or four seconds, he grabbed the quick release on the wing tanks.

Travis watched as holes magically appeared in the metal wing covering. Bullets punched ragged gashes in the fuselage with muted popping sounds as they swept across the last two hundred yards. Cody never flinched. Impervious to the withering fire, he held the airplane straight and level, glued to his target. "Come on baby, hold on," he whispered. "Just a little closer ..."

Two hundred feet from the corrugated roof of the ammo dump, Cody pulled the release and the wing tanks tumbled, seemingly in slow motion, toward the earth. One of the homemade fire bombs went crashing directly through the tin roof of the ammo dump. The other splashed across the backside of the compound, catching buildings and tents on fire, but its impact was dwarfed by the explosion of the dump. The Mustang had just roared over the roof of the building when the ordnance in it was catalyzed by the napalm. The explosion was horrendous, creating a fireball ten stories high and melting everything within a hundred yards of the impact. Fifty yards past that, the blast and the shrapnel blew buildings and people into unrecognizable pieces. Less than five minutes after the start of the attack by a single WWII aircraft, Delta Camp had been destroyed. Of the nine hundred men in the camp, fewer than two hundred remained unharmed and nearly four hundred had been killed. Never anticipating such an event, the colonel had made a tremendous strategic error. He had placed his ammunition depot within shouting distance of the billets for his soldiers, and he had paid for it dearly.

Resistance ceased after the fireball explosion. The survivors were interested only in getting away from the terrible carnage. Demoralized and frightened men scrambled for the safety of the woods as Cody and Travis made one final pass. They still had plenty of ammunition, but there was no need to fire, so complete was the destruction.

Cody climbed to two thousand feet and circled the compound for a moment, surveying the disaster below. He was not proud of what he had done, but he was satisfied that the threat of Rockford's army, at least in that camp, was over.

While they circled the compound, Travis turned away from the destruction below and looked to the west. His attention was captured by a dot–a fast moving dot–coming in at about five thousand feet and headed right for them.

"Cody, we've got a bandit at two o'clock, coming in hot. If I didn't know better, I'd say it was a fighter jet."

"Got him," Cody said as he banked around toward the oncoming plane.

"Cody, I don't like it. Does Rockford have fighter planes?"

"Well, come to think of it, it's been rumored that he snatched one from a training facility outside Little Rock, but I didn't put much stock in it. Now I'm beginning to wonder."

Travis grabbed the back of Cody's seat and shouted, "Get this damned plane down on the deck, *now.* He's coming for us and if he catches us high, we're screwed!"

Cody Joe jammed the throttle to the firewall and threw the aircraft over and down. The plane plummeted like a mortally wounded dove. Once again, Travis's stomach ended up somewhere near his knees, but that was okay. They were in for a fight, one in which they would be out-classed, outgunned, and battling for their lives. They needed the terrain below to confuse the F16's missiles, and diminish the enemy's speed and maneuverability advantages if they were to have any chance at all. As the jet approached, Cody brought the '51 around tight against the hills at a thousand feet.

When Fredrick Marshall had closed to three miles in his Falcon, he activated the sidewinder under his starboard wing. To use a heat-seeking sidewinder missile, he had to be fairly close; it wasn't one of the thirty-mile missiles used on most of the F15s and '16s. Besides, Marshall thought it would be better that way. He'd get to see the results first hand. In seconds, the warble in his headset went to a steady, insistent tone and the triangle on his targeter went from blinking to solid. He was locked. About a mile out, he grinned and pulled the trigger, releasing the missile.

"Surprise, surprise!" he said with a feral smile.

Cody had just leveled off when Travis saw the the puff of white smoke under the wing of the jet and watched the missile rip away, streaking toward them. "He's fired a missile, Cody! We've got a heat-seeker on us! That son of a bitch is gonna climb right up our exhaust port!"

"Maybe, maybe not," replied Cody in a voice so calm it belied his tenseness and concentration. "Hang on, I'm gonna try something." Before Travis could open his mouth, Cody turned the huge engine off and put the craft in a shallow dive, turning the exhaust port side away from the oncoming rocket. In the few seconds they had left before the missile would strike, the cold, rushing air began to cool the exhaust ports, diminishing the signal given to the heat-seeking projectile screaming toward them. At the last second, when the missile was less than two hundred yards away, Cody snapped the plane hard to the right, pulling it away at almost a right angle. The missile, unable to lock on the much diminished heat signal, streaked under their left wing, earthbound.

Travis breathed a monumental sigh of relief. "God, Cody, nice flying."

"Not done yet," Cody replied matter of factly, "he's still coming." And indeed, the jet streaked by a thousand feet above them.

The plane fell like aerodynamic lead and Cody hit the starter button as the green earth rose up at them. The engine coughed and turned, but didn't catch. "Come on, baby, come on," Cody coaxed as he hit the starter button again. The prop still windmilled and the rounded hills of Arkansas raced up at them with frightening speed.

Travis, strapped in the back with no control over what was happening, felt like a man locked in a wildly speeding roller coaster that had just thrown its tracks at the high point of its course.

Cody's voice was getting louder and more insistent through the head phones as they ate up the last two hundred feet between them and the forest below. "Come on! Come on, you son of a–" Suddenly the engine roared to life. Cody slammed the throttle forward and leveled her out, the final seconds taking them so close to the earth that the tops of the pine trees nearly took the paint off the undercarriage of the plane. "Hang on, buddy!" Cody yelled as he yanked back the stick and climbed toward his opponent one more time.

Marshall couldn't believe it–the goddamned missile must have been defective. It *missed!* Expecting to see the kill first hand, he had flown right by them when it failed to strike its target. Cursing, he turned and climbed.

The jet, twice as fast as the '51, tore open the sky as its after burners kicked in and climbed, in seconds, to five thousand feet. The '51 had barely reached a thousand feet when the jet rolled over on its wing and dropped like a steel falcon. Marshall laid his finger on the trigger of the gatling gun as he closed once more on the Mustang.

Cody, seeing the jet coming at him, snapped the plane over and dove, zig-zagging, hugging the rugged terrain in an attempt to evade. He knew that if the cannon on the Falcon locked in on him for two seconds there wouldn't be enough of his plane left for a Christmas tree ornament. Survival depended on timing–but timing was one of Cody's strong points.

Marshall dropped down on the fleeing '51 like a hawk on a pigeon. When he had closed the distance to killing range and finally locked his targeter on the elusive Mustang, he smiled and pulled the trigger of the devastating Gatling gun.

Cody, the iceman, with his concrete nervous system, waited until the last second before Marshall fired, then snapped the stick back and to the right and all but stalled, practically stopping in mid-air.

Marshall had never been in combat. He was a good National Guard pilot, but certainly not a great aviator. Unfortunately for him, he was up against a man who made the airplane a part of him–whose body fused with the metal, the leather, and the instruments. Cody's lack of fear and his natural, intrinsic understanding of flight made him closer to a bird than a man. Cody Joe was as good as they got.

Marshall was concentrating so much on the kill that he was amazed when he pulled the trigger and two things happened: First, a millisecond before the murderous cannon fire erupted from the belly of the Falcon, Cody's plane broke hard to the right and arched upward. The fusillade of projectiles passed harmlessly under the P51. Secondly, Marshall, being inexperienced, came in too hot and realized too late that he was over-shooting the Mustang, screaming right by and below it. An experienced war pilot would have hit the afterburners and been in Louisiana before the man in the '51 had a chance to think about it. Marshall did just the opposite. He chopped the throttles and hit the air brakes in order to slow the plane and bring it around quickly for another shot. That was exactly what Cody had hoped he would do.

When the jet passed beneath the Mustang, Cody slammed the throttles to the firewall and hit the water/alcohol injection system switch for that powerful extra burst of horsepower and speed. The big Rolls Royce engine whined and Cody dropped onto the tail of the slowed F16 at over five hundred and forty miles per hour, his machine guns relentlessly hammering out a tempo of destruction for the trapped jet and its careless pilot. The few moments that Marshall used to slow and control the speeding jet were fatal. As he banked out, the '51 closed on his left rear quarter and hammered the plane with a line of .50-caliber bullets from stem to stern. The glass in the cockpit shattered as the huge machine gun rounds impacted and tore through, slamming into Marshall and bouncing his body like a man attached to a live electric wire. A red mist filled his vision, and as the calm darkness of death crept over him, his last thought was: *Who the hell* was *that guy*? The jet rolled over and began a gliding trajectory toward the far mountain where, seconds later, it buried itself in a ball of smoke and flame.

The guy was William J. Cody, Jr., probably the finest light plane pilot left in what was left of the United States of America. And as he did a victory roll across the cloudless, blue, Arkansas sky, he realized that even for a man as accustomed to living his fantasies as he was, he had just experienced the ultimate dogfight–the nearly impossible challenge–and had come out on top! Cody howled like a wolf and rolled the plane again, just for the sheer hell of it.

CHAPTER 21
OF HATRED AND REVENGE

A jubilant Travis and Cody returned to the homestead to find the preacher and the sensei sitting on the steps of the front porch. One look at their faces, and Travis's excitement evaporated. "What's wrong? Where's Christina? Where's Todd?"

The preacher looked up, his eyes filled with apology. "They hit the place while we were gone. Travis, I'm sorry. Will was killed, and they shot Carlos and left him for dead. They must have taken Christina and Todd with them."

Travis felt tentacles of fear wrap around his insides and squeeze. Perhaps for the first time, he was fully aware of the width and depth of his love for those two people. They had taken his family. His *family*. At the thought of them being harmed, he was consumed by a coldly murderous detachment. He would get them back, and he would kill Rockford and anyone else who stood between him and those he loved.

Travis looked down at the preacher. "How long ago? What happened?"

"All we know is what Carlos was able to tell us, son. He's sleeping now, and lucky to be alive. Seems they shot him as he ran for the back of the house. The bullet only grazed his head, but it was enough to knock him out, and he tumbled down the cliff in the back. Like I said, it wasn't a real bad wound, but it bled a lot. He musta looked dead layin' down there on the side of the hill, with his forehead all bloody, so they left him. We found him and bandaged him up. He's a little dizzy, but he'll be okay.

"Carlos said about thirty or forty of them came out of

the woods on the run. They shot Will as he headed for the house to warn Chris. She musta' put up some kinda' fight. There were four of them dead in the living room and one dead on the front lawn. There was one more in the kitchen, but it looked like Ra got him."

At the mention of Ra, Travis panicked again, knowing that the dog would die before letting them touch Chris or the boy. "Ra, where is he? What happened to–" Just then, Ra came through the front door, moving a little slowly, and favoring his front paw. The dog limped over and nuzzled Travis gently, almost as if he sensed the tragedy in the air. Travis breathed a sigh of relief at the sight of the great, black animal, realizing once again how expansive his family had become.

"Somehow they locked Ra in the cellar," the preacher continued. "Close as I can figure it, they must have knocked him down there after he attacked the guy in the kitchen. He's got a good lump on his head but it looks like he'll be all right."

Cody put his hand on Travis's shoulder. "I'm sorry, buddy, I'm really sorry. Whatever you want to do, whatever needs to be done, you know I'm in."

The preacher stood up. "Travis, I'm sure I don't have to say it, but the sensei and I are ready when you are."

Behind him, the sensei, who was still sitting on the porch, got up. "Travis–all of you–we want the same thing, but now is not the time to go off unprepared. We need information. We have to know where they are, and what to anticipate. Cody, do you think your man in the camp can get us this information?"

Cody paused before answering. "Nine chances out of ten, he's going to know exactly what's happening. He's that good."

"Very well," said the sensei. "Then return home, and make sure your property is secure. Contact your man. Get the knowledge we need as quickly as possible and call us on the van radio tomorrow morning." The Japanese turned to Travis. "Trust me, my friend, and try to remain calm. We can only succeed if we prepare intelligently."

Travis sighed and looked up at the afternoon sky. "I know you're right, Sensei, but at this moment all I want to do is get in that van, drive into Rockford's camp, and strangle him with my bare hands. Right now, I need a large dose of your Oriental calm."

"It is there inside you, Travis. Simply go to the well and draw it up. The lives of Christina and the boy depend on your actions. Remember that."

Travis took a deep breath and exhaled slowly. "Okay, Cody, get going. Find out what you can, and we'll monitor the radio tomorrow morning. Get us what we need to know."

Once again, Cody grasped his friend's shoulder. "We can pull this off, Travis. Trust my old instincts. We'll get them back, I promise."

"Thanks," replied Travis with a wan smile.

Travis's old friend ran to his Jeep and was gone.

The three of them went inside and the preacher made a pot of their coffee. They talked for awhile, then Travis went to check on Carlos.

When he opened the door, Travis saw that Carlos was awake. He was propped up on some pillows, looking out the window, a bandana-like bandage wrapped around his head. The Cuban turned a little too quickly and winced as Travis walked over.

"Carlos, *mi amigo*, how are you?"

"*Bien, Jefe*, I be okay, just a little dizzy."

"Good. I'm glad. You didn't see what happened to Christina and Todd, did you?"

"No, *Jefe*. They shoot me and Will first, then they take the house. *Lo ciento*. I'm sorry, *Jefe*. I did not protect them."

"It's not your fault. You did your best. We'll get them back."

"*Sí, Jefe,* if we have to shoot every one of them goddamned sons-a-ma-bitchees!"

"Yes, every last one if necessary," said Travis, who reached over and patted Carlos on the back. "You just rest today, *amigo*. We'll need you soon. I'll make sure you get some supper, and I'll see you in the morning."

"*Gracias, Jefe.*"

Travis stood on the porch a half hour after sunset and looked out across the darkening valley. Torn by conflicting emotions of rage and fear, he gazed for a moment at the little cherry tree that Will had planted by the side of the house. It stood there in defiance of the darkness, its white petals blossoming, issuing a statement of serenity to the night. A light breeze carried the fragrance of the flowers across the yard and, at that moment, Travis could almost hear the sensei's calming words and confident voice filling him with peace and strength. Desperation turned to hope, and in the hope he found faith. He raised his eyes to the heavens and prayed that God grant him one last favor–the return of his family.

At seven the next morning, Travis had just begun to monitor the radio when Cody's urgent voice broke the silence. "Travis, come in. Come back to me!"

"I'm here, Cody, what is it?"

"Thank God I got you, buddy! Listen up! Rockford wasn't in the camp when we hit it yesterday. It was him and his people who killed Will and took Christina and Todd. When he got back and saw what was left of his compound, he had a conniption fit–actually several of them from what I hear. He's coming for you today with every man he has left, which I figure to be about two hundred and fifty after casualties and desertions."

"How much time do we have?"

"They're on their way now, so I figure you've got maybe two hours. I'm sending over a dozen of my men for support. They're all I've got, buddy. I'm gonna try to fuel and arm the Fifty-One again, and hit Rockford as he heads toward you. I should be able to change the odds a little, if I can get ready in time. Good luck, partner. I'll see you when the smoke clears."

Travis slammed the mike into its cradle and raced back into the house, shouting for his people. Moments later, the preacher and the sensei, along with the wounded but willing Carlos, stood in front of him. He looked over at the Cuban. "Are you all right, *amigo*?"

"*Sí, Jefe*, I be okay. I fight!"

A solemn smile touched the corners of Travis's mouth, and he nodded. "Well, this is the news," he said, "and it's not good. The colonel is still alive, and he's gone ballistic over what we did to his camp yesterday. He's coming for us in less than two hours, with every man he can muster. Even with the people Cody is sending us, we could easily be outnumbered ten or fifteen to one. I know you're my friends but, because of our friendship, I have to say this: None of you have to stay. There's a big world out there. You can get in the van and–"

"Save it, son," interrupted the preacher. "We ain't got time for no last-stand-at-the-Alamo speeches. This is our home and our fight, too, and there ain't one of us here who don't owe you his life. We ain't goin' nowhere."

Travis looked at each of his friends. They nodded.

"We fight them sons-a-ma-bitchees!"

Travis was once again filled with an elemental, deep-seated pride in the companions fate had provided him. "Okay, this is what we're going to do: They've got to come at us from the front, through the woods and along the road. We're going to rig up some surprises for them with the grenades we have left–a little something I saw done in Nam."

The sensei brought out the box of grenades, Travis got some monofilament fishing line and two rolls of duct tape from the shed, then they all headed down the dirt road to the entrance of the property.

Travis paced off about seventy-five feet into his driveway from the main road and found two big trees, one on either side of the drive. With the clear fishing line, he bound a grenade to each tree trunk, about three feet up from the ground. Then he tied the line to the pin of the first grenade, ran across to road, pulled it tight, and tied it to the pin of the other one. From there they moved about fifty yards closer to the house, where Travis showed them how to set up the second surprise. The preacher kept watch at the entrance of the driveway as Carlos, the sensei and Travis moved into the woods on both sides of the road, shinnied up each of the larger trees, and taped a grenade to the bottom side of one of the branches. They then tied a piece of fishing line from the pin, which was pulled out slightly, to a large rock, and set the rock firmly in the crook of the branch. The three men did this throughout the wooded area in front of the house. When they finished, Travis sent the other two back to the house. He found himself a protected spot in the woods, near the road, and settled in.

He hardly had a moment to relax before Eric and Derrick, the two huge twins, arrived with a dozen reinforcements. Travis intercepted them before they got into the driveway, had them park their two vehicles on an old logging road that ran across the western end of the property, then escorted them to the house. The men gathered together and discussed their defense strategy, then everyone took their positions. Travis returned to his viewpoint in the woods.

It took Cody much longer than he had expected to refuel the big plane and rearm the machine guns–so long that even the cool, nearly unshakeable Cody was in a panic by the time he climbed onto the wing and reached for the cockpit bubble. He slid back the canopy, paused for a moment, and turned to one of his maintenance people on the ground. "Get me my gun. You never know when you might need a Thompson." The weapon was tossed up to him and he casually snatched it out of the air, then jumped into the airplane. Moments later he was off the runway and headed for Rockford's convoy.

When Cody reached the area near Travis's home, he saw the line of military and civilian vehicles only minutes from their destination. He also spotted, to his dismay, another small column of two convoy trucks and a Jeep coming from Alpha Camp. After a final check of the instruments and a quick burst of the guns to insure working order, he threw the wing over and roared down on Colonel Rockford and his column.

Cody caught them in a long stretch of road about a mile before Travis's homestead. "Welcome to hell, Colonel," he whispered as he fell on the column, his machine guns chattering a staccato melody once again. As he streaked by, pieces of pavement disintegrated, vehicles exploded, and men scattered under the bombardment of the huge four-inch bullets. On the second pass, the men fired back from the protection of the woods and granite outcroppings along the road.

Halfway through the second pass, Cody took a machine gun burst through the front underside of the aircraft. The bullets tore into his radiator, taking out all but one segment of his cooling system. They also split a fuel line and, as the high-powered jets squirted the fuel, it splashed across the hot engine and ignited.

Cody had chewed them up badly. At least fifty men were dead or wounded and almost half their vehicles had been taken out, but Cody Joe and his magnificent flying machine were going down. The engine was overheating rapidly and flames were already working their way out of the engine cowling. If he didn't get down quickly, it would explode and kill him for sure.

Cody kicked the left rudder hard and, with equally heavy stick, threw the plane over the mountain and into the valley as he headed for the flat, straight road below. Unfortunately, the best piece of flat road was occupied by the small column of reinforcements coming from Alpha Camp. Cody backed off and dropped some flaps. It was already getting smoky and hot in the cockpit–he only had seconds.

The officer in the foremost truck of the convoy couldn't believe his eyes when he saw the WWII fighter plane, with smoke and flames belching out of it, coming right down at him. As Cody made his emergency approach five hundred yards in front of the column and fifty feet off the ground, he opened up with his machine guns. Few pilots in the world would have had the composure to initiate a coordinated attack while in the process of making a crash landing in a smoke-filled, burning airplane. Cody, however, was one of those pilots.

The driver of the lead truck slammed on his brakes and gaped in disbelief as twin lines of .50-caliber bullets ripped up the road in front of him and worked their way into the front of his vehicle. The huge bullets tore through the engine, the cab, and into the gas tank, which exploded in a fiery roar, throwing the destroyed vehicle on its side. Cody hit the road, bounced ten feet into the air, and came down hard a second time as he drew the stick back to lessen the impact. That time he stayed on the road, but he was still moving too fast toward the burning truck and the vehicles behind it. Unable to stop the plane before reaching the immobilized truck, and unable to get far enough off the road to avoid contact, he lost the tip of his right wing to the overturned vehicle. It slowed him considerably, spinning the nose of the plane away from the oncoming vehicles.

The men in the second truck, a hundred yards back, stared in shock as the smoking Mustang finally careened to a halt. The shock turned to terror as Cody jammed the left rudder and hit the throttle, slowly spinning the airplane around at them while simultaneously firing those devastating machine guns. Bullets danced across the field and onto the road, then into the truck, as the burning aircraft turned. When the stream of bullets reached the truck, Cody stood on the brakes and held the trigger down. The second truck was ripped apart, and exploded like the first, torching the occupants.

There was so much smoke in the cockpit that Cody couldn't see anymore and his shoes and the bottoms of his pants were catching fire. He ripped open the canopy and jumped out onto the wing just in time to see a Jeep carrying two officers come bounding around the burning truck and screech to a halt fifty feet in front of him. Without pausing, he reached into the cockpit and grabbed his Thompson. The two men had just begun to stand, drawing their sidearms, when Cody opened up from the hip, blasting out the windshield and knocking both men from the vehicle with the heavy .45 slugs. Cody jumped off the wing, ran over to the far side of the Jeep, and threw himself to the ground behind it just as the gas tank on the plane blew.

Fire and flame, and pieces of aircraft flew across the road and into the fields on both sides. When the thunder, and debris from the explosion settled, Cody Joe stood up and brushed himself off. With a sad smile and a salute to the burning remains of the of the '51, he picked up his weapon and looked at the two men on the ground next to the Jeep.

"Never know when you might need a Thompson," he said as he climbed in, started it up, and headed for his buddy Travis.

CHAPTER 22
LAST STAND

After being mauled for the second time by Cody and his airplane, the colonel was blind with fury. He whipped his soldiers back into the remaining vehicles and moved out, leaving the wounded crying, and dead where they lay.

Travis watched from his hiding place as the reorganized convoy stopped at the entrance to his property. He could see the two officers in the lead Jeep; one of which, he was certain, held his family. He felt his fingers clench so tighly that his nails bit into his palms.

Reynolds had briefed the colonel as to the layout and the grounds. The plan was simple–just drive into the clearing in front of the house, surround it, and burn them out.

Rockford was no fool, however, and he knew he was dealing with professionals. He also knew from experience that the first people into the fray were the first casualties, so he sent the trucks and his men in ahead. He followed in his Jeep with Reynolds and the driver. The first truck had barely entered the road when it hit the almost invisible monofilament line, pulling the pins from the grenades tied to the base of the two large trees. The explosion was deafening; both trees snapped in half at the base, falling across the road and the truck. Shrapnel from the grenades blew the windows out of the cab and shredded the canvas covering on the back of the truck, killing the front passengers and wounding several of the soldiers in the rear of the vehicle. The tires of the truck were cut to shreds, rendering it useless and further blocking the passageway.

Travis smiled as the explosion and pandemonium sent the officers into a rage. The road was completely blocked; the men would have to go in on foot.

Reynolds ordered everyone out and formed up in front of the ruined truck. After the first booby trap, no one was overly anxious to walk down the road, so the colonel ordered his men into the woods on both sides of the dirt track. The plan was to work their way through to the clearing, then attack on signal, the same way they had the first time. Almost two hundred men moved into the forest, headed for the fifteen men in the buildings at the clearing.

The odds weren't good, but the deadly grenade ambush lay waiting in over thirty of the trees in front of them.

As the men moved forward, Travis melted silently into the woods and worked his way back to the compound. On returning, he had four men spread out and take positions approximately twenty-five feet into the woods on the clearing side. They held quietly until the majority of Rockford's men were almost on them, then they opened up with their guns. The object was not to kill that many soldiers, but rather to bunch the enemy in the killing zone set up by the grenades. The four men cut loose with a fusillade, causing the colonel and his soldiers to stop and take cover under the trees bearing the fatal fruit. Then they retreated to the safety of the buildings in the clearing.

When Travis saw his men fall back, he knew the trap was set. He uncased and armed the last two LAWS anti-tank guns. He lifted the first one, aimed into the thick of the woods on the left side of the road and fired. Next to him, the preacher drew the second onto his shoulder and fired into the right side. The blast of the rockets knocked several of the tenuously balanced rocks from their perches in the trees. When they fell, the pins were pulled from the grenades taped to the branches. As each grenade exploded, it kicked the rock from the tree branch closest to it and repeated the deadly performance, sending thousands of pieces of shrapnel toward the men beneath. It was like being caught in the maelstrom of an intense mortar barrage. There was nowhere safe to turn as bomb after bomb detonated and the men were torn to pieces. Wounded screamed and cried, and as the grenades burst around them, the survivors stumbled in blind panic toward the clearing.

It was Reynold's ferret-like quickness that saved him and the colonel. When the explosions began, they were about halfway through the woods, off to one side. Reynolds happened to glance up and see a grenade taped to the branch of the tree in front of him. "Run, Run!" he shouted. "They've wired grenades to the trees!" The blasts closed in as they dashed for the side of the clearing while cries of the wounded echoed in their ears.

Of the two hundred men in the forest around the homestead, over a hundred were killed or incapacitated in a matter of seconds. Another forty died as they ran from the woods into the clearing and the withering fire of the defenders. The remaining sixty or so rallied and began firing at the house and the outbuildings from the protection of the trees.

Rockford and Reynolds, along with a good portion of their best men, made it past the barrage, to the edge of the woods. They dug in across from the guest trailer which sat about fifty yards from the main house.

Firing from the corner of his living room window, Travis saw the colonel separate his men and pour fire from two different directions into the small mobile home and the four men holding it. Within five minutes, three of the men had been killed and the fourth retreated to the safety of the ranch house. Rockford and his soldiers rushed in and took positions around and under the trailer. The soldiers on the other side of the clearing, taking heart when they watched the colonel's accomplishment, charged the barn and overran it, killing another four defenders. It cost them fifteen men, but they forced Carlos and the others holding the out-buildings to fall back to positions in and around the house. Rockford had just rallied his men to rush the house when the sound of a vehicle roaring down on them from behind brought everyone around.

Cody slammed the Jeep in gear and was off like a shot, leaving the smoking remains of the airplane and the burning trucks behind. Twenty minutes later, as he neared Travis's home, he could hear the exchange of gunfire and he knew the fight was on. "Hold on, Travis, hold on," he muttered as he weaved around the ruined, smoking remains of the column he had just chewed up with the Mustang.

When he reached the entrance to Travis's home, he saw that the road was blocked by the wrecked truck, but he remembered that his friend had cut a fire lane on the eastern corner of the property which led to the house. He jammed the Jeep into reverse, spun it around, and headed for the lane. Seconds later he was flying down the bumpy path, dodging stumps and practically bouncing out of the Jeep as he hit exposed roots and potholes. The sound of the fight had grown and, as he neared the clearing, he could hear men shouting, wounded crying, and the constant crackling of small-arms fire.

As fate would have it, the fire lane broke into the clearing directly behind the trailer where the colonel and his men stood preparing to charge the house and overwhelm the last of the defenders. They would have, most probably, been successful, had it not been for a William J. Cody and his trusty Thompson.

Cody, a master at snap decisions, burst into the clearing and saw the men gathered behind the trailer. Without even slowing down, he reached for his weapon, shouldered it, and opened up on the group, shooting out the remainder of the Jeep's windshield in the process.

It was disconcerting enough for those men to see some long-haired madman in a leather aviator's hat and goggles charging down on them, shouting and shooting from a roaring Jeep. It was considerably more disconcerting when one of the madman's bullet's struck the LP gas cylinder next to the trailer and it blew into a fiery ball of red-hot shrapnel.

Travis had watched the two officers gathering a group of men together at the other end of the trailer, preparing to rush the house. He knew the contest was still a roll of the dice. He was yelling at the others to get ready for the attack, when suddenly he heard the roar of a Jeep, the distinctive bark of a Thompson, and saw the propane tank ignite, taking the back half of the trailer and a good portion of Rockford's squad with it. He knelt there by the window, the cacaphony of battle raging around him, and smiled.

"Cody," he whispered.

Rockford and his soldiers were thrown to the ground from the blast, but committed and under fire, they recovered quickly and charged. Of the dozen or so men nearest the tank at the opposite end of the mobile home, eight or nine were killed instantly. The other four or five lived long enough to stagger to their feet and face the maniac with the machine gun.

The dozen soldiers who had taken the barn saw Reynolds and the colonel charging the house with the last of their men. Sensing victory, they opened up with their weapons to give them cover and charged the opposite side of the house.

Inside, the remaining defenders consisted of Eric and Derrick, two or three of their men, Travis, Carlos, the preacher, and the sensei. As the men from the barn charged, the twins, who were standing next to the kitchen door, turned and looked at each other. Wordlessly, they snapped fresh clips into their Thompsons, kicked the kitchen door off its hinges, and walked out side by side, their machine guns booming. Pieces of the porch snapped and exploded around them as they stood together like two deadly genies, Thompsons jumping in their huge hands.

One of the giants flinched slightly as he took a round in the flesh of his side. The other grit his teeth as bullets struck him in the leg and the arm, but their guns never missed a beat. When the hammers of the two weapons fell on empty chambers, there wasn't a soldier left standing in the clearing. Eric and Derrick once again looked at each other, without uttering a word, and smiled. The other side of the house had not fared as well, unfortunately.

Two of the colonel's men had thrown smoke grenades as they charged and under the cover they created, nearly a dozen of the soldiers reached the house, including Reynolds and Rockford. Travis had watched from the window as the tall, arrogant officer bellowed orders to his soldiers. He heard two of them call him colonel–finally, his enemy had a face.

Reynolds and four of the attackers broke from the charge and attempted to take the defenders from the rear of the house. The sensei and Travis saw the move and rushed to the back. The first three never made the porch as Travis and his friend magically appeared from behind two of the concrete pillars which supported the roof and cut loose with their M16s. The fourth one, along with Reynolds, had been protected from the murderous fire by the bodies of the first three. As his comrades fell, the fourth made a dive and pulled off two quick rounds as he hit the porch. One of those was wide, but the second smacked the concrete pillar next to Travis's face. The exploding particles of concrete dust struck Travis in the face and eyes, blinding him momentarily. He threw his hands up to his eyes as Reynolds and the other soldier leveled their guns. In that split second, the sensei realized Reynolds was aiming at him, and that the other soldier, five feet away and on his knees, was bringing his gun to bear on the blinded and helpless Travis. There was no way the sensei could take them both.

He made his choice—a life-and-death decision that was the consummate statement of friendship. The sensei hurled himself against Travis, knocking him through the opening where the sliding glass doors led into the living room, while firing at the man who would have killed his friend. The kneeling soldier never got off a shot as he was bounced backward through the door on the porch. Reynolds, however, got off several, two of which hit the sensei in the chest, knocking him down, his gun flying across the floor. Reynolds paused for a moment as the weapons fell silent, his eyes scanning the room. The sensei lay motionless, his eyes closed, the blood from his wounds staining his shirt a bright red. Reynolds walked over slowly, cautiously, listening to the sounds of the fight out front. He reached the Japanese, whose chest barely rose and fell, and nudged him with his boot. Satisfied the man was no threat, the soldier started to move past him to finish Travis, when suddenly the sensei's eyes snapped open and his hand snaked out behind the heel of Reynold's boot and jerked.

Taken completely by surprise, the soldier was thrown off balance and fell on top of the Japanese, who grabbed Reynolds by the front of the shirt, pulled the startled man's face to his own, and drew his short sword. He held Reynolds so tightly the man couldn't pull away and, as their noses almost touched, he whispered hoarsely, "Come meet my ancestors with me, Captain." Then he plunged the blade into the officer's stomach below the abdomen and drew it upward, opening his midsection from groin to sternum.

Reynolds screamed like a pubescent girl, struggling maniacally as the razor sharp sword sliced open his stomach muscles and he felt the warm wetness of his entrails pouring out. The sensei held the man to him with an iron grip, watching his opponent's bulging, terrified eyes begin to glaze as the life force left him and the screams ceased. Finally, when the captain quit trembling and his eyes rolled into the back of his head, the proud old Japanese pushed Reynolds off him, laid his own head on the cold, blood-covered floor and, with a sigh, closed his eyes.

Outside, two more of the colonel's men fell to the defenders as they reached the walls of the house, but the fire they poured into the windows and through the walls had taken out another two defendants. Rockford was left with less than half a dozen men. The colonel had watched Reynolds break off with his men and charge the porch. He had also heard him scream moments later. Rockford had been in war, and he knew that scream. There was no point in counting on the captain. The furious gunfire on the far side of the dwelling had grown silent, and none of his men who had charged the barn had reappeared. The odds no longer appeared so good.

Travis, who had been knocked unconscious for a moment when he hit the floor, struggled to his feet, wiping his eyes and trying desperately to clear his blurred vision. As he began to focus again, he turned in a panic toward the silence of the porch. "Sensei! Sensei!" he called as he grabbed his gun and stumbled out through the sliding doors.

His friend lay on the floor in front of him, covered in blood. Reynolds lay next to him, the whites of his eyes staring at the slowly spinning ceiling fan above him. Travis rushed to his companion's side, dropping his gun and cradling the man in his arms.

Slowly, the sensei's eyes opened once more, and when

he recognized Travis, he did his best to smile. "Ah, my friend. I am glad you are here now," he whispered. "It is time for me to join my ancestors." The sensei paused for a moment, drew a small breath and coughed, then looked up at Travis again. "It has been good to know you, Travis-san. You have shown me that Samurai is a state of mind and not a class, nor a race of people. You, are Samurai! Now give me your hand."

Travis felt hot tears running down his cheeks as he put his hand in the sensei's. Slowly, and with great effort, the Japanese brought his *katana* around and laid it in Travis's palm. "My swords are now yours. Keep them with pride and honor, and remember me, my friend, when you clean them at night."

Numbed with grief, Travis could find no words. He held his companion and brushed the hair away from the sensei's face.

The sensei drew one last ragged breath. "Do not despair of this passing, Travis. It is but a journey completed. We have walked together before and we shall walk together again." For the last time, their eyes locked and in a whisper, the words came. "*Sayonara*, my friend."

The sensei's eyes closed, his last breath passed from his body and, with a quiet, almost peaceful sigh, he joined his proud ancestors.

Cody and the preacher found Travis sitting on the floor, holding the sensei.

"Oh God, no," the big man moaned when he realized what had happened. He moved to his friend's side and gently put his arm around his shoulders. "I'm sorry, son." The preacher paused for a moment in reverence, then stood. "I'm sorry, but we need help now. They're about to break through the front. Come on, son. Come on."

Travis laid the sensei on the floor, placing the warrior's

swords by his side. He took a deep breath, then picked up his gun and turned to the preacher. "Okay, let's go finish it."

Outside the house, Rockford regrouped his remaining men. He pulled two smoke grenades from his belt, and threw one at the front steps and the other through the living room window. As the smoke poured out, he ordered the last of his soldiers into an assault on the front door of the house. They rushed the large oak door, shot off its hinges, and charged into the smoke-filled room. The colonel, however, after providing a quick barrage of covering fire, began to retreat slowly through the swirling billows, toward the trailer and the woods behind it.

Cody, Travis, and the preacher reached the smoky living room just as the soldiers broke down the door and rushed in. The attackers, outlined by the light of the doorway, were greatly disadvantaged, and paid for it. Four of the five were cut down in the crossfire created by Carlos near the bedrooms, and Travis and the others, who had come through from the back of the house. The last one, attempting to escape, turned and ran around the kitchen side of the house. He turned the corner full tilt and stumbled headlong into the twins. Before the man could recover and shoot, Derrick ripped his gun out of his hand and crushed his skull with it.

Travis quickly checked the bodies in the house, looking for the colonel. Cautiously, he moved to the door and peered out through the slowly clearing smoke. He saw the tall man in the distance, running for the woods. The adrenalin of hate slammed his system like a cocaine mainline, and without a word to anyone, he was out the door. Thirty feet from the woods, Rockford turned and saw Travis running toward him. He stopped, raised his rifle and fired. Travis watched the gun come up and rolled to his left as the automatic weapon stitched the ground where he had been seconds before. When the colonel realized he'd missed, he again swung the gun onto Travis and pulled the trigger, but the firing pin hammered an empty chamber. Having exhausted his last clip, Rockford threw down the gun and ran for the woods. Travis rose and fired, but his aim was high, and he tore the branches from the trees above Rockford's head as the soldier scrambled into the forest. Seconds later, Travis reached the edge of the woods and followed.

As Rockford raced through the trees toward his vehicles, Travis realized the man's intention, cut across to the fire lane, and ran for the road to intercept him. Unobstructed by undergrowth, he made much better time and reached the parked convoy well ahead of the colonel. He worked his way quietly down the line of vehicles to the command Jeep, lowered himself beside it, and waited. It wasn't long before Rockford came charging out of the woods, gasping with exertion. As he walked over to the Jeep, Travis stood up and leveled his gun at him. "Don't move, Colonel, or I'll kill you where you stand."

The colonel was startled at first, but when he recognized his antagonist, he recovered and smiled. "If you do, you'll never see the boy or the woman again."

Travis tensed, but kept his voice calm. "You're right, Colonel. I need you to talk to me." He pulled the trigger of his gun and tore up the ground at Rockford's feet.

The man yelled and danced back. Travis smiled. "So talk to me, Colonel. Where are they?"

Rockford regained his composure and stared back. "Do I look like a fool?" he asked. "Maybe I'll make a deal with you." His eyes flickered for a split second to Travis's left side, just behind him.

Travis dropped to the ground and turned as the lone, slightly wounded soldier at the edge of the woods raised his gun and fired. The bullets passed over Travis's head as he opened up on the man, practically cutting him in half, but in the intensity of the moment, he loosed more rounds than necessary. Suddenly the firing pin of his weapon was slapping air.

He turned, just in time to see the colonel charging, knife out, his face drawn back in a feral-like snarl. Travis rolled away, losing the grip on his gun, as the first slash of the knife caught the top of his shoulder instead of his throat. Instantly, he was out of the roll and up, spinning to face Rockford, who moved forward, his knife weaving back and forth in front of him, his eyes bright and cold. The colonel lashed out again, and Travis managed to avoid the full impact of the blade by jumping backward, hands wide and out of the way, but a thin red line appeared through the slashed fabric on the breast of his shirt.

Rockford rushed in. The knife missed Travis's eyes by inches, but in the process of snapping his head back to avoid the blade, he lost his balance and fell. As the soldier moved in for the kill, Travis, on his knees, saw the empty M16 lying an arm's length from him. Just as Rockford grabbed him by the hair and drew him up to slit his throat, Travis grasped the weapon and snapped the butt of the gun up sharply between his opponents's legs. The triumphant gleam in the colonel's eyes turned to shock as he grunted with pain.

Travis brought the gun up once more, hard, and as Rockford doubled over, Travis yanked himself free, simultaneously swinging the weapon in a swift, upward arc at his enemy's head. There was a resounding crack as the stock of the gun met jaw bone, lifting Rockford up and depositing him on his back–out cold.

Travis breathed a shaky sigh of relief, reached over and took the knife from the colonel's hand, then rose unsteadily to his feet.

Cody had gone looking for Travis when he heard the firing out on the road. He found his friend leaning against the Jeep, out of breath and bleeding. Cody Joe dressed Travis's wounds with a first aid kit from the vehicle, then together they bound the colonel spread-eagle to the hood of his own Jeep. A half hour later, when Rockford came to, he saw the two men standing over him.

Travis grabbed the colonel by the hair and jerked his head back. He had Rockford's knife in his hand and a merciless look in his eyes. "Where are they, Colonel?"

"Screw you and the horse you rode in on!" Rockford spat through bloodied teeth. "If you want to make a deal, I'll talk."

Travis's face went hard as granite. While holding Rockford by the hair with one hand, he reached around with the knife in the other. "This is the deal I'll make with you," he whispered, as he laid the blade against the side of the man's scalp, and in one clean slice, cut his ear off. As Rockford screamed, Travis slammed the soldier's head on the hood of the Jeep, then he jerked the colonel up to face him. "You've got ten seconds to tell me what I want to hear, or your eye is next. That's my best offer."

The colonel's voice came out in a gurgling, high-pitched squeal as Travis once again moved in with the knife. "No! No! Don't cut me anymore. I'll tell you. I'll show you where they are."

You're goddamned right you will," growled Travis. "Screw this up, Rockford, and it'll be the last thing you ever show anybody!"

He looked at Cody. "Hop in," he said, pointing to the driver's seat of the Jeep that Rockford was tied to.

Cody smiled. "Gonna get pretty hot for him tied to that hood."

"You're right," Travis said with a grim smile. "All the more reason for him to be in a hurry to get us where we want to go." After some preliminary directions from the now obliging colonel, they headed for Rockford's personal quarters on the periphery of Alpha Camp.

It took half an hour to reach the camp. When they came to its perimeter, the place appeared deserted. The road they were on kept them away from the main compound. In moments, the big farm house Rockford had requisitioned came into view. They parked in the circular driveway, cut the soldier loose from the Jeep, and pushed him forward. With a fractured jaw and a ruptured groin, the man limped slowly and painfully toward the front door, grateful to be free from the nearly scalding hood. Cody and Travis followed close behind, prodding him with their guns. Once inside, Rockford led them to the pantry and the door to the cellar. He removed the lock and took them down the stairs to the large room below.

Reaching the bottom of the stairs, they heard Christina call out, "Travis! Travis, over here!" The two men looked across the dimly-lit room to a dusty old couch where Christina and Todd sat, bound hand and foot. Travis's heart leaped into his throat at the sight of the two, and he and Cody rushed over to untie their bonds. In their excitement, they left the colonel standing by himself at the base of the stairs.

As the two men worked on the ropes, Rockford slid slowly over to the underside of the stairway and reached a hand under the staircase to a hidden shelf, and the gun that lay on it.

Christina's attention was devoted to Travis as he slipped off her ropes and held her. Todd looked up as Cody worked on the ropes that still held him and saw the colonel bring out the gun. For a second he was drawn back in time, to a sinking boat and the eyes of his father; to the blood in the raft, and his mother as she closed her eyes and died. He could not, he would not, let that happen again. At that moment, something slipped inside the cogs of his psyche; something snapped and cantered loose, freeing the imprisoned machinery of his mind.

He drew a breath and screamed, "Look out, Travis! Behind you!"

The colonel was just snapping back the slide on the automatic pistol as Cody turned and reached for his Thompson. With that same triumphant gleam in his eyes, Rockford brought his gun to bear on Travis who, unable to reach his weapon in time, had moved in front of Christina to protect her. Rockford pulled the trigger as Cody stepped in front of Travis while firing. The reports of the weapons in the closed cellar were deafening, but in a second it was over. The big .45 slugs from Cody's gun had slammed the colonel against the back wall. As the man's knees buckled and he slid down the blood-smeared bricks, he stared in disbelief when he realized that Travis was still standing.

Cody brought his weapon down slowly and turned to his friend with a strange, troubled look in his eyes. "You okay?" he whispered. Travis was about to reply when he saw the single hole in the breast of his partner's worn flight jacket, and the bloodstain spreading from it. Travis reached for his friend just as Cody's legs gave out, and he collapsed to the floor.

In a second, Travis was at his side, rolling him onto his back and unzipping the blood-soaked jacket. He ripped off his own shirt and pressed it to the wound, lifting Cody's head and shoulders onto his lap. Cody Joe opened his eyes, and coughed painfully. "Don't worry, old buddy. No one lives forever," he whispered, looking up at his shocked friend.

"Don't talk, Cody, don't talk. We're gonna get you help, get you out of here."

Cody wheezed in a gurgling breath as his punctured lung began to fill with blood. “Don’t think it’s gonna do much good, buddy, but it’s okay. Been a hell of a life; lived more than any two people I know, ’cept maybe you.” Cody closed his eyes for a moment and drew another tortured breath, then opened them again. A small trickle of blood escaped the corner of his mouth as he looked up at Travis once more. “You and I, we’ve been around enough to know that this ain’t the last dance. If I don’t see you later, my friend, I’ll see you again.” He smiled, and his eyes closed.

Travis lifted his friend into his arms and headed up the stairs for the Jeep.

EPILOGUE

The warm winds of an early spring blew across the land and new life sprang from barren winter branches with astonishing speed, as if nature itself was announcing its determination to survive. The winter's survivors welcomed the warmth and promise of the new season with rekindled hope, and the intrinsic desire to rebuild and create anew.

The world had been dramatically changed. Entire countries had disappeared, continents were reshaped, and new, unexplored lands had risen from the sea. Yet, through all the chaos and tragedy, man's spirit had endured.

A spiritual harmony had begun to settle over the land in a fashion not seen in this country for the longest of times. Never before, perhaps, to such a degree, had mankind uniformly decided that a change in the way we see our neighbor was necessary for the spiritual evolution and the physical survival of the race called man.

There was still no cohesive federal government, in the sense that it offered aid or continuity to the remaining states in America, but a new capital of these less than United States was being established in central Nebraska, and the surviving president had sent emissaries to the states in an initial attempt toward re-organization. Governor Turner, with the help of Judge Harcourt and a handful of like-minded politicians, had begun to re-organize Arkansas's political infrastructure.

Interstate commerce was appearing again, and intrastate commerce, in the parts of the country less damaged, was beginning to grow. The land and the people had survived the worst, and recovery was underway.

Travis stood on his porch and watched Todd laughing and shouting as he played on the lawn with Ra. The preacher helped Christina as she knelt in her cherished garden, coaxing up tomatoes, cucumbers, and various other vegetables that would carry them through the year. Only a few yards away, her mare frolicked with its new colt. She glanced at them and smiled.

He looked out over the yard, and his eyes settled on the little cherry tree, blooming brilliantly in the warm spring sun, its fragrance floating across the homestead. At that moment, he couldn't help but think of the two men the tree represented: The one who bought it for him with a gold Krugerrand, and the one he gave it to. Cody, the small, energized ball of fire with a Viking's yellow hair, an easy smile, and more courage and heart than the greatest storybook heroes; and, of course, the sensei–that quiet, proud Japanese who taught Travis more about life, and about himself, than any other person he had encountered this lifetime.

Just then, Cody walked through the sliding glass doors leading to the porch, a glass of Will's wine in his hand. He was somewhat thinner than he used to be, and his breath came a little shorter from the badly damaged lung, but the fire in his eyes and the ready smile hadn't changed at all. On that fateful day, almost a year ago, Travis had raced him to the medical center in Mena, and once again, William J. Cody's luck had held as the doctors saved his life on the operating table.

Cody smiled as Travis turned toward him. He often found his friend here. He understood, and knew to give him his times of remembrance.

As Travis nodded, he glanced back through the sliding doors at the two swords that hung above the mantel on the fireplace. He thought of the serene, powerfully confident man who had given them to him. Standing there, he felt the Oriental calm settle over him, as it did so often now. He sensed the sensei's soft voice speaking to him, as he had so many times before from the cockpit of the boat they had sailed together.

"The road to the light is long, Travis, and there are many stops along the way. We share these interludes with kindred spirits, time and time again. Like two small branches of the cherry tree, the winds of time and the lessons of Karma will brush us together occasionally. Through the seasons of experience and learning we grow, sharing the fruit of our wisdom with those who have traveled far enough along the path to hunger for it. This is the way of life, Travis.

"Whenever you take joy in the blossoms of my tree and smell their fragrance, I will be there to share it with you.

"We shall meet again my friend. *Sayonara.*"

About the Author

Michael Reisig was born in Enid, Oklahoma, in 1948.

The first son of a military family, he was raised in Europe and California before moving to Florida. He attended high school and college in the Tampa Bay area.

After college, he relocated to the Florida Keys, established a commercial diving business, and traveled extensively throughout the southern hemisphere, diving, treasure hunting, adventuring, and writing about his travels.

His other interests include flying, martial arts and fishing.

He presently resides in the Ouachita Mountains of Arkansas. He is Outdoors Editor and staff writer for the *Mena Star*, and continues to pen his novels.

Reisig is also the author of the *Intrepid Arkansas Traveler*, a guide to the Arkansas outdoors that contains a collection of his Dave Barry-style newspaper columns, anecdotes and short stories.

The Intrepid Arkansas Traveler, by Michael Reisig

A comprehensive guide to the Arkansas outdoors, puncuated with tall tales and anecdotes by the Traveler himself.

"If it's fun and it's in Arkansas, it's in here. Reisig's stories are gut-laugh stuff."

–John Corbitt, Managing Editor, *Mena Star.*

The Hawks of Kamalon, by Michael Reisig
Publication date: May, 1999 from Write Way Publishing, Denver, CO.

Great Britain, Summer, 1944

A small squadron of British and American aircraft depart at dawn on a long-range strike into Germany, but as they cross the English Channel, the squadron vanishes.

Drawn thousands of light-years across the galaxy by Kamalon's "Sensitive Mothers," ten men and eight aircraft are greeted by a roaring crowd in a field before the provincial capitol, on the continent of Azra; a land in desperate need of champions.

Captain Ross Murdock and the '51 Squadron are cast into a whirlwind adventure of intrigue, treachery, and romance as they are "culled" back and forth across the universe, outwitting and outrunning the Germans, while they attempt to foil the invasion of Azra by the neighboring continent of Krete.

The Hawks of Kamalon is a heart-hammering adventure in the classic tradition of Robert Heinlein, but it also examines the parameters of faith and friendship, the qualities that define civilization, and the width and depth of spirit.

For further information, get the book:
Basic Preparedness
A "How-To" Guide for Preparedness & Self-Reliant Living

($16.95 + $2.50 s/h), from the Survival Center
1-800-321-2900 or 1-360-458-6778

Basic Prespareduess tells you how to prepare for The Shift, and the Survival Center catalog tells you where to get the supplies needed to prepare for this event.